Past FORWARD

VOLUME TWO

Chautona Havig

~With much thanks to "Jillow"~

Who knew that an offer of help would turn out like this? Hope you don't regret it! Meanwhile, I cannot tell you how much I appreciate the time and humor you've invested in me and in my work. God Bless You.

Books by Chautona Havig

The Rockland Chronicles

Noble Pursuits
Discovering Hope
Argosy Junction
Thirty Days Hath...

The Aggie Series

Ready or Not
For Keeps
Here We Come

Past Forward- A Serial Novel

Volume 1
Volume 2
Volume 3

Historical Fiction

Allerednic: A Regency Cinderella Tale—in Reverse

The Annals of Wynnewood

Shadows and Secrets
Cloaked in Secrets
Beneath the Cloak

The Not-So-Fairy Tales

Princess Paisley
Everard (Coming 2012)

CHAPTER 39

The porch swing rocked gently in the crisp air. Steaming cups of chamomile tea warmed their fingers as they chatted, huddled under a warm quilt. Willow's head nestled into the shoulder near her ear, and she reveled in the strength and security there. It felt good to have affection again.

The anger that had held her captive in its relentless grasp during the past few weeks seemed more manageable at times like this. The day was over, the work done, and for half an hour in the moonlight with steaming cups of calming tea, Willow and Lily could talk about everything that hurt without Willow's emotions raging out of control. She loved these times. They reminded her so much of her long talks with her mother. If only the pain and fatigue in her heart was as manageable as that of her leg.

"I don't know what all to do. I have planned for more work next year—not less."

Lily pushed Saige away from her feet before asking, "Why?"

"I can. I can sell everything I don't need myself, so it'll keep me busy."

"Busy enough to help you forget—" Lily began, her hesitation audible. "Are you sure that's wise?"

"Actually, it's not that. Not really. It's just that I'll be doing the work anyway, so why not give Jill what she needs at the same time?"

"I've wondered about a few things…"

"Such as?"

Willow listened as Lily explained how interested people were about life on the farm whenever they heard about it. She told about the schoolteachers who had come to her wondering if Willow would allow a fieldtrip to her farm. She shared how encouraged she'd been by Kari's journals and the faith that Willow's mother obviously had. She mentioned the fruits, the vegetables, and the crafts that, while just another part of Willow's existence, were fresh and exciting to those who didn't live with them for survival.

"Have you ever named your farm?"

Willow shook her head. "No. We joked about it when we read *Anne of Green Gables* or *Rebecca of Sunnybrook Farm,* but—"

"I think that's the first thing you should do."

"Really?"

Lily nodded. "Yep. And then I think you should consider publishing your mother's journals—either as a compilation of years or as an autobiography journal style."

"Who would want to read Mother's journals but me?"

"You truly have no idea how unique your life is; do you?"

Willow wasn't a fool. Of course, her life was different. She lived it and saw how those around her lived. What she didn't understand was the attraction to the novel for novelty's sake.

"I know that I live differently. Chad made that glaringly obvious with his continual questions of why I didn't do this or that as sacrifices to the infernal god of time!"

"Don't be ugly."

For a moment, Lily's words scratched at the hardened door of her heart. The woman—so near her own mother's age—rarely corrected her, but of late, she had shown little patience with Willow's latent antagonism toward Chad. Lily seemed tired of it. "Do you have any idea how often he asked me why I didn't want to save time on this or that?"

"Do you have any idea how much of his own personal time he devoted to ensuring you didn't lose your harvest?"

"I tried to pay him—" she protested.

"You kicked him in the gut."

A smile spread across her face but she hid it from Lily. "Literally."

"What?"

"I kicked him in the gut the night before —"

"Before you lost your senses?" Lily interrupted, each word laced with irritation.

"I understand Chad is your little pet, and you feel badly that I don't worship at —"

Lily stood and moved toward the front door as if she'd rather go to bed than listen to any more. "Your anger has rotted into bitterness. You're taking it out on the wrong person. Attack Satan with your grief — not the people who have shown you nothing but love and affection in the face of your loss." She paused and turned back, her own emotions taking hold. "Let Jesus take these broken pieces of your heart and create stained glass art from them. Don't use them as weapons against the people who love you."

Tears overcame her — again. "Why do I get this way? I hate it! Why do you think I pushed Chad away?"

"Because you don't trust him."

Willow shook her head, watching the shadow move on the moonlit porch. "But I do —" Her voice quieted. "I think I don't trust me."

Lily returned, sank back down into the swing, and rewrapped the blanket around them. Willow dissolved into a fresh wave of tears. Between sobs and choking back sobs, she confessed, "I miss him."

"Let me call."

Her heart froze at the thought. "No."

Chad's shoulders slumped. "You've got to be kidding me. Now?"

"I thought it's what you've been workin' for, Chad. They called and asked for my best rookie. I told them that was you." The chief leaned against his desk, both palms flat on the top as though ready to shove it across the room.

Hands stuffed in his pockets, Chad shuffled his feet. "When would I start?"

"Thirty days."

He kicked his toe against the chair in front of him. "When do I have to decide?"

Varney sat quietly for what felt like hours. At last, he spoke. "Chad, son, it sounds to me like you already did."

The words twisted in his gut. The decision—it could affect every hope he had for his career. He wanted to shout, "I'll take it!" but instead he grit his teeth and muttered, "Yeah."

Chief Varney came around the corner of the desk and clapped a hand on his shoulder. "Well, I'm a little surprised, but I can't say I'm sorry. You're good for this place."

As Chad stepped out of the office, he heard the chief call for Martinez. It felt like a kick in the gut. He'd worked so hard for that job. He wanted that job. But until he knew Willow would be ok…

Her words flooded his memory as he grabbed his hat and the keys to his cruiser. *"No, Chad, I don't need a ride home."*

"Come on, Willow, this is ridiculous — "

"Well, ridiculous or not, I want to walk. I can do it now, so I want to," she argued.

"You'll be hurting by the time you get halfway there. You're going to overdo it — "

A crowd of people outside the church and across the street in the park overheard it and glanced their way. "Well it's my life to overdo, isn't it? You know, I am beginning to understand why my mother avoided people!"

He'd stepped forward, put an arm on her shoulder. "Willow, I'm sorry, but — "

"Just go away, Chad. Leave me alone. I'm tired of being your little project. I think it's time you found a new one. I'm not interested."

Tom Allen had stepped in and reminded her of all Chad had done to help her since her mother's death, particularly since her accident but had only fueled Willow's anger even further. She'd reached into her purse, pulled out a large wad of bills and tossed it onto the ground at his feet, turned, and fled weeping.

10

Even now, weeks later, Chad remembered the limp in her awkward gait and the anguish in her voice. When her anger and her rejection pierced deepest, her earlier words soothed. *"That's why you're safe to attack."* Until she no longer needed someone to bear the brunt of her pain, Chad wasn't going anywhere.

Chad felt Luke's eyes on him as he buffed, polished, and generally avoided what both men knew; the headstones were finished—had been for days. "Chad, you're going to wear that thing out. Just take it out there."

"She doesn't want it from me—not now."

"Yes she does. She wants you to keep fighting for her."

Chad stared at Luke with new interest. "Does Aggie flip like that?"

"Yes... well, not the same but they all have at times. Also, she has the children to hold onto. She has Mom and the church, Tina and William. And, she's had a few more months to deal with it."

"I'm so out of my element, but—"

"She's alone," Luke finished. "The aloneness strips you raw just to watch it."

"Yes! How'd you know?" The moment he spoke, Chad felt the foolishness of his words as they knocked the wind from him. "Dumb question."

They loaded the headstones into his truck, and Chad stood, leaning his head against his door. "How do I do this? She'll throw me off the property—"

"Just go put it on the grave. Don't ask. Just do it. She'll be glad... eventually."

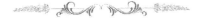

The shovel pierced the ground. Piles of dirt fell beside him as he made room for the headstone. Time continued as he dug, as if the pain represented by those slabs of wood meant nothing to the rest of the world. He worked slowly, each shovelful deliberately and precisely removed before he planned the next—a pathetic attempt to drag out the process in hopes she'd come see—yield. She didn't. Procrastination failed, he settled Kari's headstone into place, and moments later, the smaller marker for Othello stood proudly beside Kari's.

He sat, leaning against the tree and admiring his handiwork. Had he chosen the right wording? Was making one for Othello too much? The Finleys considered animals pets, not family. Chad shook his head as if to clear it. He had to stop second-guessing himself. The sun wrapped him in a warm cocoon, and the autumn breezes rustled the golden oak leaves above him, until Chad Tesdall fell asleep.

"Why won't he just leave!" Willow's fury neared epic proportions. "What is he doing out there?"

Though her leg and foot still didn't have the strength it once did, she went about her fall housecleaning as though unencumbered, only the pain that the mirror showed around her eyes proving that the effects of the injury still lingered. She swept the attic ceilings, wiped the walls, dusted and oiled the stored furniture, removed the rugs, beat them to within an inch of their existence, and when all was spotless, covered everything up there with the roll of sheeting plastic Chad had brought her weeks earlier. Just seeing that plastic irritated her. She didn't want it. In fact, she wanted to toss it at Chad's head.

From the porch, she glared at Chad's truck and nearly went crazy trying to see exactly what Chad was doing. He seemed to be sitting there at her mother's grave, which infuriated her further. "He's probably whining to Mother. *Tattling!*"

Half an hour later after dragging the rugs back up two flights of stairs (and ordering the memories of how helpful Chad had been the last time she'd beaten the rugs from her thoughts), Willow lost her patience and stormed out the front door. She called for Saige, but the dog seemed to have vanished.

Halfway across the field, Willow saw Chad rise from the base of the tree and walk toward his truck. Just before he climbed over the fence, he waved at her, paused for a response, and jumped over the fence. His truck roared to life, and he backed onto the highway. Tires squealed as he sped away from the farm.

"Yeah. You go. Go and stay gone. Everyone needs to just go away and stay away."

Her anger melted slightly as she saw the headstone. The handwork on it—so lovely. The carved lettering, the small cross at the top, and the well-oiled wood appealed to her love of beauty. The hand-carved inscription tore at her heart.

Kari Anne Finley
*Mother * Mentor * Friend*
Beloved

It was perfect, every word expertly chosen, placed, and the result was lovely. She wanted to thank him, but as seconds passed, her heart hardened again.

Darkness fell as she sat in the same spot Chad vacated hours earlier and poured out her soul to the Lord. Anger permeated her thoughts so thoroughly that she truly didn't think she'd ever rid herself of the rage now anchored in her heart. In rational moments, she knew she was wrong, but her pain always swallowed her reason and left her even more bereft and heartbroken than ever.

Bill had called and come by several times, but with no answer to his knocks and calls, he went away again. She'd stopped answering her phone. Chuck had come by twice, but each time she'd stepped outside the door, hugged him, and told him to go home. Lee's visits were brief. Willow didn't care to talk, but she didn't send Lee home. Only Lily's visits did she welcome and greet without question or orders to leave.

She no longer went to church and knew her rare visits to town reminded longtime residents of her mother—head down and her eyes focused on the destination, never meeting another's eyes if she could help it. Much of her adaptation to life around her was now lost in a cocoon of self-preservation—much like Kari's.

Hunger drove her into the house. Saige's side-swaggle walk failed to amuse her as it usually did. Her beef stew simmered on the stove, the bottom sticking to the pan but not yet burned. "That was close," Willow muttered to herself. She glared at the Dutch oven. "It's *his* fault."

The first bite was halfway to her mouth when she heard Chad's truck barrel into the yard and stop short. She'd recognize the sound anywhere, although it had been weeks since he'd come this close to the house. Before she could stand to order him from the property, he filled the doorway.

"Look. You can hate me. You can blame me for everything that has gone wrong in your life. I don't really care. Well, that's not true, but I understand. But the one thing that I asked you to do is keep your phone on and—"

She was on her feet by the time he finished speaking. "I don't have—"

Chad took two steps and their shoes nearly touched. "Yeah, ya do."

"Who do you think—"

"I'm a friend. A real one. I'm that one in Proverbs that'll hurt you if it's best for you and apparently, it is! You cannot live here alone without any way to call for help. Period."

"I did for nearly twenty-three years."

Chad stuffed his hands in his pockets in what she recognized as an attempt to keep them from throttling her. "And if you hadn't had the—" He swallowed and Willow wondered if he'd swear. He never had before, but... He continued without sullying their ears. "—thing with you, you'd be dead now. Dead. Do you get that? Do you realize you would have died if you had lain out there for hours? That was an artery you cut, woman!"

"It's my life to lose!" she flung back at him.

His voice, quieter and gentler than she could have imagined, and much more so than he'd ever been, broke a tiny hole in the wall she'd erected around her. "No it isn't."

"What?" she whispered, confused and weary.

"It's not your life anymore. You gave it to Jesus."

"I don't want to hear that."

A trace of a smile hovered around the corners of Chad's lips. "Where's the phone?"

"In the basket on my bedside table."

"Eat your dinner. I'll go get it."

Willow watched, stunned at his interference, as Chad strode from the room and out of sight. She sank into her chair and lifted the same spoonful of stew to her lips. She couldn't taste a thing. The rich gravy, the carrots, potatoes, tomatoes, and onions — she tasted none of it.

Chad stopped in the doorway, saw her bowl, and went to get her other one. He ladled himself a healthy amount of stew, grabbed a slab of sourdough bread, buttered it, and sat down at the table next to her. "I wondered about that. Your minutes lapsed."

Confused and somewhat annoyed, Willow watched as he ate her stew, pulled a new minutes card from his wallet, and added them to her phone. As if to be certain that everything was in working order, he grabbed his own phone and dialed. Her phone rang, and he pushed it across the table.

"Answer it."

"That's crazy."

He cocked one eyebrow at her. "Answer it."

She glared at him as she picked up the phone. "I'd say hello, but what's the point?"

"The point is that you can give me the silent treatment. You can wail, kick, scream, and fight me every step of the way, but I'm not leaving you alone anymore. You're not thinking clearly. No one should hurt alone."

"I have Lily."

"When she has time and until you decide you don't want her around either. I know what happens, and it's not happening anymore."

"I'll call the police."

Chad grinned as he took his last bite and stood to rinse it in the sink. "That'll work just great, because they won't have to send anyone out."

15

CHAPTER 40

Clyde McFarland pulled into Willow's long drive the last Thursday in October. Willow's note lay on the seat beside him, as if reminding him that everything had changed. The tattered edges of the note showed the wear of frequent rereading. For almost twenty years, Kari Finley had walked into Fairbury and called him, asking him to pick up their cow for butchering. This year, a handwritten note, signed by the girl, had arrived to request his services. The loss of Kari hit him hard—surprisingly so—but the cell phone number as a postscript... That hurt. Cell phones and the Finley farm did not mix.

As he rounded the curved driveway and pulled up to the house, he saw a truck parked in the yard. Surely, Willow hadn't bought a truck! His heart sank just a little—and then further as a man strolled across the back yard to the pasture gate. More than the loss of Kari and the addition of modern communication technology had changed around the old place. It saddend him to see it.

Willow strode toward him in the same familiar work boots, flannel shirt, and jeans. Some things hadn't changed. Clyde McFarland thought she was the freshest, most appealing young woman he'd seen in years. His eyes slid toward the young man at the gate. If expressions could be believed, the young fellow at the gate thought so too. Autumn winds whipped Willow's hair across her face, and Clyde snickered as the man whipped out a digital camera, snapped a picture of her swinging over the gate, and stowed it in his pocket before she had a chance to notice.

"Mornin', Willa. I was sorry to hear about Ms. Kari. She was one of the finest women I've ever met." His heart constricted as he watched her swallow hard and blink back sudden tears. It was still raw. How long had it been?

She gave him a watery smile. "Thanks. Mother liked you — trusted you. Mother didn't trust very many people."

"It was an honor to know her," Clyde said. He meant it too. He pointed to the trailer. "You want me to take care of this?"

Willow shook her head and grabbed a length of rope coiled on the fence post. "No thanks. I'll get her." The animal followed Willow to the trailer, and as "Dinner" climbed up the ramp, she patted the cow's nose. "I'll miss you, girl."

Clyde glanced at her sharply. The Finley women didn't "miss" their food. "Are you sure —"

"Of course. Thanks. I'll get the trash from the shed."

He'd arrived every other day for nearly a week. She'd yet to speak to him. He ate her food, milked her goat when he could beat her to it, and brought wood from the woodlot that she subsequently split and stacked. It drove him crazy how much she fought his help, but Chad had determined not to let her angst affect him.

Willow had ignored him since the moment he arrived, but Chad went about his work, watching the man with the livestock trailer with a bit of a suspicious eye. A part of him felt a little ridiculous — sort of like an overprotective brother or father who assumes the world is out to get his little girl. Still, this man was used to dealing with Kari, and from what Chad had learned of Kari, the woman frightened people. Willow wouldn't scare anyone who didn't know her well.

He watched, concerned, as she led the animal up the ramp and closed the rear gate on the trailer. That pause — the touch of Dinner's nose. It seemed so out of character. Clyde the butcher

18

seemed to think so too if his expression was worth anything.

Willow banged the side of the trailer to let Clyde know all was secure and then disappeared around the corner of the barn. Concerned—again—he moved to follow once the truck was out of his way. Instead, it drove to the end of the barn behind Wilhelmina's pen. Surely they weren't—they didn't eat— Chad swallowed hard. Before his stomach could begin churning the acids that rose and burned his throat as he imagined what he might have eaten with goat in it, Willow opened a small door in the barn—one he'd never noticed.

The trailer had two stalls. The second opened with an escape door and in there went two boxes and a barrel of what sounded like broken glass. Gunnysacks followed. He'd watched her burn trash—often, but he'd never considered that there might be trash she couldn't burn. Kari had provided for every aspect of their lives. The last bag rolled across the trailer floor as she shut the door. It was a very small amount of trash—hardly enough to consider, but it was gone.

The process was remarkably short. From the time McFarland arrived until he disappeared around the curve of the drive, hardly twenty minutes had passed. Chad watched her, waiting to see how she handled herself, and then climbed into his truck with a wave. She didn't acknowledge it—not that he thought she would.

His truck bounced over the lane. It was time to re-grade it. Just as he turned onto the highway, another livestock trailer arrived. *A new cow already?*

Willow, on the other hand, took a deep breath the moment his truck disappeared around the bend. Chad was gone; she could be off her guard. She fought the idea, but Chad's presence and help was comforting. Although she knew it was ridiculous, her deep rage held her in bondage. A sound sent her gaze toward the window.

"He's back?" she whimpered. "I thought he had to work."

Chad jerked the back door open and walked to the sink, grabbing his cell phone from the window. She shook her head at him and said, "Oh that's funny. That's really funny."

He winked at her as he passed. "Yeah, but I came back and

got it. I practice what I preach."

After Chad drove away, again, Willow went out back for more thrilling log-splitting fun. She stood log after log on the chopping stump, swung the axe, and stacked the smaller pieces on the back porch. The work went slowly — as tedious as she could possibly imagine. Exasperated, she slammed the axe into the splitting stump and left it there.

She jogged inside for her fishing rod, tackle box, and a thermos full of water. Ten yards away, she set them down and jogged back for a picnic blanket. She planned to sit and fish until she fell asleep from sheer boredom. Boredom, she had discovered, was a highly underrated commodity in today's society.

At the fishing hole, she spread her blanket, attached her fly, and settled herself along the bank of the stream. The fish weren't biting, which didn't surprise Willow. She listened to the birds twitter and the squirrels chatter and watched as golden leaves dropped around her. The infusion of raw nature on her soul had a more soothing impact than anything she could attempt to contrive. In the middle of nature's symphony, she fell asleep.

By the time she awoke, darkness covered the countryside and stars twinkled overhead. She lay there reveling in the beauty of the night sky, remembering other times that she'd slept under the same tree. If she was honest with herself, and that was something Willow refused to be just then, she would have admitted that she dreaded the return home. Her mother had always sat on the back steps petting Othello — Bumpkin in those earlier years — waiting. No matter how late she returned or how many fish she brought back with her, Mother had never complained.

Slowly, Willow retraced her steps home — every movement so familiar she could have made it blindfolded. The slight incline, all the way from the water's edge to the corner of the barn, was harder to climb than usual. Her left leg balked at the uphill climb. *I need to work more on those exercises,* she scolded herself.

By the time she neared the house, she noticed a strange

light as it flashed by the back door. At the corner of the barn, she paused. The light flashed again, and Willow recognized Chad's profile. Why was he back again? He'd been leaving her at least every other day or night. If he started to make it a daily habit again, she'd take it up with Chief Varney. *That'll show him.*

Once she reached the back step, Willow sat next to him and stared out into the darkness just he did. "Do you need something?"

"I just wondered how you were doing."

"You've got your phone…"

He sent her a sidelong glance. "I didn't know if you had it with you when I got here, so—"

"A few numbers and a send button would have told—"

Chad sighed. "I didn't want to know this time."

Remorse filled her heart. She'd brought him to this. He wasn't willing to call because of the likelihood that she'd react— badly. "Oh, Chad—"

He stood. "Glad you're fine." Without another word, he walked toward his truck.

"Chad?"

He turned. "Yeah?"

Willow reached into her pocket and pulled out her cell phone. Sliding it open, she showed him the light. "Got it."

Chad remained unmoved for several seconds and then retraced his steps until he stood just inches from her. Willow searched his face for some kind of indication of his thoughts. At last, and to her relief, he stuffed his hands in his pockets and gave her half a smile. "Thank you."

The screen door creaked as he stepped inside. Strange that he'd never heard it squeak. Willow heard nothing. The tears he had expected were actually deep, heart-breaking sobs. He knelt beside her, and patted her back. "Shh. It's going to be ok. It really is going to be ok."

Willow jumped, startled, and then flung herself at him. A fresh torrent of tears soaked Chad's shirt in seconds. "What—

why are you—" she swallowed hard, "why are you back tonight? Again."

"I had a feeling..." He couldn't finish. Her sobs drowned out any words he attempted. Not knowing what else to do, Chad sat awkwardly on the chaise, one leg uncomfortably higher than the other, and passed her bits of toilet paper, brushed her hair from her face, and made sympathetic noises. *Why didn't I send Lily?* he whimpered to himself. *I liked it better when she was getting close to Bill, and it looked like she wasn't quite so alone.*

"You know," she sniffled and grabbed another wad of toilet paper. "I'm so glad you're the one who lives here and not Bill."

"Why?" he asked, though he wasn't certain he wanted to hear the answer.

"Because you don't expect anything of me. Bill wanted me to become someone else, so I could be who he thought I should be. Chuck has his heart on his shoe, and I have to be sure to nurture it without stepping on it accidentally. But you, except for occasional bouts of clinginess—"

"Clingy!" Chad leaned back in surprise.

"Well, you did make showing up on my doorstep a habit..."

"You invited me! You specifically stood on that porch and said, 'I'd like to have people come over,'" he protested.

The tears stopped, hovering like a cloud ready to burst again, but she laughed. "I said stop in; I didn't say *move* in!"

"Hey! I didn't move in until you couldn't wal—" he began. "Um, let's try that again. I didn't *move* in, I was just consistently available when you needed help."

As if from out of nowhere, she asked, "Do you have a good name for a new goat? Willie is almost dry, so I need to trade her in—"

"You trade-in goats?"

Chad's appalled tone sent another wave of laughter over her. "Well, sure. We get a new goat every time the current one goes dry. We have an arrangement with a breeder in Brant's Corners."

22

"Why don't you wait and see what it looks like? I can't imagine naming an animal before I saw it. Didn't you say your mother looked in an animal's eyes?"

The moment he spoke, Chad regretted his question. She'd just come out of a crying jag, and it seemed that now he'd start a new one with his bungling. She just wanted to see her mother—to talk to her. Kari was an amazing woman. He would have liked—a sigh escaped.

"Chad, what is it?"

"*It* is selfishness."

"I don't understand. You sound—even look—sad."

His chuckle did not comfort her. It sounded cynical. "Well, you pegged it about right. I was sitting here thinking about how much I wish I had met your mother—about how often I think, 'Aunt Libby would have loved her,' and then I realized how selfish and pathetic I am to dare to want something for myself that should be my wish for you."

"Should you want what God didn't choose for me though? Is it right to do that?"

"Isn't that what grief is? Are you saying grief is wrong?"

Her hands flew into the air waving in protest. "No! That's not what I mean. And anyway, isn't grief just a manifestation of the rift caused by death that we weren't designed to handle in the first place?"

"That seems to imply that we're flawed, Willow."

"Well we are—"

"I mean the original design was."

"No, but we were designed for a life that we don't have." She struggled to sit upright as she explained her thoughts. "It's like what happened to me in Rockland. I was 'designed' for life on this farm and then 'woke up' in Rockland. It's—oh, I can't remember what it is called—some kind of shock."

"Culture shock."

"That's it!" she exclaimed. "We have culture shock with death, because we weren't created to suffer that loss."

She stood. "You look miserable. Let's go for a walk."

"Where?" Chad just wanted to go home, but Willow's thawed reaction to him wasn't something to ignore.

23

"To the swing. You can push me. You like to push people around."

"I do not!"

Their good-natured argument continued out the door, down the steps, and around the barn to the tree. Willow settled herself carefully in the swing and tiptoed back until her feet couldn't reach any further. "Oh, it's chilly. I should have brought my jacket."

"Take mine," Chad insisted wriggling out of it. "I'm not creating a personal breeze."

"Bossy," she accused as she stopped the swing and thrust her arms into the warm flannel-lined sleeves of his denim jacket. "Hey, this is warm. I thought it'd be cold. Denim isn't the warmest fabric."

"Don't you have flannel-lined jeans?"

"Well—"

"I rest my case. Denim jackets need liners the same as every other jacket," he informed her with mock haughtiness.

"Know-it-all."

She pushed back and released the swing again. Chad pushed it as it swung back to him and said, "I thought I was Mr. Bossy."

"That too."

The crisp night air stung his nose as he stood there, pushing the swing higher and higher. From his vantage point, it seemed as though the next shove would send her flying through the night sky. The jostling of the tree branch shook leaves that sprinkled down on them from the tree. It was the scene of movies—mushy, ridiculous chick flicks that his mother and sister loved.

Words tumbled from him—ones he didn't care to share. "You know, I don't like telling people what to do. I'm better at following orders than giving them."

"You're in a strange job for that," she retorted.

"My high school guidance counselor gave me one of those career aptitude tests."

"What are they?"

He regretted mentioning it. "Well, they just ask you a

24

bunch of questions, and based upon your answers, they give you career advice. I scored high on law enforcement except in one area."

"What was that?"

"Leadership. I'm not naturally a take-charge kind of guy."

"Could have fooled me." Willow's voice held a tone of amusement.

"They put you through all kinds of psychological profiling before they let you in the academy, and I had to talk to the psychologist about my resistance to taking charge when I have 'natural leadership skills and instincts.'"

"That doesn't make sense."

He shivered as he pushed the swing again. "Well, basically I know how to be bossy, I'm willing to be bossy if I have to, but I only do it if I have to or if it's my job."

"So what part of your job is it to boss me around?"

Chad sounded like he was laughing as he shouted, "I'm not bossy!"

Willow jumped from the swing, landing eight feet away. Her calf screamed its protest, but she forced herself to ignore it. Jumping from swings was a normal part of her life. She had to try it some time. She spun in place and muttered, "Are too."

Chad took a step closer and crossed his arms over his chest. "Am not."

Not to be outdone, Willow took a step closer as well as she said, "Are too."

Mentally, she calculated the distance to the fence. If she could make it there before him, she'd beat him to the house. However, with her gimpy leg, she knew it was a risk. Somehow, she had to get a head start, or she would have no chance of winning a footrace against someone taller, stronger, and without a leg with nerve damage.

Chad's, "I. Am. Not!" growled back at her as he took another step toward her.

The swing. She had to keep the swing between them.

25

Stepping slightly away from the fence and toward the swing and Chad, she put her hands on her hips and insisted, "You are too."

"Am not."

He was almost close enough. One more step. Without a word, she crossed her arms to match his and took the largest step she could without looking too obvious. She nodded. "Mmm hmm."

As though choreographed perfectly, he stepped to the swing and placed his arms on the ropes, shaking his head. Willow pounced. She twisted the seat of the swing, making an 'x' in the rope and shoved it over his head. Chad shouted in protest. "Are too!"

She ran. Without a glance to see how successful she'd been, she thundered across the grassy field, nearly vaulted the fence, and raced across the front yard. Once in the house, she locked the door, but seeing Chad racing for the back door, she hurried through the room, knocking over a chair in the kitchen. The lock turned in place just as Chad's hand touched the knob.

"That's not fair! You have my jacket."

"Mother always said that life isn't fair."

"I'm freezing out here," he protested.

"You were fine at the tree," she countered.

"That's what you think," he muttered under his breath. How she heard it, Willow didn't know. "It's called dying to self. It's what I do."

"Admit you're bossy and you get your jacket back."

"Admit you're obnoxious and I'll consider it."

She unlatched the door and strode into the living room. With his jacket hung from one finger, she turned and asked, "You admit you're bossy?"

"I will concede that when provoked, I can be, um— confidently protective."

"That's the new term for bossy. Got it."

He glared and took another step closer. "And you are…"

"You think that I am obnoxious."

"You are." He snatched his jacket from her. "And don't you forget it."

"See. You prove my point beautifully."

Chad opened the door and stepped onto the porch as he pulled the jacket over his arms. "That's what you think." At the bottom of the steps, he waved. "Goodnight."

"Chad?"

He paused. "Hmm?"

"Thanks for coming. I feel better."

"That was the goal. Night." He opened the door to his truck and slid onto the seat, watching for a light to come on somewhere in the house. *Come on. I'm watching for her to light something somewhere and we both know it.*

As he started his truck, he groaned, slamming the palm of his hand against the steering wheel. *I can't get rid of her! Even when I can, I can't. Why did I come back? She told me to stay away! Why. Can't. I. Just. Stay. Away?* He started the engine, muttering, "and I am *not* bossy!"

As Chad drove toward the highway, he rubbed an itchy jaw against his collar. The slightest whiff of lavender teased his senses. Great. Now his favorite jacket smelled like her. A grin split his face. Yeah. *Smelled* like her. She smelled. Good smells counted as smelly, right? His life wasn't one of those sappy books with phrases like, "The fragrance of her permeated his thoughts, his dreams, his heart."

"Oh, puke."

CHAPTER 41

Lee's voice rose to an excited pitch. "So I went in and I told them—I said, 'Look, she's a fabulous designer, and she made those samples in no time, by hand, from her sick bed no less. You know you want them.'"

"And that impressed them?" Willow filled the freezer with packages of beef, organized from front to back.

"Well no, not that. Suki said that without someone to run the store, they didn't have a use for the designs. Oh, and that their first designer and she were 'professionally incompatible,' so they decided they wanted an all-in-one kind of person if they were going to expand."

"That makes sense—can you hand me that roast?"

"Why are you mixing up the meat?" she asked as she passed the lump of beef.

"It's just how we do it."

Lee shrugged and eagerly returned to her topic of choice. "Anyway. I told them that I'd love the job of managing the store and collaborating with you. They'll consider it in a meeting with us."

"Really? I thought it was all or nothing?"

Practically jumping and squealing, Lee grabbed Willow's hands. "I know! Isn't it great!"

The loading of the freezer went quicker than ever. With half a cow stored for the winter and the previously frozen vegetables moved to the veggie freezer, Willow grabbed a slab of brisket and followed Lee into the house, chattering about the possibilities.

"So I wouldn't have to leave the farm?"

"Nope. I'd bring out the fabric swatch books as often as I could, and if we had to meet with a sales rep, you could just come in for the day."

Willow glanced around her, smiling. "You were right. I belong here, but this is so exciting! I can do both. I can live my life, and I can play with clothes!" After a moment, her brow furrowed. "Why do they want *me*? Why isn't the designer for the women's store doing the children's wear?"

Lee shrugged as she accepted a glass from Willow. "He doesn't want to. He's working on a collection of his own as well as Boho, so..."

They discussed their plans for hours. Lee had to press Willow to make some of the designs a little less practical for an upscale shop, but once she caught the vision, Willow managed to create ideas that kept the illusion of custom design with couture detailing but requiring simple construction. Sundresses, tops, shorts, capris, and skirts appeared on her sketchpad.

"Wait. What about your salon?"

Lee shook her head. "I have two great stylists. If I get a manager, I can just check the books and inventory on Sunday nights and be fine.

Their eyes met. Lee reached across the table to shake Willow's hand. "I'm excited. I'll have Suki's bosses draw up the papers."

February 1997-

Town drives me crazy. There is so much busyness — so much stress and haste. I sense it in myself sometimes. There's always this drive to be going and doing, and to some extent, it is necessary. Sometimes, when I see how many more new conveniences there are, I wonder why people don't have more time. Why do people work so hard with "labor and time saving devices" and yet have less time than ever?

And the quest for stuff seems insatiable. First people rented those

30

huge laser disks that were the size of record albums and three times thicker. Then came not only the VCR but also the Beta. Some people had both at once. Now it seems like everyone is moving to these new DVDs. With every new "upgrade." I hear and read more about how people can have more because they take up less space. There's nothing wrong with it, but where does it end?

Willow, on the other hand, is untouched by it all. I smugly thought it was my brilliant discourses on the subject over the years, but I wonder now if it isn't just that she's naturally content. At her age, I was so bored unless I was going, going, going. I was too old for the things most little girls enjoy and too young for teenaged pursuits. I was stuck in a limbo created by our modern lifestyle. I didn't want that for Willow.

She, on the other hand, is stuck in both worlds. That child keeps us in fish. She can butcher a chicken twice as fast as I can, and she tills the soil like there's no tomorrow. The books she reads would have been far beyond my comprehension, and I certainly wouldn't have found them interesting. However, she swings for hours. She makes daisy chains, roams the property with Bumpkin, and spends hours creating alternate realities for her little dolls in their house. Oh and of course, Triple Chinese Checkers. It bothered her that four of the triangles weren't used so she created yet another way to fry my neurotransmitters. We play three colors and try to wipe out our opponent without killing off our players. Her strategy is brilliant I'm sure. I just wish I knew what it was so I could beat her.

Valentine's Day, 1997-

Continuing my goal of infusing the holidays into her consciousness this year, I mailed Willow a store-bought Valentine. She was so excited when she brought up the mail (ok, she always is. It's not like we get much). I thought she'd find it a little silly, but the novelty factor helped.

Oh my! She's been holed up in her room for the past two hours and just brought me her Valentine for me. She copied every aspect of it perfectly. She made an envelope, a stamp – complete with curfed edges, a "seal," made from melting candle wax no less, and then the card. She was obviously influenced by the one I gave her, but like everything she does, she took it to another level. The embossed tussie-mussie on the

31

front of the purchased card morphed into a 3-D basket when I opened this card. All those hours of making snowflakes paid off. It is truly a work of art. Her poem, on the other hand, while charming and therefore in my mothering eyes perfect, was less than inspiring.

*I think that I shall never see
A Mother loved as much as thee.
Without you I would be bereft
Oh Lord, don't take her from me yet.*

I didn't know I was so near to the grave. Somehow, I didn't laugh. Well, not until I heard her titter from the other room. Then we had the biggest tickle-fest and pillow fight in the history of the Finley family. I confess, I won. What can I say?

Chad read the journals from his couch. Sprawled comfortably with one leg over the back and the other barely resting on the floor, his favorite Keith Urban CD playing softly in his MP3 player, he'd spent the majority of his afternoon lost in Kari's world. Willow had thoughtfully dropped them off with a jar of homemade—could it be any other kind?—chicken soup on her way to Rockland for a business meeting with Renee, Bill, and Lee.

He grabbed another tissue and sneezed, dropping the journal as he did. His head exploded. After two days of sick leave, he was ready to go crazy. His stomach rumbled, but the effort required to drag himself from the couch and reheat the soup was more than he thought he wanted to expend. His stomach growled again. He reached for another tissue and found the box empty.

"Well, if I have to get up," he mumbled to himself, "at least I can kill a chicken with my tissue." His head shook, confused. "Wait, that doesn't sound right. Whatever. I'll eat."

He found a quart-canning jar in the fridge with the richest smelling broth he'd ever imagined. Homemade noodles floated in the mixture. Carrots, celery, onions, and what smelled like hearty dose of garlic, mingled in the simmering pot sending his stomach rumbles to new levels of discontent. He stepped away and his stuffed nose smelled nothing. A step closer—mmm.

There it was. He'd eaten better in the past six months, excluding about six weeks of culinary and personal misery, than he had since he left home for the police academy.

He rifled through his sparsely populated cupboards for crackers, but Cheese Nips didn't sound appetizing with chicken soup. Her loaf of bread tempted him, but instead, he filled a glass of water and carried it to the floor by the couch. A last glance at the fridge sent him back for a bottle of Sprite. Colds were cured by Sprite and chicken soup. It was a Jewish proverb or something. He'd read it somewhere. Well, the chicken soup part, but he knew that if that proverbial Jewish mama had ever had Sprite, it would have been added to the prescription.

He inhaled the soup and glanced toward the stove. So far away and yet so tempting. A wave of sleepiness washed over him. He'd better at least put it away or he'd wake up to spoiled and wasted soup and that would be criminal. As local law enforcement, it was his duty to prevent crime, not commit it. Yes, he must eat the soup. Oh, drat. How sad.

Hours later, he awoke and found Willow sitting on the floor, across the room, covered in his comforter, and reading one of her mother's journals. "Hey, whatcha up to?"

"I'm cold."

"I can see that. Are you sick?"

She shook her head. "No, but I will be if I walk home." She reached down and pulled the comforter over her leg. It looked funny, that leg.

"What happened to your jeans?"

"I don't know," she said irritably. "I've lost my tote bag with my jeans, warmer jacket, hat, water bottles—"

Chad sat up concerned. "What about your purse?"

"I had it out to pay for the bus ticket. That's actually when I found my bag missing. I think it was stolen."

"I'll take you home."

Shaking her head, she motioned for him to stay seated. "I don't want that. You're sick. I just thought maybe you knew who might be able to drive me home and if someone might have a jacket that I can borrow until I can order a new one. I need that jacket."

Phone in hand, Chad did a quick Google search and dialed the feed store. When no one answered, he dialed the chief's house and asked for Terry's last name. Within minutes, he'd arranged a jacket to be delivered, to his door, and as fast as Terry Boucher could get it there. "Chief sounds worse than me, so I didn't ask if Darla could go. I'll take you."

"That's ok, with a better jacket, I'll be ok. Do you have a pair of sweat pants I could put on over my skirt. I'd be shaped funny but warmer."

Chuckling, Chad stood, wobbled, and then shuffled to his bedroom. "As much as I'd love to see that, forget it. Besides, maybe..." he wheedled, "if I take you home... you'll be merciful and share some more of your soup."

Before she could protest, he shut the door behind him. A sigh of exhaustion escaped the moment he hid behind the door. He didn't want to drive. He actually didn't really want more soup right then. All he wanted was to close his curtains, crawl into bed, and sleep—for a very long time. However, he knew how hard it was for Willow to ask for help. If she asked, she needed it. Period. By the time he found someone available, he could have driven her there himself.

Terry's knock came swifter than he expected. Chad gulped at the price, but Willow didn't hesitate. She wrote her check, albeit painfully slowly, and thanked the older man profusely. "I don't think Mother knew you sold Carhartt. I know we bought her last one from a catalog."

"That's when I started selling them. The jacket didn't arrive, so she asked if I'd be able to find a reputable dealer. Your financial guy took care of it I think. Everyone wanted your mom's jacket, so I started carrying them."

"Well, I appreciate it. Mother caught her sleeve on fire last time she wore it, so she was going to get a new one." Her voice caught before she added, "I bet she would have bought it from you."

As the door shut behind Terry, Willow turned back to Chad. "Are you sure? I can walk now, or maybe one of the other officers—"

"Let's go."

Almost from the moment they climbed into his truck, it was too quiet. Chad nudged her and said, "Talk to me. I need to stay awake. Tell me about your meeting."

"Well, I signed the contract. Renee and Bill both agreed it was a sound deal for all of us. I produce twenty-four pieces ready for display by December first. I guess they'll provide all the materials, have someone pick them up for me, and the store opens January seventh."

"And they're paying you enough?"

"I think it's more than generous. They offered me a flat price per item for my labor and designing time, and then I get a commission on every piece sold plus a bonus at different levels." She smiled excitedly. "They even took my advice and are pre-making eight of the styles. I said that parents would probably want to be able to buy something last minute too, so they're going to keep a limited stock."

"This store interests you." He was intrigued by her insights and enthusiasm in the planning process. Chad wanted to question her about whether she'd made the right decision about staying in Fairbury, but exhaustion barely allowed him to drive. This was a bad idea. He was two blinks from an accident.

Willow, apparently unaware of Chad's fuzzy thinking, chattered about the logo they had designed and the plan for a play corner for the children. "Oh and they liked my name suggestion."

He felt groggy… the blur of the road blending into the blur in his mind. He heard something — something familiar. "Chad?"

"Huh?" He swerved slightly and turned into her driveway.

"Chad! You almost hit the corner of that fence!"

His eyes flew open wider. "Did I? I didn't notice that."

At her door, Willow begged Chad to come in and stay but he refused. She rushed in, filled another jar with soup, and hurried back out to his truck, shivering in the cold night air. "Now you call me when you get home so I know you're not dead on the side of the road somewhere."

"Yes, Mother."

"That's not funny. Call me."

35

Willow prayed earnestly as she milked Willie, fed and bedded down the chickens, and filled "Belinda-the-new-cow's" water trough. She checked her phone twice as she strained the milk and sterilized the bucket. No call.

By the time she'd eaten a bowl of soup, washed her dishes, and cleaned out the sink, she was nervous. Thirty minutes later, she called. No answer. She tried repeatedly for the next half hour but with no better results. An hour and a half was too long to drive five and a half miles.

She could call the police and ask them to check his house or the highway, but would he get in trouble? Could it hurt his job if they knew he drove while sleepy? What could she say that was truthful without giving it away? Chuck and Bill were too far away. She could walk there before—

Without a second thought, she changed clothes, put on her warmest jeans and her new jacket, grabbed gloves, hat, flashlight, and at the last second, stuffed them in a tote bag with their first aid kit. It was bulky, but if he'd hurt himself... She tried his number again. Nothing. Perhaps she should call Pastor Allen. Would he feel obliged to report Chad though? If only she knew the protocol on those kinds of things. Nope. She was walking. It wasn't worth the risk.

Willow was furious, both with herself and with Chad. This was unnecessary. A gust of wind howled against her kitchen window. "Great. Now wind too. I thought I smelled that northern gale coming," she muttered to an empty room as she banked the fire in the stove.

She stuffed the tote bag in her jacket, pulled the strings tight around her hips, and stuck her arms in the straps before she zipped up the coat. Gloves slid comfortingly over her fingers. Her ear warmers came next, followed by her warmest felted hat. Finally, she knotted a scarf over the entire head ensemble to ensure the wind didn't snatch it.

She called at nearly every mile. Where moonlight shone, she tucked the flashlight back in her jacket, but when it dipped behind trees or behind a cloud, she whipped out and trudged along the highway. Twice she heard a car, saw lights, and flattened herself in the ditch until the vehicle disappeared around a bend, feeling just a little foolish. Were Mother's orders logical at a time like that? She didn't know. Still she trudged onward. According to Bill's way of thinking, you wouldn't offer a stranger a ride anyway, and that probably went double for late at night.

By the convenience store, she was nearing panic. Where could he be? At the corner of Market and Elm Streets, she tried to blend into the hedge as Martinez made his last circle of the town square before his shift ended, his headlights sweeping just a few feet from her. She trudged to the apartment on Bramble Row, growing more concerned with each step but the sight of Chad's truck parked crookedly at the curb both annoyed and relieved her.

"That man!"

She pounded on his door but Chad didn't answer. The door was locked. She crossed the hall and listened. Someone was inside talking, so she knocked on the door. A man answered, but appeared to be alone. It took her a moment to realize that the voices were probably from a TV. *I have to watch something sometime,* she thought irrelevantly and asked, "Do you know if Chad's home?"

"Thought I heard him a while ago, why?"

"He's not answering his phone."

The man rubbed a potbelly and grinned. "Well, a guy does have to sleep. Maybe he turned it off."

"He's awfully sick. I just want to make sure he's ok, but he won't answer his door or his phone."

"Sick, you say?"

"Fever, chills, sneezing—" Willow began.

"Sounds like the influenza. Supposed to be bad this year. I got a key for his place around here somewheres. He gave it to me a while back, but where—" A light came into the man's eyes. "I know. I saw it just the other day when I was scrounging up change for a paper. It's in the medicine cabinet. I'll be right back."

Willow couldn't fathom why someone would put a house key in a medicine cabinet or why he'd look there for loose change. When he brought her the key, she quickly opened Chad's door and brought it back. "He wanted you to have the key so—"

"That's nice of you ma'am. Want me to go check on him?"

"If I need you, I'll knock. Thanks."

"I was sick and wanted to sleep, so I turned it off!"

"And when I turned mine off, I got my head chewed off! You said you'd call!"

Chad stuffed his hands where his pockets should be but came up empty. "I forgot. I was tired, sleepy, and I'm not used to having to check in with Mommy!"

"Gee," she retorted, "that sounds extremely familiar. I thought you were dead or at least had the courtesy of being mostly dead on the side of the road."

"Well, I'm mostly dead in my bed so will you just go away?"

Willow's head snapped back as though punched. "I'll do that." She paused, glaring at him before adding, "Don't ever hold me to a standard you won't keep to yourself again. Ever."

At the door, she turned back. "And turn your phone on, or next time I walk five miles in cold wind you'll feel it. I assure you."

CHAPTER 42

Chad bolted upright in bed, his heart pounding, and his mind whirling. He took a deep breath. It was just a dream. His head felt clearer than it had in days.

What a dream! *Sending Willow out into the cold after a long walk like that, it was unconscionable.* He frowned. Where had the word unconscionable come from? He didn't talk or think with gold-plated words. Only the knowledge that he'd never do such a thing kept him from being sickened by his own somnolent hallucinations.

Was this some kind of warning from the Lord? Was he being overbearing about her safety? He had no right; he knew that. He had no rights whatsoever. An imaginary taste of his own medicine might just be what the Lord had prescribed to open his eyes.

He stood, amazed at several minutes of consciousness without sneezing, and waited for a wave of dizziness. Feeling silly when it didn't come, Chad stretched. His muscles felt tight and unused, but other than that, he felt back to normal, almost.

After tooth de-fuzzification, he hurried into the kitchen—starved. A jar of soup on the counter stopped him cold in his tracks. "I thought I ate that," he muttered. "How strange. I must have dreamed that too—"

A dirty pot, bowl, and splatters on the counter assured him that he didn't dream anything of the kind. Memories flooded his mind. The drive to Willow's, the concern in her eyes, the blare of a semi's horn at the curve just before the Fairbury turn-off. He'd really driven after all. Not good. He could have killed someone.

He gripped the counter as Willow's face loomed over him. He could still feel the aching shakes as she fought to wake him up. His mind watched in horror as her eyes went from fear and concern to anger and disbelief. He'd broken her trust. Nothing hurt him more than the idea that he foolishly put people in danger—except maybe that he'd disappointed Willow.

He shook his head. He didn't want to think about that. "Take a shower and work from there, man. This is bad."

"Chief, I can come in, but I need to take a drive out to the Finley place first." Chad paused listening to the Chief's concerns. "No really, I know it's my day off, but Joe and Judith worked their days off to cover me. I can at least cover one of them."

He slid his phone shut and glanced at his watch. Two hours before work. His eyes traveled to his closet. Should he change now and leave straight from Willow's for work? A glance at the soup jar on his counter clinched it. He'd change first. She might not throw leftovers on him if he was dressed in his uniform. As he reached for his uniform, he sighed. Only one clean one left. He couldn't risk it.

Thirty minutes later, he drove up the long driveway wearing jeans, a sweatshirt, and his uniform safe on the seat of his truck. The sound of her axe told him she was chopping wood. Again. The last thing he wanted to do was tousle with an axe-wielding angry woman like Willow.

He stood off to the side as Willow split wood like a pro. That thought amused him. She was a pro. Splitting wood kept her warm and fed all winter. Her life depended on it. Literally.

As she tossed another piece of wood into the wheelbarrow, he could have sworn she raised one eyebrow at him. He swallowed hard. "So I came to tell you about this dream I had."

"Really?"

Chad stuffed his hands in his pockets. "Yeah. I woke up in a panic because I dreamed that you walked all the way to my house to make sure I was ok, and I just kicked you out."

"Really now?"

This wasn't good. She managed to add a new word but the old one still hung there— taunting him. "I was so relieved to wake up and realize it was a dream. Well, until I went in my kitchen and saw a jar of soup on my counter—and an empty one in the sink."

"Humph."

"So, I grabbed some work clothes and drove straight out here to see if I really did what I'm afraid I did, or if my dreams are just more vivid than I realized."

"Get me some water, will you?"

The request surprised him. He'd expected sarcastic remarks about feeling better, angry comments about having to work hard to warm up after her walk, but a request was the last thing he'd expected. "Sure."

Water dripped from his nose, chin, and all over his sweatshirt seconds after he handed her the glass. "What—"

"I've read in books about women doing that. It always sounded so satisfying, but I never thought I'd have an occasion to do it."

Chad shivered and brushed water from his sweatshirt, thanking the Lord for dirty laundry protecting his uniform. "Willow, there's no excuse for what I did—"

"That's for sure."

"—but I am very sorry. I wouldn't have ever done anything like that consciously."

She dropped the axe and leaned her hands on her knees, her eyes barely raised to his face. "I was terrified. I can't lose any more people in my life. I don't have enough to spare."

"Forgive me?"

Without thinking, Chad arranged his features into the practiced boyish earnestness combined with masculine charm that worked so well on his mother. To his chagrin, and his relief, it worked. Willow rolled her eyes, threw up her hands, and said, "Oh, you're impossible. Come in, I have cherry bars."

41

Cherry bars. He'd sent her home in freezing weather and she had cherry bars. What was wrong with this picture?

Just as he stepped inside the door, she thrust a plate in his hands with a glazed cookie bar on it. Chad took the plate and stood near the stove, trying to dry his sweatshirt. "This is good. Almond."

"I had some dried cherries once, so Mother and I tried to come up with a recipe we liked. I think they're good."

"Good," he agreed between bites.

"I shouldn't have thrown water on you out there in the cold. It's a fine way to get you sick while your resistance is already down." She sighed. "I'm sorry, Chad."

"I send you home in the cold and you're sorry." He shook his head and added, "Look. Let's consider it behind us. I'm getting the better end of the bargain, but..."

She seated herself at the table and pulled out marking pens and a piece of paper she'd been embellishing. Small flowers slowly appeared scattered across the paper. Willow talked as she drew the flowers, sometimes meeting his eyes while still coloring in a leaf or a petal.

"Is there anything you can't do?"

"What's that supposed to mean?"

His index finger thumped on the table, just once, next to the paper. "That's what I mean. You cook, you preserve, you work the land, you butcher animals, you draw, sew, and create strategic versions of games that require incredible mental skills. What can't you do?"

"Music."

"You sing..."

"Not well, though. I sound ok, great compared to Alexa Hartfield actually, but still, it's just a generic voice. I can't play an instrument of any kind."

The longing in her voice, the idea that she hadn't learned something that she sounded interested in—it surprised him. "Why not? That sounds like just the kind of thing you'd do on a winter's evening."

"Mother was adamant. We couldn't learn from a book, so we didn't learn."

42

"I don't understand. Why not just pick up an instrument and play with it until you figured it out. I mean, the first people who ever used an instrument had to do that."

With a sigh that deepened that longing, she shook her head. "Mother said that you'd learn terrible habits if you weren't taught to hold your mouth or your fingers correctly, and it'd only leave you disappointed when it limited you or made it impossible to learn."

"How sad."

"It is how it is. Mother was always right about these things, so I just learned to focus in other areas." The traces of yearning in Willow's voice almost hurt him.

"Is there something you wanted to learn?"

With a smile that struck him as sad, Willow shook her head. "I never let myself think about it."

Kari had made one mistake in the world she created on their farm. She developed a love of learning, beauty, grace, and artistry in their lives. Every year was an exercise in living life as richly and fully as they could. Learning new things became a way of life, but somehow she'd managed to stall this area. Chad hoped to find why and how in her journals. It seemed out of character for her.

Chad stood rinsing his plate as he did. "I am sorry to hear that. I think you'd enjoy it." He rose, glancing at his watch. "I've got to get to work."

As he stepped out the back door, Willow's voice stopped him. "I thought of something else."

"What?"

"Money. I don't get it."

He stared at her in surprise. "But you have such a head for numbers!"

"I can't seem to translate it into practicality. I'm really glad mother had such a good financial advisor."

Chad returned the table and leaned against the back of his chair. When her eyes rose to him, questioning, he said, "Willow, your financial guy is only as good as your understanding of what he does."

"… financial guy is only as good as your understanding of what he does."

Chad's words pounded her mind from every corner. He must be right. Bill was trustworthy, but Willow knew her mother watched their accounts carefully. She could add, subtract, multiply; basic math skills were a breeze. The abstract concepts of applying those numbers in daily living were another story. Counting dollars was not a problem, but assigning value to items made no sense to her.

That evening, she poured over Kari's accounting journals and Bill's monthly and semi-annual statements. Chad found her at the kitchen table, hands cupped protectively over her head and tears of frustration threatening to overcome her at any minute. "Hey, what're you doing?"

"Trying to understand it all. There are all of these numbers; they all make sense on paper but not in my head."

"Well, I only have an hour but—"

She shoved the journals off the table. "But why can't I understand it? I'm not stupid!"

"Hey—" He touched her arm lightly. "Hey, look at me. You are right. You're not stupid. But you've lived a life where you never actually used money. Value of items is personal to you instead of collective."

She blinked slowly, tightening the hands over her head. "Ok, you're losing me already."

"Well, for example, what would you pay for my truck?"

She looked at him blankly. Willow Finley had no interest in his truck. "I don't know. I'm sure trucks are expensive—all that metal and stuff."

"Ok, so how much would you pay for it?"

"Nothing. I don't want it."

Chad whirled the other chair around and sat backwards in it. "Well, if you did—"

"Um, probably a few hundred dollars. Maybe even a thousand."

"Oh, how I wish! I'd keep more of my paycheck every

month."

She shook her head. "I don't understand. What does it have to do with your paycheck?"

"Well, that truck was almost twenty-five thousand dollars before down-payment and trade-in. I have to pay four hundred dollars a month. By the time I get another chance at the job in Rockland, it'll be paid off."

Her eyes widened. "How can you afford that?"

"I don't have many expenses. My apartment's cheap and includes utilities. I decided I'd buy it with today's dollars instead of tomorrow's."

"But it's so much money. That's what we spend on living a year on expensive years, look!"

"Oh, Willow, you and your mother had so few living expenses compared to most Americans. You had no car insurance, car payments, no mortgage, almost no food budget— Those are the big ticket budget items."

She pointed out her mother's expenditures, mystified by the price of things. "Seeds. Look at the price of seeds! They're so inexpensive. You pay four hundred dollars a *month* for just a tiny piece of a truck but we don't pay that much a year for *seeds*!" None of it made sense. "Food is so much more important than that truck."

Chad glanced at his watch. "I'll come back tomorrow afternoon. We'll do this—you and me. You *can* learn it. You've just never had to, and I think—"

Her head snapped up instinctively. "What?"

"I think that now you've been exposed to it a little more, you'll get it."

A smile lit her face. "Of course. I just need time. And I can ask my lawyer to look over new account sheets to make sure she agrees with Bill's decisions until I understand it, can't I?"

Chad nodded. "Or, I can look for you. I took some economics and financial classes in college."

She gathered the papers and shoved them in a pile, dumping her mother's journals on top. "I'll just wait until you can help me understand then." Relieved, she jumped up to add a log to the stove as she said, "I need to remember to teach it all to whoever I put in my will." She sighed. "Yeah, Bill said I have to make a will." Her eyes widened. "Wait, I was going to leave it to you anyway, so I don't have to teach you anything."

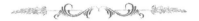

Chad's cruiser sped toward Brunswick with another drunk in the back seat, but his mind was on Willow. He'd deceived her. Deliberately. He'd chosen to use truth to hide truth. Kari Finley had chosen not to help her daughter understand money. She'd known of Willow's educational gap; that was obvious. And he'd hidden that fact from her.

"Lord, now what?"

"You shay shumpin' to me?"

Glancing into his rearview mirror, Chad shook his head. "I'm sorry. Talking to the Almighty."

The drunk's head lolled to one side and a snore followed. Chad's mind reverted to his prayer but he kept it internal. *"I lied to her, Lord. What do I do about that? Do I confess? Do I just tell her some other time? Do I keep my mouth shut? I don't know. I know Kari had her reasons. Surely, they're in the journals somewhere. Find it and let her read it herself?"*

He prayed all the way to Brunswick. An hour later, minus a drunk and with a strong odor of Lysol-tainted vomit in his car, Chad zipped past the Finley farm and breathed easier as he saw it enshrouded in darkness. She was sleeping again. Sleep meant she wasn't worrying. Now if he only could.

He entered his apartment at ten forty-five and stared at his phone. Without a second thought, he punched number four and waited. "Luke? I've got a problem."

With a thud, Chad dropped a stack of papers, catalogs, magazines, and newspapers on her coffee table. "Welcome to American Consumerism 101."

"What is all of this?"

"Well, these," Chad held up a stack of papers, "are

46

examples of household budgets. They represent every demographic—from those at poverty level to those making six and seven figures. Aggie knew where to look and even found ones that show how much people spend on specific things like shoes, eating in restaurants, and haircuts."

As she flipped through a few of the papers, Willow felt instantly overwhelmed. "And the newspapers?"

"They show what's happening in the economy."

"Catalogs?"

"To give you a sense of the difference in prices of things. There are some ads in the papers too. You can compare the price of a pair of running shoes from Wal-Mart vs. the catalogs and then look at the budget summaries."

Her eyes blinked. "Why would I do that?"

"Well, from that you could learn what kind of quality different people could afford." Chad could see she didn't understand him. "For instance, a man making twenty-five thousand dollars a year can't afford to spend one hundred dollars for a pair of leather athletic shoes from a store in the mall. He's more likely to go to Wal-Mart and buy a cheap pair for twenty dollars."

"But that doesn't make sense," she protested.

"Why not? He can't afford to spend five times the money on a pair of shoes."

"He can't afford not to."

"I don't think you understand. Let me try—"

Annoyed, Willow slapped the papers against her thighs. "No, *you* don't understand. I assume the leather shoes are better made?"

"Well yes,"

"And will last much longer?" she continued.

"Yes, but—"

"And they're probably better for his feet too. More comfortable maybe, and have good support?"

Chad threw up his hands in surrender. "Yes, all of that, but—"

"That's exactly why he can't afford the twenty dollar pair. A person, who doesn't have money to spare, can't afford to

47

waste what he does spend on disposable products. He needs to get the best value for his money. The inferior shoe will wear out sooner and probably damage his socks, is less likely to be repairable, and more likely to protect his feet."

"But when you don't have the money —"

Speaking very slowly, as though explaining something very difficult to a child, Willow interrupted. "The wise thing to do is wear the old shoes as long as possible. Tape them with duct tape or eat less expensive food, whatever you can do to save those extra dollars until you can afford that first pair of better shoes. Then, you start saving for the next pair the minute you buy them so you're ready next time, but throwing money away on inferior shoes is the rich man's way of spending."

"Rich man's!"

"Of course," she insisted. "only the rich can afford to buy cheap things and replace them often. The poor must buy quality, or they'll spend all their money replacing the junk they bought in the first place."

"That's an interesting philosophy."

She shrugged and flipped through advertisements. "It's common sense."

"Uncommon sense. I don't know anyone who would expect me to buy more expensive shoes than say, Alexa Hartfield."

"Is she rich?"

His laughter made her look up sharply. "Why was that funny?"

"Alexa Hartfield has to have millions. Every one of her books has been on the bestseller lists for weeks and weeks. They've made movies from her books. She has to be loaded."

Willow waited for him to finish but Chad started to show her something in one of the reports he had. "You didn't finish."

"Finish what?" Confusion seemed to be the mask du jour.

"Your sentence. You said, 'She has to be loaded' but you didn't say with what."

An indulgent smile replaced the questioning twist to his lips. "Money. She must be very wealthy."

"And you think she spends more money on her shoes than

48

you do on yours."

"Well, I spend more on mine than a married guy with a kid or two would at my salary."

"It's just so foolish, though."

They debated her rich man/poor man philosophy in between his examples of spending, but his explanation fell flat. Chad had come ready to teach her like a class project, but Willow wasn't accustomed to a lecturing style of education. After half an hour, he knew he'd lost her.

"Why don't we put these away for now and next time I'm here, we can do some more. If I try to push you too much, you'll end up with a massive brain freeze."

Willow stared at the pile of papers and glanced up at Chad. After another glance at the individualized reference library provided for her, Willow shook her head. "I'm sorry. You went to a lot of work, and I feel ungrateful, but I don't want to do this. I just realized something."

"What's that?"

"I don't have to understand it all. I just have to make sure the numbers work the same as they have been. As long as rates of increase are comparable, and as long as reports arrive on time and everything, then it doesn't matter if I know why we earn seven percent instead of seventy. I don't need to know why I can spend ten thousand, twenty thousand, or five hundred thousand dollars a year. What I need to know is how much I can spend and how to budget. If I know how much everything is, that shouldn't be too hard."

He'd pushed too hard. Chad sensed it. He'd pushed her away from something she wanted to learn. The thought bothered him for many reasons. Little was beyond her; he'd just cemented one of those little things. As he examined himself, he realized that part of the pang he felt was because for once, he had something relevant to teach her and it wasn't going to happen.

"Well, we can talk about it later. How about Chinese Checkers?"

Willow glanced at the sky. "It's almost time for me to make dinner. Why don't you set it up in the kitchen and I'll play while I cook."

The game started slowly. With hands covered in beef she pulverized into a flat thin piece of meat, she directed him which one of her pieces to move, often taking several tries for him to grab the right marble. He almost accused her of doing it deliberately but her mind went too fast at the beginning of the game for him to have that luxury.

"What are you doing with that meat anyway? There won't be anything left of it if you keep that up."

"Green at the left tip one to the right — I'm making pizza."

"Pizza!"

"Yeah. I think it's going to be good. Blue middle row one left next."

Chad didn't have the heart to tell her that beef wasn't a substitute for pepperoni. He watched as she simmered the beef in her skillet — the wood cook stove sending radiating warmth through the room. Willow checked the oven temperature and smiled.

Amazed, and amused, Chad watched as she spread slices of bread with butter, arranged them on a cookie sheet, laid the beef on top of each one, smothered them in sauce and cheese, and slid the whole sheet in the oven. "That looks good."

"I added beef to them to make them more substantial. The other pizza tasted wonderful but I need more protein."

"Most people use dough for the crust."

"I thought about it, but I have bread and it seems silly to make dough when I already have something that'll work. Red jump green on the right."

As she mixed a salad and called out moves, pausing between leaves of lettuce to calculate the consequences of different choices, the scent of toasting pizzaishness sent his senses reeling. "That smells wonderful."

"Should be done in a minute."

"How do you know it's not burning? There's no glass to see —"

She looked confused. "Do you check stuff in your oven all the time?"

"Well no, but the box says how long and what

temperature..."

"Well, I say how long and keep it at the right temperature, so I don't see why I need a window into my oven. White jump green, black, and yellow."

"How do you do that?" he said frustrated as he dropped marbles in the drawer tray of the checkerboard.

"Do what?"

"Talk about ovens, temperatures, and manage to take out two of mine and only one of yours, while still making it into your home space."

"I may not know how much about the market value of marbles, but I know how to move them."

CHAPTER 43

April 15 2004-

Another year, another tax return signed, sealed, and postmarked. Bill is kind to indulge me by mailing it to me, so I can mail it in with that postmark hand stamped by Fran Kraus herself. I wonder if she knows that I know her name. She sees me a handful of times a year. I quit going in the Post Office in December. The first few years she asked about my Christmas cards. Then she quit asking and just looked pityingly at me. I chose to forgo it all.

I've been feeling guilty about Willow's lack of education in the finance department. If I was a better mother, I would help her learn it, but she has such a good head on her shoulders. Her logic regarding how she values things is sound, and the monetary value she places on things has to do with their worth to her as an individual rather than their worth to society. She'll never be a slave to consumerism. Why mess with that?

In my defense, I have tried to whet her interest. When I order, I have her check my math so she is at least familiar with what I pay for things, although, I really don't think she notices or cares. The not-so-little-anymore twerp sure finds my math errors, though. She can do such complex mathematical calculations in her head! It had been so long since I used a calculator that mine was dead when Bill Franklin needed it.

We've crossed the two million mark. This is good. This is very good. I think she'll be well provided for now. I don't know why, but I can never picture myself old here. I still feel like the twenty-year-old that I was when I came. Too old for my body and too young to know

53

what I was doing. I think part of me died that October. That's a lie. Most of me died. Part of me lived.

Libby Sullivan's eyes filled with sympathetic tears. "How very alone she was."

"Willow is like that now. Not in the same way, of course; she doesn't suffer from festering wounds that refuse to heal—"

"You're talking like Kari now."

"I know. She influences my thoughts, my actions," he ducked his head, "and even my dreams."

Libby listened for some time and then spoke. "Chad, I don't know exactly how important Willow is to you personally, but there is something you should know."

His mind still focused on the journal entry, Chad nodded absently. "Mmm hmm."

"Chad!"

His head sapped up sharply. "What?"

"Did you hear me?"

"What?"

Nudging his foot with hers, Libby Sullivan tried again. The slow, distinct way she formed her words reminded him of Luke. "I said, I don't know how important Willow is to you right now but here is something you ought to know."

"What's that?"

"Willow doesn't need the complications of romantic entanglements in her life right now. She needs time to adjust to basic friendships first. She's never had that."

"Aunt Libby, I'm not in—I mean I don't care about—well, no that's—"

"Chad," she interrupted laughing. "Take a deep breath. I'm not going to dance around you at Thanksgiving and taunt 'Chaddie's got a gurl-friend' like Cheri did that year when you were what, twelve?"

"Well, I was just taken aback. Do you think I've given her the wrong impression?"

"Well honestly, I don't know her well enough to be sure," she began. "But Willow doesn't seem like someone desperate for romance. She's not likely to assume any more than you

54

specifically state. You've made her sound very literal."

Swallowed hard, relieved. He was slowly growing to enjoy his new friendship but the idea of sending an inaccurate message bothered him. He'd done that once in high school; he'd never make that mistake again if he could help it.

"Chaddie-my-Laddie?"

"Yes Aunt Libby, Libby, Libby-on-the-Label."

Her eyes narrowed. "Don't mock me my boy." She reached across the couch and grabbed Chad's hand just as she had when he'd poured out his heart after speaking disrespectfully to his mother, after lying to his basketball coach, and when Linnea Burrell accused him of trifling with her affections. "Willow isn't Linnea. You've been gun-shy of anyone with hair below the ears ever since. Relax and enjoy your friendship."

Chad took the journals, stood, and thanked his Aunt Libby. "I can't wait for Luke any longer, but tell him I stopped by."

"Chad?"

"Yeah?"

Libby walked to the door, her arm in her nephew's and hugging him fiercely before he stepped outside. "Go talk to your father. He's a wise man. He can help you. Luke is a good man. He's my son, and I love him. But Chad, your father can give you something Luke can't—experience. Go talk to him."

"Dad still feels rejected because I chose college and the academy. I can't seem to talk to him anymore."

Libby let the screen close behind Chad before she suggested, "Go to his store. Ask if you can talk to him in his office—on his turf. Let him see you seek him out. He'll listen and he'll help you."

"Mr. Tesdall, please come to register seven. Mr. Tesdall, to register seven. Thank you."

Christopher Tesdall glanced down at the monitor for register seven and bolted from his chair at the sight of Chad standing there. For his son to arrive at his store for any reason—well, only one thing could cause that. Emergency. It took until he reached the flaps that separated the store from the stockroom, to talk himself down. If it was a real emergency, someone would have called—surely. Still, panic left an acrid taste in his mouth by the time he reached his son's side.

Chad stiffened at his awkward hug. "Hey, good to see you. Is something wrong?"

"Can we talk in your office?"

"Why?" Christopher's eyes were constantly roaming the store checking for slacking baggers, overly full lines, and any hint of untidiness. He ran the cleanest store in the Rockland metro area, and he was proud of that.

"Dad, I really need your help."

"Come on then," Christopher agreed, adding defensively, "You'd think with the money I spent on your education, I'd be the one coming to you."

He led Chad through the store. The awkwardness between them grew, deepening the chasm that had formed in their late teen years. All his hard work, saving every penny he could, the hours searching for every grant or scholarship available to his children—it all flooded his mind. The loans— Chad's grades hadn't been what Cheri and Chris' had been. They'd taken a second mortgage on the house to cover what their savings failed to do. He glanced over his shoulder. Chad's head was down, looking defeated. He'd never known; they hadn't told him. A new thought hit him. It wasn't that, was it? He'd discovered that they hid the source of his college tuition?

The idea was ludicrous. Still, maybe it would have bridged the horrible crevasse that divided him from his son. If he succeeded there, perhaps the others... Memories of debates over psychology shamed him. He never understood what they were talking about, and their ready acceptance of what seemed like indoctrination, destroying everything he and Marianne had tried to instill in them—it hurt. He felt ignorant, even backward at times.

An employee stopped him, asking a question, the respect

56

and deference shown almost like a salve to a festering wound. In his store, his employees and bosses alike respected him. He knew his job, and he did it well. He predicted food trends months in advance, the rise and fall of prices, and if a particular brand-trial would succeed or flop. He managed nearly three hundred employees and their schedules. Yet with all of these skills, he felt awkward around his children.

"So," he began as he opened his office door, "what brings you to my store." He winced inwardly at the unnecessary emphasis on "my." *Way to alienate your son further, you idiot.*

Chad sank into the closest chair, trying to stuff his hands in his pockets, but of course, he couldn't. "Oh, Pop..."

Chad's instinctive use of the old pet name "Pop" cut him. His son needed him. "What's up?"

"Did mom tell you about Willow?"

"The girl that lost her mother a while back?" Christopher prayed his son hadn't lost his senses and gotten a young woman pregnant. Marianne thought Chad had finally found a nice girl, but then Marianne thought that about every girl he ever spoke to or about these days.

"Yeah. She's—well she's different."

Marianne was right. He had gotten soft on this one. Christopher just hoped she wasn't from some snooty family. Maybe she could build a bridge where he'd failed. "Your mother thought you were becoming... attracted to her."

Christopher knew he was on the wrong track the second Chad slid down in his seat, his fists shoved into his pockets. Even seated in a chair, the old habit held fast. "Her too?"

"I take it your mom's mistaken again."

"That's an understatement. Willow is not looking for, and nor does she need, any romantic entanglements."

"That's a strange way to put it—romantic entanglements. More of that degree talking, I suspect."

"Just something Au—I heard recently."

"So why are you here?"

"Oh, Pop, I don't know what to do with her. She's amazing. Really, you should meet her. I think you'd like her. She runs that little farm of theirs like it was breathing."

"And this is a problem?"

Chad looked embarrassed. Was he telling the truth about his feelings for this girl? His answer made even less sense. "She's been isolated. Severely. She only knew her mother. No one else."

"No family, huh?"

"Extensive family in Rockland and some in Chicago, I think, but no, she didn't know anyone."

Leaning his arms on his desk and clasping his hands out in front of him, Christopher tried for a little clarification. "Didn't know... how?"

"The only contact number we had to call was her financial advisor."

"Poor little rich kid, huh?" It figured.

"Well, yes and no. She has millions, but she doesn't comprehend what that means."

Understanding dawned. The poor girl. Her mother should have made better preparations than leaving it to an understaffed police force like Fairbury to take care of her child. "How severe is it?"

"Is what?"

"Her mental condition. Can she live there alone or—"

Chad's laughter surprised him. "She's not mentally challenged like you mean."

"None of this makes any sense, Chad."

"Well, she's almost like an Amish girl thrust into our world, except that there was no community for her. Just her mother."

"She saved?"

"Yes. I didn't want to go back out there at first, but I arrogantly thought that maybe I was supposed to expose her to Jesus. Instead I got a sight of faith I've never imagined."

"So why didn't the church—" Christopher began.

"How can the church do anything with someone they've never met?"

"How can someone claiming to belong to Christ avoid His body? That's like the hand saying to the leg, 'I don't want to bother with you.'"

58

He listened as his son explained all about Kari, their unique situation, and their life. As they spoke, he asked questions that only seemed to frustrate Chad. Though he did listen to the current problem regarding money, his mind mulled Kari's history. "She has a couple million invested somewhere because of some guy named Steve, who is a creep, and this Steve had a dad with enough money floating around to fork over a certified check for her mom to get out of town. Sounds like *the* Steven Solari."

"Television guy? The one whose son died a few years ago — murdered?"

"Probably a coincidence," he suggested. There was no reason to get his son curious about a man like Solari. "So this is all interesting, and I'm glad you wanted to share with me, but can you tell me what the point is?"

Chad explained his problem. It didn't make sense, but when Chad said, "She truly thinks her annual seed budget should be more than my annual car payments," Christopher lost his patience.

"How'd this girl ever get through school?"

"Willow never went to school. Her mother tried, though not hard enough I'll grant you, to teach her monetary value, but she liked that her daughter wasn't affected by modern consumerism."

After mulling that idea over for a moment, he shook his head. "So, in other words, she's a poster child for why homeschooling is a bad idea."

"I wouldn't say that. In some ways, she has a better education than I do, and really, how many live that isolated? I think they usually have extended family, friends, churches, other homeschoolers... This is more of an example of why extreme isolationism or sheltering is not a good idea. When they get into the so-called 'real world' they're vulnerable."

Willow forgotten, Christopher jumped on that. "Why 'so-called?'"

"The force has taught me that there are a lot of different 'real worlds' out there. The rich kids don't have a clue about life in the inner city real world. The town of Fairbury interacts in

59

the big city, but they don't really know what it's like to live there. And then there's Willow. If you don't do it yourself to survive, then she's clueless."

Christopher didn't want the conversation to end. It was the first man-to-man discussion he'd had with Chad since high school where neither of them was on the defensive. He felt petty knowing he relished his son's need and desire for his advice.

"Hmm... I think you're being wise to be concerned. This Bill may be a good man, but good men make mistakes, and unfortunately, sometimes they give into temptation. He knew Willow's mom was watching him carefully, but he has to know the daughter doesn't have a clue. That's an awful lot of temptation."

"How do I help her understand without losing her unique perspective? I don't want to take away who she is."

They talked—re-bonded. Years of division dissolved into a level meeting ground of mutual respect. While the store ran like the smoothly oiled machine that it was, father and son fixed the kinks in the machine of their relationship; though not a smooth operation yet, it ran again. No matter how short-lived, Christopher was determined to enjoy every second of it.

The intercom paged Christopher once more, ending their discussion. "I've got to go, son, but I'm glad you came. Bring her home at Thanksgiving. This girl needs a family, and Cheri always wanted a sister."

"Dad, I told you—"

"We'll informally adopt her—no marriage licenses necessary."

CHAPTER 44

The rhythmic pounding of feet on the treadmill helped dull the drumming in his head. Two months hadn't erased her footprint in his life. Seeing her at the meeting was hard—painful. Why did it have to be so difficult? Why did he care as much as he did? He'd known her for years. Why couldn't he see her as the young daughter of a former client?

Even now, he could feel her arm on his when making a request or encouraging him in some way. He saw her eyes roaming over his apartment, remembering the expression on her face after her first bite of sushi and the earnest way she listened to his thoughts on the lake project, until Bill thought he'd go crazy with the memories. If she'd only been willing to give it a chance…

His hand shoved the lever to "off," nearly breaking it in the process. What was wrong with him? In just a few weeks of contact with her, he'd fallen for Willow in a way he never had for anyone else. It was ridiculous, premature, and he knew it. He also knew it was genuine and the loss of what might have been hurt him more than any of his actual relationships ever had.

He tried to be pragmatic about it, but the fact remained that his heart was heavy. She'd learned to be comfortable in the city—well, learned not to be afraid of it. She liked the store, the museums, and the botanical gardens—Bill sighed. He'd never taken her to the zoo. He hated broken promises.

Without allowing himself to consider the consequences, Bill dialed her number. After several minutes of idle chatter about her fall preparations, her progress on the designs, and the apparent success of her physical therapy, Bill mentioned the weather forecast. "It's supposed to be in the mid-sixties on Saturday..."

"Wow. I thought maybe we were done with warmer weather."

"I promised you a trip to the zoo this fall. I think this is the last Saturday we'll get a good view of all the animals." Several seconds passed as he waited for a response—any response. At last, Bill hesitantly added, "I'm not trying to make you feel uncomfortable. I wouldn't pressure you—I just," his tone dropped to a whisper. "I missed you."

"I'll come."

A full minute passed before he could bring himself to ask the one question he needed to know most, "Are you coming because I asked, or because you want to come?"

"I want to come because you asked.

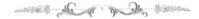

The road to Fairbury had never seemed so long. His car whizzed around the curves and finally into Willow's driveway. He hoped she was home—the thought made him laugh. Of course, she was home. Where would she go and how would she get there?

He didn't see anyone in the house, the barn, or anywhere nearby. He sighed at the sight of the wood stacked against the house. She'd cut, split, and stacked it all. Why did she live like this? He didn't understand. Saige yapped at him from the barn, but he ignored it.

Just as he turned to leave, he heard a voice. "Chuck! Hey!"

Down past the barn, coming up from the trees, Chuck saw Willow carrying a bow over one shoulder and something unidentifiable on the other. As they met in the middle, he realized that she carried a turkey. "Did you shoot that thing?"

"Yep. For Thanksgiving. Mother always cleaned it after I

shot it." She winked at him. "Do you want to clean it for me?"

"I wouldn't know how, but I'll help you eat it."

She eyed him suspiciously. "Was that an invitation for an invitation for Thanksgiving?"

He swallowed hard. Honest or go for the kill? One look in her eyes and he tried a novel approach—honesty. "It was a hint for one—I guess." Ok, partial honesty.

Willow grinned. "You're on. You bring the cranberry sauce."

"Do you make pumpkin pie?"

"Of course," she exclaimed insulted.

"Sweet potatoes and marshmallow crème?"

Her nose wrinkled. "Ew."

"I accept."

At the barn, Chuck watched as she put several huge pots on the stove and filled them with water. He grew sick as she tore out a few feathers and then cut the bird removing the entrails. Weak, he sat down, turning, his head as her knife dug into the neck and she reached for the crop.

"That is so disgusting. Forget that, it's vile. Maybe tofu turkey isn't such a bad idea."

"We make great turkey and dressing. Oh and gravy—our gravy is great."

Half an hour, and a doused turkey later, Willow talked to him as she plucked it. "What's your favorite animal?"

"The one that is leaving me alone," he groused as he attempted subtlety, shoving the dog away."

"I mean at the zoo."

"Zoos are great," Chuck said. "They stick the animals where they can't bother you, but you can look at them if you feel like it."

"Don't be obnoxious."

"Look who's talking obnoxious," he whined. This dog—"

Willow interrupted him. "You didn't say which one was your favorite."

Chuck stared at her, stunned. "I think that's a first."

"First of what?"

He took a deep breath, stuffing down rising emotions. "No

one ever asks me a question twice." He dropped his head before he met her curious gaze. "They're usually relieved that the question died."

"Well, if I didn't want to know, I wouldn't have asked, so of course I asked again."

"I like flamingos."

"Oh, do they have flamingos?"

Seeing the question in her eyes, he decided to answer it before she asked. "They're bold, beautiful, and so graceful."

The sun set with the color of flamingos streaking through the clouds as she finally shoved the turkey in the freezer and wiped her arm across her forehead. "I need a shower."

"Hey, after that shower, we can go get something to eat and see a movie or something... We could even go to Brunswick and go bowling if you like?"

"I've never been to Brunswick."

Chuck grinned. She hadn't said no. "Go take that shower."

"Go milk Willie."

His grin grew as he adjusted his suggestion. "Milk the goat, and then take your shower."

"So if you get three strikes it's a turkey? Are you kidding me?" Willow's laughter brought smiles to people all around them.

"Well, I thought it was appropriate."

"So you got your turkey today and I got mine," she chortled. Willow picked up her ball. "My turn. No gutters."

"You miss the gutter, and I'll buy you ice cream when we're done."

"I'll miss," she insisted as she swung the ball. The second it rolled into the gutter, she set her hands on her hips, swiveled and glared at him. "Next swing."

"Bowl."

"Whatever."

He poked her rib. "You're sounding kinda modern."

"Is that good or bad?"

64

"Indifferent."

She grinned. "I told Chad you were indifferent to me. You just proved me right. You might be my new hero. I am discovering that I like being right." Her next ball rolled painfully slowly down the lane. It wove slightly back and forth and hit the center pin. Four pins toppled, one wobbled but didn't fall. She stood disgusted before turning away muttering, "Slacker."

Chuck grinned. Only Willow Finley would insult a bowling pin for not falling over as expected. "I owe you ice cream. And you have now broken the ten point mark!"

"Is there a prize for getting the least amount of points? I think I'd win."

"Want me to have them blow up the bumpers?"

She looked at him blankly. "Bumpers?"

"Long tubes that fill up the gutters and make the ball bounce around until it knocks over pins."

"What a cheater's way of not learning. Sounds like something for little kids like those training wheels I wanted and Chad wouldn't get me."

"Well…" Chuck wasn't sure it was a good idea to mention that they were for children.

"And besides, I think I could manage to consistently just miss it at the back up there anyway."

By the end of the game, she'd racked up an impressive seventeen points. "I want ice cream. I think this game must be like woodwork. I can't do it."

"Sure you can—once you get used to it and your leg heals a bit more."

"You think my leg—"

Chuck was sure of it. "I can see it in the way you move up the lane. Walking on the street you hardly limp at all now, but here where both floor and shoes are slick, you favor it more."

As Willow removed her shoes, she glanced down the lane. Grabbing Chuck's ball, as well as hers, she returned them to the racks. On the way back to his car, Willow nudged Chuck. "We have to do this again. I'm going to learn this. Does Fairbury have an alley?"

65

He shook his head. "Nope."

"Drat."

"Are you sure it's a good idea? I mean—" Chad tried again. "Aunt Libby said something the other day that I thought made a lot of sense."

"What'd she say?"

Just her tone told him how much his aunt's opinion seemed to matter to her. It seemed a bit premature, considering how little time they'd spent together. Then again, Aunt Libby was one of those women who made friends for life in the space of an hour.

"Well," he began awkwardly. How do you tell someone that you aren't interested in her as much as some might wish you were? "Aunt Libby was warning me, she was afraid I might— well, that spending so much time together—"

"She thought you were following in Bill's footsteps."

"Right—well, she thought I might anyway. And she warned me. She said that you needed time to have real friends without any romantic strings attached. I think she's right."

Willow assured him she wasn't looking for anything of the kind. "Bill knows I'm not moving there; I know he's not moving here. Romance just isn't going to happen. And Mrs. Sullivan is right. There's too much in my life that is new for me to add any more." She smiled as if she had a secret. "Except for maybe bowling."

"Bowling?"

"Yeah," she said, still smiling. "I went bowling in Brunswick with Chuck last night. I got a score of seventeen, ate ice cream, and walked the streets of Brunswick. It's bigger than Fairbury, but it's not as big as Rockland, I don't think. I saw the police station. Is that where you go sometimes?"

"Yeah. So you went out with Chuck, huh?"

He didn't hear the rest of the conversation. While his responses must have been reasonably normal, Chad's mind spun out in unreasonable directions. Why was he perfectly

66

content with the idea of Bill and Willow spending a day together, but the idea of her enjoying herself with Chuck kicked him in the gut? It didn't make sense and he knew it.

As he climbed into his truck, Chad remembered something. He slammed the door shut and punched her number. Through the living room window, he could see her silhouette as she answered the phone. "I forgot."

"What?"

"I talked to my dad yesterday and he invited you to Thanksgiving at our house."

Chad didn't know what he'd expected her to say. He understood that she might not be interested in spending her day with a group of strangers, but he'd hoped she might. Her answer, however, surprised him. "I can't."

"Oh."

"I invited Chuck to eat at my house. Actually, he kind of invited himself."

Shaking his head in amazement, Chad sighed. "That sounds like Chuck."

Disappointment filled Willow's voice. "I wish I had known. I wouldn't have gone turkey hunting and then the topic wouldn't have come up, and I wouldn't have invited him."

"You *want* to come?" That surprised him.

"Of course, but I can't just call Chuck and say, 'Sorry, I got a better invitation.'"

"*He would,*" Chad thought irritably. "See if Chuck wants to come to my house too."

"Really? I know you don't like him."

He stifled the surprise in his voice. "I never said that."

"Chad, you didn't have to. Anyone could tell. Chuck's deliberately blind much of the time, but he's not stupid."

"*That's what you think.*" Aloud, he assured her his invitation was genuine. "Call and see if he'll consider dinner with the Tesdall-Sullivan clan."

Just as he started to click off the phone, Willow's voice rushed back onto the line. "Hey, does your mom need a turkey?"

CHAPTER 45

"So, where do we want to go first?"

Willow glanced over the brochure map and finally chose the Asia Park. "I want to see tigers and the pandas."

Before they entered, he handed her a digital camera. "Use this. I'll get your pictures printed for you, but this way you can take all you want without running out of film."

Bill led the way through the simulated bamboo gates and into the Asian portion of the zoo. The peafowl were one of the first things they saw. "They're smaller than I always imagined. I thought they'd be bigger somehow. The tail is long, but look at that little body!"

As they wandered through the zoo, Willow delighted Bill with her observations and the innumerable pictures she took. Tigers were favorites. Not too large or small, they satisfied her imagination and expectations perfectly. The pandas did not fare so well. The moment she reached the enclosure, Willow sank onto a bench; her arms drooped dejectedly.

"They're so big!"

Bill couldn't imagine what the problem was. "They're smaller than all the other bears—"

"But I always thought they were little—like koalas. They're too big." Her eyes grew wide. "Oh no! Are koalas big too?"

As they went through the continents, Willow's comments amused more than just Bill. She spent twenty minutes staring at

69

the giraffes, awestruck by their height and apparent gentleness. "Wouldn't it be amazing to be God and be able to create something so magnificent? Look at that! Everything defies nature. Evolution would never have a chance to develop a neck like that—the species would have died out first."

Bill's indulgent smile annoyed her. He shook his head and tried to show that the choice of food may have come after the neck growth. "It doesn't have to work the other way around."

"Why would the neck grow for food that it doesn't know it wants? That's just ridiculous."

A sense of wonder enshrouded her at the sight of the gorillas. "Look! There you can see where the idea of evolution could take hold."

Bill stared at her in shock. "Do what?"

"I didn't say I agreed, but when you look at them—the way they interact and their features—you can see where people got the idea anyway. I never understand the nothing to something to slime to slop to worm to man connection, but if you skip all of that and just look at him and you, you can actually see a connection."

"Gee thanks."

Laughing, she hooked her arm in his and moved to the aviary. The flamingos in all their showiness made her think of Chuck, and she made sure Bill took a picture of her with them. From one place to the next, her zoology lessons literally came alive. She commented on the animal noises and stood in amazement at the immense size of animals like elephants and hippopotami.

"I think I could live here. Can you imagine taking care of these creatures? It's like a small piece of Eden right in the middle of the city!"

Nothing else that Willow could have said would have made the impact on him that her comfort in the zoo did. She talked with several of the zookeepers, asked intelligent questions, and in the course of the afternoon, learned more about the care of exotic animals than most people know about their household pets. Despite his desire for her to enjoy herself, Bill's interest flagged in the mid to late afternoon. As the sun began to set, Willow finally tore away from the Artic wolves and followed Bill to the car.

"Oh that was incredible. I have to go back. Do they let the animals out all winter? Maybe I can take the bus into the city. I have less work in winter."

As they pulled into Rockland traffic, Bill carefully broached the subject that had been whirling through his mind. "Have you considered that you'd enjoy being a zookeeper?"

"Oh wouldn't that be wonderful! Taking care of animals so far from where they originated? All the breeding programs and the—"

She rhapsodized all the way to the farm. Bill asking questions and making suggestions for further study kept her excitement level high, but at the sight of home, she switched the focus of her delight to her farm. "I love this place. The trees, the fields, the animals. And, it's so close to the zoo!"

Bill felt like banging his head on the steering wheel. Every time he thought he had her thinking in a different direction and working hard to do it without coercion, she refocused on home. It was enough to make him want to drive home and never leave the city again. Almost.

"Come in, I have a chicken in the crockpot."

Her kitchen felt as cold as the outdoors. Bill fought the temptation to let his teeth chatter while she built fires in the stoves. He felt useless. Chad would probably be in there loading everything for her, but all he could do was stand around, hands thrust in his jacket pockets, with his teeth trying to whittle each other down to a nub. Even Chuck probably knew how to stack a fireplace or a stove. Bill felt ridiculous. Even if the self-absorbed man did know something as practical as how to lay a fire, he wouldn't ever think of doing it when someone else was there to do it for him.

"S—sorry I'm no help."

"It's just cold in here because I haven't been cooking. Why don't you go out to the barn and get the crockpot."

Bill almost choked on the idea that her food was cooking in the barn. "Why is it out there?"

"Electricity. I don't use it often, but I do have one so when

71

I want to use it, I do it in the kitchen in the barn."

After his jaw connected to his knees and repositioned itself, Bill asked the question of the day. "Why not just turn on the electricity in the house then?"

"We just don't use the electricity in the house."

Bill stumbled down the steps and into the yard. Saige bounced around his ankles nearly tripping him. He'd never been so thankful for moonlight in his life. How did she see to get out there?

He snapped on a light just inside the barn door and sighed in relief as a floodlight filled the yard. Another light brightened the barn and a third lit the way to the kitchen. With his jacket sleeves as potholders, Bill returned to the house, feeling much more comfortable in the lights from the barn than he'd ever felt at night at Willow's home.

"I found the floodlight."

"I noticed. Can you fill plates for us while I milk Willie?"

Without waiting for an answer, Willow exited into the bright lights of the yard. Bill heard her shout to someone, but by the time he got to the door, he knew who was there. Chad had arrived. This wasn't good. Seconds later, the lights that illuminated the house disappeared leaving the kitchen lit only by an oil lantern. Though soft and beautiful, Finley lamplight left too many shadows for his comfort level.

Chad burst into the kitchen, rubbing his hands together and shivering. "Man it got cold fast! How are you?"

"Supposed to be doing something with this chicken but —"

Apparently oblivious to the fact that Bill answered a question he hadn't asked, Chad shook off his jacket and peeked into the stove. He grabbed the stove poker, jabbed the wood inside a few times to stir up the fire, and then came to where Bill poked ineffectively at the chicken. Almost as if assessing the situation as a crime scene, he took in the room, the food, and the stove, and reached for the platter on the hutch, nudging Bill out of the way.

"I'll take care of it. Why don't you sit down? You've been on your feet all day."

Bill sat and answered what seemed like insipid questions

about the animals and Willow's reactions to them, while Chad removed the chicken, carved it onto two plates, and dished up the vegetables. He poured milk, buttered bread, and set the table as Bill talked about lions, tigers, and bears—not to mention a few birds. Silverware appeared on the table followed by salt and pepper.

It was evident, within seconds of Chad's arrival, that he belonged there. The man's comfort level in the house was completely different than Bill's, and he felt it. He watched uncomfortably as Chad went into the living room, stirred up the wood stove, adjusted the window coverings, and pounded up the stairs and minutes later, hurried down again. When Willow came in the kitchen, Chad asked about the chickens and then pulled on his jacket, commenting that he thought she hadn't been gone long enough.

"I'll get them. You sit and eat. You must be starved."

Willow hadn't touched the fire since she'd returned from the barn. Bill watched as she shrugged out of her jacket, stepped out of the boots she'd worn, and held her hands over the stove to warm them. They worked together like old friends. She knew exactly what he'd done in her absence; he knew exactly what to do. Bill was out of place.

With an abrupt shove of his chair, Bill stood. "I need to go. Thanks for coming with me today."

"Is something wrong?"

Bill shook his head awkwardly. "No, not really, it's just—" he rubbed his chin, before reaching into his pocket and grabbing is keys. "I don't fit out here. I—I'm sorry. Thanks again."

He paused as he passed her. While she stood with a pie in her hands, Bill placed his hands on her shoulders, and gave a half-hearted smile. "You're good for me. I think—I think I'm just better as your financial advisor than I am as a friend." He kissed the top of her head and whispered, "Bye, Willow."

Several minutes later, Chad brought a basket of eggs into the kitchen and found Willow sitting in her usual chair, a pie in her lap. "He left."

"Where'd he go?"

"Home. For good."

Confused, Chad tried again. "Did something go wrong today?"

She shrugged. "I had so much fun. We talked and dreamed all the way home and then I came in from the milking and he left."

"It's probably my fault. I intruded on his date. I'm sorry. I just thought the lights—"

"He loved those lights," Willow began. "It wasn't you. It was him. He hates it out here. I thought he'd gotten over that." She looked at the plates of food. "Have you eaten?"

With his jacket off and hanging over the chair, Chad sank into the chair and watched as Willow ate mechanically. "I'm sorry. I don't know what to say."

"Say you'll teach me a new game, because I'm not in the mood for Chinese checkers."

"What do you have that you don't know how to play?"

"Nothing," she admitted. "But surely you have something."

Chad pictured his closet with a box of papers that he hadn't looked at since he'd set it there the day he moved into the apartment. His kitchen cupboards were empty. He had nothing but a television, some paintball gear... video games...

"I'll be back in a while," he said, jumping up from his chair.

"Eat first and then go. I'll take a shower while you're gone."

"Yahtzee again! How do you do that?"

Willow's grin spread as she passed the dice cup. "Your turn."

After three rolls, Chad marked a zero for his twos. In typical Willow style, they played the entire sheet as one game. She had said she didn't see why they should only play one column when they could play six. The game migrated from the kitchen table, to the couch, and finally to the floor in front of the woodstove. Lying on their stomachs, they faced each other like gunslingers in the old west.

"Small straight. Thirty points."

"My mom calls that a little straight," Chad commented irrelevantly.

"Tell me about her."

An involuntary smile grew on Chad's face. He loved his mother and knew Willow could see it just watching him as he thought about her. "Mom is the greatest. She's one of those women who seem a little ditzy at times and appears to be a pushover, but mom's sharp as a tack. We didn't get away with anything."

"Will she like me?"

"I can't wait for you to meet her. I think you're going to hit it off great."

The uncertainty in her voice surprised him as she pressed. "She's a city woman though, right? Are you sure she won't be uncomfortable around someone like me? I mean—"

Chad covered the dice cup with his hand stopping her roll. "Willow, not everyone is like Bill. Bill's not a bad guy. I think he just feels so out of place here, and some people don't adapt well. Most people adapt at least a little to whatever surroundings they're in, but I think Bill just can't. He's very one-track. Focused. Do you know what I mean?"

Nodding, Willow pulled the cup from under Chad's hand and shook it. One full house later, she passed it back to Chad and said, "I don't know. I think maybe Mother was right. Maybe friendships aren't a good idea."

The lost tone in her voice found its way to a place in Chad's heart that he'd guarded well. She'd lost her mother. Then, in taking a risk in areas her mother had avoided, she'd opened her heart to friends and had already lost one. How much loss would she suffer before she gave up on people entirely, or worse, grew bitter and changed the person at the core of who she was?

He thought of Rockland, the police force, and his career. Memories of conversations with Luke, the chief, his father, and his mother flooded into Chad's mind. Sheriff. He could become

75

a sheriff. He could stay on the Fairbury force for the rest of his life. Brunswick was close. Was her friendship enough of a reason to potentially change the course of his life? Then again, how could he not? How could he leave her alone and vulnerable?

"Willow, friends are worth it. Even when you lose them, they're worth it. Some of us just have better sticking power than others. I'm not going anywhere."

"Of course you are," she protested as she recorded four sixes in her four of a kind. "You're moving to Rockland in just under four years if you get half a chance."

"I already turned down Rockland. As far as I've planned, I'm staying right here in Fairbury. I might even start looking for a house in a couple of years. I can afford it better here."

She passed the dice cup to him thoughtfully. "You turned down a chance at Rockland? Why?"

Squirming, he shook the cup much harder than necessary and managed four twos. At least he had one column of twos left. As he wrote the number down, he tried to formulate an answer. He had to word things carefully or she might misunderstand him. If he said she was the reason, Willow might feel guilty or worse, assume a romantic attachment that Chad didn't have, didn't want, and wanted to avoid at all costs. His aunt Libby was right, as usual, and he intended to benefit from her wise counsel.

"I wasn't ready for it, and the longer time passes, the more I realize that I wasn't seeing the job I have right here, right now. I need to own and respect the job I have before I search for something 'bigger,' and I have a feeling that day isn't going to come. This job gets bigger the longer I'm at it."

"Well, you might not leave yet," she began, "But Bill's gone, Lee's going, I always feel awkward with Mrs. Varney, Lily is a dear friend, but I've heard something about them moving to be nearer her parents, and even Chuck doesn't come around often."

The game continued without much talking for some time. As columns filled, they tallied scores, each of them fiercely competitive until the sheets were completely filled. In the end,

76

Willow and her streak of Yahtzees won by a huge margin.

"You win. This time. I'll beat you next time," Chad added as he went to add another log to the stove.

Willow's smile lit her face, and in the glow of the oil lantern, it was a lovely sight. "There *will* be a next game, won't there?" she mused quietly to herself.

Chad's hand rested on her head for a moment before he turned to leave. "Even if I did move to Rockland tomorrow, there'd be a next game before the month was out. I don't have many friends, Willow. I don't make them easily. But when I have a friend, I *am* a friend. Period."

CHAPTER 46

"… so they want to come out and interview you. I didn't give them your number without asking first, but it'd be such great publicity for the store."

Lee practically bounced as she talked to Willow after church the next morning. Willow's mind, still on the sermon and wondering where the "one-anothering" that Pastor Allen spoke of fit into her world, nodded absently and agreed. "Sure, that's fine."

"Oh thank you! I wasn't sure… I know you're private and all that, but—" Lee hugged her quickly and skittered out the door phone in hand and dialing someone.

Willow disappeared into the bathroom and changed her shoes in the stall. She'd learned that if anyone saw her changing shoes, they'd feel obligated to offer her a ride home. As thoughtful as their gestures were, most of the time she looked forward to the walk. She was used to an active life doing for herself. The speed in which others lived theirs, she found wearying.

Her conversation with Chad still tumbled in her thoughts. Identifying the extremes was easy. If she avoided all people, that would be selfish and unhealthy. Her mother's situation was unique, and while she'd made the best decision for her, it wasn't the best decision for Willow. However, she led a busy life. Her responsibilities filled most of her time, and what was left was precious to her. She needed to invest in friendships that allowed her to be herself.

She had no doubts. Chad was a friend. He'd be her friend regardless of where he went or what he did. There was a lot of comfort in knowing that someone else out there cared about her. She'd hoped, she'd even prayed, that somehow the contact with her family at the funeral might spark at least a cordial, even if infrequent, relationship with them, but she hadn't heard from any of them since. It didn't hurt—she wasn't one to mourn the loss of that which she'd never had. However, in hindsight, Chad was more family-like than anyone she could have imagined.

She rounded the corner and onto the highway deep in thought. Libby was a wonderful friend. She was the kind of woman that Willow knew would be there if she could, and if not, her prayers would include Willow regardless. But Lily— somehow Willow instinctively knew that if Lily did move near St. Louis to be closer to her parents, her friendship would slowly fade. Lily wasn't an unfaithful friend as much as one who was so busy with the here and now that she found little time for the "back then."

Lost in her own world of sorting relationships, Willow didn't notice a sedan creeping along the highway beside her. As she mentally worked out ways to reciprocate visits to Libby, send letters to Lily, and reminded herself to pray for Lee and Bill in Rockland, the driver watched her. Eventually, Willow glanced up into the laughing eyes of Chad.

"What are you doing?"

"Waiting to see how long it'd take you to notice me. Hop in; I'll give you a lift home."

She shook her head. "No, thank you. I really do just need the walk."

Chad smiled and waved before he rolled up the window and accelerated. Half a mile down the road, he whipped the car around and came back. "Are you ok? Last night still bothering you?"

"I'm fine," she assured him. "I'm just enjoying the day. Thanks."

As Chad zipped down the highway back toward Fairbury,

80

he realized that for once, he didn't doubt someone when they said they were fine. Willow hadn't yet learned to say what she didn't fully mean. He prayed she never would.

The man on her porch made Willow feel uncomfortable. She'd granted the interview, although she only vaguely remembered agreeing to it. Now that Robert Belier sat on her porch swing, asking her questions that seemed completely unrelated to her work as a designer for *Boho Deux*, she wished she hadn't agreed.

"My mother bought our farm twenty-four years ago."

A truck barreled up the driveway and Chad raced from it looking for something seriously wrong. Willow sat on the porch swing with a strange man, but she didn't seem agitated or upset. Taking the porch steps two at a time, he leaned against the railing and manufactured a smile.

"Chad, this is Robert Belier from the Rockland Chronicle. He's here to do an interview for something with the store."

Chad nodded at the reporter, commented on a nice day for an interview, and pointed at the door. "Willow, I need to talk to you for a minute if you don't mind?" He glanced once more at Robert. "Please forgive the interruption. It's urgent."

Robert stood and waved her into the house. "Mind if I take a walk around? Take a few pictures?"

"That's fine," Willow agreed.

Inside, Chad backed her against the door and hissed, "What's wrong! I broke nearly every law there is getting here. I expected wild dogs, broken bones, or at least a nice healthy barn fire, and you're sitting out there sipping coffee—"

"Tea. Don't drink coffee."

"—tea with some reporter!"

"He made me uncomfortable." The vulnerability in her tone almost hit home, but Chad's adrenaline still controlled him.

"So you dial 9-1-1?"

"I didn't!" she protested hotly. "I dialed 1. For Chad. I

81

texted 9-1-1. See. I have this phone thing down to an exact science!"

"I didn't even know you knew how to text!"

Looking quite pleased with herself, Willow admitted, "Lee taught me how while we waited for the lawyers the other day."

"But why 9-1-1? I thought you were injured. You scared me half to death."

Her wicked grin told him what she'd say before she uttered a word. "Then you're not even *mostly* dead yet. You're fine."

"I'm waiting."

The innocent look on Willow's face was priceless. "For what?"

"For the 4-1-1 on the 9-1-1."

"Well, I don't know about 4-1-1. You only taught me 9-1-1, but I needed help and couldn't let him see me calling you, so I called with my phone in my pocket. 9-1-1 was all I could be sure I'd get right."

"You did that sight unseen? Impressive. So why am I here?"

Willow's green eyes turned grey. Chad watched as her face crumpled before him and tears threatened. "I just felt—" She swallowed hard brushing the dampness from her eyes impatiently. "I feel so stupid and ridiculous, but he makes me uncomfortable. I don't trust him; I was afraid to tell him to go away."

"Aww, Willow, why? He would have gone."

She swallowed again, forcing a lump back down her throat. "I wasn't sure I could get to the gun in time if he didn't."

Amazed to see such a strong woman reduced to such fragility, Chad wrapped his arms around her protectively. The trembling her heavy jacket had hidden was more than evident now that he was so near. "Shh... it's ok. He's not going to hurt you. I'll get rid of him."

She jumped back, shaking her head. "I need to do this interview now that I agreed to it, but if you could stay..."

"I'll stay on one condition."

"What?"

82

"You start keeping coffee in the house. It's too cold for water, and hot tea and I don't mix."

"Deal."

Chad reached for the knob, but Willow stopped him. "I'm sorry, Chad. I feel so silly. I don't know what is wrong with me, but I don't like this man."

Her eyes, red with suppressed tears and from rubbing, pleaded with him making her seem more vulnerable than ever. Chad, fighting to reconcile this woman with the one who had put Chuck in his place and who butchered chickens without mercy, sent her upstairs. "I'll go find him. You go wash your face or whatever you do to get rid of red eyes. What do I tell him?"

"Anything you like. I trust you."

Outside, Chad saw Robert Belier wandering around the yard and speaking into a hand-held recorder. "Hey, Willow will be out in a minute. She had some things to do first."

"She's fascinating. What can you tell me about her life here? Why did they choose such a remote existence?"

"Willow lives five miles from town—I'd hardly call that remote."

"She lives at the end of an incredibly long driveway, it's well known around Fairbury that until her mother died, no one knew anything about them except to stay off of their property, and even now, she turned down a lucrative job in Rockland to stay here. Why?"

Chad began to understand Willow's dislike. "Well, I'd hardly call managing a children's clothing store 'lucrative.' It isn't chump change but—"

"Compared to her income here selling a few vegetables—" Robert insisted argumentatively.

Patience thin, Chad chose to answer the original question. "Kari Finley moved here when she decided she wanted a more deliberate lifestyle. Her journals speak of living life similarly to Thoreau's 'sucking the marrow out of life.'"

"So it didn't have anything to do with being single, pregnant, and from a middle class evangelical family in the eighties?"

83

"Her decision for this life was, I am sure, influenced by what she wanted for her child, but she left the city because of what she hoped to find here."

Robert nodded and continued. "How did she learn all of this?"

"Forgive me if I'm rude, but what does this have to do with Willow designing for *Boho*?"

"Nothing really."

"So why are you asking these questions?" Chad queried pointedly.

"This article isn't about her designs or *Boho Deux*. This article is about Willow Finley the designer. It's part of a three part series we're doing for the opening of the children's annex of Boho. We're doing one on the original store and their success, one on Willow Finley—who she is and how it will reflect in her clothing—and one on the new store and what it has to offer the discerning shopper in Rockland."

Chad's bubble deflated. Willow obviously didn't know why he'd come. "I see. I'm not sure Willow was aware of that when she agreed to the interview."

"Well, today's reader doesn't want to know what school someone went to or how they are just like everyone else but different. Today's reader wants to know who someone is at their core. They want to understand who and what they are—and do."

Shaking his head, Chad stuffed his hands in his pockets. "I don't know exactly what that means, but I do know that living here with her mother, and the way they lived, definitely had a huge impact on why Willow is such an excellent designer."

When Willow joined them several minutes later, she invited Robert into the house. "Come on in. I'll show you around the house."

For the next hour, Robert toured the Finley home, heard stories of her childhood, watched the interaction between Chad and Willow, and filled his digital recorder with almost enough information for a book outline. The craft room held several mannequins with partially completed samples hanging on them. Even Chad, who had no eye for photography, could see that the picture would be incredible.

Robert Belier stopped at the end of the driveway and took a picture of the Finley farm. The house and barn, barely visible behind richly colored trees with leaves that rained down at regular intervals, sat nestled in the fields. A tree to his right caught his attention, and he climbed over the fence for a closer look.

CHAPTER 47

Chad grabbed an armful of wood before he entered Willow's kitchen. "Hey, need this in here or in there?"

"Here's fine. Then you can get out." There was no humor in Willow's voice.

"Um, is something wrong?"

"And take that article with you," she added without elaboration.

Chad stacked the wood next to the stove and picked up the Style magazine that came in Sunday's papers. Open to a picture of Willow's farm, the title caught his eye, and just as he realized that she stared at him with swords in her eyes, he sank into a chair to read the article.

On Walden Farm

Just outside the quaint town of Fairbury, with its weekly Farmer's Market, old-fashioned town square, and uniformed cops walking a beat, sits a small farm nestled among rambling hills and fields. A dog greeted me at the end of a long driveway, barking and bouncing as most overgrown puppies do. Meet Saige, the latest member of the Finley family. Willow Finley met me on the porch with a tray of tea and homemade almond-cherry bars. A taste of heaven on earth, I assure you.

Some twenty-odd years ago, Willow's mother, Kari Anne Finley, disappeared from Rockland, leaving her family worried and concerned for her safety, and moved to the farm, pregnant with Willow. After several years of no contact, and when all leads to her whereabouts failed, they assumed the worst had happened and tried to pick up the pieces of their lives without her. This spring, however, news arrived that Kari had been living within an hour's drive of their front door for nearly twenty-four years.

Instead, hidden away from society, Kari and Willow grew their food, raised animals for food, and when not engaged in backbreaking labor for survival, spent hours creating beauty in every corner of their lives. I saw hand hooked rugs, quilts, candles, soap, and every scrap of paper in their home embellished in some unique way. The hand painted "wallpaper" in the old-fashioned parlor is just slightly more stunning than the hand-carved door and window trimming. Willow describes her life as a tribute to Thoreau's "... liv[ing] life deliberately... sucking the marrow out of life."

While we sat around a woodstove that heated the water for our tea, Willow described her education, the skills she developed over the years, and the beautiful life they lived. Some have compared their life to the Amish, but Willow is quick to remind us that her mother rejected the Amish because of their theology and the limits set in how one can live their lives. I found a much stronger parallel to the life of famous author and illustrator, Tasha Tudor.

You may wonder; what does all of this have to do with Rockland Metro Style? How does a life so far removed from the streets of our city affect us in any way? We don't look to New Cheltenham for lifestyle choices or fashion sense, why a small farm outside of the modern equivalent of the fictional Mayberry, North Carolina?

Since the death of her mother, Willow has expanded the scope of her farm. She now sells her produce in Fairbury's weekly Farmer's Market, and soon, her children's clothing designs will be available in Boho Deux. This trendy store, catty-cornered from Boho Chic on Boutique Row, will feature all the style we've come to expect from the highly successful garment center but designed for younger fashion connoisseurs.

When I spoke to the manager of the upcoming store, Lee Wu, I asked how someone so far removed from society, and with no fashion exposure, much less experience, was considered for such an important position, Lee was animated in her defense of their decision. In fact, according to Ms. Wu, without Willow's assistance, Lee wouldn't have the job she now holds as general manager of Boho Deux.

"The owners of Boho wanted a complete package — designer and manager. Willow said no. As much as she loved the design aspect of the job, she wasn't willing to move from her farm, so she suggested the current set-up."

It's hard to imagine a completely un-socialized farmgirl without even a high school diploma as the sole designer for an exclusive children's boutique, but it's true. The reaction to her designs has been overwhelmingly positive. I am far from a fashion expert, but the pieces I saw in the little craft room in the second floor bedroom of Willow's farmhouse were far nicer than anything I've seen on my nieces and all were definitely unique. Far from the crafty bumpkinesque pieces one would expect, they're hip, cool, and yet hold a trace of the whimsy that seems to be missing from most modern children's wear.

As I drove away from what I have affectionately dubbed Walden Farm, a lone tree in a pasture next to the driveway captured my attention. Had it been a willow tree, it would have been poetic in its eloquence. Instead, a hearty oak, sprawling yet protective, spreads its branches over a relatively new grave. The hand carved headstone nearly tore my heart. There was no mention of the family left behind, the epitaph simply reads, "Mother, Friend, Mentor."

Since returning to Rockland, I think I have a better idea of what happened to tear Kari so abruptly from her family. It wasn't the heartless tantrum of an angry daughter, or a cult-like rejection of modernity. Kari Finley was horribly damaged that autumn. Those close to Willow insist that after a brutal rape, the family of her attacker paid her handsomely to leave town. Such a strong woman is unlikely to accept a threat like that, but we all have our Achilles heel. For Kari Finley, the safety of the baby conceived in rage and violence was more important than anything else.

Such a hard beginning. Does Willow ever wonder how her mother could stand to look at her? Did she ever feel the rejection that Kari surely must have felt? If she did, just as her mother before her, Willow Finley has risen above it. She's a strong, beautiful young woman with an immensely successful career ahead of her. I wish her well — and I'd love the recipe for those almond-cherry bars.

The paper dropped from his hands. Before Chad could choke out a response, Willow's voice, low and terrible, pierced his consciousness. "My name is Willow Anne Finley. You killed my reputation. Get out of my life."

The slight attempt at humor didn't cover her pain as much as she'd hoped. She felt betrayed by the one person she thought she could trust. Choking back the tears she had fought all morning, Willow tried again. "Chad, go. I am serious. This is just too much."

"You blame me?" he murmured in disbelief.

"You gave most of the interview out there. I told you to tell him anything. I take responsibility for that and the fact that I trusted you when my mother taught me better. I won't make that mistake again."

"He asked me why your mother bought this farm," Chad began. When she looked ready to flee, he rose, holding her arm to keep her from leaving. "I told him your mother wanted to live a quieter life out of the city. I never mentioned her attack, her family, or the rich guy."

Willow wrenched away glaring at him. "How else—"

Chad shoved his hands into his pockets as he paced. "I don't know! I can't believe you think I would do this!"

"Well I don't want to think that, but the facts are that you talked to him, and he wrote it. Lee is thrilled, and I am terrified."

That was unexpected. He understood anger at the breach of privacy, but fear... He led her to the couch and gave her a gentle nudge. "Sit. Let's talk."

Times like this reminded Chad of why he hadn't wanted to make a friend of Willow in the first place. He didn't have the patience for problems. His work was problem prevention and resolution. The last thing he needed was more conflict on his days off. He'd predicted that she'd be time consuming, frustrating, and irritating. He'd been right.

His words from the previous week echoed through his conscience. He couldn't let her down, and if he was honest with himself, most of the time, he didn't want to. "Why are you afraid?"

"Mother left to protect me. She thought if that man knew I existed that I'd be in danger. The idea of someone like that reading this article seems crazy but—"

90

Chad sat at her feet and took her hands in his. "I think your mother misunderstood what that man meant when he gave her that money."

"She said he told her—"

Very patiently, Chad tried to explain the situation as he saw it. "She could have had the guy arrested. He'd have done time, I'm sure."

"Done time?"

"Gone to prison. Probably for three to five years. If the man was willing to pay her off, I'm thinking he knew other people would come forward with similar stories."

"Ok." She clearly didn't understand what Chad was trying to explain.

"The more people who accused him of rape, the longer his jail sentence. If she pressed charges, it would make the paper, and that starts the snowball. Guys like that don't write checks that big for a single situation. They have high-priced lawyers to take care of things like that. But multiple problems—"

"So you're saying you think this man hurt more women than just my mother!"

Chad stared at the white knuckles on Willow's hands. His fingers were slowly growing numb as she squeezed the blood from them. "I'm saying that no man pays out a million dollars because his son drank too much and attacked a woman. He pays off someone who has the ability to beat his lawyers in court."

"What does that have to do with me?"

"That is my point, Willow. He never considered you. He didn't pay your mother to get out of town or else; he paid your mother to keep her mouth shut. That check stub was insurance. If your mother decided to go after them, his lawyers would have shredded her in court—if she could have gotten a D.A. to even look at a case with money involved."

"Who is D.A.?"

Life with a woman who had never watched a television crime show—just so foreign. "District Attorney. For the record, the A.D.A is the assistant District Attorney."

"So this man wouldn't have hurt me?"

91

"No, and he's not likely to now. It was a mutual agreement. 'You leave my family alone and we'll leave you alone.'"

She relaxed her grip. "But mother—"

"Was a wounded woman whose own sense of self-preservation made her overreact to a terrifying situation. It's a reasonable scenario. She's battered, wounded, and terrified. Psychologically speaking, she was a prime candidate for a breakdown, but she rose above it. All that strength she exuded was a coping mechanism."

Laughter was the last thing he'd expected. Willow's hands covered her face, her shoulders shook, but laughter filled the room. "What?"

"Farm girl. He called me a farm girl. I've been looking for the right time to call you farm boy and ask you to saddle my horse or something, and he calls me farm girl."

"I think that should be your new nickname."

Another chortle escaped before Willow gasped, "As. You. Wish."

Lynne Solari collapsed on the couch next to her husband. Their trip to Florida had ended in an argument, tears, and the silent treatment on the flight home. Once in their own home, she realized that he'd lose his stained air of civility unless she attempted to smooth the waters. He'd been horrible, but she knew the cause. Where she soothed her pain with shopping and spas, Steve attacked.

"I'm sorry. I knew you didn't like Terrell. I shouldn't have invited him."

His answer came in the form of the Style magazine dropped in her lap. She smiled. He'd be fine by morning. Curled against him with her feet tucked under her, she opened the magazine to read the latest scandals and to see if the charity ball had been a success with Connie in charge. Minutes later, she was lost in the story of a young woman making her stamp on the Rockland fashion scene.

"Hey, you should read this, Steve. It's so sad."

"Mmm hmm."

She thrust the paper on top of his financial pages. "Can you believe someone paid her mother off after their son raped her?"

Steve set the papers aside and wrapped his arms around his wife. "Some things, I don't care to read about, and sensationalizing crime is one of them. Besides, who can focus on something like that with a wife like you around?"

Several hours later, once he was certain his wife's sleeping pill would keep her asleep for hours, he crept downstairs to read the article carefully. The name was right. The time, the circumstances—everything was right. She couldn't have known there was a child when he spoke to her. She still had bruises on her arms and a split lip.

A baby. He'd been such a failure as a father and wasn't much better as a husband, but that cheeky girl had raised a baby all alone. As weird as their life was, the girl had done well for herself. A baby. His granddaughter. He had a granddaughter.

Lynne would feel cheated. She'd always wanted grandchildren, but Steve's string of girlfriends had at least had the sense not to get pregnant. No little granddaughters to buy pretty clothes for and take to tearooms wearing big hats and pearls. No little boys to take to ball games. Willow Finley was too old for those things now, but she was old enough to marry and have children of her own. It sounded like she was domestic enough to want a family. If he was careful, perhaps he could forge a relationship. Money talked, and Willow's mother had listened well.

Steve folded the paper carefully and slipped it into his briefcase. He'd hand it over to Wilson in the morning. Wilson would know how to handle it.

His son's face mocked him from the mantle. Expressionless eyes that had antagonized him since Steve Jr. was just a toddler stared hollowly across the room. He wanted to miss his son. For his wife's sake, if nothing else, he wanted to mourn the loss of his only child. Instead, he mourned the loss of the son he

93

wanted and never had.

"Is the girl a fool? What was she thinking giving an interview like this? How does she know we were looking for her? We hardly saw her at that joke of a funeral."

Carol swallowed hard and tried to keep her pain to herself. Willow's letter, however innocently sent, had been almost as gut wrenching as Kari's complete disappearance. She'd left no note, her car abandoned in a parking lot, and their financial resources hadn't been sufficient to keep up the search. For years, she'd imagined her daughter lying dead in a ditch, discarded by a serial killer, or wandering the halls of a psychiatric ward, the victim of amnesia or delusions.

Instead, she lived an hour away, on a farm they'd passed a dozen times over the years. If only David had let her stop and ask to use their bathroom that time she'd needed one so badly. If only their car had gotten a flat on Kari's side of the Fairbury turnoff. If only they'd come to Fairbury's market more often — surely they'd have seen her. If only.

"Don't do it to yourself, Carol."

"She was right there — all those years. Why didn't she tell us? Why didn't she care?"

David Finley stood behind his wife's chair kneading her shoulders and praying for wisdom. "I think she did care. I think —" his voice broke at the mental image of his beautiful daughter broken by circumstances. "I think she was hurting so much, she couldn't see the pain she would cause anyone else."

"Why didn't we look close? We searched the city, Chicago, New Orleans, St. Louis — all those private investigators in all those cities and she was right here."

A guttural groan escaped before David could prevent it. Carol's face stared up at him in alarm. "What?"

"We concentrated our search here in hospitals and the morgue. I never imagined she'd runaway to Fairbury, so I assumed if she was here, she was —"

"Dead. Me too."

After several painfully long minutes, Carol's voice broke the silence between them. "What do we do now? We haven't talked about it, and I understood why but now... Our friends will know. The family will ask. What can we do?"

"I can't think about it right now. It's too much."

"She's family."

His voice strained as David whispered, "I know."

"She's Kari's daughter."

"She's a stranger."

Carol stood, fire in her eyes as she faced her husband. "That isn't her fault. Whatever Kari did—right or wrong—it's not that child's fault!"

"She's not a child!"

"She is to me!" Carol protested before she rushed from the room, tears blinding her as she ran.

The mask of sternness slipped from his face, revealing the pain he'd hidden from his wife. The funeral had been a farce. They'd all come out of curiosity and in the hope of closure that had eluded them over the years. Willow's brusque manner and lack of interest in them as people steeled his heart toward her. Kari had broken his heart—her daughter would probably shred it.

That officer hadn't made sense. Nothing the young man said fit any of the scenarios they'd tried. People didn't pay unworthy girls to stay away from their foolish sons anymore. Had Willow not been an exact copy of his mother, David wouldn't have allowed himself to believe she was truly Kari's daughter.

He'd expected appeals for money. Every time a personal letter arrived, he expected to see her name as the sender, but nothing came. Now he knew why. The money was real and Kari had obviously not squandered it. She'd always been a hoarder. David hoped Willow took after her.

The article mocked him. She'd shared much too much information with the reporter. Did she know how foolish she'd been? Was she truly as ignorant as the officer had implied? If she hadn't given the interview, who had? Was the officer paid for information? Maybe someone in the town?

Sighing, he folded the article and slipped it into his briefcase. He'd make a few discreet inquiries. For Carol's sake, he'd see if his granddaughter was someone they should get to know or if they were better off considering her dead.

CHAPTER 48

Chad's phone rang. The chief, Judith, and Joe watched amused as his face lit up at the sight of the number on the screen. Oblivious to the show he provided for an amused station, Chad answered cheerfully. "Hey. What'cha doing today?"

Willow's cryptic reply came in the form of a garbled whisper. "Wharf do away?"

"Wharf what?" The muffled sounds of slick fabric and a zipper zipping wrinkled his brow. He protested. "What is this?"

Another whisper came. "What are *you* doing today?"

Though barely audible, this one, Chad understood. "I'm working. Just heading out in a minute."

"Car or on foot?"

"What are you doing?"

"I need you to help me get a deer home."

"I'm working, Willow! I can't just—"

Her impatient voice interrupted. "Isn't it against some law to shoot a deer and leave it?"

"Well yeah, but—"

Four hands flew to holsters as a clearly audible gunshot rang out from Chad's phone. "Got him," Willow gloated, her voice normal. "Either come help me with this deer, or I'll report me, and you'll have to come out and arrest me."

"Willow! I can't go driving out there—"

The Chief waved him to the door, "Go help her."

"But I'm on duty!"

"Well, this is your duty. Now get out there, but no flirting. Get the job done and get back on the road. It's a tough job, but somebody has to help the damsel in distress."

"Damsel in distress, my foot," Chad muttered as he glared at the phone and then back up at Joe. "Why can't Joe do it?"

Joe pushed the station door open. "Because I'm on beat today—which, I might add, you were gloating about just a few minutes ago."

He knew when he was beaten. "Fine!"

The Chief waited until Chad swung the door open irritably and then said, "That's, 'Fine, sir!' to you, son.'"

The five miles from the station to Willow's house took half the time it should have. As he drove, Chad realized that she'd been hunting and called just as she was ready to pull the trigger—called to make sure he was around to help her move the deer. "Of all the irritating things—"

He stared at the barn. Of course, she wasn't home. She'd called from hunting. Where would Willow—Chad flipped open his phone and punched her number. The phone rang and slipped to voice mail. "Willow, I'm at your barn, but I don't know where to find you." He paused. Years of TV shows tempted him until he decided to do a little mental tormenting. "I need a twenty on your location."

"Well, let's see you stew a bit over that one anyway," he muttered to himself. He stuffed the phone in his pocket and went to find her garden cart. He'd wheel it to her and they could—the cart was gone.

Saige dropped a knotted rope at his feet and jumped excitedly as Chad picked it up and threw it. For five minutes, Chad threw, Saige retrieved, and the anger that had tried to take root in Chad's heart slowly melted. The brisk morning, the stiff breeze, and the scent of autumn surrounded him. Could any place on earth be more perfect?

After another glance at his phone, Chad stepped into the kitchen. Coffee sounded good—perfect while he waited. The sight of the kitchen table stopped him short. He wasn't accustomed to anything out of place in Willow's home. She wasn't persnickety about things, but a lifetime of putting things away instead of just "down" tends to keep your living space tidy.

A glass and oak framed display case lay open on the messy table. She'd added a leaf or two to the table and spread her things all over it. A family of tiny dolls lined the edge of the windowsill. Ticking fabric and florist foam brick with indentations of every doll lay in a heap beside the glass case. Her fly-tying vice sat nearby with a few flies lying in and near the case.

Understanding hit him in an instant. He stepped back outside, ignoring the stoves that probably needed attention, and sat on the porch step. Saige looked up at him and Chad felt reproached. "Well, how was I supposed to know? Who told her my birthday was coming anyway?" He glared at what he perceived as a reproachful look on Saige's face. "I didn't even get any coffee!"

He jumped nervously as his phone rang. "Where are you! I've been waiting—"

"I got another one. Couldn't answer. What's a twenty?"

Chad chuckled. He'd already forgotten his attempt at payback. "It's just something you hear a lot in TV shows. It means I can't see you, so where are you?"

"How would I ever have gotten that? I was wondering what you thought I should do with twenty deer!" She grunted before she said, "Ok, so walk down past the chicken coop to the fence. Follow it straight across the creek and then follow the line of trees. I'll yell when I see you."

"Going north?"

Silence hung between them for several seconds before she stammered, "Um, yeah. Sure."

Chad strode away from the house at a brisk pace; Saige followed. He shooed the animal back to the yard, and to his amazement, the dog went, head hanging and a look of despondence on her face. "Sorry, girl. If Willow didn't take you, I'm not going to."

The bridge—just a few logs tethered together with rope and tied to trees and the fence—surprised him. Then again, how

99

else would they carry back an animal like that? He followed the tree line, looking and listening for Willow. It wasn't far.

"Hey, Chad!"

Just inside the trees, Chad found Willow removing the entrails of a second deer. "What are you going to do with two deer?"

"Give them to the Mr. McFarland. He gives us the loins and keeps the rest."

"The butcher?" Her explanation annoyed him. The arrangements they had with the butcher seemed to be much more advantageous to Clyde McFarland than could possibly be equitable. "That seems like an awfully nice deal for him."

"It's better now. We used to cut off the loins ourselves, and Mother would walk to town and call him to come take away the rest, but he finally convinced her to let him do the work."

"What does he do with the extra meat? Does he pay you for it?"

Her head whipped up as she retorted indignantly, "Of course not! He does us the favor of butchering our deer for us, and we expect payment?"

"He keeps most of the deer!"

"No," she answered with studied patience, "We give him most of the deer. Without him, we'd have to butcher the whole thing ourselves and get a few more dogs to eat it all, or we'd have to allow people to come hunt on our land. The deer get thick in there some years."

A familiar feeling swept over him—understanding the incomprehensible. This was another one of what he'd dubbed as "Willowisms." Along with why saving time is so important and why buy what you can make, why charge for what you can give away seemed to be at the top of the chain.

"Let's load them up then."

"We can only take one at a time."

Chad bit his lip. He bit it from the trees, across the stream, over the fields, and to the tree near the chicken coop. Here, Willow strung the deer up by his feet without much help from Chad.

"You know, you could have just strung him up in one of

100

the trees out there, pushed the cart under him, and lowered him into it..."

"But—" Chagrin masked her face "I never thought of that. All those years I walked back to get mother's help and neither of us thought of that. It would have saved so much time, which of course, is a precious commodity isn't it?" she teased. "I'll remember that next time though. That'll save you a trip."

Chad felt terrible. He hadn't intended to make her feel like a burden. "Hey, Willow, I didn't mean it like that—I just know how much you like to do things for yourself, and it amused me that you hadn't thought of that."

The blank look on her face unnerved him. "What?"

"Well, I didn't mean to make you feel bad—"

"I don't feel bad. I asked for help, like you're always insisting that I do, I might add. You gave me a better way to do it in the future. What's the problem?"

What indeed? He grabbed the cart handles and nodded toward the general direction of the other animal. "Nothing. Let's go get the other deer."

Once back with the second deer, Willow pointed absently to the kitchen. "I need a drink of water, would you mind getting me some?"

Chad nodded, trying to fabricate a way to warn her that he shouldn't go into her house as he shuffled toward the house. "Hey!"

He whirled around and nearly knocked her over. "What?"

"I need the tarps in the barn. They're up in the loft over the kitchen. I'll wash my hands, get me water, and call." She swallowed hard, rushing on as if to keep him from talking. "You've been gone long enough—" She glanced at his uniform. "And you have blood on your pants. I'm really sorry. It seemed like a good idea at the time."

"I'm not upset, Willow. It's fine."

She bit her lip. "But—"

"Look, don't give it another thought. I don't want you nervous about calling when you need something now —"

"'I wasn't nervous. Maybe I was a little 'concerned,' but that's not the same thing.'"

His laughter echoed through the yard as he jogged to the barn for the tarps. Chad met Willow at her back door, handed her several, and whispered as she waited for the butcher to answer the phone, "'Good afternoon, Willow. Good work. Sleep well. I'll most likely kill you in the morning.'"

"Very funny."

"Just a little punny."

Her eye cocked at him as she left a message for Clyde. The moment she slid her phone shut, she quipped. "'No more rhymes now, I mean it.'"

"'Anybody want a peanut?'"

Chad found himself on the beat after all. A call from home sent Joe from town, and he drew the short straw. Six o'clock would never come. He was tired, cold, hungry, and all he could think of was the chili he'd heard Willow mention. Venison chili. She'd complained about having to use beef in her chili. She liked it best with venison.

After confiscating Aiden Cox's skateboard, again, he trudged to the station, dialing Willow's number as he went. "Hey, did I hear you mention chili?"

"Yep, you coming?"

Chad passed *Confections* and grinned. "I'll bring cheesecake."

"I'll wait for you. What time do you get off? You can name the new goat too."

As she clicked the phone shut, Willow groaned. "What on earth could cheesecake taste like? That just sounds disgusting! Maybe it's Swiss cheese…"

She glanced at the table, realizing she'd have to clear it off before he came. The clock chimed four-thirty. She still had time to finish screwing in the cup hooks before she put it all away. Once finished, Willow scooped up her dollhouse family and wrapped them in a kitchen towel. Shivering in the attic, she slipped them under the plastic that now covered the dollhouse and hurried back downstairs. A glance at the old ticking fabric showed definite faded spots. She poked at it and found it too weak to be worth saving, so she tossed it into the stove. A second glance at the foam sent her outside to the incinerator. Toxic fumes weren't worth avoiding shivers.

With a small smile of satisfaction, Willow hung the flies from the hooks to see how they'd look. Ten flies to go. It was a large display case, but it was worth it. Chad would be both pleased and surprised. She ran a finger along the smooth oak of the case. Doubt crept into her heart. Mother had given it to her for her eighteenth birthday. Could she give it away without regret?

Chad's empty bland apartment filled her mind. She knew he'd never made it a home because he'd never planned to stay, but recent conversations sounded as if he now planned to stay in Fairbury, and if he did, he'd need a homier feeling apartment. The case would be practical and beautiful. He'd appreciate that, and she wanted to give him something that truly was hers—a gift that cost her something.

She stashed Mother's shadow box, the completed flies, and the gift box she'd created in the craft room, hidden under a pile of fabric. She left the tie vise on the table and checked the clock. There was time to finish the fly she'd been making that morning. Midway through a second tie, she glanced at the clock. He'd be leaving work soon!

Cornbread. Time to make cornbread. With unnecessary speed, Willow whipped an apron over her head, tying it on as she hurried to grab a mixing bowl. The pantry, colder than most of the house, gave her the shivers as she hurried in to retrieve cornmeal and flour. Chad entered the kitchen just as she slipped her cast iron frying pan into the oven.

"Ok, this is incredibly domestic. I feel like I should call out, 'Hi honey, I'm home!'"

Feeling as blank as her expression probably looked, she stared at him. "Why?"

"Well, um—never mind. Milked the new goat yet?"

"Yes," she answered absently, as she checked the coals in the stove and added a stick. "But you could go see if you have a name for her."

Chad felt trapped in a strange time warp. The room, toasty thanks to the heat of the stove, looked ripped from one of the prairie novels his cousins had loved as teens. Willow, on the other hand, wearing jeans, a flannel shirt, and hair tied in braids on each side of her head, looked too modern as she frowned at her cell phone and shoved it back in her pocket.

"Lee likes to send nonsensical text messages."

"Most people just call them texts."

She shrugged. "Whatever they're called, she likes them."

"For example?"

"She just sent one that said, 'Ever have a margarita?'"

That wasn't something he'd ever considered. "Have you?"

"No. Alcohol, right? Salt on glasses?"

"Yep." Chad wondered why Lee would ask. "Does Lee want to take you out for drinks or something?"

"I doubt it. I think she enjoys seeing what I do and don't know. I'm a sideshow at a carnival to a lot of people."

He started to protest. It wasn't fair to say something like that, but Chad knew there was more truth to it than he wanted to think about. Eager for a distraction, he glanced at the table and pointed to the vice. "Been tying flies again?"

"A few. What do you think?"

Her nonchalance almost convinced him that he'd seen nothing amiss earlier. "I like it. Those wings are amazing."

Without another word, and before she could say anything to trip him, Chad hustled back out into the yard and over to the goat pen. A sweet faced doe blinked at him with wide eyes as he hung over the pen gate. Her coloring was similar to a dun and white paint pony and made him think of Apache braves chasing antelope or other game on their ponies.

"You look like a painted lady to me, but I don't think Willow will go for Brothelette. Maybe Gomer."

Reaching for the kitchen switch, Chad accidentally snapped on the floodlights. The yard lit up like a football stadium. The garden had been covered with mulch and a new area roped off for a new patch the next year. The chicken coop had been rotated for reasons that Chad didn't understand. The mulch pile was covered and another square roped off — for what he didn't know. A sliding door into the barn left room for the goat to come in out of the cold and, to his surprise, the clothesline had no ropes.

Out of curiosity, he peeked around the front of the house and saw the porch swing down. The front porch looked awkward without the friendly swing swaying in the breeze. He bent low, and poked at the dirt in the flowerbed. After two more, he determined that likely all of the flowerbeds were heavily mulched and ready for the first snow. The sheer magnitude of work overwhelmed him. *How can people get the erroneous idea that housewives just lie around all day eating bonbons and watching soap operas?* One look at Willow's work list and he wanted a nap.

"Chad! Dinner's ready."

"Coming!" His response was as natural as her call. He dashed into the barn, snapped off the light, and closed the doors behind him. Inside the house, he hurried to wash his hands. "Hey, you've got the place all buttoned down for winter. Where'd you put the swing?"

"It's in the barn hanging from the center beam. Butter?"

As they ate, Chad told her about his day, about how Wayne had officially pulled in the daisy-barrow that day, and how he'd missed the attempted robbery of the convenience store. "I couldn't believe it when Joe told me. They got a call from the pay phone. The guy said, 'Do not call the cops. This is a hold-up. Put all your cash in a bag, bring it out to pump seven, put it on the ground, and go straight back into the building.'"

"Really? Why would they do that? What is the inducement?"

"Well that's just the thing," Chad explained. "There is none. By time he was done talking, Joe was in his car, and by the time the attendant brought out a bag full of trash and set it outside the pump, Joe had a gun on the perp."

Shaking her head, she passed Chad the cornbread basket.

"More?"

"Save room for cheesecake."

Her eyebrow rose. "Just what is in cheesecake other than, I assume, cheese?"

"You've never had cheesecake?"

"Umm obviously not..."

Chad shoved back his chair and motioned for her to stay. "I'll be right back. Right back. This is going to be so great."

She sighed. Something about the idea seemed fishy. Maybe it was like caviar or escargot. Maybe it was raw yak curds or something equally disgusting. Surely someone like Chad wouldn't be adventuresome like that. It sounded more like a Bill kind of food.

The back door burst open and Chad whipped it shut with his foot as he entered. "You just sit there. I'll cut it. I can't believe you've never had cheesecake. It's like the prince of desserts!"

The piece of cake he placed in front of her looked like a pie. It had a crust like a pie, was thin like a pie, and unlike most cakes, had no frosting or icing. She grabbed her fork and took a bite. Putting it off wasn't going to do her any good. She would either take a bite or she wouldn't, and since he bought it for her, there was no way she wouldn't.

Chad's face nearly exploded in anticipation. "Well?"

"That is delicious. What kind of cheese is it?"

"Cream cheese."

"I've never heard of that kind. Mother brought home cheddar sometimes—and Swiss, but she never mentioned cream cheese. I wonder if I could make it?"

Chad shrugged and took a bite of his slice of cake. "No idea, but isn't it good?"

Willow nodded but she no longer noticed the flavor, texture, or even the existence of her cake. Her thoughts were delightfully engaged in the realization that Chad didn't suggest that she just buy the cheese. Chad accepted, at first suggestion, the idea that making cream cheese was something she might like to do.

CHAPTER 49

Thanksgiving Eve, Chad sat at her table, telling her what they'd learned about the man with the botched robbery. "It's kind of sad. I guess his kid needed a prescription filled and they're living paycheck to paycheck—no money to fill an eighty dollar prescription."

Willow dropped her flour sifter and reached for the teapot on the hutch. A wad of money appeared on the table before him before he knew what she'd done. "Make sure he gets that. How long will he be in jail? Does his wife need money to make up for work he'll miss?"

His eyes flitted from the roll of bills and sink where she washed her hands before returning to her dough. "He's not going to jail."

She paused before grabbing the bowl of activated yeast and pouring it into the bowl. "That's wrong. He tried to rob a store."

"Yes, but the owner refused to press charges. We can't make anything stick without his testimony, so the chief let Clay go."

She stopped, her hand buried in the dough as she stared at him. "He broke the law."

"Yes."

"He should be charged with a crime."

"Yes, but if we won't be able to prove to a jury that it happened, he will get off. That costs taxpayers a lot of money.

So, the chief gave him a warning and let him go. I don't think he'll try anything like that again."

Mixing resumed, but Chad sensed that her opinion wasn't changed. Only Willow would dump money to help a man while expecting him incarcerated for an attempted crime. Her voice broke through his thoughts. "You told him if he needed help, that you'd cover it, didn't you?"

He should have known she'd guess it. "Well…"

Strips of fabric were piled on the table. He found himself winding them around his fingers. The roll of bills taunted him. He pushed back the chair, grabbing it and carrying it to the hutch, but Willow's voice stopped him. "Take it to him."

"We covered it. The kid has her medicine, and everything is good."

"Until the next thing happens to upset their budget. If they get ahead a bit, maybe eighty dollars won't drive him to desperation." His hesitation prompted another comment. "If you don't shove that in your pocket, I will."

Chad cleared his throat. She couldn't possibly know how wrong that sounded. *Thank you, Jesus,* he moaned inwardly. Desperate to change the subject, he stuffed the money in his jacket pocket and then realized that it was likely the pocket she meant. *Fool.* Aloud he said, "I spoke to Chuck. He's going to come straight to my house after something at church in Brunswick, unless you want him to come here and get you."

"Do you think it would be rude if I didn't?"

He knew she didn't like riding with Chuck. "Not at all."

"Good! Then I'll ride with you."

Chad heard the happiness in her voice and was grateful for Chuck's church plans. He glanced at her, curious about her opinion of something that had troubled him of late. "I've been wondering. Do you think Chuck really knows the Lord? He's been going church all these years, he's very faithful in his attendance, but he is so self-centered."

Her voice dropped. "I don't know," she began. Her hands kneaded the bread expertly as they talked. "I can't tell if he just hasn't been taught or what. I do know that he needs someone who believes in him. Maybe he doesn't realize that Jesus

108

believes in him."

"Don't you think you have that a little backwards?"

Willow's laughter sounded forced. "Not really. I think we forget that Jesus is there rooting for us. He's our advocate."

Chad stopped playing with the pieces of fabric she'd been using to make her rug. "What is it? I can see it. What's wrong?"

"Anger," she gasped. "It's welling up inside me again. I can feel it. I hate the feeling and last time—"

Torn between conflicting ideas of how to handle this part of her grieving, Chad watched as she squeezed the dough into her fists and then slammed it back down on the counter. "I have an idea. I'll be right back."

"Don't you have to be at work soon?"

"I think I have time," he assured her glancing at his watch.

He returned within half an hour, carrying several boxes into the barn. Once he had his plan set up, he called to her. She stood on the back porch until he beckoned her into the barn.

"What?"

"Open the box."

A newspaper-wrapped plate emerged, and Willow unwrapped it as she pulled it from the box. "A plate?"

"Next time you want to lash out at someone, you just come out here, unwrap as many plates as you need, and smash them in the barrel."

Her eyebrows drew together as she tried to understand. "What a waste—"

"No more waste than sitting in my closet. I have like a dozen sets of dishes in there."

"How'd you get so many—why?"

"When I moved here, everyone and their brother gave me some. Aunts, old ladies at church..." Chad shrugged. "Fairbury doesn't have a thrift store, so they just sat in my storage unit.

She eyed the plate contemplatively. "Do you really think destroying a plate is going to help?" she challenged.

"Yep."

To his surprise, she raised the plate over her head with both hands and slammed it into the bottom of the barrel with all the force she could muster. Shards flew everywhere and a couple managed to shoot out of the barrel, causing her to jump backwards protectively. Chad reached for a pair of goggles. "Maybe these would be a good idea, just in case."

To his amusement, Willow shoved them on her head and over her eyes before grabbing another plate and smashing it into the barrel. After the third plate, Chad patted her back and murmured something about going to work, but she was too intent on unwrapping the next plate to notice. He jogged past the house, remembered the bread, and hurried inside.

The bread had risen—but whether high enough, he didn't know. Two greased bread pans sat waiting for use. Unsure if it was the right thing to do, but unwilling to interrupt Willow now, Chad washed his hands, divided the bread, shaped it into clumsy looking loaves, and covered the pans with a towel as he'd seen his mother do.

Willow didn't even hear his truck start. On her eighth plate, tears running down her face, she systematically smashed plates and ground out her grief in deep guttural moans that only she and the Lord understood. The "whys" of her loss finally broke the surface of her grief, sending her to her knees, clutching a plate. "I just want my mother back, Lord! I just want a mother again."

Thanksgiving -

Today seems like my first real Thanksgiving here. That first year, I was busy ripping out wires and sanding down floors. Last year, I froze, trying to chop wood faster than I burned it. But this year, it feels like I have something to be thankful for. That is very wrong of me. I've always had reasons to feel gratitude. In the beginning, I had a safe place to live. I was near enough family that if something went terribly wrong I could have appealed to them for help. I had the money to keep us alive, and the intelligence to figure out how. Last year I kept warm by chopping! I had wood to chop. Of course the first logs weren't much use. Oh how they smoked. I'm glad I found a few dead trees, or I would have had to order wood from somewhere.

110

*I tried singing **Over the River** to Willow, but I couldn't do it. She'll never go to grandmother's house for a holiday. I decided that I must make our holidays treasured events. I have made pumpkin pies all week. It feels so wrong, but after a bite of each, I tossed them in the incinerator. I wanted to enjoy pie on Thanksgiving, so once I mastered pies in that cook stove, I moved to roasting chicken. I have enough frozen chicken for meals to last me a month – or two, but I have learned how to roast the perfect chicken. It's utterly delicious. However, my cranberry sauce failed. I finally walked to town with Willow strapped to my back and bought two cans. So, dinner was simple – chicken instead of turkey, corn (Willow ate all five kernels too), stuffing, rolls, gravy, and cranberry sauce. We're both full to bursting, but isn't that part of why we're thankful? I distinctly remember Miss Graves talking about "bounty" and "gratitude" in regards to Thanksgiving. She used bounty in every form it can possibly be used.*

*I read her the books I purchased on Thanksgiving. I know she doesn't understand half what I'm reading, but I decided to read them aloud to her anyway. I have a feeling I'll be doing a lot of that. She loved **Five Kernels of Corn**. I've never seen anything like it. She sat still as a cat waiting to pounce, and every time I said "five kernels of corn," she bounced like I'd told her we were having ice cream!*

The weather was awful today – not something I was particularly thankful for. The roads were slick and two cars ended up in the ditch nearby. I felt cruel, but I didn't answer the door. One man pounded demanding the use of my phone, but I told him I didn't have a phone and if he didn't leave, I'd come out with my gun. So, while I wasn't thankful for today's weather, I was thankful for a warm house, a gun to protect us with, and interesting books to read.

Actually, I've been thinking of a lot of things to be thankful for, and I thought I'd list them. I can compare every year and see if my opinions change or grow.

~The Lord. Without Him, I truly would be nothing.

~A trustworthy financial planner. Mr. Burke has already proven himself faithful.

~A world of information and the resources to purchase what I need.

*~**Mother Earth News**. I'd be lost without that new-age blarney-filled treasure trove.*

~My daughter. I would never have had the courage to buck the modern American lifestyle without her.

~A love of beauty — this really helps keep me going.

I think mentally, I will be counting our years from Thanksgiving to Thanksgiving. I think I'll also move the calendar out of the kitchen and into the pantry. I think, when I am struggling, it is too tempting to start counting days away. For a year or two, it can stay where I have to make a deliberate effort to look at it. By that time, Willow will need to learn the days of the year and the months and seasons. By then, surely, I will have grown accustomed to life lived rather than existed.

Chad's truck interrupted her reading. She'd planned to read all of her mother's Thanksgiving entries but had overslept and frost overnight had sent her into the fields to retrieve the lambs and cow. Gomer, the "painted lady" had dried up during the past week, leaving her free from milking.

Bursting in from the cold, Chad shivered. "Oh it's cold out there. We could have snow this week!"

Willow set the journal back on the table and hesitated. Moving from under her soft warm afghan and quilt was not something she relished. "Is your truck warm? It was so cool all summer that—"

"It has a heater. My truck is warmer than this room. You're letting the fire die out."

"Don't want it going while I'm gone. Mother was particular about that. She said the risk of loss of everything wasn't worth the half an hour of comfort when we were away from the house."

With a shrug, Chad brought her coat from near the stove and held it out. "Well get into your coat quickly then."

"I need to put out the ice blocks and then I'm ready."

Afraid to ask, Chad watched as she pulled warm gloves on and carried large plastic containers full of water outside. Curiosity bested him and shaking his head, he asked, "What exactly are those for?"

"Ice. For the icebox in summer. We fill the ice room with them."

"Why not use the ice maker in your freezer?"

"We don't have an ice maker in ours. It's a waste of space when we can get ice free all winter without using up valuable freezer space."

It made sense, but didn't. A new idea occurred to him. "So why didn't you carry them out there after you filled them up? Or better yet, use the hose."

"Mother didn't like the hose for this. Sometimes we drink the ice, and the hose lies out there in the dirt all the time..."

"You're ignoring my first question."

A foolish expression crossed her face. "Because, if you must know, I had to go to the bathroom when I was done filling them and I got sidetracked with the journals until I was warm and cozy on the couch, and then I didn't *want* to get up."

"Now that is the most refreshing thing you've said in a long time."

The corner of her mouth twisted as she considered his words. "What do you mean?"

"It's just that usually you do everything, by the book, regardless of whether or not you really want to do it. This time you just skipped the whole thing and did your own thing. I love it."

He grabbed the loaves of bread and bouquet of dried flowers she'd arranged for his mother and grinned at her. "Ready to go?"

"Ready."

They stepped outside the door and Willow reached to twist the spigot a fraction of a turn. "I don't want the pipes to freeze."

"What about inside?"

She grinned. "It's dripping slowly upstairs — filling the bathtub."

Somehow, Chad knew that she'd use that water for the animals or to feed some growing thing somewhere. Before he could ask, another thought danced around the edges of his consciousness. "Hey, where's Saige?"

"She's off chasing rabbits. She's getting pretty good at it. I found remains of two of them the other day."

113

"Awww I'm sorry."

Chad's attempt at sympathy failed. Willow looked at him as if he was crazy and said, "Why?"

"Well, you sounded discouraged, and that must be pretty gross—"

"Well, I am a little discouraged. All that meat I have for her, and she's off getting her own food. I really need to consider getting another dog for her."

He slammed the truck door shut and sauntered around to his side of the vehicle. The dog leaves rabbit entrails where she can find them and her only concern is the wasted dog food in her freezer. "Wow," he muttered. "Wow."

CHAPTER 50

The clock on Chad's dashboard slowly changed numbers. Seven thirty-five changed to seven thirty-six. A mile passed. Willow's nervousness increased. Chad noticed but said little as the trees and fields gave way to the Rockland Loop. She was probably just nervous—a new place and all.

As he pulled onto the Loop, he skirted the city, out toward the suburbs. Willow seemed to notice. "This is different."

"Yeah, we live in Westbury—the old side."

"I see."

It didn't take the world's most astute person to realize that Willow wasn't her normal carefree self. "Are you alright?"

"No."

Three points for honesty anyway, Chad thought to himself. "What's wrong?"

"Rockland smothers me. It'll pass. At least you don't have all those horribly tall buildings." She sighed. "Bill's apartment. I love and hate it."

"Once we get in the house, you'll probably feel better. You're used to houses, and ours isn't all that different from yours."

"Tell me about who all will be there."

Diversion. She wanted diversion; he could do that. "Well, let's see. There's Mom and Dad of course and Chris and Cheri. Then Aunt Libby and Luke will be there—"

"Oh, are they bringing Aggie and the children?"

Chad shook his head and made a left onto yet another residential street that to Willow probably looked exactly like every other street they'd crossed. "Aggie went up north to see her parents for Thanksgiving."

"I see. So Luke and Libby, anyone else?"

He told her about his goofy uncle Ed, about his grandmother and grandfather—how they never said anything remotely pleasant to each other—and reminded her that Chuck was coming. By the time he finished describing the guests, he pulled his truck up in front of a large white house with tall round pillars.

"Wow."

Amused that she used a word usually uttered about her, Chad smiled. "It's nice. Pretentious for such a small house."

"Small!"

"Yeah. It looks bigger than it is. They did that deliberately. It's something about how they designed the façade."

"How do you know all that? It's fascinating." Willow's voice sounded more nervous than fascinated.

"We studied architectural styles in high school as part of our postmodern studies. My teacher was a hippie liberal who hated teaching in suburbia, so he spent all his time trash talking our town and our lives."

In such a short time, she'd adjusted to so many new things, including waiting for him to open her door. Of all days, today he had to do that. His mother stood on the porch, watching. She'd kill him if he didn't. He took the loaves from her and nudged her toward the house. "Come on. Mom doesn't bite."

Willow's eyes widened. "Do some people do that? Bite?" She backed away just a bit."

"No. It's just a saying—" A smirk twitched her cheek and Chad groaned. "Oh, you got me. I couldn't believe—"

"Sometimes people just assume that because I'm different that I'm stupid. I've gotten Chuck a lot, but it's hard to trip you up. You know me too well."

"You know I don't think you're stupid, right?" He swallowed hard. If he had let her think…

Before she could respond, Marianne Tesdall wrapped her

116

arms around her son. "Chaddie-my-Laddie!"

"Mom, you're dead."

"And this must be Willow," his mother continued as though Chad hadn't threatened her with imminent demise. "Come in, come in. I want you to meet Christopher!"

"Chad's brother?"

"Oh no," Marianne explained, "Chris is Chad's brother. Christopher is my husband— Chaddie's Daddie!"

"Mom!" Chad groaned and shrugged at Willow. "She likes to torment me with that."

As Marianne led Willow to the den, Willow's head turned to Chad and mouthed, *"Chaddie-my-laddie?"*

"That's it; I'm never bringing home a girlfriend. Just a friend is too humiliating!"

"What'd you say, Cha—"

"Enough Cheri, or I'll sick Chuck on you."

"Bring him on," his sister challenged. "I hear he's a doozy. Why'd you invite him, again?"

"Because Willow was stuck with him, and dad wanted to meet her."

Cheri met and held Chad's eyes for several seconds and then shook her head. "You know mom is hoping—"

"Yeah, I know. I thought maybe if she met Willow, she'd see that it's not going to happen." He glanced down at the basket of post-it notes and pens. "I'd better take this to her and rescue her from their 'discreet interrogation.'"

As Chad disappeared around the corner, Cheri smiled to herself. "That is very interesting –my-laddie."

"What'd you say?" Chris stood at the bottom of the stairs with an unreadable expression on his face.

"Chad's friend, who happens to be a girl, who is not his girlfriend, but is."

"What?"

"Exactly, my brother. You said it well." Cheri nodded for emphasis.

"Chad's protesting too much?"

"See, now aren't you glad you have me to keep your psychology toes sharp and agile?"

Chris grinned. "This I gotta see."

She grabbed his arm. "Just back off, though. We want to see it all, and if he suspects—"

"You are wicked, little sis."

Cheri grinned. "But smarter than your average sibling."

"Oh, that was low."

Unaware of the scheming behind the scenes, Chad made small talk with his parents before he pulled Willow away, holding up the basket as an excuse. "Once people start arriving, everyone will be fighting over it, so we'll just get it out of the way now."

Willow shrugged and followed Chad to the kitchen table. Cinnamon rolls and a glass pitcher of juice with clear plastic cups in a stack beside it filled the center of the table. "Hungry?"

Willow nodded looking for a plate. Chad scooped a cinnamon roll onto a napkin and handed her a plastic fork. "Mom's cinnamon rolls are the best!"

"Ok, so what is the basket for, and why did you try to get me away from your father?"

Chad hadn't anticipated her perceptiveness. "Well," he began. How do you tell a woman that he didn't want his family to start making wedding plans just because you brought her home? "Remember how mom was hoping for something—"

"I see." A glance at her told him she did see. Before he could respond, she added, "And the basket?"

"It's a tradition. We don't have a lot—every year is different in most respects but turkey at someone's house and the Thanksgiving basket are two anyway."

"Ok, that explains a lot. I completely understand the purpose of it now."

Her sarcasm wasn't lost on him. "Sorry. It's actually very simple. We write down a word or two on these papers to describe what we're thankful for."

"So if I was thankful for my new car, I'd write down 'my new car?'"

Shaking his head, Chad said, "No it's not just that. The goal is to write down something you're thankful for that reflects you as a person but isn't so specific that you might as well put

118

your name on it."

"I don't say who I am?"

Suddenly, Chad realized he'd jumped into the middle of an explanation. "No. Sorry. See what we do is, during dinner, we pass the basket around the table, and everyone draws a paper from it. Then, based on the answer, we guess who wrote it."

Rephrasing the explanation, Willow tried for clarification. "So, I write down family. Somehow, that tells everyone something about me so it makes it easy for them to guess it was me instead of everyone else around the table who might have written down family?"

"Well, sort of, yes. For instance, last year when I graduated from the academy, I wrote down, 'donuts.'"

Silently, Willow sat waiting for him to finish. Chad, on the other hand, still amazed at his brilliance, waited expectantly for understanding to dawn. She finally shrugged. "That's it? Donuts?"

"Yeah. It was a stroke of genius since we'd had them for breakfast that morning, and dad bought them so mom didn't have to bake anything. Everyone thought it was mom!"

"That makes sense. What do donuts have to do with graduating as a police officer?"

"Police? Donuts? See?"

Her eyebrows rose expectantly. "See what?"

Chad groaned. Of course, she didn't understand. She wouldn't know the cliché about officers and donuts. It wouldn't make any sense to her at all. "Well, see, there is this joke that all officers do is sit in donut shop parking lots, eat donuts, and drink coffee so if you ever need a policeman, you need to go to the nearest donut shop."

"Oh." She smiled. "That was a good choice then. So if I am thankful for Saige, I'd say 'herbs' or 'spicy friends'?"

"Exactly!"

Without a word, she took the paper and peeled a sticky note from the pad. "It's all sticky."

"Yeah. Write on the side that's sticky and then fold the edges to meet that way no one can read the words and think

119

about them before dinner."

While she searched for the perfect words, Chad poured them each a glass of orange juice and passed her another napkin. Willow shook her head. "No thanks, that one was enough."

"I thought you'd like a napkin for your fingers. You're holding your hands like you want to wash them."

"May I?" Without waiting for an answer, she hurried to the sink and rinsed the icing from her fingers. She retrieved the plastic fork and rinsed it as well. "Do you have a fireplace or something for the paper?"

"Under the sink." When she hesitated, he nodded. "Right there." Chad rose, crossed the floor, and dumped his empty cup in the bag with the rest of the garbage. Though he sensed hesitation in her, he ignored it. "Come on, let's go play Ping-Pong."

He returned the basket to the hall table and then led Willow down the basement stairs, where Chris and Cheri appeared to be in the middle of a game — appeared but it looked suspicious to him. "I play winner so Willow can watch. She can play next winner — that'll be me, but hey."

"In your dreams Chaddie m'boy."

"That's Laddie, Chris. You've been away from home too long," Cheri taunted.

"I still know how to give ice cube massages, girl," Chad growled warningly.

As his siblings battled their way to match point, Chad explained how to play the game, and pointed out good moves and bad ones. After several questions, Willow said she thought she understood the basic rules. "Let's see you play."

Chris and Chad took their places while Cheri dragged a couple of lawn chairs from the corner of the basement. "Here. This'll be good." She leaned in and whispered, "I let Chris win so I could watch this. I love how Chad whoops Chris every time. Drives Chris nuts."

"I can't help wonder..." a ball whizzed through the air and hit a support pole behind Willow's head, "what that poor ball did to deserve such vicious treatment."

Cheri stood and grabbed another ball from a bucket nearby. "You dinged that one, Chad."

Willow watched as Cheri tossed it into the garbage near the dryer. "May I look at it?"

The ball had a crescent shaped dent in it. "Wow. How—"

"The edge of the paddle. See how he slices through the air with that swing?"

"Yes."

Cheri grinned. "It works great most of the time, but once in a while the ball hits the edge instead of the flat of the paddle and the ball is a goner."

Willow's first game was tame compared to the others. She focused on swinging the paddle, hitting the ball, and trying to aim it where Chad had to work to return it. While they gently volleyed, Chad working hard not to send his returns zinging across the net and into the wall at the back of the room, Cheri and Chris watched amused.

Cheri pointed out a bulge in Willow's sweater pocket. "The ball," she whispered, "she kept it."

The pace picked up gradually. Willow's confidence grew and occasionally she slammed the ball across the net, but Chad always returned it with equal force that she couldn't meet. In no time, the game was nineteen to zero. Though tempted to give her a point, Chad knew she'd resent it. Game point. She returned a difficult serve and managed, albeit accidentally, to put an unexpected spin to the ball.

A light of understanding dawned. She returned several difficult balls but eventually lost, twenty-one to one. "You won't beat me so easily next time."

Chad's face challenged her. Cheri saw it and insisted Willow take her turn. "You have to keep going while you've got your rhythm."

Chris nodded emphatically. "It'll take you half a game to get back in the groove. Switch sides and play again."

Chad won twenty-one to fourteen. By the end of the game, Willow's confidence soared and she managed to hold off game point with several points before he sent a slice right under her paddle. "Yes!"

"Good game!" She handed the paddle to Cheri and pointed to the stairs. "Do you mind if I go get a drink of water?"

"No, sure! Want me to get it for you?"

She shook her head and started for the steps. "Chad, do you want more orange juice or water or something?"

"Juice would be good, thanks."

Willow glanced at Chris and Cheri. "Drinks? Juice..." Their shaking heads answered for them.

She was half way up the stairs before Chad jerked his head at Chris. "Go make sure Mom doesn't pounce, will you?"

In the kitchen, Willow reached for another cup and frowned. Chris watched, amazed and slightly disgusted, as Willow glanced in the trash, saw Chad's cup still sitting on top, and retrieved it. He started to protest, but she grabbed a bottle of dish soap from the counter, read the label, read the back of the label, and smiled to herself. Seconds later, a freshly washed and dry disposable cup filled with juice sat on the counter.

She washed her own juice cup, filled with water, and started to drink but Chris stopped her. "Wait. You don't want to drink from the tap. It's nasty chlorinated stuff. This little spigot has filtered water."

Willow watched as he filled her cup with the approved substance and smiled. "Drinking water here. Washing—"

"Tap."

"If it's not good to drink, why is it ok to wash with it? Residue—"

"Well, the tap water won't hurt you," Chris explained. "It just tastes awful, because they put the chlorine in it to kill bacteria."

He'd watched her for almost an hour and Willow fascinated him. As a psychologist, she represented an unstudied section of humanity. He knew nothing of people who lived cloistered from society. She reminded him of studies of Amish children who entered the "English" world, and yet unlike the defectors, she wasn't racing to embrace the world around her. Instead, she rather seemed intrigued by it.

"So..." he stopped. How does one begin a conversation with someone whose entrance into what some might consider

122

"real life" began with the death of her only other human contact?

"Is there something you want to know but feel awkward asking?"

"I wasn't sure how to strike up a conversation, and then once I did, I found myself inserting my foot into my mouth." Willow's glance at Chris' dock shoes amused him. "That's just a saying. You know, 'open mouth, insert foot.'"

" Mother always said that if you want to have friends, you must be friendly. That's probably why we never had any friends. We weren't very friendly." Before he could ask if she felt that his question was unfriendly, she said, "So I don't see how asking a friendly question would be worthy of stuffing a sock in your mouth."

So, she knew "stuff a sock in it." Interesting. "Well, you seem friendly enough to me."

Her laughter brought Marianne and Christopher in from the den where they were waiting for the beginning of the Macy's Thanksgiving Parade. "Come in guys, it's about to start."

Willow held up Chad's cup. "I'll be right there. I promised Chad some more juice, and then I'll come right back. To Chris she smiled apologetically. "I'm sorry. I think my joke failed."

"I'll take that to Chad. Go ahead and get a good seat while you can. Uncle Ed will be here any minute, and you never know where he'll park himself."

Downstairs, Chris handed Chad his cup of juice, waited until Chad took a big gulp, and informed him of its origin. "Why did she pull that cup from the trash?"

Chad spewed the contents of his mouth all over Chris' RU sweatshirt. "She did what!"

"She washed it of course, but—"

"Chris!" Even the parade observers upstairs should have heard Chad's protest.

"But why did she take it out of the garbage in the first place?"

Chad studied the cup warily. "She washed it? Are you sure?"

"I watched her. She went into the kitchen, walked straight for the trashcan, pulled it out, read the soap bottle—who reads soap bottles anyway—and then washed it, dried it, and refilled it."

A shout from downstairs sent six eyes rolling. Cheri groaned. "The parade is starting. We can't miss another five hundred tissue paper-covered vehicles."

Chad paused as he brushed by his brother. "Sorry about your shirt, man."

"Where are you going in such a hurry?"

"I have a chance to watch Willow watch a parade for the first time? No way am I missing a second of that."

The doorbell rang. "Get that, will you, Cheri?"

The remaining Tesdall siblings exchanged amused glances as Chad hurried up the stairs. "Yep. This is going to be interesting," Cheri declared.

From across the room, Chad watched Willow wilt. A constant stream of questions bombarded her from all sides. Uncle Ed delighted in asking her questions that they all knew she couldn't answer. Libby tried to buffer them, but excitement over Luke's impending engagement distracted her. Chuck and Cheri battled over Stratego and music genres, while Chad's grandparents "enjoyed" their ritual sparring in between peppering Willow with questions about life on the farm.

The clock chimed the half hour. He glanced at his watch and made a decision. Dinner wasn't for another hour and a half. It was time to take Willow away from the house for a little bit. Marianne passed on her way to the kitchen and Chad stopped her. "Do you need anything from the store? Willow needs a break. She's getting overloaded."

"I forgot margarine for Grandma. You know how she'll complain. I was going to send Chris, but—"

"We'll get it."

His uncle started a new round of questioning. "Uncle Ed," he interrupted abruptly. "Mom needs something from the store, and I thought Willow might like the drive."

"Get me some Maalox will you? Your mother's stuffing always does me in."

"Maalox. Got it. Willow, you want to come?"

The grateful look on her face was all the answer he needed. They bundled back into their coats and hurried outside. Immediately, Willow took a deep breath. "I love fresh air."

"It's city air, Willow. It's not that fresh!"

"Compared to inside —" she paused. "That's probably not a polite thing to say, is it?"

"It's honest anyway," Chad reassured her. "Let's go."

She watched him navigate the streets for a moment before remarking, "I don't see how you can tell where you're going. The houses all look alike; the streets all look alike!"

"Well, the streets have different names you know," he teased as he turned onto Chester Blvd.

Within minutes, he parked in front of his father's store and led Willow inside. "This is the store dad manages," he explained as he led her down the bread aisle toward the cold cases in the back of the store.

After a few feet, Willow stood and stared at the dozens of bread options. Her eyes blurred at the sheer volume of food. Jars upon jars of jams, jellies, and preserves flanked the breads, bagels, English muffins, buns, and rolls. Peanut butter jars lined the other side. She counted eleven brands, three sizes per brand, and forced herself to stop when she realized that each brand and size came in crunchy and creamy as well as some in other options.

"What's wrong?"

"There's so much food! Look at all the bread! Mother told me about supermarkets, but this is incredible. It's like J.C. Penney and their skirts but it's bread. That's a lot of peanut butter!"

Two pre-teen girls passed them, giggling and staring. Chad pulled her arm gently toward the back wall. "The butter is back here. C'mon."

The back wall of dairy products assaulted her senses as well. Gallons upon gallons of milk, cream, half and half, and all related products seemed to stare at her from the cases. "I've never imagined—"

Chad stared at her, confused. "It's not as big as this or anything, but the market in Fairbury..."

"I've never been inside. Is it like this?"

He nodded. "It's wonderful isn't it?" In one place, everything you need to keep you fed and healthy."

Willow wandered down the back aisles staring at boxes of cake mix, stuffing mix, canned pumpkin, canned cranberry sauce, marshmallows... the list was endless. The meat counter looked like a sea of red and white meats, sausages, and fish. "Look at all the—" Her eyes found the meat cold case and widened. "More!"

All through the store, she wandered the aisles until she reached the produce section. "Oh, wow. Wow!"

Light fingers trailed across lettuce, spinach, celery, and tomatoes. Awestruck, she picked up eggplant, zucchini, and asparagus. "How?"

"Produce is shipped from all over the country and even the world."

The aisle of medications and hygiene sent her mind reeling. "All of this is for what?"

She picked up a bottle of pain reliever. Several competitor bottles announced that their product solved all of life's pains and aches. Bottles and boxes announced relief of constipation, indigestion, coughs, sneezing, dry eyes, and toothaches. Vitamins filled shelves assuring her that she'd be healthier and live longer if she just took their little pills.

"What—"

Chad grabbed a bottle of Maalox and steered her to the checkout stand. "Uncle Ed can't digest mom's stuffing."

"Then why does he eat it?"

The cashier failed to stifle a snort. "Well, I don't know. I guess because he likes it."

"But if it makes him need this stuff," she poked the bottle just as the checker swiped it across the scanner. "Is food worth it? There are other things that he likes to eat, surely!"

Stella glanced at Chad. "Well, Chad, she has a point."

"You know him?" Willow's voice was filled with surprise.

"Sure. His dad is my boss and the ogre who makes me work on Thanksgiving!"

Compassion filled Willow's face. "I'm sorry. That's terrible! I didn't think about it, but working on Thanksgiving— that's terrible!"

"Just joking. I always ask for Thanksgiving. I get triple time and my family is too far away to visit so why not?"

"Triple time? That's even worse!"

Chad nudged her amused and winked at Stella. "That means she makes three times more per hour than usual."

As they walked to Chad's truck, Willow wondered aloud. "What do people do with all the time they save? If they're not growing food, baking their bread, and canning the food they grow, then why doesn't everyone have more time?"

"I guess they're working to be able to afford to pay someone else to do that for them."

"I think I'm supposed to be amazed," she began, "but I can't help but think that it's sad somehow."

CHAPTER 51

The family seemed to erupt in cheers, hugging one another as Willow and Chad entered. "Well, I'm glad you're happy to see us but —" Chad began.

"Luke's engaged! Aggie said yes! He's coming back late tonight with video footage of the proposal," Cheri squealed excitedly.

Libby beamed at Willow. "I'm going to be an instant grandma all over again! Can you stay and watch it with us tomorrow?"

"Yeah!" Cheri's enthusiasm infected them all. "After the guys get back from their shopping frenzy, we can have pizza and tease Luke!"

Seeing the uncertainty in Willow's eyes, Libby thought she understood. "Oh, how silly of me. Chad's here. He can't take care of the animals if you're not home. I'll find a way to bring it to you."

Chad pulled Willow aside. "Judith or Joe — even Martinez would go out and make sure the animals had water and food. I know they would. Do you want to stay overnight and see the tape?"

"I couldn't ask —"

"Look, if you had to milk the goat, I wouldn't have suggested it, but anyone can sprinkle feed for chickens and dump some alfalfa for goats and sheep and a cow."

Chad's grandmother passed by saying, "Well if Aggie

knows what's good for her, she'll renege and run. Misery. She's asking for misery."

Willow's patience with the constant berating and negativity was gone. "I think that's a horrible thing to say." She said coolly, and to Chad's ears, with terrifying calmness. "Luke is a good man and will cherish her."

Silence descended over the room. Everyone waited for Grandmother Tesdall to pounce. Misery welled in Willow's heart. She hadn't meant to say what she thought aloud. "I'm sorry, Mrs. Tesdall. I shouldn't have said that."

"But you think it," the irascible woman countered.

"Yes, but thinking something doesn't give us the right to be rude, and I'm sorry."

"You don't like me very much, do you?"

Willow heard a few gasps and blushed. "Actually, I don't know you. I don't like the way you talk to your husband, though, and I don't think you know Luke very well if you think Aggie would be better off without him."

Chad felt like sinking into the floor. His grandmother would explode. But to everyone's surprise, she laughed. "I like you, girl. You've got spunk." She turned to Chad and said, "Keep this one. She's worth a hundred of the princesses out there."

Grandpa Tesdall paused beside her and kissed Willow's cheek as he followed his wife into the living room. She laid a hand on his arm and smiled into his eyes. "Mr. Tesdall, try kindness. I think it'll gentle her. Someone somewhere said something that made her feel weak or foolish for being proud of her husband, and she's just protecting herself."

Cheri hurried to where Chad and Willow discussed something in hushed tones. "Hey, is he convincing you to stay?"

"Well—"

"Oh come on, you've never had a slumber party! We can so do it! I'll give you a facial; we'll roll our hair, and watch the chickiest chick flicks I can find."

"Chris, can I come home with you?" Chad wailed with mock horror.

130

"No way bro, you're staying." To Willow she added, "We'll torture him. It'll be great."

The constant ribbing of sibling relationships, so utterly foreign, fascinated her. Their banter bordered on vicious, but a deep closeness and obvious love overrode any unflattering impressions. "Chad's my ride. If he's staying, I'm staying."

Chad grinned. "I'll call Judith."

Chuck pulled Cheri from the room and down to the basement. "Ok, what gives? You've been taking pictures of them all day and now you're pushing her to stay."

Cheri's smile lit up her face hiding the slight scar along her upper lip. "I want to see if I'm right—and I am—and pictures are for proving things to those who are a little resistant to the idea."

"Blackmail?"

Hooking her arm in his, Cheri climbed the stairs. "Kind of reverse blackmail. This helps the victim."

"Willow, I'm going to go dress for dinner; come up and talk with me."

Chad heard Cheri from the other side of the room but couldn't catch Willow's eyes quickly enough. Willow followed Cheri upstairs, taking her own tote bag with her. "Oh brother," he muttered to himself.

Willow found Cheri's room fascinating. The walls were plastered with travel posters and overlapping those, were prayer cards of missionaries from that area. India had missionaries in Mumbai, Delhi, Thane, Jaipur, and Agra. As she spun in a circle, she saw posters of Peru, Cambodia, South Africa, and New Guinea.

"You want to travel."

"Sort of—I want to be a traveling missionary kid tutor."

Impressed but clueless, Willow asked the obvious question. "What exactly do you do as a traveling missionary tutor?"

"Well, I want to serve missionary families instead of

131

serving as a missionary. So, I want to travel to different families and help with their kids' education. So many of these families home school—it's not like they have a choice—but life can be exhausting enough as a missionary without adding more to it. I just want to come help and give mom and dad a rest while I tackle the humps their kids can't get over."

"That sounds wonderful! Is there an organization that you go through, or—"

"I don't know. I haven't looked that far yet. My job now is to get my education."

Willow nodded appreciatively. "So how did you decide to do this?"

While Cheri changed for dinner, she told about her summer of persecution in high school and how it inspired her to want to serve in missions. "But I think I'd be best helping the families."

"I can't imagine that kind of experience stimulating a desire for me to risk that kind of persecution again."

"It was awful. The constant pressure to recant, to deny the Lord, the hard labor, the sleeplessness, and the fear—"

"But they didn't hurt you…" Willow hardly got the words out of her mouth.

"Not really. Just hard physical labor and sleep deprivation—some hunger but not too much. A few of the girls got propositioned, though. Offered an easier time for favors."

"How did you escape?" Again, Willow found it impossible to hide her horror.

"You know where it says in first Corinthians that you won't be tempted without a way of escape? Well, there was. One by one, we all got out and back to our homes. It changed all of us."

Just hearing the story of the camp bus hijacking terrified Willow. "My mother moved from Rockland because of a horrible experience. People think she was wrong to protect— isolate us even—but I am glad. To endure something like—"

"It's a privilege if it's for Jesus who endured so much worse. Trust me, if you lived through it, you would have stood firm and come out a much stronger Christian. We all did."

"Right here in America. Who would have imagined!"

Their discussion moved to more pleasant topics as Cheri swiped a mascara brush over her eyelashes and put on a light coat of lip-gloss. Willow felt damp from over warmth and pulled a fresh shirt and her tin of deodorant powder from her tote bag. "I'll be right back."

When she returned, Cheri caught the slight whiff of lavender as Willow crossed the room. "Is that your perfume? It smells so clean."

"Deodorant."

"What brand?"

Willow handed her tin of deodorant powder to Cheri and began unbraiding her hair. Cheri, intrigued by powdered deodorant, asked how she made it. "It smells so nice!"

"It's just a fifty-fifty solution of baking soda and cornstarch with some crushed lavender. Mother liked dried mint better."

"I'll have to remember that when traveling. I might not be able to find my favorite brand, but cornstarch and baking soda should be easy enough to bring on a plane or buy at a store."

Willow flipped her hair over her head and rubbed the scalp well. As she reached for her brush, Cheri cried, "No! What are you doing?"

"Brushing my mess."

"But it looks great like that. Why ruin it?"

The memory of Chad's reaction at the mid-summer's faire caught her off guard. "He wasn't teasing."

"What?"

"Chad said something once when I unbraided my hair, and I thought he was mocking me—you know, in fun."

Adding this tidbit to her growing arsenal, Cheri nodded hands on hips. "Well he was right. You look cool."

"But if I don't brush it out, it'll stay kinky and wavy. My hair doesn't hold curl anymore, but it does kink well from a braid."

Cheri ran her fingers through her own hair demonstrating how to arrange it. "Just run your fingers through to tame the couple of snarls and let it hang. If you had bangs, it might be a bit bushy but this works. It has that Sandra Bullock slash Drew

Barrymore appeal—tousled but not messy."

Willow adjusted her skirt, tried to forget about her messy hair, and stood ready for inspection. "Will I do?"

"That skirt is to die for. With boots, you'd be a walking advertisement for Boho. I've got to go see how that skirt looks on me in my size."

"This one didn't come from there, but I'll make you one if you like."

Cheri squealed and pushed Willow from the room. "Oh I'm going to like having you in the family."

"But I'm not—"

"Pop said we're adopting you as one of the family." As Willow's face drew tight with concern, Cheri added reassuringly, "He said no marriage license required!"

As they started down the stairs, Cheri nudged her gently. "Look, Chuck is trying to be patient with Uncle Ed."

"That's not like him at all," Willow began, but Cheri cut her off.

"And if Chad's Adam's apple bobs, you'll know I was right about that hair."

Willow tried not to look. A significant part of her didn't want to know, but like anyone, when told not to look, it was impossible to avoid. Chad glanced up from a photo album he shared with his grandmother and swallowed hard. He scooted closer to his grandmother to make room and jerked his head to the spot next to him.

"Come see how cute I was."

Cheri grinned and pushed Willow towards the couch as she quipped, "Emphasis on the *was*, brother o' my laddie."

Willow's attention was immediately on the children in the pictures. She recognized Zeke and Libby and even Grandmother Tesdall, but miniature versions of Cheri, Chris, and Chad held her attention.

At a quarter after six, Marianne called everyone to the table. Chad motioned for Willow to stay seated as he led his grandmother to her chair. His thoughtfulness and gentleness, while expected by Wanda Tesdall, charmed Willow. He returned immediately and escorted her to the table commenting

134

quietly that her hair looked nice.

"Cheri told me not to brush it out."

"Seems like I said something like that once, and you ignored me."

"Well, frankly, I'm not sure I agree with either one of you, and I don't think I care if I look like Sandra or Barry someone or another, but I wasn't going to be difficult about something so minor while a guest in your home."

As he pushed in her chair, Chad murmured, "I'll remember to wait until you're at my house next time I want you to do something."

Willow stared down at her plate, curious as to why one of the little folded squares was on top.

"Ok, does everyone have a paper?" From the tone of his voice, she could tell that Christopher loved this part of Thanksgiving. Her eyes followed his as he said, "Libby, why don't you read yours first?"

"Ok, my words are practical wisdom. If I thought she'd be thankful for herself, I think I'd say it was Willow's—it fits her perfectly—but I think she's a little too modest for that."

"Hear, hear!" Chuck cried with loud applause. Cheri pulled his arms down and told him to shut up, sending titters around the table.

"Well, I don't know," Libby continued. "It has to be about someone other than the person so someone is thankful for someone else who is wise. I—" She paused. "I know. And I'm not telling."

"It's you! Someone said you're wise. I've always said it," Marianne announced triumphantly.

Willow asked to see the note. "Well, it's not Chad's handwriting, or I would have said Chad. He's always saying how wise his father is and how much common sense he has, so I would have guessed it was Chad being thankful for his father's wisdom."

"You're never coming back," Chad protested. "You're too good."

"But, it wasn't his handwriting."

Libby smiled. "He disguised it well. Good one, Chad."

Seeing her brother choke up with emotion, Libby patted Ed's arm and encouraged him to go next.

Around the table, people guessed until Grandfather Tesdall read "commencement." "My guess is Cheri since she graduates this spring."

"Nope! I was crayons remember?"

Chris nudged Cheri and they exchanged knowing glances as Chad's hand slipped from the table and squeezed Willow's under the cloth. Chris piped up. "I think it's Willow. She began a new life this year, and she's practicing thankfulness for it."

"Practicing!" Chad protested.

"He's right," she answered quietly. "I am deliberately thankful. It's not spontaneous gratitude, but when I think about all the good that has come from the changes in my life, as much as I wish I could go back to last spring, I also don't. I just wish I could have the changes *and* Mother."

The kitchen buzzer buzzed, sending nervous chuckles around the table. Chad's mother smiled. "Rolls are done; we can continue after dinner is served. Cheri?"

Libby rose with Cheri and Marianne and disappeared into the kitchen. One look at Willow's face told Chad she was about to lose control. Without a word, he stood and pulled out her chair for her. "Excuse us."

Taking her hand, he led her from the room, up the stairs, and into the guest room shutting the door behind them. Tears were already splashing down her cheeks. "I'm sorry Chad — it's such a happy day for everyone, and I'm just being ungrateful."

He held her as she cried until a new thought crossed his mind. "I didn't think, Willow. I know how important holidays were to you and your mother. I didn't think about the fact that this is your first big holiday without her."

Her sobs grew deeper and more heart-wrenching. Chad tried to comfort her but was unable to be much help. He pushed her onto the end of the bed and handed her a pillow. "Hold onto that. Just hold on for a minute."

Downstairs, he grabbed Libby's arm and pulled her away from the sideboard, whispering something in her ear. Libby's eyes glanced at the stairs, and she nodded. She untied her apron, tossed it over the back of her chair, and hurried up the stairs to the guest room.

As sorry as Cheri was for Willow's pain, she couldn't help a certain amount of satisfaction over the wet patches and wrinkled spots from obvious grips on Chad's shirt. One look at her mother squelched that satisfaction. Marianne, however, looked unnerved, and she knew why. The last time Chad had shown half the care and concern for someone that he showed for Willow, Linnea Burrell had accused him of shredding her heart for the fun of it.

CHAPTER 52

Christopher Tesdall called a final goodbye to his brother, Ed as he drove away, and shut the door. "Well, another year, another Thanksgiving."

"Luke just called, he'll be over at four to pick up you guys," Marianne called from the kitchen.

"It's just sick."

"What is," Willow asked curiously.

"They'll be out in the freezing cold for a few cheap deals."

The blank expression on Willow's face didn't change. "Where are they going and why?"

Chad shoved a Black Friday ad at her as he plopped on the carpet at Willow's feet. "Day after Thanksgiving sales. Mom and Cheri hate 'em. Doesn't make sense but they do. Dad, Chris, and I love 'em. All Christmas shopping done in one stop, at the best prices, and we make the retailers happy by giving them a great sales day. However, our shopping fiends don't like it."

"You like to shop but not tomorrow?"

Marianne's impatience with her husband and sons was evident. "They don't shop, they hunt. The store is the hunting grounds, the items are the game, and their speed is their weapon. They get in, go for the kill, and get out. No thought whatsoever in their purchase. Just grab, wrap, and bow."

"Ooh good one Mom!"

"So, are you a 'drag it out as long as possible and spend

twice as much time and money' like the girls, or do you have a little common sense like us," Chris challenged.

"I don't think I'm either. I think I'm more of a 'make it up as I go' kind of giver."

"What does that mean?"

"Cheri, that means she's a diplomat," Christopher insisted. "Smart girl, this one."

"No, I just wouldn't know where to look or what to buy." She glanced at Chad and snickered. "I think I'd just stand in the store, spin in circles, and walk out without anything."

"So you didn't celebrate or did mail order or what?"

Willow passed Chad a pillow. "We made a lot of our gifts."

Intrigued, Christopher leaned back in his recliner, one arm behind his head, and encouraged her to tell them more. "What did you get for Christmas last year?"

Smiling at the memory of her mother's excitement, Willow said, "Fishing line."

Smiles and nods plastered the faces around them until Chad said, "You look like it was one of your favorite presents ever, why?"

"Because it was her last one, stupid," Cheri muttered jabbing her brother in the ribs.

"No, because it was such a sacrifice for her."

Marianne, Cheri, and Chris stared at one another in horror. "Why a sacrifice?" Chad's probing surprised her at first, and then Willow realized what he must be doing.

"Well, because it wasn't just about buying more fishing line. We probably had plenty. With that gift, she gave some of her free time so I could spend the summer fishing. It was something to look forward to." She turned to Chris, "What was your favorite Christmas present?"

"Charlie."

"You loved that crazy robot!" Cheri exclaimed. "I woke up every morning for ages hearing, 'Greetings, what shall we do today?' in that awful digital monotone."

Chris grinned at the memory. "That robot has saved me from much heartache. Any woman who comes into my house and disses Charlie doesn't get invited back." He nudged his sister. "How about you?"

Unlike Chris, Cheri had to think about her answer. "My first instinct was to say my *Diaper Darlin' Dolly*. I really liked feeding her and changing her diapers, but I truly think my favorite gift was camp."

A hush descended over the room. Willow knew instinctively that Cheri meant the camp she'd been prevented from attending by the bus hijackers. Christopher rubbed his hand across his forehead surreptitiously wiping away tears as he did. "You have no idea how hard we prayed over that decision. We always wonder if you resent us for it."

"Of course not! It was the best summer of my life. It was horrible but so wonderful. I guess I never thanked you. I'm sorry."

Amazed, Willow watched as Cheri flung herself into her father's arms settling into them on his lap. Her heart tugged in directions she'd never imagined. The relationship of father and daughter was something she couldn't fathom. It was—she smiled at the first word that came to mind—inconceivable. Imagining her relationship with the Lord as an equivalent failed. The idea of the Lord's arms wrapped around her so lovingly and protectively was impossible to grasp.

Self-recrimination also flooded Willow's heart. The story of Cheri's abduction and persecution horrified Willow. She'd been thankful for a protective mother and a sheltered world where that kind of harm was nearly impossible. Even seeing the growth that Cheri obviously experienced didn't warm Willow to the idea that such beauty and good could come from a horrifying experience, and she certainly was willing to be a weaker Christian if it meant safety from spiritual torture.

Anxious to change the subject, Willow nudged Chad's knee with her foot. "What was your favorite gift?"

"My sheriff set."

Chris and Cheri erupted in laughter. While they joked about him never growing up, Willow watched a silent exchange between Chad and his father. "Why is it so funny? I would think that's a perfect gift for him."

"He was sixteen!" gasped Cheri as she went off into further gales of laughter. "He never did get that it was a joke."

Willow's quiet voice pierced through the hilarity. "I think that you two missed the punch line then."

"Huh?"

Chad shook his head. "Don't worry about it, Willow."

"I will worry about it!" she insisted. "Your parents gave him that set as a way of telling Chad that they'd support him in his dream even if they didn't understand it, and I think it's beautiful."

The Tesdall family watched amused as Chad squeezed Willow's foot and smiled gratefully at her. "It's ok. They know what I mean even if these twits don't get it."

Calling for hot chocolate orders, Cheri escaped to the kitchen to avoid showing her amusement. Marianne, desperate to change the discussion before her emotions spun out of control, redirected the questions back to Willow. "Your gifts seem unique Willow, what other gifts have you received?"

"From Mother?"

"Well, I assumed—"

Smiling brightly, Willow plunged into a description of birthdays, Valentine's Days, and Christmases. "Well, I think some of my favorites were probably my tree blocks, Chinese Checkers, and my shower cap."

"You got a shower cap for Christmas?" Marianne's disbelief was almost comical.

"The year mother put in a shower for me she gave me a shower cap for Christmas. I love that shower cap. I still have it."

"Why is it so special to you?" The psychologist in Chris came out in full force.

"Because it was mother saying that she embraced the shower, not just tolerated it. Mother didn't like showers. She loved baths, but she put that showerhead in just for me."

Cheri, calling from the kitchen, asked, "What are tree blocks?"

"Mother took the smallest branches from trees we used for wood and cut logs, intersections, slices for floors and things like that, sanded them, oiled them well, and gave them to me.

142

They're like building blocks that create a tree house or fort or whatever you want it to be. I still bring it and my fairies out and decorate it with tea lights at Christmas." She frowned and murmured, "I wonder if I should make more tea lights…"

"Fairies?"

"Mother made them. I made angel fairies one year but they weren't as pretty as Mother's."

The clock chimed ten before the men finally dragged themselves off to bed. Willow and Cheri changed into pajamas and started the slumber party rituals while Marianne mixed a batch of brownies. The night had just begun.

Thirty minutes later, Willow sat with a bowl of popcorn, a batch of brownies, and green goop on her face watching the fascinating world of internet communication as Meg Ryan and Tom Hanks sparred over caviar. Cheri rolled her hair in hot rollers and peeled the goop from Willow's face leaving it red and raw; however, after a slathering of deep moisturizing cream, she felt rejuvenated.

By the time Joe Fox and Kathleen Kelly faced off in the coffee shop, Willow's hair bounced around her head in curls that rapidly drooped into nearly non-existent waves. "I told you my hair didn't curl. It kinks, but not curls."

After Brinkley brought the couple together, Cheri led Willow to the guest room and turned down the covers. "I'm really glad you came, Willow," she began. "You're good for us. You're really good for Chad, but you've been good for us as well."

Unsure of what else to say, Willow smiled half-heartedly and whispered, "Thank you. I've enjoyed being here."

Once Cheri left, Willow curled under the covers and reached for the lamp only to remember that there was none. She scrambled from the bed, snapped off the light switch, banged her knee into the footboard, and crawled back into bed muttering, "It's illogical to put the switch across the room so you have to cross it blindly when you're already tired. Lamps are better."

Sleep held back—taunting her. The bed was comfortable, the pillows fluffy, and Cheri's pajamas were the most

143

comfortable thing Willow had ever worn to bed, but her mind refused to quiet down and let her rest. The hum of the furnace and the periodic blasts of air rattled vent covers, keeping her mind spinning. Sirens wailed now and then, and dogs barked and howled at odd times.

A crack of light appeared from the door. "Willow? You sleeping?"

She started to sit up, but Chad opened the door further and waved her back in bed. "Don't get up," he whispered. "I just wanted to make sure you were comfortable and that mom and Cheri didn't pester you."

"You're supposed to be asleep. You have to get up in a few hours."

After shoving Willow's shoe under the door to keep it open, Chad sat on the floor in front of her nightstand, wrapped his arms around his knees. "I'm used to it. Did you like the movie? I think I heard *You've Got Mail.*"

"It was nice. I didn't understand a lot of it. They were talking on computers somehow. Makes no sense to me."

"I like Tom Hanks."

"Who is that?"

A comfortable sense of the new familiar settled around them. Willow didn't fit in his world and comments like that were delightful reminders of that. "Joe Fox. His real name is Tom Hanks."

"I didn't like how they got divorced. That was sad."

"Who, Joe's father? I didn't like that whole sub-plot. It wasn't necessary to the advancement of the story at all."

Her head shook and the light streaming in from the hall made interesting shadows on the wall as she gesticulated. "No, Joe and Kathleen. Why did they each have to be married? Couldn't they have just been single people? The infidelity made me feel icky."

Chad's heart dropped. He hadn't thought about how she'd see things. Had he been more perceptive, he could have prevented her from being exposed to things he knew her mother had deliberately avoided or at the least, warned her of content first. "Willow, they weren't married. Neither one of them was married."

"I guess I don't understand why they made it seem like they were then. Either way, it wasn't necessary. That Frank was a great character, though. I liked what they did with him." She snickered. "'Thank yer.'"

Chad rested his back against the nightstand, feeling like things were right in his world again. "Thanks for understanding about my sheriff set."

"I like the relationship you have with Chris and Cheri. It's endearing most of the time. I just think sometimes you don't seem to know when to be serious and when to be silly."

"I think you'll find that we act most silly when we feel most serious."

He sensed a question in her. The temptation to urge tiptoed to his heart but he chased it away again. She'd ask when she was ready. It came sooner than he expected — almost in a rush.

"How can Cheri be so grateful for such an awful experience? What happened to her when she went to camp that time — it terrifies me. I don't think I could be thankful for it."

Chad ached to explain it in depth. The family had given their word that they would keep those weeks of Cheri's life private. "Willow, I can't tell you all I want to about that time. It's not my story to tell. I can tell you that I truly believe if you lived it as Cheri did, you'd say the same thing that she does. It changed her life, for the better, and she would do it over again in a heartbeat."

"I don't think so, Chad. I've learned from this that I am weaker than I ever imagined. It scares me to think that such a thing can happen in this country. I just want to go home, hide out on my farm, and forget the world and the people in it if it means I'll be safe from that kind of persecution. I don't think I'm prepared for difficult times."

Chad sought her hand, praying. Not prepared for difficult times — her life, in the eyes of so many, was a series of difficult times, and yet he understood what she meant. As he wove their fingers together, he prayed aloud. Asking for faith, understanding, and boldness in Christ, Chad prayed for guidance and wisdom. Eventually, he felt her hand slacken and her breathing grow soft and rhythmic. He stood at the side of her bed, watching her sleep for a moment, before turning to leave the room. His mother's silhouette blocked the doorway.

"Is she ok, Chaddie?"

"She feels inadequate as a Christian."

The surprise in his mother's voice told him what she'd say before she whispered, "How is that possible?"

"Cheri's persecution really hit home. It's the antithesis of what the Finley farm is all about. Where Cheri embraces her painful circumstances, Willow flees them as her mother taught her. Seeing the other side..."

Marianne followed her son into his room, pulled the covers over him and laying one hand on his cheek said, "I'm proud of you, son. I cannot begin to tell you how proud I am of you."

CHAPTER 53

The men bustled into the house with their "kill" and dusted off the first flakes of winter. As Chad shrugged out of his coat, the corners of his mouth tugged upwards slightly at the sight of Willow's flower arrangement. He'd have to thank his mom later.

"Hey, Marianne? Guess what I found!"

"Shhh," his mom fussed as she rushed from the kitchen looking extra chipper and festive.

"What?" Christopher's stage whisper wasn't much quieter than his yell.

"Willow's still asleep. You guys be quiet, or I'll send you down to the basement."

"What about breakfast? I'm starving!" Chris whined in his best mock toddler voice.

Ignoring her son, Marianne wrapped her arms around her nephew. "Congratulations, Luke, I can't wait to meet her. You need to bring everyone over some afternoon soon."

"Aunt Mari, I'd rethink that invitation if I were you. We're not a visit, after all. We're an invasion."

"Good," she quipped leading her nephew to the kitchen. "Then we surrender!"

Pineapple chunks and cheese cubes sat on the counter as a pre-breakfast appetizer, but after one pass by the four hungry men, only toothpicks and two dirty plates remained. "Mom, got any of your cinnamon rolls left?" Chad was hungry enough to wake Willow deliberately so they could eat."

"No, and I'm not putting in the casserole until I hear some movement from upstairs."

"Where's Cheri?"

"She's down in the basement, digging out the tree. Chris, why don't you go help her? Chad, you could get the ornaments…"

The guys disappeared from the kitchen and a knowing look passed between them. At the foot of the basement stairs, Chad paused. "You go down; I'll be there in a minute. I just want to make sure she's not up there wondering when we're all going to wake up. I can just see her doing that."

"Don't let mom catch you!" Chris warned as he thundered down the stairs.

Chad peeked into Willow's room and almost snorted aloud. No wonder Willow still slept soundly. The blinds were down, the curtains drawn, and only one tiny, daring ray of sunlight managed to peek through any of the cracks. He leaned against the doorjamb and watched her sleep, wondering what about the picture bothered him. Then he realized. Most people assume a rested peaceful look in their sleep that you rarely see on their faces. Willow just looked like Willow with her eyes closed. The peace in her heart and the life she led, while hard and requiring much labor, was peace lived daily. He'd never noticed how clearly it showed in her face until he watched her sleep.

A hand on his shoulder made him jump. He looked down into his mother's warning eyes and hugged her, whispering as he did, "Look at her face, Mom. She looks just as gentle and peaceful awake as she does asleep."

Marianne turned him from the door and pushed him towards he stairs with a mock scowl. "Get down there and help," she hissed menacingly. "Or I'll bring out the hidden albums. I think Willow would get a huge kick out of a certain little baby boy watering my roses in the buff."

Chad jogged down the stairs. His mother had claimed for years that she had certain pictures squirreled away for opportune blackmail, and though none of the Tesdall children

148

had ever found them, they also weren't willing to risk it. She peeked in at Willow and smiled as the young woman stretched, rolled over, and resumed her rhythmic breathing.

She breathed a prayer as she turned from the room. "Lord, I always thought it'd take something drastic to pull Chad out of his shell, but I never realized it'd be a good drastic. With his job—" she sighed under her breath. "My faith was weak again. I've got that down to a science. Think we could work on some strengthening exercises now?"

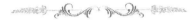

Willow awoke. Again. Her head felt fuzzy from lack of movement. She wanted fresh air and a walk. Maybe if she got dressed, she'd catch the men before they left. She hadn't planned on a shopping trip, and it would likely slow them down, but after waking several times and finding it still dark, she was ready to give up.

Not a sound reached her as she wrapped Cheri's spare robe around her. She'd have to slip into Cheri's room and snatch her clothes. As she passed the top of the stairs, light shone from the first floor and oddly enough, it looked like it was coming from outside.

Quickly, she padded downstairs and glanced out the narrow window that flanked the door. Light filtered into the room, and snowflakes fell steadily on the lawn and shrubs. She remembered a clock on the oven, so Willow hurried to see what time it really was, but as she stepped in the kitchen, she stopped short.

"Oh excuse me," she gasped, blushing. She turned to rush from the room and the sight of Christopher and Marianne wrapped in each other's arms, kissing.

"Willow, did you need something?" Marianne asked without moving from her husband's arms.

She didn't even turn around as she said, "Oh, no, I was just going to see what time it is. It was so dark in my room that I thought it was night still."

With each word, she inched from the room uncomfortably.

Marianne smiled apologetically. "I'm sorry. I went in before I went to bed and closed it up so the light wouldn't bother you. I'm putting a casserole in. Would you like to take a shower while it bakes?"

"Um—" Her eyes traveled uncomfortably to Christopher's hands as they massaged his wife's arms.

Taking the casserole from the fridge, Marianne shoved it in the oven and punched the timer. "Come on. I'm sure Cheri has some sweats or something that'll fit you."

All the way up the stairs, Marianne's mind whirled. Should she apologize for making Willow feel uncomfortable? As she chattered about Cheri's wardrobe options, she tried to read Willow's body language to determine how to respond. She wasn't ashamed of the display of affection but neither did she care to make a guest uncomfortable.

"Oh look, Cheri bought these last year and never wore them. I'm not sure why..." Marianne prattled about the velour warm up suit and t-shirt as she found clothes, toothbrush, and towels and placed them in the bathroom.

As soon as Willow shut the door, she hurried downstairs. The shouts of her sons and husband sent her back upstairs. "Well, you didn't tell me you were wrapping! Chad, Christopher, I need you."

Seated around the couch, Marianne explained the scenario with a hint of a blush on her cheeks. The Tesdalls weren't prudes. They showed genuine affection, occasionally more passionate when privacy was probable, but they were always discreet and tasteful. Willow's discomfort seemed more pronounced than when a niece, nephew, or even one of Cheri's friends burst into the house.

As he listened to his mother explain the situation, Chad chuckled. "Care to share with us Chad?" his father asked, instinctively knowing it was going to be interesting.

"I just remember when she said after we saw the *Princess Bride*. There is that line about the five perfect kisses, and she said, 'What's so big about a kiss anyway? Two lips smashed against each other. Whoop-dee-doo.' I told her she'd think differently someday."

"Smashed lips!" Christopher laughter joined Marianne's muffled titters. She tried to hush him, but it didn't work.

"Chad, what do you think? I started to apologize for making her uncomfortable, but you've seen us, we're not—well—"

"No, I don't think you have anything to apologize for. As much as Cheri, Chris, and I complain, we really do like knowing you're still—"

"You're as bad as she is," Chad's father teased. "It's called being in love. You should try it sometime."

At the sight of her son's embarrassment, Marianne stepped in and redirected the conversation. She'd watched the knowing looks between Chris and Cheri, heard the speculations of the family, and even Libby had mentioned that she hoped when enough time had passed and Willow was ready for the right man in her life, that it would be Chad. If he felt half the pressure that she did, Chad would run. They could thank Linnea for that.

"So, Chad, what do you think? I'm not going to lie, and I won't apologize for showing proper affection for my husband, but if I need to apologize for making her feel uncomfortable..."

He sat lost in thought before shaking his head. "No, you shouldn't mention it at all. In fact, I'd appreciate it if you'd be a little extra affectionate. Willow needs to see it. I'll try not to gag."

"What do you mean 'Willow needs to see it?'"

"Just that she hasn't. Can you imagine never having seen a husband and wife, any husband and wife, kiss? Can you imagine never hearing your father say, 'I love you?' Things that are so commonplace for us are earth shattering for her. I can't even begin to describe our discussion of her showing affection for men!"

This piqued Marianne's interest. "Oh no, that's something I want to hear. I've watched you with her Chad, and the only reason I haven't said anything is because I trust that you know what you're doing."

As he tried to explain, Chad stuffed his hands in his pockets leaning back into the chair. "It's strange, Mom. Because of who she is, I can't treat her like anyone I've ever known.

151

Mom, I slept over at her house — a few times — when no one else was there! Granted, most of those times were during the day because I worked night shift but still."

"And why did you think that was a good idea?"

Marianne saw the hurt in her son's eyes and hoped he wouldn't become defensive. Christopher could sound so accusatory when he didn't know how to handle things. She needn't have worried.

"She was injured. She has no one. I could milk the goats and was strong enough to help her up and down the stairs." He sighed and in that involuntary escape of air, Marianne saw that he didn't think they'd understand. "I was who she trusted. I couldn't *not* do it, Pop."

She watched Christopher fight his tendency to put everything in a carefully packaged box. She had often told him as they reared their children, "You can't decide how everything should go and then force it to go that way. Sometimes you have to use discernment instead of rules." In fact, the rare times that she disagreed with him in decisions regarding their children had always come down to that one concept. "Just because the scenario doesn't fit your idea of the perfect script, doesn't mean it needs to be written out of the play." Now she wondered if he would control himself before he alienated his son.

"You probably know best, and it's never wrong to serve the body of Christ. How you do it — well, still. I can't — "

It killed her to watch him struggle. Their son had opened himself up to them, knowing that his father might open his mental lecture list and pull out the appropriate one for the occasion. To her relief, Christopher stuffed it down. "Anyway, tell us about the affection problem."

Chad told about the conversation he'd had with Willow. His parents sat dumbstruck as he described her nonchalant attitude of holding the hands of three men in almost as many days without the slightest idea that it would mean anything more than friendly reassurance and appreciation. "You know how you always said you could tell when a girl's father quit showing her affection around their teen years?"

Christopher nodded — a look of dismay on his face. "You

don't think…"

"Well, no. I don't think Willow is in danger of trading her virtue for male attention, but considering she's never had any, I think she is both oblivious to it being any different than female affection as well as having a deep need for it. If she didn't so thoroughly disassociate herself from any hint of romance, I couldn't be the big brother slash friend that I am without having another Linnea on my hands."

"Oh I'm sick of that girl's name! I'm sick of her impact on our family! I'm sick that our son, my kind-hearted, handsome son, has run from every decent girl he's ever met thanks to that—"

Her husband silenced her with a low murmur, "Enough, Marianne. Don't let the bitterness back."

Before anyone could speak, the bathroom door squeaked. Chad leaned forward and whispered, "Don't walk around lip-locked, just be affectionate like you always are… just a bit more often!

"Morning, Willow!"

Willow brought her towel downstairs brushing her hair as she came. "What should I do with the towel? The racks are full up there."

Marianne jumped to grab it. "I'll take it. Would you like some juice? I'd offer you fruit or cheese, but the guys inhaled it when they got back."

"Where is everyone?"

Chad smiled from his spot on the couch. "Downstairs. They're wrapping gifts. I'm supposed to be down there, but I had a few things to discuss with Mom and Dad."

"Well you go down and wrap; I'll get Willow to help me with breakfast."

On cue, Christopher passed through the kitchen as Marianne checked the casserole, murmured something into his wife's ear, kissed her cheek, and followed his son down the basement steps. Smiling to herself and half-forgetting her earlier concern, she winked at Willow. "What a man will do to get a meal."

"So what I can I do?" Eagerly, Willow looked around the

153

room for anything to focus on other than Marianne's face.

"Is something wrong?" Marianne doubted Chad's confidence that affection would be good for Willow to see. "Can you reach in that cupboard—no the next one. Yes. Can you get me um six... no, seven of those plates?"

"Sure." There was a pause before Willow added, "I wonder where our extra plates are."

"What did you say?"

As she handed Marianne the plates, Willow explained their limited dish situation. "I know we have replacements— anytime something broke there'd be a replacement in the cupboard the next meal. I never thought of it before, but Mother must have them somewhere. I wonder why she didn't just keep them in the cupboard."

Feeling unusually insightful, Marianne Tesdall saw Kari more accurately than most ever did. "I think your mother wanted a visual reminder that she only had enough emotional stamina for two people 'at her table' so to speak."

Tears sprung to Willow's eyes, but rather than being overcome by them, she smiled. "Two people at her table. That's perfect. Chad has almost become family—the brother Mother would never have had for me. I still have two people at my table most of the time. God is good."

"Oh Luke, I'm glad you got that on tape. Your double single knee proposal is unique; I'll give you that. Of course, I'd give anything to be able to hear you, but the comments of the children and the aunts were priceless."

"I laughed so hard watching that. When Tavish said to get the smelling salts..." Luke mused thoughtfully.

Cheri's romance radar was in high gear. "So did you choose a date? Do you know where—"

"Can you give him twenty-four hours before you plan his life, Cheri?" Chris' nudge was anything but gentle.

The room erupted in laughter at Luke's discouraged, "I doubt I can get her to find time before Christmas, but—"

Willow's voice, though quiet, cut through the pandemonium. "I wish you well, Luke. I'll be praying for you and for Aggie."

Luke squeezed her shoulder as he moved to refill his glass. "Thank you, Willow."

A sidelong glance at the Tesdalls made Willow's stomach flop in that horribly uncomfortable manner it had adopted that morning. Marianne stood, leaning her back into her husband's chest, Christopher's arms around her waist. They seemed to share a private joke between them, reminding her of the married couples she'd read about in books. There was something special—different about their relationship that both intrigued and frightened her.

Until she'd been bombarded with hints about her presumed budding romance with Chad, the idea of romance hadn't bothered her much. Bill made illusions to it, and she found the attention pleasant, but now, in the Tesdall home where deeper relationships were both casual and serious, she shied away from them.

"Willow, I've got to be at work by six, and I didn't pick up my uniforms—I think we should go soon. With the snow, the roads—"

"Ready whenever you are." She turned immediately to find her tote bag, but Christopher's voice stopped her.

"Chad, can I see you in the den before you go?"

She watched nervously as the two men disappeared into the room and a pocket door slid shut behind them. Willow had no doubt that the Tesdall family liked her. Their warmth toward her was genuine; she was confident on that score. However, something in Christopher's manner told her that he was concerned for Chad.

Unaware that Willow even noticed the exchange, Christopher sat his son down for a conversation he'd rather not have. "Chad, I'd give anything to avoid this…"

Anticipating his father's words, Chad's shoulders slumped. "I'm sorry. I know I've been a disappointment to you in so many ways, but—"

"Don't assume you know what I'm going to say. I'm pretty

sure you don't." Christopher leaned forward, his hands clasped together. "You know, I've been praying about you and Willow since the day you came to the store. I've struggled with it because I have no doubt that the Lord brought you into Willow's life for a reason and not just to help her. She's been good for you too."

As he continued, Christopher watched his son struggle against becoming defensive. They'd had the best visit since Chad left for college. Old wounds had been stitched and were healing. Was it wise to risk tearing them open again? Even as he thought, Christopher continued. "… I'm not concerned about where things are now. I know you think I'm going to condemn you for your choices concerning her, but I'm not. I see why you've done what you've done, and I'm proud of you for it."

Swallowing hard, Chad raised his eyes to meet his father's. "I cannot tell you how much that means to me."

"Which," Christopher continued, "is why I'm going to say something you probably don't want to hear, but I want you to listen close to what I *am* saying and not add in what I'm *not*."

Chad nodded. "Bad habit of mine."

"Your relationship with Willow is a lot like yours with Cheri. I don't see the same kind teasing, but I suspect that part of that is that she's not comfortable here, and I know she's still a little fragile. You see her as a sister; you treat her as a best friend. This is good."

"But…"

"But she isn't your sister. She's a sister in Christ, I grant you, but she is not your sister. The day will come, probably sooner than either of you are prepared to think about, when one or both of you will marry."

"Pop, please—"

"Listen to me, son. If you keep things how they are, I don't foresee any real problems. However, if you continue to treat her like Cheri, the time will come when you're watching movies with your arm draped around her shoulder, or she'll fall asleep half curled against your chest or your lap just like Cheri does. That may be innocent, and I trust you to search your heart about those things and to listen to the Holy Spirit's promptings." Christopher took a deep breath and prayed his son really listened. "But her husband isn't going to want to come home and find you casually affectionate with his wife."

"I don't think that's a problem. I can't see her marrying, but if she did, I'd never—"

"Your wife wouldn't necessarily like it either."

Chad's head whipped up sharply. "How can you think I'd ever—"

"I know you wouldn't. That's not the problem. I am trying to set up a picture in your mind. If you are not careful about how you show affection—and I know you—you're going to keep her feeling secure by any means you know. It's who you are and who you've always been. I wouldn't want you to change it. But if you keep seeing her as another sister instead of a single woman, then the day one of you marries, she loses another important relationship."

"Well I wouldn't just abandon her, Pop!"

"No, but you'd pull away. It's a natural response and a right one. But it'd mean another loss in a young woman who can't afford any more losses."

Taking a deep breath, Chad asked for clarification. "Ok, can you tell me in as few and as simple words as possible, what you're suggesting?"

"Be her friend, Chad. Be there for her. But keep your relationship to something that can continue, just as it is or awfully close to it, in case one of you marries." Glad to have the burden of his heart off his chest and on the table, Christopher stood. "Of course, you'd solve all your problems if you simply married her yourself in the next decade or two."

"Don't count on it."

157

CHAPTER 54

Saturday morning Willow awoke to sun streaming through her windows and a few inches of snow on the ground. Wrapped in her favorite robe and feet swaddled in wooly warmness, she stood at the window and enjoyed the beauty of fields of snow. The dusting over the tree branches gave the farm the feel of fairyland, sighing contentedly at the sight.

Willow loved snow in the fields and hated it in the yard. What looked like a white blanket of cotton over fields, became a slushy mess after a few tramps to the barn, to feed the chickens, chickens, and back again. The first day of snow was always a treat in the Finley home—almost a holiday. On that day, they ignored the extra work, extra mess, and concentrated on the beauty, because the rest of winter would demand they pay attention to it. They made snow ice cream, drank hot chocolate, ate chicken soup, and huddled next to the stove reading, knitting, or simply daydreaming.

The clock struck seven. If she didn't hurry, the day would be gone before she could relax and enjoy it! Willow pulled on her favorite jeans, t-shirt, and chamois flannel shirt. As she hurried downstairs, her fingers expertly braided her hair into a long French braid. Near the backdoor, her boots and over-boots sat ready for wear.

By the time she left the kitchen, the stove crackled, the teakettle warmed, a bowl of dry oats waited for the kettle, and a Dutch oven of water sat waiting for heat to do its job. Outside,

Saige barked her welcome and rolled playfully in the snow. Ice containers waited for a trip downstairs to the ice cellar. She shivered in the brisk air but knew that with a few minutes work, she'd warm up enough to shed a coat if she wore one.

Grabbing the snow shovel from the barn wall, Willow cleared a wide strip from the chicken yard and threw open the door. The huge thermometer on the side of the coop read twenty-six degrees. "Kind of cold ladies, but there's some bare dirt out there if you want to run around —" The birds were out of their coop before she could say cold. "Don't say I didn't warn you."

In the barn, she spread a fresh layer of straw in the stalls opposite the inhabited ones and moved the animals across the aisle. Water, hay, a little grain for the cow and the barn animals were all set.

Willow grabbed a chicken, container of soup, and packet of dog meat from the freezer. She poured some milk in the cat pans and glanced around the barn with one final look. She hadn't seen the barn cats for a week or two, but they'd be waiting for milk again now that it was cooler. A mouse scurried from one hay bale to the next. "They'd better catch that thing, or I'm cutting off their room and board," she muttered as she slid the upper barn window open and then shut the door.

In the house, she poured water from the teakettle into her cup and added her tea ball. Barely covering the oats with boiling water, she set a plate on top and retrieved a jar of peaches from the pantry. Willow scooped several sliced of peaches onto the plate, replaced the jar lid, and stowed the jar in the icebox. It needed more ice. "How fitting," she muttered as she hurried down for another block.

Her chicken in the pot, oats down the hatch, and kitchen cleaned up and looking spiffy, Willow shrugged off her flannel shirt and boots, slipped back on her slippers, and sighed. It was a beautiful day. By nine o'clock, she curled herself on the chaise to Alexa Hartfield's book, sipping tea between pages.

Her eyes closed and she listened to the sounds of her house. The fire crackled in the stove, Saige barked outside, and as she opened her eyes to read once more, she heard the gentle

160

shushing of the page as she turned it. There was no laughter, no thumping up and down the stairs, no one calling for Mom to help with this or that, or good-natured protests of unfair treatment. There was no furnace to make a strange clicking noise just before the whoosh of warm air shot through the vents. No sirens wailed; no car doors thumped; all was quiet in her world.

Just after noon, she stretched as she stood to heat her lunch and noticed the mail truck slow down as it neared the end of the lane. Grabbing her keys, her flannel shirt, and a thick sweater, Willow pulled on her boots and stepped outside. "Want to grab the mail with me, Saige?"

Willow rarely made the trip to gather the mail. Sometimes weeks went by without a single letter or catalog, but if they saw the truck stop, the Finley women would take a break in their day and walk to the mailbox to see what might be in it. Down the lane, she trudged through slushy snow, Saige dashing in circles, racing ahead of her and then zipping back to urge her onward. She pulled her keys from her pocket and unlocked the box. The memory of a day long ago when she was just a child came flooding back to her.

"Mother, what's wrong with the mail – there are ants!"

"Some fool thought it would be fun to dump a can of Coke inside the mailbox."

The little girl frowned, her face screwing up into a picture of fury. "That's just wrong. It's not their property."

The mother tossed several pieces into the stove and set a third aside. "I agree."

"Ants are getting on the counter."

"Brush them into the sink and wash them down. Get every single one off the letter. I need that one."

Before the week was out, mother and daughter worked side-by-side at the end of the drive, covering the mailbox with a concrete box and a locking door. The girl was certain they'd never get mail again. "But how will the mailman get the mail in if it's locked."

"I'll take a key to Fran in Fairbury."

"Do I have to go?"

The mother paused, wiping sweat from her forehead with the

161

back of her hand. "I don't think so. You did well last time, but no fishing either. Just stay on the ground and near the house. If it can hurt you, don't do it. Not while I'm not here to help."

"I guess I could play with my fairies…"

"Make them a Christmas tree. It'll be here before you know it."

"It's months away!"

"Even so," the mother said. "There. That oughtta hold off delinquents."

"What's a delinquent?"

"A person who needs regular doses of a specific vitamin."

They were halfway back to the house before the girl asked the question that had to be asked. "What vitamin, Mother?"

"Vitamin?"

"Are the delinquents deficient in? What vitamin?"

"Matthew 7:12."

"That's a Bible verse – the golden rule."

"My mother used to call that verse the golden vitamin – sure to cure whatever ails bad behavior."

Two letters and a new catalog from Hancock's of Paducah—it was a good day. The name on the return address of one of the letters made her heart race and she hurried home to read it. The other letter looked like a bill of some sort.

Seated on the couch, with the light streaming in from the window, Willow opened the letter from David and Carol Finley.

Dear Willow,

As Thanksgiving nears, I find myself thinking of you all alone in that large house and wondering how you are doing. Do you have Thanksgiving traditions or plans? How did Kari celebrate holidays with you, and now that she isn't with you, what will you do?

These are thoughts that fill my mind as I make shopping lists. I smiled when I wrote down marshmallow crème. Oh, how your mother hated sweet potato casserole. I'll buy a yam and bake it for her. I always do. I've done that for twenty-four Thanksgivings now. No one eats it; they don't like it. I just can't bring myself not to bake it for her, and this year, I guess I'll bake it for you, because now there's no hope that she'll ever walk through that door and tell us the nightmare is over.

162

How I want to invite you to spend a few days with us, and yet your grandfather and I aren't ready for it. I hope you can understand that. We steeled our hearts to the pain of losing Kari, and some of that steel bars us from you, but we want to unlock those doors. We just don't know how yet.

We saw your interview in the newspaper. I was surprised at how freely you discussed the circumstances of your birth and Kari's disappearance. It has opened a floodgate of questions for us that we weren't prepared to handle. I don't say this as a means of reproach but as a request. Please leave us out of anything like that in the future. We don't care to relive those times, but our media gossip-driven culture doesn't respect that.

Do you ever come into the city? Perhaps we could meet at one of those quiet little tea rooms and talk on neutral ground with no pressure. I would like that. I have a granddaughter that I don't know, and that grieves me.

You have cousins, you know. Kyle has three children. Jonathan is just a year younger than you — almost twenty-three. Peter is nineteen, and Bethel Anne is fifteen. Your Uncle Kyle and Aunt Sheryl live in Hillsdale where Kyle is a loan manager for the bank. Cheryl is an RN in the oncology department.

This letter is already longer than I intended. I find that when I start writing, I have a hard time stopping. Kari used to be that way. I have a shelf of journals and diaries from age six to age twenty and every letter she wrote home from camp. I can't tell you how much those have comforted me over the years.

I pray for you, Willow. I hope you know the Lord and how precious you are to Him.

Grandma

Tears splashed on the letter before Willow realized she was crying. Again. How tired she was of her unpredictable emotional state! It was a good letter — good and honest. It didn't offer or expect more of her than was reasonable. After a second reading, she laid it aside. Chad would like to read it.

The bill she expected to be for her leg. Now and then, a bill for some medical personnel that she couldn't remember and didn't care about would arrive, and she forwarded them all to Bill happily. However, this time, it wasn't a bill. A check fell from the folds of a letter as she opened it. Made out to her in the amount of two hundred fifty thousand dollars, the cashier's check was signed by Steven J. Solari. She read the letter suspiciously.

Willow Anne Finley,

An interesting article came across my desk recently. Upon verification of a few simple facts, I have proven to my satisfaction that you are my granddaughter.

Had I any idea of your existence all of these years, I would have, of course, contributed financially to your upbringing. While I cannot undo the past, I can try to make up for it by aiding your future. You will find a check enclosed. They claim it costs 150,000-200,000 to raise a child from birth to eighteen, but college adds a significant amount to that, and I have allowed for that as well.

I know what you must think of my son. You can't possibly think anything that I already haven't. He was a severe disappointment to both his mother and me. Now that he is gone, we are alone, growing older every year, and finding it lonely without our son or the children he could have had.

I know I should not hope that you'd consider meeting with us at some point, but I do. My numbers are on the card I've enclosed. Please call any time. I haven't told my wife about you. She'd be crushed if she knew she had a grandchild and then you chose not to let her be a part of your life. I cannot do that to her. Whatever you may think of us, I am not my son, and my wife is a kind, gentle woman.

Sincerely,
Steven Solari

Willow's first inclination was to throw check and letter into the fire. Her hands felt soiled having touched them. A cold sweat sent shivers down her spine, but Willow refused to allow her emotions to control her. She smoothed and folded both letters before returning them to their envelopes. In the kitchen, she slipped them between the salt and peppershakers, grabbed the strainer and stockpot, and carried the Dutch oven to the sink. Time to make soup and eat lunch. She'd handle emotions later.

Chad found her sitting at the kitchen table surrounded by a fabric catalog, paper, pen, and a couple of letters—clearly in shock. "Willow?"

"I can't believe it. I just can't believe it!"

"What!"

With a dejected gesture, she waved her hand at the mess on the table and dropped her head on her arms. Chad picked up the letters and read them. The letter from the Finleys, while lacking in the warmth and urging he hoped they'd show, encouraged him. Perhaps Willow was on her way to being a part of her family. However, at the sight of the check and the letter from Steven Solari, Chad's blood pressure reached dangerous levels.

"What an absolutely inexcusable—"

"I know! How could I have done something so stupid!"

"Aww Willow, it's not your fault. You didn't tell that reporter anything—"

Her shocked face stopped him. "Reporter? What are you talking about?"

"Solari's letter. His contacting you is unconscionable."

"Oh that," she dismissed. "I'm still processing those."

"Well," he tried again, "If that's not the problem, what is?"

"I was so upset about it all that I went through my fabric catalog, wrote down every piece of fabric I liked and bought them all!"

"This is bad why?"

"Let me rephrase then. I just spent over three hundred dollars on fabric that I don't need just because I didn't want to think about the implications of those letters." As he opened his mouth to reply, she added quickly, "And I *called* to place my order! We don't *do* that!"

Despite a heroic attempt to suppress them, chuckles followed her horrified ejaculation. "So she *is* a normal woman after all!"

"What do you mean?"

"It's common knowledge, Willow, that a significant

165

portion of American women deal with stress by their favorite sport—shopping."

Her amazement was evident. "What am I going to do with three hundred dollars' worth of fabric? I don't need any clothes for ages yet!"

"Make them for someone else. Make clothes for Aggie's children or for Christmas presents, or make quilts or whatever else you can do that you do but you never let yourself do that you wanna do…"

"But three hundred—"

Chad picked up the Solari's check. "Well, you could always cash this…"

"That is just—it's just—just *not* funny."

Changing the subject, Chad made a show of sniffing the air. "Do I smell chicken soup?"

"Yeah. I almost forgot to add the vegetables."

"Is that bread?"

She tossed him the potholders. "Here. It's probably done."

He'd underestimated the effect her mini shopping spree had on her. Silently he pulled the bread from the oven, ladled soup from the Dutch oven, sliced and buttered the bread, squishing the loaf in the process, and cleared the table for dinner. As he worked, he saw some of what his father had warned him. His natural inclination was to wrap an arm around her shoulders and reassure her but now…

Impatiently he brushed aside his new misgivings. He'd take it to the Lord later, but right now, she needed a bit of strength that she couldn't manufacture for herself and subconsciously, she was probably expecting it. As he placed her bowl in front of her, he sat on his heels at her side and draped an arm around her shoulders. He waited for her to meet his gaze and then smiled into her eyes.

"It's ok, Willow. You can afford an occasional extravagance. Be thankful that it won't mean not eating for a month and let it go. Now you know you're just as vulnerable as the next person, and you'll be prepared."

As she took a bite of her soup, she grinned back at him. "Maybe I should be stupid more often. This is nice. I wasted my

166

day moping about those letters. My snow day was a bust."

"It'll snow again."

"But it won't be the first snow."

Chad remembered an entry from Kari's journals about snow days. "Oh, I think you can just pretend like this one didn't happen. You weren't even home when it started snowing so you really should wait for one where it's actually snowing."

"That's cheating!"

"Not," he hedged, "When *you* make the rules."

That night, in his apartment, Chad prayed. For what seemed like hours, he poured out his heart to the Lord regarding his life, Willow's life, and whatever their relationship was. His father was right. He saw her as another little sister to pester, protect, and occasionally pamper. He treated her much as he had Cheri when she'd returned from "the pit."

However, something wasn't right in his spirit. He knew his father's cautions had unsettled him on another level. He bared his soul to the Lord and peeked inside himself, wondering why the idea of Willow marrying was so distasteful to him but found no answers. He didn't love her. Well, not as he saw his father loved his mother. So many confusing thoughts whirled through his mind but always returned to the same question. What would happen if Willow did marry? The idea that once would have sent him clicking his heels for joy as he escaped the confines of a friendship he hadn't sought, now filled him with dread that life could change so drastically.

He slid open his phone. As he waited for Luke to answer, Chad grabbed the last Coke from his fridge and settled into the corner of his couch, his free hand massaging his temple. "Hey Luke. Got a few?"

"Couch is open. Will this be cash or credit?"

"How's my tab?"

"Staggering, but I'll let it slide," Luke agreed with mock reluctance."

"You have the gift of giving."

"But not the gift of gab so why don't you do the talking?"

"Of course, it's Willow again. You were right to send me back there..." Chad waited for Luke's response but then smiled as he realized if he waited, his minutes would be flying off his phone. "Dad thinks I need to be there for her as well, but—" He sighed. It seemed so logical when he was thinking to himself, but aloud it sounded strange.

For ten minutes, Chad shared the conversation he'd had with his father and then with the Lord. He told Luke about his misgivings at the idea of Willow marrying and that the longer time went on, the more convinced he was that perhaps he shouldn't marry. "That'd take care of one of us anyway. Maybe if I was just upfront with her. Would it sound weird to tell her, 'Look, you're like my other little sister and I want to keep treating you like that, but if you ever get married, I'm probably going to have to change how I show it?'" Even as he spoke, he knew it sounded ridiculous—pathetic.

Again, silence reigned. Each minute that passed sounded like an old-time cash register's "cha-ching" in his ear. Finally, Luke answered. "I understand Uncle Christopher's concerns, and I think they are valid. I also see your point and yes, that'd probably work, but before you say anything or change anything in your relationship..."

Chad waited again. He waited. And waited. "Yes?"

"I think there is something else you could consider. It'd solve both the problem of how you respond to Willow when she marries and how you respond to the fact of her marriage."

"That's why I pay you the big bucks."

"Well actually—"

"Now, now, don't get all wrapped up in the details, just give me your solution, oh wise Swami of mine," Chad teased as he relaxed sinking into the couch again and feeling like life was all right again. As a child, he'd always felt that if mom or dad couldn't solve a problem it was ok. That's what God made Luke for—his own personal problem solver.

"Marry her yourself, Chad."

"Oh, not you too!"

A pregnant pause passed before Luke continued. "I'm not

talking about heart throbs and romance, although I recommend them highly..." Luke cleared his throat. "I just think that a good friendship like yours is a good enough reason to marry."

"Marry so that no one else can. Somehow that doesn't sound very 'giving myself up for my wife' kind of thing."

Luke tried again, pausing often as he usually did. "Chad, you love Willow. You love her in the most important way for a husband to love his wife. You serve her. You 'agape' her. This is exactly what she needs. That is giving yourself up for her, and you do it daily. You've done it since the first day you drove away from her farm, over to Ferndale, and bought that cell phone so she wasn't alone and unable to get help if she needed it. You didn't want to go but you did."

He took a deep breath. This wasn't what he'd expected to hear and Chad wasn't sure he wanted to hear anymore. "And ten years down the road when she meets the man she should have married—the man who can love her both as a servant husband and as Solomon, she'll resent me for removing the chance for her to have the kind of marriage she should have dreamed about her whole life."

Luke's quiet calm voice came across the line and touched Chad's heart in a way that nothing had ever affected it. "Chad, once she marries you—or anyone else for that matter—there is no 'man she should have married' down the road. And, perhaps the reason she hasn't dreamed of the perfect romantic 'happily ever after' fairytale is because the Lord was preparing her for a life with a stodgy old guy named Chad." Luke paused. "I'll send a bill next week. Night—"

"Wait, there's something else."

"Now what?"

Knowing he was setting himself up for major teasing, Chad forged onward bravely. "I got Willow's Christmas present in the mail today, and there's a problem."

"What is that?"

"It's not assembled."

Laughter rang out across the airwaves and taunted Chad as Luke retorted, "Then assemble it, man."

"It's wood."

169

"That was low. Wood as in raw wood, wood as in screw together wood, or wood as in, stain it and go?"

Chad grinned. He had Luke interested. He needed that advantage before he confessed his goof. "Well, kind of all three minus the screws but add the glue."

"What is it?"

"A dulcimer kit?"

Sighing, Luke replied sarcastically. "Why do you sound like that's a question and you don't know."

"Because I'm waiting to be bashed over the head with it."

"Why did you buy a kit? You always hated models."

"I didn't know I did. I went back to the website after I bought it and in tiny print it says, 'not assembled.' Apparently that means it's a kit rather than you need to string it and pop the pegs in and you're ready to go."

Luke's response was disheartening. "You'd better get to work. It's just barely a month away—"

"Will you help me?"

"Will you take Laird home while Aggie and I are off wherever we end up going after the wedding?"

Chad grinned. A week with a teenaged boy and no women to complain about what they ate. This would be fun. "Of course! That'll be great. What are you doing with the other kids?"

"Well, I don't know. I'm trying to find a way to send a few here and there so that it's not too much work for any one person. Mom'll keep whoever is left, but I don't want to overwork her, and I want to be gone for a couple of weeks so—"

"What about Willow? Think Aggie would let them go to Willow's farm? I think they'd have fun."

"I'll get back to you on that. On a scale of one to ten, what do you think she'd say to a request like that?" Luke held his breath expectantly.

"Nine point five at the lowest."

"I'll stop by this week and look at your mess—er gift."

"Will I ever be out of debt, Luke?"

"Start praying. If Aggie says yes and Willow agrees, we'll call you paid in full."

"Yes!"

170

CHAPTER 55

For a week, Willow left the letters on the kitchen table, open and easily perused. She mucked barn stalls and prayed. She cleaned the chicken coop and prayed. She cooked, knitted, hooked her rug, and prayed. She milked the new goat, which Chad christened "Ditto," and prayed. Then, she prayed some more.

For hours, she worked on the foundation site for her forthcoming greenhouse. Her original plans had been scrapped for a lean-to design kit that she'd found in one of her mother's stacks of catalogs. It was more expensive and larger than she'd planned, but the added advantage of putting it next to the barn and close to the house was enough incentive to move fences and arrange plans for a larger scale operation than ever. She'd have lettuce in January just like Mr. Tesdall's big grocery store. Oh, and she prayed with every shovel, every moved wire, and every nail.

Saturday, a week after the letters arrived, was December first. She awoke with a child-like delight that not even the loss of her mother's help and camaraderie tempered. Chad was coming to spend the day, the goat was giving milk like nothing she'd ever had, and she'd gotten a call from the greenhouse company that her kit was on its way.

After breakfast, she cleaned the kitchen and left a pile of pancakes warming on the stove for whenever Chad arrived. She hurried upstairs, feeling quite girlish, and into the attic pulling down the box of artificial greenery. Chad found her tying "pine" swags across the front porch, wrapping the posts, and adding large deep red bows to the pivotal places.

"Hey, looks great! What do I do?" he called as he jumped from the truck.

"I've got pancakes on the stove if you're hungry first."

"Be back to help you when they're gone," he promised.

By the time Chad returned, the front porch looked like a Thomas Kincade Christmas painting. Willow greeted him without preamble. "Can you go up into the attic and get the box in the middle of the floor marked, 'Porch tree'?"

"You have a tree for your porch?"

"Humor me. I want my tree."

He hurried upstairs, returning minutes later with the large box. Amazed, he watched as she screwed a long pole into a traditional tree stand. "It's leaning to the left."

"Straighten it will you?"

As he held the pole straight, he asked the obvious question. "Is there a reason you are putting your tree out here?"

"It's for the birds."

"Then why do it?"

"For the birds," Willow repeated. "You need to clean your ears."

"Sooooo," Chad asked once more, "Why do the birds need their own tree?"

"They don't. It just gets them to come close enough to the house that I can watch them from the couch. The chickadees are quite friendly and entertaining when the jays aren't around."

"Ahh. I see you still have the letters out." Willow seemed to wilt before his eyes, making Chad feel like a heel.

"I know. I keep praying and praying about it, and I don't know... At times like this, I really miss Mother's confidence. She'd know what to do, and she'd just do it."

"I think your indecision is because you know your mother's judgment was clouded by fear, and you don't want to repeat that."

They worked together as she assembled her unusual tree. Branches slid into drilled holes in the "trunk," and when she didn't like something, she pulled it out, tried a different one, and stood back to see the result. Chad was curious. "Where'd you get this tree?"

"Mother bought several the first few years, trying to find one that didn't get mangled in storage. Later she cut the rejects apart to make two perfect trees. This one used to be in the spare room during December. I'd wake up Christmas morning and the tree would be all set up and decorated for me as a surprise."

"You didn't decorate with your mother?" The idea didn't fit what he knew of the Finley women.

"I helped with the downstairs tree, but you know how little hands are. They don't make for an attractive look when the top third or half is almost bare. This way I got to help, and Mother got to have a perfect tree too."

"So how did it end up out front?"

Willow smiled remembering. "I decorated the living room tree one year when mother was sick, and she liked it, so she told me to take the other one back to the attic and confessed why she'd always had two." She stood back from the tree and nodded satisfied. "That's perfect. I'll make the ornaments later. I want to get started on the living room and I'm cold!"

Inside, Chad helped her carry down boxes of decorations from the attic. With her guidance, Chad wrapped the banisters in imitation evergreen, commenting all the while that he'd expected live trees and décor. "I can't believe you have all this fake stuff."

"With all the dry heat in here, what else could we do?"

The logic couldn't be denied so Chad wrapped, humming *The Holly and the Ivy* as he retraced his steps and tied ribbons at regular intervals. His festive mood seemed to heighten Willow's enjoyment. She disappeared into the library several minutes later, he heard the scratchy sound of an old Victrola playing and Bing Crosby's voice crooning about a *White Christmas*.

He clambered down the stairs and leaned against the doorjamb as she sorted albums. "You have a Victrola. I forgot about that. Come on."

He grabbed her hand and twirled her into the living room half-waltzing, half two stepping as he did. "Come on, it's

173

Christmas!"

"Not yet it isn't."

"So," he continued as though she hadn't argued the point. "Are you up for company on Christmas?"

"Why?" The song ended and she put on another before going back to decorate the windows again.

"Because I have to work from ten till six the morning of Christmas eve and then again from two until ten."

Her eyes sought his from across the room looking miserable. "That is terrible. Why —"

"Hey, they gave my first Christmas off. Most places wouldn't do that for a rookie. It's my turn, so I took the short break so Judith could have more of the day free."

"You're a good man, Chad."

"Well," he teased, "It's about time that you figured that out. I've been telling you for months — "

"There is a box on the table labeled popcorn strings, can you get it and start hanging them?"

"You saved popcorn strings?"

Willow's laughter blended with *Up On the Housetop* perfectly. "No, silly, they're crocheted. We worked on them all summer one year."

The strings were amazing. From just a few feet away, you'd never know the "popcorn" was crochet thread and the "cranberries" were wooden beads. Chad looped and draped expertly thanks to a Christmas fanatic of a mother and a perfectionist sister.

"Stairs are done. Next?"

"Doorways," she replied without even glancing at his handiwork. He felt a little miffed that she didn't care admire—er—inspect the work, but a question from her interrupted his thoughts. "So the ladies' Bible study is having a gift drawing. I have someone I'm supposed to buy for. We can't spend any more than twenty dollars, but I'm confused."

"Sounds pretty straight forward. What's the problem?"

"Well, is that twenty dollars for the gift, for materials to make a gift, and for people who buy everything, what about their wrapping paper and their card? Do they count that as part of the twenty—"

Chad dropped the length of evergreen and went to switch out the album as she chattered. Beneath the question was the real one—the one he knew she couldn't seem to articulate—probably because she didn't know it herself. If Willow knew the real question, she would have just asked it. "Willow, are you concerned about the gift itself, the limits, or who you got as a name?"

"All of it. I'm not supposed to tell who it is, but I guess that's so the girls can't do a process of elimination thing. I could tell you, right?"

"Right. Who'd you get?"

"Lee," she admitted ruefully. "I already made her a skirt, but I don't know exactly how much I spent making it. I've never paid much attention to that."

"Lee loves your tote bags. I've heard her talk about swiping one of yours when you're not looking. Maybe you could make one to match the skirt."

"I can't give her both, it'd be over that limit—"

"So give her the tote for the exchange and give her the skirt because you were going to do it anyway." Chad didn't quite see the difficulty, but he listened and decorated doorways like a pro.

"That might work."

"Now what?" he queried as he admired the festive air in the house. Who wouldn't love such attention to Christmassy detail?

"Can you take that table by the window and carry it up to the spare room?"

Chad emptied the table of its vase of dried flowers and hand-embroidered doily, and hefted it over his head, carefully avoiding the ceiling. He shook his head in disbelief as he saw a pile of old blankets protecting both the floor and the wall and a woodpile on top of it. Only Willow Finley had a woodpile inside *and* outside her house."

Once she had rearranged the living room a little, Willow called for tree number two and began assembling it to someone singing "Silent Night." "Hey, would you put the branches in?

175

I'll set up candles if you can get the branches in for me."

For the next hour, they worked silently but in a harmony even Chad couldn't deny. Wordlessly, they passed each other things they needed, often before the other realized it, and a feeling of familiarity stirred in Chad's heart. It reminded him of his parents. They often worked for hours on a project, never speaking, always complimenting one another in their actions, until, when they completed the job, they stepped back, arms around each other, and admired the final product. Maybe dad and Luke—

"Chad? If you have to work Christmas, how will you get any rest? You go to bed after six and have to be up and at work by two. I don't see how—"

"I have a plan if you want to hear it."

"Well obviously," she teased, "or I wouldn't have asked."

"Mom and Dad are going to do Christmas on New Year's Eve so I can be there—you're invited by the way. I thought if you felt like company, they could come spend the day with you. I'd come here after work, take a nap, spend a couple of hours with you guys, and then go to work again. We could have dinner during my lunch hour." He grinned at the agreeable expression on her face before he added, "I know Mom would help."

"I love it. I'll write your mother a letter today!"

Willow set down her ornaments, hurried upstairs, and returned with a box of hand embellished stationary. Curled on the couch and surrounded by evidence of Christmas, Willow wrote a letter of invitation to Chad's parents and handed it to him for approval.

Mr. and Mrs. Tesdall,
Chad has told me of his work schedule on Christmas Day, and I wondered if you would like to come to my house for the day. Chad plans to have dinner with me, and your company would bless him as well, I am sure.
I am hoping to hear that you'll come,
Willow Anne Finley

While he read, she worked on another letter. He waited

176

rather impatiently for Willow to finish and exchanged the letters eagerly. As he read the second letter, Willow folded the first letter, slipped it into an envelope, and addressed it, waiting patiently for Chad to finish reading her second one.

Dear Grandmother Finley,

I was pleased to receive your letter last week. I've been praying over your suggestion since then, and I think a trip to the city might be fun and a good way to meet you. I know you were here for Mother's funeral, but I don't remember much about that day.

If it would be convenient for you, I could come into Rockland next Friday, December 7, and meet you wherever you'd like, assuming you contact me in time. I can't leave before seven in the morning and must be home before seven at night, but otherwise, I can adjust my schedule to yours.

Respectfully,

Willow Anne Finley

"You could add your phone number in a post script so she can just call, and you don't have to worry about mail problems."

"Oh," she exclaimed delightedly, "I'll do that. Is there anything else you'd change or add?"

"I don't understand why you didn't tell her that you didn't give that sensationalist reporter the interview she thinks you did."

Willow fidgeted with her letter for a minute. "I didn't see how it would help them with the pain of anything, so why bring it up again?"

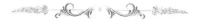

After dinner, when all of the boxes and containers were safely stored back in the attic closet, Willow made hot chocolate, brought out the sugar cookies she'd made the night before, and set them on the end table. Reaching for her Bible, she handed it to Chad. "Would you read Luke?"

Chad took the Bible awkwardly. He'd always hated

177

reading aloud. "Well—"

"Please?"

The pleading in her tone and the eagerness of her expression was impossible to deny. He took the Bible and turned to Luke as he watched her walk around the room lighting the dozens of tiny candles everywhere. Flame by tiny flame, she transformed her homey living room into a veritable fairyland.

She sat at his feet and grabbed a box he hadn't noticed from under the table. Chad smiled as he noticed hand drawn holly and berries decorating the box. The Finley women even decorated boxes! *"In those days a decree went out from Caesar Augustus..."*

As he read, his voice halting and faltering at times, Willow arranged her tree blocks, tea light candles, and fairies into an arrangement on the table. *"... While they were there, the time came for her to have her child, and she gave birth to her firstborn son. She wrapped him in swaddling clothes and laid him in a manger, because there was no room for them in the inn."*

Log upon log she designed her house, occasionally changing this section or that, after testing the stability of the "floor." *"...Do not be afraid; for behold, I proclaim to you good news of great joy that will be for all the people.'"*

Once each floor was complete, she added tiny trees, stars, and snowflakes, creating a winter wonderland on her coffee table. *"...'Glory to God in the highest and on earth peace to those on whom his favor rests.'"*

Tea light candles came next, her hand measuring the heat from each candle to ensure it didn't overheat any portion of the structure. *"... And Mary kept all these things, reflecting on them in her heart."*

At last, once she arranged everything exactly how she wanted, she nestled each fairy in a special place in the house. Satisfied with her work, Willow leaned against Chad's legs and the couch, listening as he finished reading the passage. *"... 'Now, Master, you may let your servant go in peace, according to your word, for my eyes have seen your salvation, which you prepared in sight of all the peoples, a light for revelation to the Gentiles, and glory for your people, Israel.'"*

Only the occasional crackle of wood in the woodstove broke the absolute silence and stillness around them. Candlelight flickered, sending delightful shadows dancing across the room, but still they sat. Both pondered, like Mary, the thoughts in their hearts.

Willow tried to imagine a Christmas without her mother. She remembered the singing as they made cookies, the secrets, the fun in choosing the perfect gift, and the anticipation of almost their favorite day of the year. A tear splashed onto her cheek, then another one. Her heart heavy at the finality of yet another chapter in her life, she turned her head into Chad's knee, rested her arm across it, and laid her head down, weeping softly.

Unaware of Willow's distress, Chad's eyes roamed over the room. He couldn't help but marvel at the childhood Willow had stored in her heart. The tree was bedecked with ornaments that were priceless in both their artistic intricacy and the love and time invested to create them. Her toys were a part of her adult world and yet no one could accuse Willow of immaturity or childishness. Child-like at times? Definitely.

What a life her children would have! His mind's eye saw her sitting at that very coffee table, helping a little girl with pigtails build the perfect structure to house new fairies, angels, and, of course, candles. He pictured them writing and illustrating their own stories, and he wondered if Willow had books in her library that had never been seen or read by anyone but her or her mother. *"Every child should live like this,"* he thought to himself. Then as an afterthought, he allowed one other thought to invade his mind. *"Or at least, I want mine to."*

About that same time, he felt a damp spot on his knee and heard her sniffle. "Aww, Willow, I'm sorry."

"It's ok. I just cry over everything these days. I'm getting used to it. It used to hurt more to cry," Another heart-rending sniffle tore at him as she continued. "But now it's like washing a burn—it's soothing, but you know it will hurt again soon enough—too soon."

Chad's hand smoothed her hair, but he said nothing. Neither of them knew how long they sat there, not talking, but enjoying the sights surrounding them. "Merry Christmas, Willow," Chad whispered.

CHAPTER 56

"Ok, Luke, now what?" Chad wiped his brow, thrilled that he'd managed to get the body of the dulcimer assembled.

"Sand."

Chad sighed. He hated sanding. However, Luke pushed a chair his way and handed him a ball of steel wool. As he rubbed the wood to a glassy smooth polish, Chad talked. He talked about his dreams, his goals, and how it seemed that every day he walked further away from them to the opposite extreme of life.

"I mean, I always thought I'd become a cop. I did and I'm not sorry—really. I want to be a cop. I just thought I'd be doing drug busts, or maybe negotiate hostage situations, or even internal affairs. Instead, I ended up in Fairbury, and I turned down my shot at the east side precinct."

"Do you regret it?"

"No, that's just it. I don't. I keep seeing myself as part of the Fairbury police for a long time." While he had Luke's ear, he rambled about his apartment, how everyone complained of him living in limbo, and how now he didn't know where to start, what to do, and where to go. "Dad's right it would be easier, but I don't know. I don't know what I want. I just know that every day my life just seems more perfect than the last."

"You just told me how much you love what is right in front of you, yet you reject it."

Chad set the dulcimer on the workbench and stood. "I

know. It's just so ridiculous."

"Have you considered talking to her about it?"

A stunned look took Chad's features hostage. "I'm—" he stammered, "I'm just supposed to say, 'hey, why don't we get married and then we don't have to worry about what happens to our friendship if one of us gets married.' Oh yeah, that makes sense."

"Well, I'd give her a long time to think about it, and I'd probably make sure you don't sound like you're doing her a favor," he teased. "Think about it."

Warmth radiated in the room, but it wasn't just the stove. Chad almost hated himself for loving everything about it—the quiet camaraderie, the scent of a meal cooking, and knowing that she had looked forward to his arrival. The domesticity of it pricked his conscience, but not enough to make him resent it. Rather, he embraced it just a little more.

"Oh, I talked to my mom, and she wants you to come for the day on Friday."

"Well the last bus leaves for Fairbury—"

"That's another thing," he interrupted. "I get Friday off, and I don't have to be at work until six on Saturday. We could stay over—"

"I have a goat—"

Grinning, Chad interrupted again. "But I have a solution!"

"What's that?"

"I bring the oldest Allen kid out here, and we teach him how to do it. That way, if you need to be gone, you have someone you can call if I can't do it."

"Why not just come home?" Willow liked the idea of more time with Chad's mother but didn't quite understand making long term plans to be gone from home more often.

"Let's face it, most of the time, you can't. Most of the time it's not just about someone to bring in the chickens or milk the goat. You're usually very busy and need to be here, but this time of year is your opportunity to build relationships with

182

people, and if that means being away from home, then why not?"

"I don't know..." she hedged. "Friday is your birthday. Your mother would probably prefer to have you there without me."

"Are you calling Mom a liar? Her exact words were, and I quote, 'Tell Willow I want to take her to little India and a few of the craft stores while she's in town.'"

Willow passed Chad his plate of roasted chicken and vegetables. "Do you think he can learn it?"

"Who?"

"The Allen's boy—Caleb."

"You'll go?"

"I have to meet Grandmother at the Mad Hatter—what a name—at eleven-thirty."

It was as if he could read her mind. While they ate, he watched her expression as she worked through her thoughts and feelings. He knew she considered it irresponsible to leave work. Would milking a goat fall into a category with making candles and planting a garden or was it closer to mail delivery—nice if someone else does it, but she'd go into town if necessary?

"Should I let Grandmother borrow Mother's journals? I was thinking especially of the early ones."

His brain tried to switch gears and almost slipped. He took a drink of his milk, hardly noticing the difference in flavor for once, before he answered. "No. I think she'd enjoy reading them, and I know they'd be a lot of encouragement to her, but you don't know this woman. People change. She might not be the same person your mother loved and trusted."

"You're right. They're not something I can loan and not expect back. Mother used to say, 'Never loan what you wouldn't give away.' I'm not sure why she said that. Who would I have loaned anything to? I didn't *know* anyone."

Chad sensed her dissatisfaction. "You know, you could let me take them into town and make copies of them."

"Copies?"

Those random things that Kari had never explained

jumped out at the oddest times. It was logical, when he considered it, that Kari might not have needed to explain the function and purpose of a copy machine. "Just a machine that takes a picture and prints it."

Fascinated by the idea of instant reproductions of anything on paper, Willow sighed. "I want to see one of those machines work sometime."

Without another ·word, she left her half-full plate, returning minutes later with her mother's first two journals. "Thanks."

After dinner, Chad helped wash the dishes, and while Willow mopped the floor, he loaded the stoves for the night, before pulling on his jacket. Work called. "I'll bring Caleb out tomorrow around four-thirty, ok?"

"That'd be great. Thanks."

Once she heard the crunch of his tires on the new layer of snow, Willow crept from the kitchen and retrieved her knitting bag from the library. Though she was tempted to sit down and start knitting, Willow forced herself to climb the stairs and change into pajamas. Once on the couch, she smiled. Every candle glowed brightly in the room. Chad's thoughtfulness warmed her heart and made the room seem less empty.

"Lord, I am lonely. Summer wasn't so bad. Fall was bearable. Winter…" She stuffed down a sob, "I don't know if I can make it until spring."

Her knitting needles clicked at speeds she rarely tried to achieve as she worked the final packet and collar of Chad's birthday sweater. If she worked her fastest, she could get it done and be able to block it overnight. She held the piece up in the light and studied it. The heathered oatmeal merino yarn was perfect. She'd fallen in love with the Aran sweater with an Irish collar years earlier, and rejoiced when she noticed Chad's birthday on his driver's license one day.

The quiet seemed oppressive. She tried singing but felt even lonelier than ever as her voice echoed in empty rooms with no harmony accompanying her. Anxious to finish, Willow knitted faster. She dropped stitches, ripped out small sections, and tried again, determined to go to bed as soon as possible.

In bed, a silent house made sense. The stark emptiness around her felt comfortable and normal when cuddled in bed with blankets and pillows around her. During the day, she and her mother had spent so much of their time doing their own things that it wasn't unusual to be alone during the day. However, from dinner until they parted for bed, she'd had someone to talk to—to read with, and to share her dreams.

"I want my Mother," she whispered mournfully as she wove the last yarn end into the sweater. "I am tired of being alone."

Chad arrived at four-thirty with Caleb Allen and burst into the empty kitchen. "She's not here—"

"Someone is in the barn, I think. What smells so good?"

Under the lid of the Dutch oven, Chad found a roast. "Oh man, roast."

"She eats well anyway."

"She eats a lot! She works hard, and in summer puts away twice as much as I do."

The "men" found Willow in the summer kitchen dipping candles. Chad watched amazed as she dipped the candles in her large pot, into ice water, and back again in the pot. Paper cups lined the counters and rows of tiny tea lights sat cooling in paper-lined trays.

Willow didn't even turn away from her work as she said, "Sorry, Chad, can you show him what to do? I got a late start today, and now I'm really behind."

"Only if I'm invited to dinner."

"Sure. You're both—"

Caleb grinned but shook his head. "I wish I could, but Mom's making my favorite casserole. I've been bugging her about it for weeks, so I need to be there."

Chad stood close to the stove and watched as Willow dipped her candles in the tallow, dipped them in the ice bath, and then back to the tallow vat again. "What's in there?"

"Tallow—beef fat from the cow, beeswax, alum, and some

185

cinnamon oil."

"Odd, I thought I smelled lavender." He sniffed the pot. Definitely cinnamon. *"Must be your hair,"* he thought to himself.

"I am done with the plain and the lavender, but I like cinnamon for December and February."

Chad caught Caleb giving him a knowing look and shook his head, his eyes demanding, *Don't get ideas, boy. That last thing we need is Fairbury gossip spreading faster than usual.* Caleb nodded in apparent agreement.

As he led the boy outside, Chad noticed Willow humming the tune she'd loved so much from his Argosy Junction CD. He glanced back, took in the candles that filled the room, and wondered just how many she'd made that day. How did she manage to get so much done without her mother's help?

At first, Caleb's milking left more milk in the animal than in the bucket. Chad stripped one teat and showed the boy how to use enough force without hurting Ditto. Caleb tried again, listening to each instruction, following them all until he felt more confident. "What happens if I don't get it right? The animal gets sick, doesn't it?"

"That's why you'll do it properly tomorrow. You know there won't be anyone to pick up the slack. That said," Chad pulled out his phone and punched a bunch of keys. "—if you have any doubts, if there isn't close to this much milk, call Luke. He'll help."

"Why didn't you just ask him?" Caleb's eyes grew wide. "I wasn't complaining, or anything. I just wondered why risk it with a kid..."

"Because Willow will be more willing to use you than Luke. You'll let her pay you. She won't feel like she's putting you out. Luke is family—"

"I thought she didn't have family."

Chad tried again. "He's my cousin. He's my family and my parents are doing their best to convince her to become an honorary Tesdall/Sullivan."

"You could make that official, you know..."

"Don't even go there." The warning he tried to interject into his tone sounded more like panic to him. *You've got to get a*

186

grip.

"I'm just sayin'…"

Willow wasn't in the summer kitchen when they returned to sterilize the buckets, but a pot of water boiled for them. Caleb's eyes widened. "She's good."

"Yep."

"I gotta go home. Just strain it and put it in the fridge, right?"

"Right. I'll do it." Chad pulled his keys from his pocket and twisted Willow's key from the ring. "Here's this one. Check the water too, while you're gone. Make sure the pipes aren't frozen."

"And break any ice in the water troughs, right?"

Chad grinned. "You've got it. You'll be great. Thanks."

As Caleb stepped from the barn, he glanced around him. "This is a nice place—big for one person."

"Big for two, but it works for them."

The boy stared at Chad for a moment before he said, "Worked, you mean. It worked for them. Looks to me like it only works if they have help." Before Chad could reply, he added, "Gotta go before Mom hollers at me."

Caleb's words reverberated in his mind, ricocheting off memories that proved the boy's point. It seemed as if no matter what he said or did, the point always came back to a warped version of the verse in Genesis. *It's not good that Willow should be alone…*

"Why don't you wash up?" she said as he stepped inside the back door. "Dinner's done."

He pulled off his jacket, hanging it over hers on the hook. Somehow, he'd never been able to use the hook where Kari's had once hung. After drying his hands, he took the roast platter from her and nudged her toward the table. "Sit. You look beat."

"I am. Long day."

"My mom used to joke about how she slaved over a hot stove all day. You actually did that." As he spoke, he sliced the meat, putting several on her plate. "Roll?"

"Yeah—" She rose to get them, but he stopped her. "I'll get it. You're resting."

Several times during the meal, Chad had to nudge her hand or her foot, prompting her to eat. As for him, the meat seemed to melt in his mouth, the vegetables were cooked exactly how he liked them—not too done, not too raw. Her mashed potatoes had flakes of skin that should have given them a lumpy texture. He'd never had better potatoes. And the gravy… his eyes closed as he took another bite, savoring the flavors.

The moment she finished eating, Chad sent Willow upstairs. "You take a shower. I'll take care of the stoves and wash dishes."

"That seems a bit disproportionate."

"You just fed me the best meal I've probably ever had. I call it even." He grinned at her as he pushed her from the room. "Go."

The moment he heard the water come on, he pulled out her loom and the tray of fabric strips, setting them by the couch. Maybe if it were there, she'd sit when she came back downstairs. The stoves, all three of them, came next. By the time he started on the dishes, she'd returned. "I'll dry."

"Go sit down."

She shook her head, snapping his leg with the dishtowel. "We'll work together. I like having someone to work with at night."

"I like having someone to work with at night." Her words pricked his heart. Why did he resist what could be such a good thing? *Is it so wrong that I would like the chance to find a girl, fall in love, and then get married?*

She stared at him as if waiting for a response. "What?"

"I asked if you wanted chocolate cake."

"Later. I'm stuffed."

Once in the living room, Willow's eyes widened. "Oh you got it out. Thanks!" She sat on her rug loom and grabbed a handful of pieces. "I dumped my tray yesterday, and now they're all a mess."

Without a word, Chad started sorting her colors while Willow chattered freely about her day, the candles, and the pattern of her rug. "I'm so excited. It'll match the other one. I've

188

never been especially fond of that long tree one in my room."

"Then why did you make it?"

"Well, I thought I'd like it when I made it. It just looked so... not what I wanted when it was done."

"What will you do with it?" For Chad, the idea that Willow would replace something before she'd worn it out seemed impossible.

"Well, I'll probably add it to the dead ones in the attic. Mother thought they acted like insulation to help keep the house warmer, so we put our old ones up there. I shouldn't have done this. It's really wasteful; the rug is just barely wearing on the edges—"

"I wondered—" It felt rude to ask, but Chad could picture the rug between his couch and the bar that separated his living room from his kitchen. If it looked half as good as he imagined, it'd be great—not too feminine. His family couldn't complain about the lack of décor with something like that on his floor.

"So, what would a guy have to do to convince you to let him have the rug when you're done with it?"

Her head snapped up from the frame where her hands deftly worked the wool strips in and out of the backing. "You want it?"

"I think it'd look cool between the couch and my bar—"

"Sure! Take it home tonight."

Chad shook his head, murmuring something about being patient, but she didn't seem to hear him. Amused, he listened as she went off on another tangent, sharing plans for replacing the rugs in the library with book quote rugs. "It'll be forever before those rugs wear out, so I have time to choose my quotes."

After a few more moments of silence, she sighed contentedly. "It's nice to have someone to talk to. This week has been especially lonely at night."

Chad's throat constricted and his mouth went dry. He'd just been mulling that their relationship was perfect the way it was and he didn't need to introduce anything as pressure-filled as marriage into the recipe. "Aww, Willow," he choked. "I'm sorry. I didn't realize—"

"It wasn't so bad in summer and fall, but it's so quiet in

189

here at night. I like the solitude sometimes, but other times it's just—just—" she paused before whispering, "awful."

His hand covered hers. "This is exactly why going to Rockland is a good idea." The word quiet bounced through his mind for a while. "Hey, would audio books be enjoyable?"

"Audio books?"

"Books read aloud and on CD or MP3." A blank look masked her face. He waited several seconds and tried again. "Would you enjoy listening to books read aloud by others?"

She reached for her Alexa Hartfield novel, but he waved her back. "I'm not reading it. Reading aloud isn't my thing, but I can take care of too much quiet when you want to work on something."

She shrugged and grabbed another pile of blue wool from his knee. "It sounds wonderful. I don't really understand, but if you think it's a good idea, take my card and go buy it before I go crazy."

CHAPTER 57

Flakes fell around him as Chad rounded the corner. At times like these, his mind escaped to Rockland and imagined cruisers with heaters—stakeouts even. There simply was no appeal to walking a beat along Fairbury's commercial sidewalks.

Wayne at the Pettler finished shoveling his sidewalk just as Chad passed. "Hey, Chad, mind carrying this around the corner to Michelle over at the Mail Box? I just got a rush order."

He took the shovel, swung the top over his shoulder, and sauntered down the sidewalk, feeling like an overpaid and glorified errand boy. *"Your attitude stinks, Chad,"* his conscience accused.

"Another year in limbo," he mentally retorted. "Morning, Mrs. Costas."

"Good morning Chad. You're such a good boy. We're lucky to have you while we can."

"While you can?"

Mrs. Costas tucked her scarf in a little more snugly and smiled dolefully at him. "Before Rockland calls you away. We eventually lose all of our nice boys to Rockland. Except Joe. He's going to stay forever, I think."

Chad grinned at the older woman, giving her a glimpse of the dimple that few ever saw. "I'm not going anywhere, Mrs. Costas. I've decided to stay here with Joe and keep the varmints out of Dodge, er, Fairbury."

"Well, that is a wonderful thing to hear. I hope you do."

In front of The Mail Box, snow was packed and slick. A woman carrying a box to be shipped reached the front, sighed as her shoe slipped, and turned around again, muttering, "I give up."

"Ma'am?"

The woman turned. "Yeah?"

"I'll help you in and shovel out the front before you're done."

As he spoke, Chad chopped at the icy surface of the snow and then shoveled a strip away from the entrance. Opening the door, he set the shovel down and took her package. "Watch your step. I've got this; just get in where it's warm. "Michelle?" he called as he ushered the reluctant customer inside the warm building."

"Back here. I've got your copies and I need to talk to — Oh, hello, Mrs. Klein. Need to ship that?"

Chad set the box on the counter and disappeared out front to finish shoveling the area in front of Michelle's shop. The merchants on Center Street had complained about her lack of diligence in keeping her section of the street clear, but Chad knew she tried. If he couldn't spend a minute helping, what kind of man was he?

When he finished, he popped his head in the door and told her she was set for a few days. "If you keep a shovel out there, I can take care of it before or after work."

"Oh I couldn't ask you to —"

"You didn't. I volunteered." He turned to leave, but she stopped him.

"Do you have a minute? I have your copies.

The sight of the "copies" Michele brought him left him nearly speechless. "What —"

"I couldn't just run them off in black and white. Not after I read some of them."

"You read —"

Blushing, Michele tried to explain. "I didn't mean to — not at first. I ran everything off, went to put the rubber band around them, and dropped everything. I tried to reorganize them, but

192

there were no page numbers, so I had to read to make sentences make sense and then I couldn't put them down."

"Kari is like that isn't she?"

"Kari?" Michelle wondered aloud.

"Willow's mother. Those are her journals."

"Oh my," Michelle began, "I've never read anything like it. I wrote a note—" she pulled an envelope from beneath the counter, "—apologizing. I felt terrible once I realized how much of it I read, but that woman's faith touched me like nothing I've read in a long time."

"So you printed them in color?"

Looking somewhat chagrined, Michelle shook her head. "Not all of them. Just the prettiest and," she choked, blushing. "—my favorites. Do you think Willow will be upset?"

"No. She'll probably offer to loan you the rest."

Michelle took back the letter and opened it. "I sort of suggested that but not quite the way you mean."

"Huh?"

Grinning, she showed him the letter she'd written to Willow. "*Dear Miss Finley,*" Chad read to himself.

I need to apologize. After I printed the pages from your mother's journals, I dropped them everywhere. Normally it wouldn't have been a big deal, but I had a fan going to dry some things, and it just blew the papers all over my workroom.

They aren't numbered, so getting them back in order required a little reading at the beginning and end of each page. Once I started, I just couldn't stop. These are some powerful journals. They moved me, challenged in my faith, and left me hungering to know more about who your mother was and how she lived.

I know that there are sections of these journals that must be incredibly private, but they're so personally written and illustrated, not to mention inspiring, that I truly believe they would bless many people. Please consider publishing at least a compilation of them. The right printer could make a facsimile copy of the pages you were willing to share if you chose.

Please pray about it, and if you need help, I am here waiting to serve.

Sincerely,
Michelle Ferguson

"Wow."

Michelle nodded. "Yep. That's exactly how I felt when I read them. Wow."

Willow drew streamers, confetti, and tiny number twenty-sixes all over the butcher paper on her table. Chad watched, sipping his coffee, as she spent at least an hour creating the perfect wrapping paper for a box that didn't look anything like the display box he'd seen. "Come on, how about twenty questions?"

"Nope," she answered as she grabbed a metallic gold pen and added occasional swirls across the pale blue paper. It looked festive. "You can wait to find out with the rest of your presents. Your mother warned me that you'd pester me about it."

He glanced at his watch. Why had bringing Caleb out here at six in the morning seemed like a good idea? "I'm hungry."

"You're the one who told me not to cook." She stuck her tongue out at him. "You're the one who insisted that I needed an Old MacDonald's biscuit with eggs and cheese."

"I didn't know we wouldn't be leaving until ten!"

Willow stood, paint pen in hand, glanced at the living room clock for a moment, and returned. Taking the paint pen, she swiped it across his nose and went back to creating her masterpiece. "It's not even eight yet."

Chad jumped up to wash the paint from his nose. "What'd you do that for!"

"So you'd have something to do to get your mind off of presents. There."

Chad passed her the tape, but she shook her head. "It's not dry yet. I'll work on Grandmother's now." After a glance at his face, she added, "I'd go check the mirror if I were you. I think you need some soap."

By the time he returned, she had filled a large gift bag with one of the prettiest afghans in the house. She threaded ribbon through the grommets in the bag and tied a lovely bow. "What is that for?"

"Grandmother. I think Mother would have wanted her to have one of her afghans."

"You can't replace that, Willow."

"I don't need to. I have others, Mother's journals, and, a lifetime of memories. I realized last night that God gave me more years with Mother than Grandmother."

"Speaking of which—" Chad jumped up excitedly. "Be right back. You won't believe this."

The brown paper "bag" rustled as she pulled the spiral-bound stack of paper from it. The cover looked exactly like the cover of Kari's journal, although the pages were mostly black and white. She ran her hand over it, smoothing the page. "This is amazing! I should have her do all of them like this. I could get one for me and one for Grandmother. That would protect Mother's journals and…"

He heard the hint of tears in her voice, and passed her Michelle's letter. "Well?"

"I'll have to think about it but not today. I can't think about it today."

"Be Scarlett O'Hara. Think about it tomorrow." He reached into his pocket and pulled out a small bag. "Here, I got that MP3 player I was taking about. I put Alexa's latest book on it, so when you are done with it, let me know, and I'll take you down to the library and show you how to download more."

Willow stared at the little ear buds, the thin cord, and the bright pink little box as though an alien from another planet. "How do I?"

"I knew you'd ask, so I even brought the instructions," he teased as he whipped them out of his other pocket and handed them to her."

"I think I'm ready then. I have clothes, gift for Grandmother, one for you—even though I might just give it to Chris if you keep pestering me!" Grinning, she handed him his box.

"You just want to torture me. Well," Chad insisted, "it

195

won't work. We're off to Ferndale!"

"Why Ferndale?" she questioned as she wrapped a shawl-like thing around her shoulders, draping it over her head.

"Wow." He hadn't meant to say it, but the combination of stylish attire, carefree attitude, and a hint of a windswept look after she flung her hair back over her shoulders stirred something in him he hadn't expected—and refused to acknowledge. *Good thing she brushed out her hair,"* he groused inwardly.

"Isn't it beautiful! Mother wove it last winter."

"Wait," Chad grasped at anything to take his mind off his reaction to her. "You weave too? Is there anything you don't do?"

Willow opened the door, grabbed both gifts, and pointed to her duffle bag. "Well, we can't weave anymore. I broke it last year trying to carry it downstairs. Cut myself terribly too. I have a nasty scar—"

He waited until they were near the end of the drive before he asked, "So what'd you do with it?"

"With what?"

Chad turned out of the driveway and onto the highway. "The loom. The broken one. What'd you do with it?"

"It's in the attic in a box in pieces. Mother was going to try to fix it this winter, but—"

"I'll take it to Luke. Maybe he can help me fix it."

Willow shifted in her seat. "So tell me about Old MacDonald's. Is it like Marcello's or the Diner, or the sushi place..."

"Uh, none of the above. It's fast food."

"They're fast. That's good, but we have three hours," Willow protested.

"No, they're a fast food place."

"And that means—"

That was bizarre. How could he explain the concept of fast food to someone who has no clue not only what it is, but also why you'd want it? After several failed attempts at describing it, Chad suggested she wait and see for herself.

As he pulled into the parking lot, Chad tried to see the

196

restaurant from Willow's perspective. The first thing he saw was the garish red and yellow sign. Strange how it had never seemed garish before... The huge maze of a jungle gym seemed to swallow the front of the building and the parking lot was almost overflowing with cars.

Inside, he followed her eyes as she took in the dining area. Plastic plants, plastic tables, hard plastic chairs welded to those tables, and plastic trays. Garbage cans in bins near the front door—a man dumped a tray half-filled with food and a cup on top in the garbage as they passed. What did she think of the waste? He ached to ask but simply couldn't.

Chad stood in line behind several others while Willow glanced around the restaurant. It didn't' appeal to her—he could see that. What was it? The bored indifference masked by hyper-cheerfulness, typical of most fast food places, should intrigue her even if only because of the novelty. The girl behind the counter gave him his total, jerking Chad from his musings. He took the change, added a few bills, and shoved them in the box for the Ronald McDonald House.

As he stepped aside to allow the next person to order, Chad beckoned her to follow. "Willow, over here."

"Why did you put money in the box? Is it like the tip cup at the deli? What's the Ronald McDonald House?"

"It's a charity McDonald's sponsors. They have 'houses' that are like hotels near major medical centers for families to stay in when their child is sick. Mom and Dad stayed in one when Cheri was hurt as a baby. They only had the one car back then, so it was that or not see her. It's just what we do. We *always* put money in the RMH box."

"Oh that is wonderful. I'd—"

The employee behind the counter handed Chad a tray. Willow watched amused as he asked for salt and the girl overtly flirted with him. As they sat in the nearest booth, Willow grinned. "I've finally seen it."

"Seen what?"

"Flirting. She was definitely flirting."

Chad tossed a glance in the general direction of the cash registers and shrugged. "I guess. Obviously you weren't paying attention at Thanksgiving."

"Why?" Willow unwrapped her "sandwich" and stared at it.

"Cheri spent fifty-percent of her day flirting with Chuck Majors."

"And the other fifty-percent?"

Cheri had once hinted at her own cache of blackmail photos. He didn't really believe she had them, but also wasn't ready to risk being wrong. He shrugged and muttered, "Just being her normal irritating little pipsqueak self."

"Flirting with Chuck. Hmm."

Something her tone disturbed him. "Does it bother you?"

"I think it's delightful."

A boy carrying a cup of orange juice tripped over shoelaces and fell against their table. Chad managed to jump from his chair before his clothes were soaked, but his food didn't fare as well. "You ok, buddy?"

"Aw, man! Moooom… I need another orange juice!"

Chad stared at the juice-sodden McMuffin and grabbed the tray. "Be right back."

"I'll get—"

Willow started to rise, but he waved her back. "No. Eat while it's hot. I'll get it."

Willow watched as he dumped the tray and went to order a new one. She unwrapped her food—a sandwich of sorts using a biscuit for bread. It sounded like a good idea at the time. As she peeled back the top of the biscuit, she stared at the eggs— unsure.

"What's wrong?"

"Are these eggs?"

"Yeeeesss…"

"They don't look like eggs. They're all flat and foldy. How do they get them like that?"

Flirty girl called Chad's number. Willow watched as he chatted with the girl. When he returned, he was grinning. "Ha! I got the freshest ones."

"What?"

"Andrea says that the eggs on your biscuit are made from

real eggs, folded, and frozen. They just heat them up here. Mine is cooked on the griddle in a round mold."

"Who is Andrea?"

A bit of red tinged Chad's ears. "The server. I asked about the eggs for you."

"And," she tried not to smirk, "how did you manage to get her name?"

"It's on her name tag..."

Willow choked on the bite of biscuit she took in an attempt to hide her smile. "Aahh—"

Chad nodded at her food, his mouth full of his own sandwich. "So, what do you think?"

Never had she chewed anything so slowly. The textures alone—strange. "Well, the biscuit is good—delicious really. Nice and crispy outside and flaky inside. It's just..."

"What?"

"Something tastes off. I think it's the butter. I don't think I like cow butter."

"—talk 'bout—'sting funny," he muttered.

"What?"

"Nothing."

"Oh, no." She reached across and snatched his sandwich from him. "No muffin for you unless you tell me what you said."

He took a bite from his odd-looking hash browns. It was like a fried potato cake rather than actual hash browns. "Ok, fine. I just said that you were the one to talk about milk products tasting funny."

"Why is that?"

"Goat milk is much stronger than cow. I haven't tasted it in the butter, though." He frowned. "Maybe they use margarine."

"Plastic?" Her nose wrinkled and she pushed her sandwich away, staring at it.

"Margarine."

"Mother called fake food 'plastic food.'"

Chad sighed as he retrieved his sandwich from her. "That was an Internet legend. The one molecule thing. They say it about everything eventually. The only thing it's true of are Hollywood actresses."

"What? Molecule?"

"Oh, I thought—never mind."

He seemed put out. Willow nudged his foot with hers and said, "But the sausage is pretty good too. The cheese is weird."

"Well, it's—" He snickered, choking on his bite of food. "You're going to go home and make this, aren't you? You'll make English muffins, biscuits, and put real butter, real scrambled eggs, a poached egg, goat cheese—stuff from your farm on these things and call it a breakfast, won't you?"

"Well, why not?"

He dropped his sandwich and leaned forward. "I want to hear you say why."

"What?"

"Come on, say it."

"I just want to see what they taste like with real food. I think it'll be good."

He shook his head. "I love it. Real food." His eyes roamed the room. "So what do you think of the restaurant."

She took a bite of her sandwich, giving herself time to formulate a polite answer. "I think it doesn't connect well with the outside, but it seems... easy to clean."

"Easy to clean?"

"Sure. Hard surfaces everywhere—look how fast she wipes down the tables and sweeps under them." That statement sparked a new thought. "When you said fast food, I kept thinking of service—taking the order and getting the food out, and it was, but..." She swallowed a big gulp of water, not liking the strange greasy feeling around her lips. "Napkin?"

He grabbed for them, but they were gone. "Must have used them all. Let me get some." When he returned, he passed her a stack big enough for a family and said, "But what?"

"But—huh?"

"You said you thought it was about the food and then you said 'but...' What were you going to say?"

"Oh!" She took another swig of water after wiping the opening clean of grease. "I just realized that there was more to it than that. It's fast in everything, isn't it? Eat fast, clean fast, cook fast, serve fast, leave fast." She pointed to the play area. "Do kids play fast too?"

"Yeah... They play by moving fast, but it's probably the one thing that slows down leaving around here. Kids screaming to stay while mom and dad just want to go."

They cleaned up their mess, and as Willow stepped from the restaurant, she said, "I like McDonald's."

Chad's expression spoke before he did. "What? You didn't like the food, the interior, and the fact that Andrea flirted with me, but you like the restaurant. That doesn't make sense."

"They gave me a good idea for breakfast when I go fishing and they have the hotels for sick families. Yes, I like them." She hesitated before adding, "And if you like Andrea flirting with you, then isn't that all that matters?"

Willow sat in the waiting area of the tearoom, picking at her skirt with unsteady fingers. Each time the door opened, she glanced up, sighed, and dropped her eyes. She pulled out her phone and frowned as she saw the time. Ten minutes late. How long should she wait?

Just as she decided to call and ask Marianne her opinion, the door open and a woman stepped inside. She could be — maybe. The woman's eyes met hers as she skirted the room to reach Willow's side. "I'm sorry I am late. The stupid traffic is horrendous today. I'll get our table."

Mozart played lightly in the background as Willow and Carol Finley wove through the tearoom behind their server. At a little table near a window, they sat and accepted their menus. Neither spoke as they chose their tea and sandwiches. Once they gave the server their orders, Carol crossed her legs, leaned back in her chair, and appraised Willow openly.

"You look like my mother-in-law. Actually, you look *exactly* like her."

"Mother mentioned that once."

Awkwardness hung over the table like a heavy blanket.

Willow felt smothered by it and suspected that her grandmother did too. Desperate to break the ice, Willow passed the gift bag across the floor. "I brought you a couple of things I thought you might like."

"I didn't bring you—"

She frowned, shaking her head. "I didn't expect you to. In the bag there's a copy of two of mother's journals—of the first two years—and an afghan she made a couple of years ago. It was her favorite, and she mentioned a few times that she thought you would like it." Her hands fidgeted as she added, feeling very awkward, "So I brought it."

Carol Finley pulled the pages from the bag and dabbed tears from her eyes. "I don't know why," she sniffled, "I thought it'd be a good idea to meet in public. I'm going to make a fool out of myself."

"I'm sorry."

After taking a sip of her tea, Carol asked, "Willow, why did you come?"

"I don't know."

"Do you mind if I open the afghan at home? I don't think I'll make it through—"

"That would probably be best. It's large." Willow swallowed hard. "I just wanted you to have something of Mother's."

"I'm surprised you call her mother. She always hated that name. The only time she used it with me was when she was irritated, and then it was, 'Mother! I can't believe...'" Carol dabbed at her eyes again. "I was mom."

"Sometimes I think our life started as a sort of penance for Mother, and through the years, she learned to embrace it. Perhaps she realized what a beautiful word mother is when she realized she could never say it again."

There was no doubt in her mind that her grandmother found the visit as awkward as she did. She recognized the signs of someone uneasy with her frankness. It hurt, despite her self-admonition to be true to who her mother taught her to be. Verification came in Carol's next statement.

"You're a very unusual young woman, Willow. How did

Kari educate you?"

"She just did."

Carol rephrased. "I mean, did she use a correspondence course, what?"

"I just learned as we lived."

Again, Carol tried to explain herself, "But, for example, how did you learn multiplication?"

"Skipping steps as I went upstairs to my room, grouping things by fours or threes—just by living. I think I'll copy the excerpts of Mother's journals that talk about it and mail them to you. I'm not very good at explaining it. To me, it was just life."

"So different from the Kari we knew. She was such a traditionalist…" Carol's voice broke. "I'll never forget that call."

"Call?"

"The police called when they found her car abandoned. It was registered to David. We started looking…" Tears filled the woman's eyes again. "For so long. We looked for so long, but nothing."

A lump rose in Willow's throat. "I'm sorry."

"Well, it's not your fault, now is it? Sometimes the pain shows up at the oddest times."

That concept, Willow understood. "It happens to me too. Someone asks about Mother, and it seems perfectly natural. I see the spot where her cup used to sit, and I fall apart."

"It was like that with your letter."

"My letter?"

"I—" Carol stumbled over a few words before she managed to speak a coherent sentence. "I fell apart when I got that letter—and I thought it was a prank at first. At the funeral, I hardly cried, but then after talking to the officer, I sobbed all the way home."

As if she hadn't just dropped an emotional bomb on Willow, Carol swiftly changed the subject. "Tell me about your officer."

"My officer?" The possessive pronoun produced an unwelcome sinking in her heart.

"David, your grandfather, is convinced that there's something going on with you and the officer—the one from the funeral."

"Chad..." she answered, her mind reeling with the implications of her grandmother's assumptions. "Sorry. I hadn't thought of him as mine or as an officer. I mean, I know he is, but to me he's just Chad."

"Well, how did you meet him?"

Willow's natural resistance to intrusion flared. "Why do you want to know? I'm not sure what that has to do with anything."

"You don't need to get defensive. We're not about to jump into your life and start trying to run it. I was just making conversation."

Taking a deep breath, Willow tried to calm herself as she answered. "I didn't mean to be defensive. That day is still very difficult for me."

"Difficult—oh!" Carol choked down the sip of tea she'd taken. "I'm sorry. I didn't know—the memories. I didn't mean to make—tell me about your farm."

After that, the conversation, while superficial, flowed more naturally. She described the farm, what they grew, their projects, and how they kept busy. As Carol tried to envision the size of the garden or the wallpaper Kari painted, Willow sighed. "I should have brought a photo album to show you."

"That would be nice to see some time."

It would be so simple to invite them to visit. The words hovered in the back of her throat, almost taunting her—daring her—to issue an invitation, but she hesitated. Once she made that overture, she would hurt them if she chose not to continue a relationship with them. They'd been hurt so much already— the stories Carol told...

"Perhaps you would like to visit sometime." The moment she spoke, Willow wished the words back again. An illegible expression crossed Carol's face, and Willow hastened to add, "It would have to be after Christmas. I would invite you before then, but I'm busy with Christmas presents, and I have guests coming for Christmas day, but maybe after the first—"

"I'll have to check with David. He's so skeptical about the wisdom of even meeting you." She must have noticed Willow's dismay, because she continued apologetically. "Kari's disappearance was very hard on us both emotionally and financially. I think he aged ten years in one."

"I understand. If you don't care to come, I'll order reprints of my favorite pictures and mail them if you like."

Willow lost all heart for the discussion. "I think we're monopolizing this table. I should go. Thank you for inviting me, Grandmother. I hope it hasn't been too difficult for you."

She rose, grasped the other woman's hand briefly, turned, and disappeared into the crowd near the front of the tearoom. When Carol called for their check, she found it paid in full with an ample tip added for the extra time at the table. Picking up her bag, Carol hurried to her car, pulled the afghan from the tissue wrappings, and sobbed into it. The white lacy afghan was almost identical to one she'd coveted so many years ago. It smelled of lavender, and yet somehow, when she inhaled she caught a slight whiff of the essence of Kari.

"Mr. Solari will see you now." The voluptuous receptionist sashayed across the floor, opened the door to an immense office, and introduced her. "Willow Finley, sir."

Steven Solari had never expected Willow Finley to arrive at his office. When his letter brought no response, he had assumed that he would have to find another way to ingratiate himself to her. "Willow —"

"I think Miss Finley is more appropriate."

"For a man to call his own granddaughter —" Steve began, but Willow cut him off.

"Excuse me, but I am not here to discuss genetics or genealogy."

"Then why are you here Will-ow Finley."

From within her purse, Willow withdrew his check. "I came to return this. While I appreciate the sentiment that prompted your sending it, I cannot accept it. I've lived my whole life on your money. I don't want more of it now."

"It must be running low by now. Let me try —"

"Actually, Mother invested it well, and I truly have no need of it. Perhaps you should consider sending it to my maternal grandparents. I just learned that they spent a significant amount of their savings and retirement looking for Mother after you threatened her."

Impatiently, Steven slid the check into his drawer. "Had I wanted to look for her, I could have found her in less than a week. Property records, utility bills—it doesn't take a genius—"

Willow turned on her heel to leave, making one last reply. "They didn't look for her alive here in Rockland. They searched records in other states, but they assumed if Mother was close, it was because she was dead. I heard what my grandparents went through today. When I think that my existence caused everyone so much pain—"

Her voice broke and she opened the door, but not before Steve caught up with her and blocked it, pushing it shut. "I don't understand why she ran away when she needed help most. We could have been supportive of her even if her parents—"

"She left," Willow ground out through unshed tears, "because she assumed a threat behind your payoff. She feared for my life if you learned of my existence."

The girl's words stunned him. He'd warned Kari Finley, it was true. However, he'd only tried to prevent her from returning often for repeated handouts. In fact, he always been a little surprised that she'd never come again. "But I never said, or even implied—" Steve protested hotly.

Willow whirled and glared at him. "Mr. Solari, my mother was a broken and battered woman. According to her journals, she still had bruises the day she saw you. You couldn't have missed them. How do you expect a woman so utterly debased to think clearly?"

He tried another tactic. Perhaps if she pitied him... "She protected you. I understand and respect that. I protected my son too, but unlike you, it just made things worse. Your mother was a much better parent—"

"Excuse me, Mr. Solari; I'd like to leave."

Despite his desire to force her to stay and listen, Steve

stepped aside. As she opened the door once more, Steve couldn't resist asking one more question. "Were you afraid to come here today?"

"Terrified." Her words sounded sarcastic, but he saw that she spoke the truth.

"Now that you've seen that we won't hurt you, perhaps we can discuss dinner sometime..."

"I don't think so," she whispered and slipped from the room.

Steve Solari crossed his arms and grinned at the sight of his retreating granddaughter's back. This might be easier than he thought.

CHAPTER 58

"Chad?"

Something in her tone put Chad on alert. "What's wrong?"

"I'm at the corner of," she paused looking at street names. "Sixth Avenue and California. I see a bank building, a big office building of some kind, and Starbucks — it says coffee."

"Ok… um, are you ready for Mom to come get you?"

A sniffle alarmed him. "Um, do you think she'd mind if we went later or tomorrow or next year?" Her tone grew strained — pained.

"I'm on my way. Go inside Starbucks and order a Caramel Macchiato or one of those Peppermint Mocha things. I'll be there as soon as I can."

"Ok." She sounded lost and hurt. "Hurry, Chad. I want to go home."

Chad was in his truck and on his way before she hung up the phone. He punched his mother's cell number and waited impatiently for her to pick up. "Mom?"

"Yeah?"

"First, pray. Something went wrong with the meeting. Willow is a mess. She's asking to go home, and the Willow I know would have just gotten on the subway, bought a bus ticket, and gone home. She wouldn't call for help."

"Well maybe she didn't know where the subway station is. It's probably nothing — "

"She was downtown in the financial district." As he spoke,

the hair on Chad's neck stood at attention.

"Did she say where?"

"Sixth and California."

"That's near the Solari building." Just as he started to panic, the familiar soothing reassurance that characterized her in a crisis came through the phone. "She's fine. She called. Send her to the Starbucks—"

"Already did."

"That's my boy. Bring her home. Don't let her go home if you can stop her." Just before he disconnected, his mother added, "Oh Chad,"

"Yes?"

"Happy Birthday, son."

"Chad said to get a Caramel Machiavelli or something with Peppermint. Which do you suggest?"

"You've never had Starbucks?"

"I've never had coffee," Willow admitted with a feeble attempt at a smile.

"I'd get the Peppermint Mocha Grande. The chocolate and peppermint give it a nice smooth and mild but refreshing flavor."

The counter girl sounded like an advertisement on Chad's parents' television. Once mixed and ready, a young man Willow's age called it out from the other end of the counter. "Have a nice day."

She sipped her drink, burning her tongue twice. At first, the coffee's bitterness overshadowed the flavor of the chocolate and peppermint. However, once her taste buds adjusted, and the temperature cooled a little, she inhaled the rich steamy scent between gulps, finishing it in record time. A glance at her watch showed a whopping ten minutes had passed. Surely, Chad couldn't get all the way from his house to her in less than fifteen or twenty minutes—not with all the downtown traffic.

She brought her cup back to the counter and ordered another one. To her dismay and irritation, the girl behind the counter tossed her cup and accepted her money. "I take it you liked it?"

"It was very good. I didn't think I was going to; it was a little bitter at first, but then it got better." She paused. "I didn't need a new cup. The other one was fine..."

"We have to use a fresh cup. Health regulations."

Back in her seat, once again, she again sipped at the coffee while watching the pedestrians on their way to undisclosed places, trying to forget her morning. Solari had been difficult but a necessary step. She wanted to ensure that the man was permanently out of her life and thought that the easiest way to remove him was to face him. Now she wasn't so sure. He hadn't been menacing or frightening—he seemed almost pathetic in his eagerness to forge a relationship. But something still felt off about the interview.

Grandmother Finley, however, had been much more emotionally difficult than Willow had imagined. Lost in thought and memories, she didn't notice when Chad strode into the coffee shop and pulled another chair up to her table. "Willow?"

"Oh, you got here fast."

"Traffic was on my side," he explained brushing aside unhelpful commentary. "What's wrong?"

"I want to go home."

"Mom's house is empty. Let's go there. It's closer."

How he managed it, Chad didn't know, but he got her to the truck, across town, onto the Loop, and to his parents' house in half the time it should have taken. Before he went inside, Chad sent his mother a text message asking her to give them an hour before she came home.

As they stepped in the door, she strode through the house, directly to the kitchen. He watched as she pulled a glass from the cupboard and filled it, guzzling it in just a couple of gulps. "Thirsty?"

"I had all that coffee, but I just need water. I feel jittery."

Willow's spoke at unnatural speeds. Her hands twitched, her eyes roamed, and she seemed to shake her head now and then, giving her the appearance of one with Parkinson's disease.

"Um Willow, what did you order?"

"Peppermintcoffeelikeyousaid. It wasgoodtoo."

"Wow. You're sensitive to caffeine I guess."

"I hope not," she confessed. "Ihadtwoofthem."

Chad's mind raced. If drunks needed coffee to counter the effects of alcohol, what did you give people for caffeine? He refilled her glass with water, sliced a chunk of cheese, and pushed her to eat, not knowing if it'd have any effect on her. "Tell me about Starbucks. How did you get way down there?"

"I took Mr. Solari his check."

"I see." He didn't see, actually. For once, he realized that his natural tendency to blast her for putting herself in a painful and vulnerable position wasn't going to do a lot of good and would probably irritate her in her hyper caffeine-induced agitated state.

"He's a small pathetic little man. It was a little embarrassing."

"Embarrassing? How?" Embarrassing wasn't the word he'd expected.

"To think that I'm related—that I share genes and DNA with a man like that—little minded and self-seeking. It was disgusting. I felt dirty just being in there."

"Solari is a powerful man, Willow."

Finishing her water in a single swallow, Willow refilled it. She started to take another drink and stopped, handing it to Chad. "Excuse me."

The effects of the coffee were already evident. Chad took the water to the living room and set it on the coffee table in front of the couch. While he waited, he glanced around the room, noticing the changes there since he'd been a child at Christmas. The advent calendar was gone. In its place on the mantel was a Christmas pyramid. His mother had always wanted one but didn't like the idea of candles and boys shoving and pushing through the house. He could almost hear her voice, *"Take it downstairs, boys!"*

The stockings were missing and replaced by swags of evergreen, white lights, and silver bells with deep blue bows. As he thought about it, he remembered that the swag had been there last year as well. The coffee table sported a large holly arrangement with pinecones and candles. His childhood home had changed completely while Willow's remained just the same.

When she returned, Chad patted the sofa next to him. "Come talk to me. I'm a little concerned."

"It was awful, Chad. Those people, my grandparents, they're still hurting." The words poured from her heart as she relived her discussion. "Mother hurt them so badly when she left, and I felt like I should apologize for her, but I know she made the best decision she could with the information she had, and I—"

"Whoa there. Just take a deep breath. No one blames you for any decisions, right or wrong, that your mother made."

"I think they do. If I didn't exist—" She jumped to her feet pacing the floor and ranting. "I should never have contacted them about mother in the first place. I should have known that it'd be reopening wounds. I was insensitive and selfish and—"

The sudden urge to kiss her into silence both shocked and amused him. *Been tortured with too many chick flicks thanks to Cheri,* he thought to himself. *Keep her sisterly. You wouldn't exactly kiss Cheri like that, and anyway, she'd consider it a whipping to have "smashed lips" at a time like this.* Aloud, and unaware that he actually spoke, he muttered a stern lecture to himself, "You've got to get people's opinions out of your head and stop letting them dictate your thoughts and actions."

"You're right. I know you are. But the things I said are true too."

"I'm what? What exactly did I say?" Panic filled his heart. Had he really spoken aloud? What if he'd said—

"You're right. I am letting other people's opinions have too much control over me." She peered at him closely. "You didn't know what you were saying?"

"I didn't know I said it aloud," he confessed and praised the Lord's mercy in not letting him have said any more.

"What else are you thinking but not saying then," she retorted glaring. "If you have opinions, why not share them like the rest of the world? I can't believe this!"

"I'm not the enemy, Willow. I often think things that I don't share. My opinion is just my opinion and it's mine to share or not. I'm not the enemy."

Willow simultaneously burst into tears and a fit of giggles. Chad watched miserably, and slightly amazed, as she wiped frantically at the streams of tears pouring down her cheeks, tittering about how silly she was.

Marianne arrived in the middle of the outburst and promptly asked, "Is she drunk?"

Willow dissolved into a fit of hysterics, punctuated with the occasional sob. Chad snickered at the sight and tried to explain. "She's on her first caffeine high, and it's a doozy. Two Peppermint Mocha's in a row."

"Oh honestly, Chad!"

"See, now I got you in trouble with your mom. I swear today—"

Desperate to stop the constant and highly out of character self-recriminations, Chad tried something else. "You're right. You really should have thought of these things. You should have known that you'd cause pain to these people, but you went anyway." The dumbstruck look on Willow's face and the fury in his mother's eyes would usually have stopped him, but Chad continued as seriously as if he was rebuking a naughty child. "I think you owe everyone an apology for your existence and for how you've ruined theirs with your presence. You're nothing but a burden to everyone around you. I think we'd all be better off if you would just go back to your farm and stay there. Your mother had the right idea. You're not meant for socializing."

"Chadwick Elliot Tesdall!"

"Mom!"

Willow's attempt to control her laughter failed. "Cha—Chad—your face."

"I cannot believe you'd be so insensitive—even in jest. I taught you better than that."

"He's right, Marianne," Willow began. "He's right. I'm being self-centered."

Shaking his head, Chad tried again. "No, that's not the

214

point I was trying to make. I was trying to point out that everyone is so wrapped up in their own hurts and grief that they don't realize the pressure on you to be everything to everyone at all times."

Marianne drew Willow to the couch and pulled her down next to her. "Listen. Chaddie's right. We're here to support you. You're not alone. You're not at fault for things you had no say in. You're just another one hurt by a horrible string of events — by a crime. If you have anything blameworthy, it'd be the crime of innocence. The last I heard, that's not even a misdemeanor."

She pointed to the stairs. "Now get your tiny fanny up those stairs and put on your jeans. Chad's taking you to the park for a while. I want you to keep him there until five o'clock and then you both come home. If you get cold, go to the mall or something."

"Why? I thought you'd want help with dinner or something," Chad asked.

"Because I want you out of here while I decorate. She's the only one who you'll listen to now."

"It's a nice park," Willow admitted. She unwrapped her ruana from around her shoulders and grabbed the coat Marianne had sent. "How about a snowball race?"

"Dare I ask?"

"What do you mean?"

He grabbed a spare hat from his pocket and pulled it down on Willow's head. "Can't have frost bitten ears. Mom'd kill me. I mean," He added, answering her question, "That you Finleys do not do anything um, normally. I have a feeling this is going to be a complicated race."

"It's a race and a fight combined. We pick a destination, find a route to it with some cover for each, pace off like in those old western movies Mother told me about, and then race to the target."

"So where do snowballs come in?"

She threw him a wicked grin. "The advantage. You throw

215

snowballs. You hit the other person and they take three paces back while you count to five. You can be moving forward on five but you can't throw before five."

"You're on. We race to the truck from the other side of the park. That way you know where you're going, and we're on even footing."

"You should have kept your advantage. I'm going to stomp you," Willow threatened.

Hand in hand, they started across the park. "Willow?"

"Hmm?" Her mind was fully engaged in strategy to give her an edge.

"I'm sorry for being so harsh with you. I didn't know how else to get you to see it but—" he swallowed the lump that tried to grow in his throat. "It was cruel."

"It's what I needed to hear. You proved yourself a faithful friend, Chad."

All the way across the park they walked, their feet crunching the snow beneath them, saying nothing. At the east entrance of the park, Chad took a deep breath. "Well, I really hated to kick you while you were already low, and now I hate it more than I did."

"Why?"

"Because I'm about to destroy you with snowballs."

She turned her back to him. Feeling terrible, he whirled her around to face him again and said penitently, "I was just—"

"Are you going to count or am I?"

Grinning, he turned his back on her and started counting. "One, two, three, four—" He took the largest steps he could manage, knowing he could likely throw a snowball farther. "—fourteen, fifteen, sixteen." Grumbling, he walked around a bench wasting perfectly good steps. "—twenty-two, twenty-three—" Realizing the advantage of the bench, he took smaller steps. "Thirty-nine... forty!"

The game commenced in an explosion of flying snowballs. Willow had scooped balls as she stepped away from him, carrying them with her as she walked. At the count of forty, she whirled and fired one after the other, hitting Chad with three of them. She ran ahead as he took his backward steps.

"I'll get you for that!"

"Gotta catch me first."

Willow raced through the park. While her agility gave her an edge, Chad's willingness to dive for cover, often still throwing snowballs, kept the playing field nearly level. Across the park they raced, swapping the lead at regular intervals. People paused and watched as they dodged, retraced steps, and threw.

The truck was in sight. Chad knew if he could reach it first, she'd demand a rematch. They had another couple of hours to kill. Hiding behind a tree, he watched her movements to see if she looked cold or tired. He wasn't willing to let her win, but if a risk put him out of the game and made her more comfortable, then he would take it.

Her cheeks were rosy, her breath he could see in regular puffs, but she was clearly not gasping for air. He noticed a few kids watching the game and made up his mind. Jumping from behind the tree, he threw several snowballs in her direction and ran for the truck. Willow dodged all the balls and tore after him, pelting the truck, the air, and finally Chad at the very second he hit the truck. Instinctively he raced back three steps and dove for the bumper barely touching it before her.

"I win!"

"Why did you back up?"

"You got me as I hit the truck. I didn't know the rules, so I didn't take a chance."

"I demand a rematch," she ordered in mock disgust.

Chad draped an arm around her shoulder and led her to the crowd of young spectators. "I have an idea..."

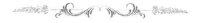

"Boy, Lance was good! I couldn't dodge his balls to save my life!"

Willow still chattered about the game as they strolled up the walk of the Tesdall home. As Chad opened the door, the entire Tesdall clan and Chuck Majors shouted, "Surprise!"

"Um—surprise? Really?"

"What else do you say when your guest of honor shows up for his party. Get with the program," Marianne chided as she bustled them into the house. "Willow, you get up there and change into something warm and dry."

Nothing Marianne could have said would have made Willow feel more at home than those words. She hugged the confused woman and hurried up the stairs to obey. By the time she returned, dinner was on the table and the family waited for her. How something so unlike anything in her home could feel so familiar made no sense to her.

She ate her dinner, barely conscious of the fact that it was delicious. When a cheesecake sporting twenty-six candles arrived, Willow realized that it must be a favorite. She'd learn to make cream cheese. Maybe his mother had a recipe.

After dinner, as Willow and Cheri helped carry plates into the kitchen, she overheard something that sparked an avalanche of drama. "Excuse me," she muttered to Cheri. "Chuck, come here."

Willow dragged Chuck from the dining room into the living room. Chad and his father sat talking about some kind of sports scores, so she dragged Chuck down the basement steps. As she left, she thought she heard Chad say, "I'm not sure what's up, but this is gonna be good."

Chuck erupted the moment she confronted him. "I don't get what your problem is, Willow! It was a compliment."

"Would you have said it to her face?"

"Well, yeah—no—well, before you started messing with my head maybe I would."

Willow's eyes flashed. "Excuse me, but before I was "messing with your head," people avoided your crass, self-centered nonsense. I'm sorry I was so mean as to assume you could rise above that."

"I don't get what is so bad. Why is ok for me to compliment her hair or clothes but I'm supposed to pretend that I don't know she has a fine set of—"

His retort died mid-sentence as she crossed her arms over her chest—and said nothing. Rather than argue the point, Willow glared at him, waiting for his senses to return.

218

Determined to prove himself right, Chuck grew more belligerent until Willow tried a new tactic.

"So what's wrong with mine?"

"What?"

"Well if it is such an acceptable practice to comment on the size, shape, or in any other way admire a woman's breasts, why ignore mine? I believe you've mentioned that you like my hair, I'm not too tall or too short, oh, and I have nice eyes if I remember. I also seem to recall something about needing my teeth whitened. So, you've fairly thoroughly assessed my other assets, why not my breasts, buttocks, and legs while you're at it?"

"Well, it's not something to say to a girl—"

Satisfied that she'd tripped him up, Willow crossed her arms and glared at him. "But I believe you said that before I meddled with your fine social skills, you would have."

"Well I wouldn't have said anything to *your* face—"

"Oh," she began patronizingly. "I see. You do have some scruples. You'll compliment a girl behind her back—even on her back*side*! But you won't be upfront with her."

"Some girls don't see the compliment—"

Willow took a step closer and practically shook him. "That's because it isn't. Cheri likes you. If you treat her like you did me at first, she'll stomp you—if her brothers don't beat her to it. For that matter, I might beat them all."

"I—"

"Are you going to try to defend yourself again?"

Chuck nodded. "I wasn't trying to be insulting. All guys talk about girls. Even Chad probably—"

"Chad!" Willow called interrupting him once more.

It took less than ten seconds for Chad to open the basement door and hurry down the steps. "What?"

"Chuck informs me that it is common practice for men to discuss different women and their physical attributes when in strictly male company. Is this true?"

Blushing, Chad shuffled his feet. He'd never thought about how it might sound out of Willow's mouth, but every man he knew spoke...appreciatively of women. "Well—"

"See!" Chuck cried like a child who found a co-culprit in a naughty escapade.

Disappointment flooded Willow's heart. "I see. I'm curious. What was the consensus on me? Do the officers think my legs pass muster? Is my backside too round or too flat? Are my breasts too disproportionate to the rest of my body?" She glared at him. "I'm disgusted!"

Willow whirled to retreat up the stairs, but Chad stopped her. "Willow, I've never—I mean we—the guys at the station—none of us, at least when I'm around, ever—"

At the smug look on Chuck's face, she nearly strangled the oaf. "You just said—"

"You asked if we discussed women's attributes. I thought you meant if we thought they were pretty or had nice hair or something. I can see Martinez being more crass about his assessments, but they all know I'd stomp 'em if they talked about a woman like that in my presence. Joe would too. And I don't want to think of what Judith would do to any of us if she found us—"

"Come on, Chad," Chuck began defensively. "You know you do it. Every guy does. We appreciate a fine body. God made us that way, and He made women the way they are so we could appreciate them. It's in the Bible!"

"Not the way you've twisted it isn't," Chad began. As if he finally understood, he stepped closer to Chuck. "What'd you say about Willow," he growled.

"Nothing—"

"If you insulted my sister—"

"It was a compliment! I've been trying to tell her than for the past ten minutes!"

Turning to Willow, Chad asked, "What did he say?"

"Ask Chris. He heard it." Why did Chuck not see the problem?

"Chris!"

"Great, the whole house will be down here before long," Chuck muttered again.

"If you did nothing wrong, Chuck," Willow began, "then there shouldn't be any reason for them not to come."

"People assume the worst about me. Even when I'm innocent, I'm guilty."

Trying a new tactic, Willow wrapped her arms around him and said, "Maybe because you're guilty often enough that they forget you can do something right too."

Chris appeared looking curious but confused. "What?"

"Chris, can you tell us exactly what Chuck said to you?"

"I didn't hear. He mumbled something, but I wasn't paying attention," he admitted.

Chris and Chad looked expectantly at Willow. "Well," Chad asked.

"Ask him. I feel icky enough without repeating it."

"It's not icky!" Chuck protested.

"Then you won't mind telling her brothers now. After all, you said it to Chris in the first place."

Shaking his head, Chuck moved toward the stairs. "I didn't mean for it to be icky but you're making it icky. I'll just go."

As Chuck's foot hit the first step, Chad stopped him. "My sister likes you, Majors. I don't know why, but she does. If you hurt her, by being inappropriate, or crass, or by walking out and leaving her to wonder what she did wrong when this is your fault, you'll regret it. Don't make that mistake."

"Right."

Chris, Chad, and Willow exchanged concerned glances as Chuck reached the top of the stairs and called out for Cheri. Seconds later, Chris excused himself, muttering something about checking on Cheri. Willow leaned against the Ping-Pong table and returned Chad's miserable gaze.

"I'm sorry, Chad. On your birthday too. I shouldn't have stepped in. It wasn't any of my business."

"You tried to help a brother in Christ."

"But did I beat him up with the log from my own eye in doing it?" she asked as she sank to the floor, exhausted.

Chad sat next to her, wanting to comfort her and yet feeling awkward at the same time. "Willow, I can't see you confronting a situation like that unless you did it out of love. Just what did he—" As she quoted Chuck's latest gaffe, Chad's

221

hands clenched at his sides. "That jerk—"

"I can see that he tried to be complimentary in his gauche way. I just knew, instinctively I guess, because Mother certainly never said anything about it, that it was wrong. Terribly wrong. I can see that he admires Cheri. You said she flirted with him, so she must see something in him, but if he said anything like that to her face, I think she'd kill him."

A deep chuckle escaped before Chad could stop it. "She'd have to beat Chris and me. And Dad," he added as an afterthought. "Not necessarily in that order."

"So if you don't talk about stuff like that, why did you look so embarrassed?"

"I don't know," Chad admitted. "Suddenly it seemed vulgar to talk about women at all."

Marianne called them upstairs. Willow stood and grinned at Chad. "So, did I ever come up in those conversations?"

"What conversations?" Chad stalled, his brain searching for a nice generic response to what he feared would be the question.

"Oh, about whether this girl or that is pretty? What was the consensus on me? I've never been able to decide."

"If you're pretty! What a joke."

She nodded thoughtfully. "Yeah. I always thought Mother was beautiful, and I don't look anywhere that nice. Bill agreed. I forgot about that."

"You're joking right?" Chad protested.

"What?"

"Get upstairs, girl! Of course, you're pretty. I swear; girls are the most aggravating creatures on the planet."

"Chad!" Cheri's voice called from the top of the stairs. "Quit flirting down there and get up here and open your presents!"

Willow cocked an eyebrow at Chad as she started up the steps. "Flirting?"

CHAPTER 59

Cheri and Chuck sat together on the couch as Willow and Chad emerged from the basement. To their surprise, Cheri kicked Chuck and motioned for him to talk to them. While Chad sat in a chair decorated with balloons and streamers, Chuck glanced miserably at Cheri and then cleared his throat.

"I owe you guys—and probably everyone else, an apology. Cheri says Willow is right, and I'm sorry." Cheri's foot shot out and kicked his shin again. "I'll make sure I'm more careful in the future."

With obvious determination to avoid the topic, Marianne passed Chad a gift. "This is from Grandma and Grandpa. They left it for you on Thanksgiving."

"Hmmm is it a Rockland Warriors sweatshirt or t-shirt?" Seconds later, he pulled a t-shirt from the box. "Two t-shirts in a row! I think they figured out that I wear those out faster." He winked at his mother and accepted the next gift.

"Oh, Chris!" He shook the box. "Ok, not a book on discovering my inner child or one hundred ways to overcome addictive tendencies…"

"You're asking for one for Christmas man…" Chris warned.

As he pulled out tickets to the next Warrior's game, Chad grinned. "You just hope I can't get the night off so you can have them. Pretty sneaky."

"Except that I already cleared the night off with your chief.

Take Willow. She's probably never been to a football game."

Chad pulled his wallet from his back pocket and slipped the tickets safely inside. "I'll do that. I'll definitely do that."

Cheri pointed at a gift bag near Chad's feet. "Open mine!"

The second Chad lifted the bag, he groaned. "Not another one!"

"Well you didn't like *PI* or *Hugo* so it was either this, *Chrome*, or *Cool Water*. I really think I should have gone with *Cool Water*."

"You should have gone with," Chad began as he pulled a box of *Burberry* from the gift bag, "with a squirt gun. It would have been very useful right now."

"But if I'd given you a squirt gun, you wouldn't want one right now, so it'd have been a waste."

Chad rattled the box. "So is this."

Willow asked to see the box and opened it. "Can I spray it?"

"Sure, stink up the place for all I care." To Cheri he added, "But I'm not wearing it."

"Every guy should have a scent. Even Chris has one."

Chad snorted. "Yeah, *Green Irish Tweed*. The name alone says, 'psychologist with a pipe.' We really should get Chris a pipe."

"I like it."

Willow's voice was quiet and thoughtful. "If I had a father, and he was anything like Mother, I think he'd smell something like this."

Marianne smiled to herself as she handed Chad her gift. "Happy Birthday Laddie."

From within a large box, Chad pulled a few black metal candle dishes, a framed picture of the family, two empty frames for "whatever pictures you want to add," and at the bottom of the box, two small matching wrought iron based lamps. "Trying to spruce up my apartment, Mom?"

"Well, if you won't..." she confessed as she passed him Christopher's box.

Christopher pushed a cardboard box with an oversized Christmas bow on it. "Happy birthday, son."

A portable battery charger brought a smile to Chad's face. His father always chose exactly that kind of gift—something practical, something you definitely wanted, but the kind of thing that you'd never buy for yourself.

"Thanks, Dad. Now if I'd only had this last week—"

"Why do you think I bought it instead of that video game Cheri suggested?"

Willow's gift brought exclamations of delight at the sight of handmade wrapping paper. "Do you always make your own paper?" Cheri asked. "Or did you just run out?"

"We always had fun making it, but I think Mother started because she didn't want to waste a trip home from town carrying wrapping paper."

"Yeah. So instead, she carries home twenty pounds of butcher paper because that's so much lighter," Chad teased as he folded the wrapping paper and set it aside.

From within the box, Chad pulled the sweater Willow had spent the past three weeks knitting. Before Chad could respond, Cheri sighed, "Ooh, that looks so Eddie Bauer—You'll have to go to New Cheltenham and walk around like a British gentleman. That's cool."

"It's amazing Willow! When did you possibly—"

"I had to do something all night when you were working!"

Chad, not knowing what else to do to show his appreciation for her hard work, unbuttoned his shirt, hung it over the back of the chair, and pulled on the sweater over his t-shirt. "It fits perfectly."

His mother looked ready to choke. He could see the ideas spinning in her mind as her eyes roamed from Willow's pleased expression to him. He hated sweaters—something his family knew quite well. If they saw him wearing it, they'd tease him. Somehow, he'd have to make sure he wore it whenever he was sure none of them would see him.

The final gift slid across the table. Chuck tried to brush it off as nothing, and sent Willow an embarrassed grin. When Chad commented he hadn't expected a gift, Chuck said, "Well, you can't go to a party without a gift, even I'm not that pathetic."

"Well..." Cheri hedged.

Chad rolled his eyes as Chuck tried to tickle Cheri as retaliation. Maybe Willow was right. Maybe he would come around. He had serious problems, but if anyone could fix him, Cheri—and a liberal dose of Willow now and then—could. Maybe he could join Cheri in foreign countries where most people wouldn't understand his social faux pas. Yeah. That might work.

Wrapped in comics with a "bow" of aluminum foil, Chad didn't know what to think as he removed the wrappings. However, at the sight of a six-pack of Dr. Pepper, he and Willow erupted in laughter. "That's a good one, Chuck. I'll keep it in my fridge so you'll come visit me and give me all the juicy gossip about my sister."

Willow laughed. "That's what I did. I didn't get any juicy gossip, but he did come and drink it for me."

Chad and Marianne walked the others to their cars, leaving Christopher and Willow inside. Groaning with exhaustion, Christopher dragged himself out of his chair and paused by Willow seated on the floor. Her eyes were riveted on the instruction book that went to Chad's battery charger. "I'm glad you came, Willow," he began. "You're good for our boy."

Willow stood and hugged him. "He's good for and to me."

Christopher hesitated and then shared what had filled his heart of late. "My son cares about you—more than he knows. He won't want to lose your friendship."

"I was foolish once and took my grief out on him. I won't risk hurting him again," she reassured him.

"Another man won't understand your relationship."

With her head cocked as she considered his words, Willow looked even younger than ever. "I think I understand." Her eyes dropped to the booklet in her hands. She took a deep breath and said, "Mr. Tesdall, I think I am too like my mother. There probably won't be that kind of man, and if there were, I'd know he was wrong the second he didn't understand. Chad's like the brother I've never had. I'm not willing to lose that."

He pulled her into another hug, kissing the top of her head as he often did with Cheri. "You're a treasure." His throat swelled with emotion. "You *are* a treasure, Willow. You're a treasure."

Without another word, Christopher climbed the stairs and disappeared into his bedroom. Willow stood watching him, feeling the void left behind. Something concerned him, and she'd tried to be reassuring, but the truth was she didn't understand what he said or why he said it.

Marianne bustled into the living room shivering and shaking a few recent flakes from her jacket as she hung it on the hook by the door. She seemed to know what her husband said, because she hugged Willow saying, "Chad has always been a little emotionally vulnerable. He's a servant, and people take advantage of that. My husband has a hard time remembering that not everyone is insensitive to Chad's needs."

"I think I understand now. Thanks." She tucked the instruction booklet back in the charger packaging and said, " I love your family."

Marianne led her to the den and pulled a movie off the shelf. "Make Chaddie watch it. He'll never admit it, but he loves this movie, and you need an introduction into modern Christmas classics."

"Marianne," Willow said wryly. "I need an introduction into *any* Christmas classics!"

Chad called to them from the living room. "Willow? Mom?"

"In the den." Winking, she added "Willow picked out a movie," as Chad filled the doorway. "I'm going to bed. Dad's whipped, and I need my beauty sleep."

Chad kissed his mother's cheek. "Hogwash. You could never sleep and still be the most beautiful mother in the world."

"Won't work, boy. Watch the movie."

"Aww, Mom! I bet it's *White Christmas,* isn't it!" Doing a little dance with his hand fanning over the top of his head, Chad cocked a hand on one hip and with an affected effeminate lisp sang, "Sthisters, Sthisters, there were never thuch…"

227

"Wrong. Now put the movie on. Night, Chaddie."

Willow, somewhat stunned by the vision of Chad prancing like a woman on heels, passed Chad the movie. "I think this is probably a better idea anyway. That was terrifying."

"*While You Were Sleeping*. I should have known. Are you sure you don't want to watch one of the Bourne movies? *Lord of the Rings*?"

Her eyes widened. "They made Tolkein into a movie?"

Chad pulled the box from her hand. "Yeah, and we'll be up until tomorrow afternoon trying to watch them all. We'd better stick to this tonight. First, popcorn. Regular or caramel?"

"We like ours with butter."

"That's regular. Be right back."

Willow followed him to get a glass of water and watched transfixed as he pulled a package from a box, removed a cellophane wrapper, and tossed the entire thing in a small oven. "Popcorn in the oven?"

"Microwave." Chad punched a button with a picture of a popped kernel.

"Ahh—can I have some water?"

Chad filled a glass and handed it to her just as the microwave beeped. "Yes! Let's go," he cheered grabbing the popcorn bowl from a shelf next to the microwave, tearing the bag open, and leading the way into the den.

"That was fast. That was—" She stood examining the microwave. "There's no flame, no heat in here—what is this thing?" Her eyes widened. "Wait. Mother said something about an appliance for heating things up. That was this, wasn't it?"

"You've never—oh my word. Of course. I brought out a package of it that night but you didn't—it didn't occur to me that you didn't know what a microwave *is*!" Her last words must have registered at that moment because he added, "Sort of didn't know anyway..."

"Well, let's watch the movie, and you can explain microwaves tomorrow."

They sat at opposite ends of the couch—Willow looking absolutely comfortable with her feet tucked under her and Chad, stiff and unnatural. The first line about Lucy's life being

228

orange sent Willow in a small fit of giggles. "I'm going to like this."

The broken window prompted a gasp and then a giggle. "If he was thinner and better looking, Joe Jr. would be Chuck!"

Seconds later, she asked, "What's she tossing on the tree?"

Once Peter fell onto the tracks, Willow sat upright—tense. She waited anxiously for someone to help and then cheered as Lucy jumped on the tracks. "She noticed how he smelled?"

Chad shrugged. "Just call her Cheri."

As Lucy introduced herself to a comatose Peter, Willow scooted next to Chad and pointed out the machines, asking questions under her breath. "I think that one was in my room…"

Chad pulled her closer and draped an arm around her. She curled comfortably against his side and watched as Lucy talked to a sleeping Peter. At the line, *Have you ever been so alone you spent your night confusing a man in a coma?* Willow sighed. "No, but I could," she whispered.

"I don't plan on being in any comas any time soon," Chad reassured her.

Willow glanced up at him, smiling into his eyes. "They remind me of your family," and seconds later, "Jack reminds me of you."

"He drives a truck. Smart guy."

Willow hated Peter's apartment. "It's almost as bare as Bill's.

"Bill's apartment looks like that?"

"Nah," she corrected. It's just empty like that—more empty really. He has wood and black and some red on the walls. It's boring."

As the story unfolded, Willow's agitation grew. "Why doesn't Saul tell them? This is cruel. And Jack! They obviously care about each other—"

"Mary mashed the potatoes. Everyone, compliment Mary so mom can stop feeling guilty," Chad quipped.

"What's the deal about the mistletoe? Why do people do that anyway?"

He shrugged. "I don't know. It's tradition. Started in

229

England or Europe—one of those 'E' places. Mom puts up a new sprig every day from Black Friday through New Year's Eve. By New Year's Day, there isn't a safe spot in the house!"

"Safe spot?"

Blushing, Chad nodded. "House rules. If two people pass under mistletoe, you *have* to kiss. Period."

"So this is a problem why?"

"The last thing a teenaged boy wants to do is kiss his big brother or little sister. It was mortifying."

A mischievous glint entered Willow's eye as she looked up into his face. "Then you should have brought home more girlfriends. *Someone* told me that people like kissing in the right scenario…"

"You're bad, Willow. You are very bad," he murmured. "Watch the movie."

Chad choked back laugher, failing miserably, through the scene where Peter and Ashley discuss her returning his "gifts." Willow, jaw connecting with her knees, sat up straight and gawked at the screen. "Did she just really grab her chest and claim Peter bought it! Do they do transplants for those too now?"

"No, implants." Between chuckles, Chad gave her a brief explanation of implants, prompting Willow to grabbed the remote.

"Ok, make it go back. You did that before, go back."

Barely containing his laughter, Chad whizzed the screen back and Ashley's voice pierced the room again. *"You gave me these too!"*

"Stop it!"

Chad backed up to the scene and froze the screen. Willow stared. Finally, disgusted, she reached and punched the play button. "That man is either a cheapskate, she was concave, or that doctor gypped them."

Willow stared as Chad doubled over in laughter, wiping tears from his eyes. Several awkward seconds passed until Chad said, "What?"

"I can see the movie in your eyes. That is so weird."

His hand reached for her chin and gently turned it to the

230

TV. "It's more enjoyable on the screen."

Without another word, Willow grabbed a couch pillow, laid it next to him, schooched down, and tried to lie down, but she didn't fit. She sat up to try the other side, but Chad took the pillow, laid it on his lap, and moved as far to the left as he could.

Hours later, Christopher found them asleep—Chad sitting awkwardly with one arm over her shoulder and Willow asleep, her head on a pillow in his lap. The opening music played repeatedly as the DVD player waited for someone to choose between "play" and "special features."

Christopher tapped his son's shoulder. "You'll sleep better if you go to bed."

Groggy, Chad blinked several times, trying to clear the mixed messages in his brain. "Did you really just say—"

This time, Christopher shook his son's shoulder gently. "Wake, up son. Go to bed. She'll be fine here. I'll leave a note on the fridge so your mom doesn't wake her up."

Chad slipped from under Willow's head and followed his father from the den. "Hey, Dad, know that part in *While You Were Sleeping*, when Ashley offers her breasts back?"

"Yeah..." Christopher hedged.

"Willow said that they got gypped."

Laughing, Christopher clapped an arm over his son's shoulder. "That girl is going to fit right in with this family."

"We're not getting married, Dad."

"Sure you are; you just haven't accepted the inevitable."

CHAPTER 60

It was a calculated risk but a risk nonetheless. Steve Solari observed, with apparent indifference, as his wife redecorated their Christmas tree for the third time this year. Every day a new catalog arrived with a better idea than the last, leaving her frantic to recreate it in her own home. This particular option was hideous.

"What do you think, Steve?"

The tone in her voice indicated that she wasn't sure. If he didn't give an Oscar winning performance, she'd start all over in the morning. "Wow!" He craned his neck as if unable not to stare. "Best one you've done yet. Not tacky with the stupid red and green everywhere.. I think your decorating talent gets better every year.

Lynne preened a bit as she stood back to better admire the tree. "I wasn't sure about the black and silver, but I think it works."

"What it needs is one of those crystal encrusted huge stars as a focal point." He knew she'd love the idea, and it'd take her a good week to find something like that. He'd buy up everything in town if it meant she'd keep looking. He'd never be frustrated at her lack of computer literacy again.

"Oh! I have one of those upstairs! I'll go get it right now!"

"First I need to talk to you about something. Come here."

"I just—"

Steven reserved a tone for the rare occasions when he

didn't have the patience to cajole. "No. Now."

She sat across from him. "What's wrong?"

"Come here. I'm not ticked, but I have... difficult news." His affection for his wife, while less than effusive, was genuine, and he didn't care to hurt her. Even his occasional infidelities over the years had never reached her ears. He ensured it.

"Steve?" The trepidation in her tone almost stopped him. Almost.

Wrapping his arm around her, he pulled a copy of the article on Willow from his pocket. "Remember this?"

"Yeah..."

"This girl, Willow Finley. Steve knew her mother. Well— he didn't know her well, but he went out with her once."

"How do you know?"

He hesitated. All of the doubts that he'd stamped down flooded his mind again. If he chose the wrong approach, it'd fail. However, if Willow was going to be a part of their lives, he had to be honest or it'd backfire. "Steve came to me about twenty-four years ago and confessed he'd been out with a girl and got drunk."

"Well, Steve didn't hold his liquor very well—" she began.

"This time it held him. He was rough with her, and she could have pressed charges."

His wife's wide horrified eyes cut him to the heart. Had Steve been alive, beating him for hurting Lynne would have been immensely satisfying. Everything hinged on where Lynne's sympathies fell.

"She didn't press charges, but I felt obligated to try to make it up to her in some way—however inadequate."

"That's not the kind of thing you can—" She paused and then gasped. "Are you trying to tell me that this Willow Finley is Steve's daughter?"

"Willow Finley is Steve's daughter. I checked it out; I met with the girl, and yes. She is his daughter."

"You met with her?" Her eyes clouded with confusion and then anger. "Why didn't you tell me? Didn't it occur to you that I might want to meet my only grandchild?"

"I didn't make the appointment with her. She came to me."

234

Lynne's eyes narrowed. "To demand more money. That's what you're trying to say, isn't it? Our granddaughter is a gold digger."

"Quite the reverse. When I discovered that my suspicions were correct, I immediately sent a check to cover her expenses to date. I'd given her mother money years ago." He saw distrust in Lynne's eyes and scrambled for anything to drag her loyalty to the Finley side. "Honestly, I think the only reason she cashed the check was because she found out she was pregnant. At the time, I thought she would keep the check to share with the police. I was ready to have it recovered if necessary."

"Willow returned the second check?"

"Yes. She said she'd lived off of our support her entire life and she didn't want any more. I respected her for it. She's a lovely girl — not beautiful, but she is attractive."

"They lived for years off of the money you gave them? How much did you give them?" Lynne demanded.

Steve took a deep breath, exhaled, and answered in the calmest voice he could muster. "A million dollars."

His wife jumped to her feet ranting and pacing wildly. "Steve got drunk one night, got a 'little' rough with some tramp, and you paid out a million dollars to keep her quiet! I don't think so. He raped her didn't he?"

"Lynne, he was drunk —"

"He was a pig! My own son —" She paused mid-sentence. "You saw her?"

"Yes."

"When? How soon after — when?"

"Two days later."

She sank onto his lap, dropping he face in his shoulder and weeping. "He hurt her badly didn't he? You wouldn't have given that kind of money if she wasn't visibly —"

"Battered, Lynne. You don't want to know. Trust me."

"How did he get to be so evil?" The tears he expected finally materialized.

Steve held his wife and wept with her. All the hopes, dreams, and plans he'd made for his son had vanished in the thrust of a knife over designer drugs. "We did our best. He just needed something we couldn't give."

"Makes you understand why people become religious. Maybe all that faith stuff really does make people behave better."

Bile rose in his throat just at the thought. "I'm not sure about that. Those religious nuts don't allow wine even though Jesus made it, sex, even though Jesus invented it, or dancing even though the 'man after God's own heart' danced. I think they're a bunch of hypocrites blaming the devil for their own devilish behavior. At least we're honest about ourselves."

"I want to meet her."

He had to tread extremely carefully or Lynne would never agree to his plan. "She doesn't want to meet us. You can't blame her, really. Her mother was treated terribly by our son, and I obviously insulted her trying to make up for twenty years of neglect."

"That's true. Maybe if I wrote her a letter. Maybe coming from a woman—"

"I doubt she'd read it, but I do have an idea. You'd have to be a little deceptive but—"

Her eyes narrowed. "What do you mean?"

"Well, I think if she could meet you—without knowing she was going to, it might make a difference. You could drive out that way, park at her gate, undo several wires under your hood, and walk to her door to use her phone."

"Why not use my cell phone?"

He sighed. She was so literal sometimes. "You'll let the battery run down before you leave."

"But I have the charger—"

"Leave it home then!" he protested. "Look Lynne, she's a simple girl in a lot of ways." He saw that it wasn't going to work. He needed another approach and he had the perfect one, using the simple but effective method of telling partial truth to perpetuate a lie. "She's intelligent, but from the sound of that article and my research, they don't even have electricity! You go out there, mess with the wires, tell her what happened—you heard a noise and tried to stop it and now you don't know what goes where again, and can she call for help?"

236

"So when she finds out who I am—"

"I'd be honest with her. I'd go right up to her door and say, 'I didn't mean to do this— I just wanted to see where you lived, but then my car started making noises so I tried to fix it— and now I think I messed something up. I'm really sorry."

"You think it'll work?"

Steven kissed his wife's temple. "Of course it'll work. Who could resist a woman like you? She has no family. Everyone needs family."

David watched his wife behind his issue of Time. She'd been agitated all evening. Either the meeting went extremely well and she was nervous about admitting it in the face of his previous antagonism, or it had gone terribly wrong. Perhaps his granddaughter wasn't a likeable person. He had to know but didn't care to ask.

"Dave—"

"Carol—"

She smiled at her husband and reached into the closet pulling out a large gift bag. As Carol handed it to him, Dave teased, "But Christmas is still two weeks away."

"It's from Willow."

Reluctantly, David pulled the snowy white afghan from the bag and shook it out around him. "It reminds me of that one you wanted years ago. I've looked for one now and then but never found it."

"Kari remembered it and made it."

"Kari made this," he exclaimed surprised. "She hated crafty things."

"Apparently she became excellent at all things crafty. Look in the bag."

David withdrew the spiraled journal and his eyes widened at the cover. As he glanced through the pages, he realized that it was a facsimile copy and that Kari had indeed become very artistic. A few words caught his attention. "... *Labor was horrible.*" He read aloud. "*I will never have another child. I won't*

237

marry, and I won't ever allow myself to be vulnerable to a man again. Childbirth is truly the curse that God promised."

Choked, he dropped the journal and pulled his wife into his arms. Tears flowed as all the years of loss and heartache flooded back into their hearts, reopening every wound caused by Kari's disappearance. "Do you feel it?" she whispered.

"Yeah."

"That's what my meeting was like."

"Oh, Carol. I should have gone."

She shook her head violently. "No. You would have reacted against her, and it wasn't her fault. She didn't do this to us."

His jaw clenched as David tried to decide if he should voice the concerns that strangled his heart. "Is it wise to bring her into our lives?" At the look on his wife's face, he tried another tactic. "What if we hurt her in the process?"

Carol moved to her favorite chair, sat across from David, and took a deep breath. "I told her I'd talk to you about going to visit her farm after the first of the year."

"And you think that is a good idea?"

"I don't know," she whispered. "I want to say yes. I want to swallow my pain and pride and throw myself into Willow's life until it no longer hurts, but I don't know if I can. She seems pleasant enough — she bought lunch."

"Oh you shouldn't have let her. We don't know how she's set financially."

"She's sitting pretty from what I gathered. Solari obviously paid off Kari and well."

"I'd love to give that man a piece of my mind."

He saw the hesitation in her eyes and it cut him. They'd never kept secrets from one another, but he could see it, hovering beneath the surface. She didn't want to tell him something. "Kari thought that Solari threatened her and subsequently the child. She left and didn't tell us because she thought if Solari knew about Willow, their lives, and probably ours I would imagine, would be in danger."

"Oh, Carol…"

"I know."

CHAPTER 61

February 2002-

Well, the Lord had the last laugh. I kept my end of the bargain. I reared my daughter in the nurture and instruction of the Lord. She's strong mentally, emotionally, and spiritually. I truly believe she'll stand firm in the face of any adversity.

And, the Lord honored my exact request. Willow is not short. At five foot five and a half, no one would call her tall, but she's definitely not short. She's not squatty. She is long, lean, and, well, willowy. However, whether as a reminder of His sovereignty or because He has a ~~wicked~~ (I can't say that about the Lord!) DIVINE sense of humor, He blessed her with a bra size I cannot comprehend. It must be in double or triple D's... or maybe G's. On a taller or larger boned woman, it wouldn't look quite as disproportionate, but on Willow, there is no doubt that she has what Kyle used to call, "a rack."

We spent all week designing and constructing a bra that'll be comfortable and support the weight. It took a lot of work, but it worked, and now she has comfortable garments that help support the girls. I tried naming them Babs and Frieda, but somehow Willow didn't see the humor. She's working on a new bra out of diaper flannel now. If it works, I want one for me. It's the softest thing I've ever felt.

On the positive side, living out here means she doesn't live with constant ogling and comments. I'm very glad I made a point to learn to sew. That first dress I made her — oh, that thing was ugly. Why did I think that I needed to dress her like a street urchin from the turn of the twentieth century? The Amish influence was hard to overcome. One of these days, I need to dig it out and show her. She'll get a kick *out of my huge stitches that tore every time she wore it. I mended that dress more than all of her other clothes combined. Times ten.*

Willow read the entry, grinning at the memory. Those days of standing before the mirror, trying a hundred ways to create a bra that was both comfortable, fit her shape, and provided adequate support, were some of the most hilarious of her life.

Her mother had found great delight in teasing her daughter about the size of her chest. "Should have given some to Ashley," she muttered to herself.

The memory of her mother trying on her bras, filling them with stuffing, was one she'd never forget. With a T-shirt pulled tight over the results, Kari had given a killer Dolly Parton imitation—at least that's what she had assured Willow. She hummed "Coat of Many Colors," remembering Mother singing it until she had memorized the words that week. She set the journals aside and muttered, "If I share mother's journals, that entry is coming out. I have some pride."

A glance at the clock told her it was time to put away her mess. Aggie would be there soon to discuss dresses for the wedding. A noise outside startled her and she jumped. Somehow, the large van had arrived without a bark from Saige. "Must be a quiet vehicle," she muttered.

Children tumbled from the van, running helter-skelter. Willow grabbed her coat and hurried to meet them. As she approached, Aggie lined her "troops" up in front of the porch and turned to Willow. "Can you give them the boundaries? Cans and can'ts and all that?"

Nodding, Willow led the children to the barn. "You can come in and visit the animals, but you cannot go in the loft if you can't touch the—" her eyes slid up the ladder, "—eighth rung." A glint in one of the twins' eyes—she suspected Cari— prompted her to add, "Without standing on something."

Tavish immediately reached and stretched just barely to the eighth. "Ok, so me and up can go but anyone shorter than me is out."

"Right," Willow agreed. "Now, out here," she began as she

led the children to the yard. "Don't go in the chicken yard. Period. I don't care if a chicken hawk eats every chicken in sight, do not open the gate." *How very like mother you sound,* she thought to herself.

Aggie looked sharply at the twins. "Did you hear that? What did she say?"

"No chickies. Not at all," Lorna echoed wisely.

A glimmer in Cari's eye seemed to prompt Aggie to say, "And if I see you even touch the fence, you'll come inside and sit on the floor with your hands in your lap. Do you understand me?"

"Yeth, Aunt Aggie," Cari whined.

Willow, anxious to avoid what looked like an impending tantrum, continued speaking. "Other than that, if you can't see the house, you've gone too far. Turn around. If you see water, come back."

Dismissed, the children dashed in several different directions, and Willow noted that Tavish pulled a book from beneath his coat as he took off for the barn. She would like that kid. Willow led Aggie inside and made her a cup of hot tea, serving her a cherry-almond bar on the side. "So, what did you have in mind?"

Aggie excused herself and hurried to the, van returning with two large plastic shopping bags. From within, she pulled the palest pastel chiffon and peach skin in several colors. "I bought both the white chiffon to go over the pastel and the pastel chiffon. I didn't know which looked best."

"And a style?"

"I was thinking something like the Shipoopie outfits at the end of *The Music Man.*"

Willow's blank expression sent Aggie into a frenzy of explanation, but she still didn't understand. "It's a movie right?"

"Yeah—"

"I'll get Chad to bring it to me and we can watch it. Meanwhile, why don't you bring the oldest inside and keep the boys out until we get her bodice constructed. I'll make the dress to fit the bodices once I know what it should look like."

Skepticism hovered in Aggie's expression, but Willow smiled. "Trust me. You'll see."

As they worked, Willow and Aggie forged a somewhat tentative friendship. Willow told amusing stories of her childhood on the farm, and Aggie told even funnier ones of her children and their escapades. By the time she finished with the dress mock-ups, Willow felt comfortable asking a few more personal questions.

"How long have you known Luke?"

"Since the end of May or first of June—somewhere in there."

"Wow, that's fast. Do you mind me asking why you decided to marry?"

Aggie sat in Willow's kitchen rocking chair, held her tea warming her hands, and observed as Willow added wood to the stove, put a chicken in the oven, all as she talked. "It was fast I guess but it didn't feel fast. When you see someone almost all day every day for months, it makes you feel like you've known them all your life somehow."

"I know what you mean, and I haven't seen Chad nearly that much. I thought it was because we'd worked together so much. It's like I woke up one day, found Mother dead, but she gave me a brother that I never knew and have always known at the same time."

Smiling, Aggie handed Willow her empty cup. "Maybe it's just the Sullivan men."

"Sullivan...Tesdall—not sure who, but there are similarities to them aren't there?"

"So did you mean you wanted to know why I want to get married or why I want to marry Luke?"

Her relief relaxed her, erasing the concerns that she might offend Aggie with her question. "Well, I think why you'd want to marry Luke is obvious. He's a good man, and if you want to marry, a good man is a wise choice. I just see someone my age—almost to the day—and I wonder why you want to marry. What about marriage appeals to you?"

"I've never thought of it that way. Most girls want to marry. My friends dreamed about husbands and weddings

242

from the time they were little. I didn't as much as some, but even I knew what kind of wedding I wanted someday."

"Are men like that too? Do they dream of marriage and wives and their wedding days?" Willow nearly whispered the question.

"Why do you ask?" When Willow didn't answer, Aggie continued. "I don't know, I've never been a guy, but I'm pretty sure most don't dream of their wedding day—wedding *night* maybe but not their wedding." The attempt at a joke, as much as Willow appreciated it as an attempt, failed. "I think most guys probably grow up expecting it, but I don't know that they spend as much time dreaming of it that women do."

"I just don't understand. At first, I thought Mother's experience warped her perceptions about things like men and marriage, but she had nineteen years or so with her parents. She loved her father. You'd think—"

"I've never been through what your mother went through, and maybe I'm being a bit naïve, but I think there was more to her rejection of men than marriage. She was violated in the worst way and Luke mentioned something about her giving birth here all alone."

"She was. It was raining and she was afraid to walk to town for help, so she stayed alone." Almost as an afterthought, Willow added, "She was so scared."

"I'm not sure that your mother was anti-marriage as much as she'd been so deeply scarred by a man. Physically she endured the attack and labor after it. She had no support—no one to tell her she wasn't crazy when she wanted to kill or maim, and no one to encourage her. Labor alone is so intense— my sister used to say she couldn't make it through labor without her husband."

"I like watching Chad's parents. They remind me of this couple I saw in a restaurant right after Mother died. They didn't talk much, but their actions—so harmonious. The Tesdalls are like that."

Aggie smiled. "I know the whole family hopes you guys will get married."

A visible shudder washed over Willow. "I hope they keep

those opinions to themselves. Chad and I have a wonderful friendship, and I don't want to lose it because all the pressure makes him think he's giving people the wrong idea." She pulled out her sketchpad and began doodling. "He's paranoid enough about that."

The phone rang. Instead of the normal ring tone, it played "Carol of the Bells," making Willow grin. "Chad! What did you do to my phone?"

"I thought you needed some holiday cheer. I've got more too."

"What?" With less two weeks until Christmas, Willow was frantically trying to slow down time to enjoy every moment.

"Tonight instead of prayer meeting, a bunch of us are going caroling. I get off in..." Chad checked his watch. "Forty minutes. I could come out, get that loom for Luke to help me with, you could feed me, we could go caroling and have hot chocolate with everyone..."

"I have venison stew on the stove," she warned.

"I like venison."

Her laughter filled the kitchen. "That's not what your mother says."

"That's because I never wanted her to know that it's her venison that I don't like. Aunt Libby's though..."

"See you soon. Someone's walking up the lane. How strange."

The festive look of the old farmhouse surprised Lynne. The peeling paint, half-missing roof, and cardboard over windows that she had imagined never materialized. Evergreen boughs swaged along a porch raining, wreaths hung inside dormer windows on the top floor, and candles flickered in the front picture window—a window that looked as if it had been cleaned only minutes earlier. The article had produced a mental image of a run down, dirty place. Goats, chickens, cows, sheep, gardens—it all sounded terribly rustic to her city sensibilities. She expected dirt and horrible smells, but at least the house and barn looked nice enough.

The front door opened as she neared the house. A young woman stepped onto the porch, closing the door behind her and stuffing her hands in her pockets. Willow Finley—it had to be. There was a slight resemblance even. Maybe Steve was right. If she played the part well, she could make this work.

Before she could rehearse her script, the woman called out to her. "Can I help you?"

Look nervous. Be apologetic. Don't let her see how hopeful you are. "I messed up my car, my cell is dead... I was hoping I could use your phone..."

Willow met her where the drive met the yard and pulled a cell phone from her jacket pocket. The young woman from the article didn't fit the mental picture of a young woman with a cell phone. "Sure. Here."

Once she gave her location to the dispatcher, Lynne returned Willow's phone, thanking her for it. "I can't believe I did this. I feel so stupid.

"What did you do?"

"I messed up my car, and of all places, in front your house."

To her surprise, Willow beckoned the woman to follow. "Come in. It's cold out here. I just need to call the police and let them know that I'm inviting in a stranger. My friend is an officer." The girl's teeth chattered as she said, "I don't usually invite strangers onto my property."

"I know. I'm sorry."

While Willow dialed her "friend," Lynne made a show of trying to ignore the conversation. It didn't sound as if the cop approved. Willow listened and then interrupted something saying, "—just until the car is fixed. I can't make her stay out there. It's cold."

Once the call was disconnected, Willow led her into the house. Her eyes took in the out of date furniture and folksy décor. The girl seemed to be really into Christmas. Fake evergreen was everywhere it could tastefully be draped. Somehow, she managed not to overdo it, but to Lynne's eyes, she danced awfully close to the line.

The sparsely decorated kitchen had inadequate cupboard space and a shocking lack of granite. Willow put a teakettle on the stove and added a stick of wood. Lynne's eyes bugged out as she watched the process. Woodstove for cooking and presumably heating — what kind of life was this? Was this how they still managed to have money left after all these years?

Willow mixed a cup of hot chocolate and handed it to her. "Here. Drink it. It'll warm your hands too." She turned to pour another cup saying, "Now what was that about my house? I didn't understand that."

For a flash of a second, Lynne considered claiming that she just wanted to see the girl in the article, leaving out their relationship. Her desire to know her granddaughter overrode her somewhat skewed scruples. "I drove out here to see your place — that's all. After reading that article about you and my husband told me what he knew, I just wanted to see. I didn't intend to come here — talk to you. Not like this."

"Why would you care about where I live? What do you mean, 'not like this?'"

"Like I said," she insisted, "I just wanted to see where you lived and everything — be sure you were ok." Lynne willed herself to calm down. She sounded panicked — much too emphatic in her protest. Deep breaths. "Then my car started making a weird noise. I pulled over down the road a ways. I didn't want you to see it." She ducked her eyes. "I wasn't ready to meet you."

Willow seemed surprised — uncertain. "I—"

Reckless, she plunged on again, "I just pulled over about a mile down the road and opened the hood. That's what my husband always does. It's always some loose wire or whatever, so I just pulled on them, testing them, but—"

"Excuse me, who are you and what does your broken car have anything to do with me?"

Lynne forced tears to her eyes. "Sorry, I talk a lot when I'm

246

nervous. I—my name is Lynne. I don't want to make trouble—really. I just wanted to see where you live. Her eyes roamed the room, lingering on the hutch. "You have a nice place here. I'm glad. I pictured you living in—well, I'm glad."

The girl's confusion gave way to irritation. Before Lynne could find a way to distract her, Willow said, "Why should you care?"

She set her cup down and rezipped her jacket. "I'll go. I didn't mean to meet you—to come. Steve said I shouldn't come out here and I didn't listen. I've ruined everything." She couldn't have timed the tear that fell down her cheeks better if she tried—and she did. Her heart sank as she saw suspicion on Willow's face.

"What is your last name?"

She inched toward the dining room. "My name is Solari—Lynne Solari. I just found out who you are the other day." As she pulled it open, she added, her voice choking, "My son—I am so sorry about Stevie."

As the woman rushed from her house, Willow stood frozen in the kitchen, wondering what she should do. Chad's cruiser tires crunched on the drive, soothing her agitated nerves. Chad would know what to do.

He burst through the door looking as if he expected to find someone dead on the floor. "Wha—where—why—"

"She left."

"I saw. Why is she crying?"

"Maybe she feels bad."

"Is there a reason she should?" He stepped into the dining room to watch the woman.

"Her son is—was—Mother's—her son—she is Lynne Solari, Steve's mother."

"And she came here expecting you to welcome her? What kind of nonsense is that?" Livid, he stormed across the house, ready to confront the woman.

Willow stopped him. "No, she says she just wanted to see where I lived—see the place—and her car broke down." She frowned. "I don't believe her, though. I think she wanted to meet me and made sure I couldn't refuse."

"Despicable."

"Perhaps," she said, "but I think it's also understandable. Her only child is dead, her only grandchild has every reason to avoid her, so she makes up an excuse. Wrong, but hardly nefarious."

"So why did you kick her out?"

"I didn't. She just left. Kind of surprised me. I mean, why would you go to all that trouble and then just leave?"

He stared out the window before asking, "Mind if I call her back. I know Fairbury tow service. It takes an hour this time of year."

"Sure. I'll make you some hot chocolate."

Chad left and returned with Lynne a few minutes later. The woman's tears flowed freely and her words made no sense. Exasperated, Willow mouthed a desperate request for him to "do something."

"Mrs. Solari—"

Sniffling, the woman shook her head. "Lynne. No one calls me missus except Steve's office manager. She only does it to make me sound old."

"So you wanted to meet Willow…"

"I didn't know if I did or not, but I wanted to see where she lived," the woman corrected.

"That's not true, and we both know it. You wanted to meet me and found a way to do it—probably with your husband's help."

"I didn't—"

Willow closed her eyes, took a deep breath, and tried again. "Mrs. Solari… I have never owned or driven a car, so I don't really know how they work. But basic common sense says you don't pull a bunch of wires out of their place simply because you wonder if one is lose enough to make the car not work." Before Lynne could protest, Willow continued. "Someone as obviously wealthy as you are would have one of those little car charger things like Chad does for his phone, so I don't buy the dead phone story."

"I forgot it."

"Where?"

Lynne shrugged. "Kitchen counter—maybe the mudroom. I don't know."

Sighing, Willow stood, grabbed Chad's chocolate mug, and refilled it. "If you'd said it was another car, I might have believed you, but it doesn't make sense to remove a car charger from a car if you're not putting it in another one."

Lynne Solari started to protest again but broke down and told the entire story. She confessed her husband's plan, their grief over their son's behavior, and the eagerness she'd felt when she realized that there was a grandchild. "Of course, I knew you wouldn't want to meet me. Who would? But I'm not Stevie. I didn't hurt your mother. I couldn't believe it when Steve told me—"

"Now that's hard to believe, Mrs. Solari," Chad protested. "A son like that, murdered in a drug deal, several civil cases against him—"

"I know. Most of it, they kept from me, but I'm not as dumb as they think I am. I just didn't know it was that bad. I knew he was into drugs and he was a bit of a womanizer, but I never imagined—" She looked sick just thinking of it. "I would have thrown him out of the house if I knew he was capable of that."

Chad's cell phone rang. He answered, listened for a moment, and disconnected. "Wade is over at your car. I'll drive you to him."

Lynne glanced back at Willow as she turned to leave the room. "I hope someday you'll forgive us. I'd like to be friends at least. You're nice. You knew I lied and deceived you, but you were still nice. Thank you."

At the door, Willow paused before she opened it. "I can't say it'll ever happen, but if I get comfortable with the idea of getting to know you, I know how to contact your husband." She waited for Lynne's teary eyes to meet hers before she added, "If you don't hear from me, I'd rather not hear from you."

"That's reasonable. Thanks. I think you must have had a wonderful mother. I wish I could have known her."

An unmistakable coolness entered Willow's voice. "That would never have been possible."

Lynne stared at the door, shocked, as it closed in her face. She glanced at Chad. "Wow."

With a grim smile, Chad led her down the steps to his cruiser. "That's the general consensus when people meet her. Inevitably they say, 'wow.'" He cleared his throat. "Mrs. Solari—"

"Lynne—"

With stronger emphasis, Chad tried again. "Mrs. Solari, I have to warn you. If you try to contact Willow without first hearing from her, I will help her file and will personally enforce a restraining order. Don't put her through it."

"I won't. I know," she began sounding resigned to a fate worse than a hangnail, "I know I seem like a pampered and spoiled woman who expects that she can have anything she wants if her husband is willing to buy it. I know that. But if there is one thing I've learned, it's that you can buy people, but you cannot buy relationships."

Chad let her out next to her car. "I'll be praying for you, Mrs. Solari. I'm very sorry for your losses. All of them."

CHAPTER 62

Willow sat curled on the couch stitching something. Fabric pieces littered the living room, sketches covered the coffee table, and small pieces of fabric sat in little straight rows waiting to be reassembled into Willow's chosen pattern. Chad had helped carry the fabric down from the craft room and chuckled at the chagrin she still showed when she remembered how she'd ordered so much, especially considering that she didn't know what she'd do with it.

"I guess I'll go get that loom and take a look at it," he commented but Willow didn't hear or acknowledge if he did.

Halfway up the stairs, Willow stopped him. "Chad, what do you wear caroling?"

"Warm clothes. Several layers. Very warm clothes. Gloves. And a warm jacket with warm—"

"I get it. No miniskirts or halter tops."

In the attic, Chad saw the drapes of plastic over everything and smiled. She'd used it, even when she was mad at him. One shelf along a wall under a window held an array of toys. Ignoring the side of the attic where Willow said the loom was, he pulled the plastic away from the shelf and smiled. It was a glimpse of her childhood. An old View Master sat next to a lidded decoupaged box of disks. He passed it up and unrolled Raggedy Ann from her tissue wrapping and then found her pal Andy in another package.

Roller skates surprised him. They were the older quad

style, but from the looks of them, very worn. There was nowhere to skate except for awkward turns in the barn. Surely, Kari wouldn't let Willow skate along the highway. Another thought occurred to him so he folded back the patchwork of area rugs, shaking his head at the sight before him. Both an oval and a straight line marked the floor. She'd skated in the attic on cold winter days.

The cold urged him to hurry with his errand and get out of there, so Chad put everything but the View Master disks back as he found them and went in search of the box of loom pieces. While Willow hand pieced geometric shapes of fabric together into one beautiful piece, Chad lumbered downstairs carrying the box. "It doesn't look too bad really. I don't know what they're supposed to look like, but to me, it looks like only one piece is actually broken—the rest just kind of came apart when that piece broke."

"That sounds like what Mother thought, but she was too upset to look at it."

Chad carried the box out to his truck, wrapped a tarp over it, and anchored it snugly against the cab. A glance at his watch told him they had an hour before time to milk, and the last thing he wanted to do was watch Willow sew fabric pieces together. If he just sat there, she'd want him to read. Maybe if he got a book and started reading before she noticed...

However, the sight of a lumpy looking Mary on a donkey with Joseph leading the way killed all attempts at sneaking a book. "Why are Joseph and Mary stuck in the library?"

"They're riding to the stable. They started on the landing and work their way down every day."

"Hmm makes sense. Hey, does your mom have a book on looms in here?"

Her voice trailed absently from the couch. "Upstairs. Craft room on the top shelf to the right."

Chad chose to ignore that not only did she know where it was but on exactly what shelf and what side of the shelf. Thirty minutes later, he stretched and waved the book at Willow. "Mind if I take this home so I can look at the pictures while I'm working?"

"Sure."

The clock ticked for several minutes before the silence drove him to speech. No wonder Willow felt smothered alone at night. "You know, I remember when I used to dread coming out here."

"I can too."

"What? No, I mean at first, I didn't really want to come out here. I was a bit perturbed with the Lord for 'making me' be a friend. I thought you were going to be so needy—" he explained.

"I know."

Chad remembered a conversation. "You called me on it that first night."

"Yes."

"But unfortunately, I felt that way for a long time."

"Until sometime around when you put in Mother's headstone. I've seen glimmers since then, but they're not the same."

Stammering, Chad confronted her. "If you knew—I mean, that first night you were irritated."

"That first night, you were a stranger, and I felt patronized. Now I know it's just a part of your character to deny yourself to serve someone else."

"Well," he retorted, "You thought I was clingy at first."

"You were. You were so sure I couldn't make it alone. I had a few bad days, and you decided I wasn't able to function without you."

Their playful banter continued through the afternoon, through dinner, and even down the stairs as Willow dressed. Remembering his admonition for lots of layers, Willow rummaged through her drawers and pulled on every article of clothing she could squeeze on. Then, remembering her mother's clothes were a little larger, she slid her mother's closet door open and pulled out a few pairs of overalls and a pair of her coveralls. She added all she could and then layered her mother's sweaters. The scent of Kari lingered just enough to taunt her with her loss. Blinking back tears, Willow ran a quick brush through her hair and tried to hurry downstairs. She nearly broke her neck waddling.

"There, think I'll be warm enough?"

Chad turned from loading the stove and shook his head laughing. "Only you—"

"You said—" she protested unbuttoning two cardigans, peeling off four sweaters, and stepping out of the coveralls. "I'm not even down to *my* clothes yet."

"If you hurry, we can go up and down a few of the best streets and see Christmas lights first."

Waddling stiff-legged up the steps, Willow pulled sweaters off as she climbed. He heard thumps and bangs as she tried to put everything away quickly. "Willow, just put them away when you get home!"

"Great idea" she fired back and shuffled downstairs carrying a couple of sweaters, three pairs of socks, and a pair of flannel lined coveralls. "Just how cold is cold? Flannel lined jeans, thermal unders and a sweater? Add another sweater? Cardigan too? How many pairs of socks? Oh, and should I bring these just in case?" she added waving the coveralls in his face.

"Wear your sweater and your coat. Bring a cardigan in case we go inside, you can warm up slowly. Gloves and hat. Double socks."

She pulled her boots on over her doubled socks and promptly pulled off the second pair. "They're warm enough. This'll drive me crazy. I have hot feet."

"Maybe we can share. You take one of my icy ones and I'll take one of your hot feet."

She grinned, tying on her boot again. "I remember when I was nine. I had a nightmare and crawled into bed with Mother. She put her icy feet on me, and I jumped right back out of bed. I thought the nightmare was better than her feet." As an afterthought she added, "She snored too."

"We'd better never get stranded together in an Alaskan avalanche."

"Why?" The thought progression escaped her mental bridges.

"I snore and have cold feet. We'd both freeze to death in

254

our individualized snowdrifts."

"Your feet would be covered by shoes, and I think imminent death might tempt me to stay a little closer—even if you did snore."

"I'll hold you to that if we're ever caught in an Alaskan avalanche."

Willow winked as she whipped her ruana around her shoulders and over her coat. "I'll even agree to a Swiss avalanche too."

"You're too kind.

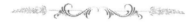

"Oh! That one is amazing! All of those blue lights on a white house—" Entranced, Willow begged him to slow down.

"But the pink bow on the door? What was with that?"

"Maybe they didn't want it to look like Independence Day with a red, white, and blue house!"

"I guess. Oh, I just remembered a house over on Larkspur. It drives the Chief crazy. They've got enough lights to rival the Las Vegas strip."

As he turned onto Larkspur, Chad pointed out the Chief's house and then Bentley's. "I like what they've done with their lawn. From what I hear, it was bare for years but Greg's the landscaping guy—" He stopped talking when Willow erupted into a fit of giggles.

"Oh my. There's no rhyme or reason to those lights! They're just encrusted on that house! Why—"

"The Chief says that they let their kids do it. All. They bought out all of the lights from the feed and seed and then the mom went to Ferndale and seriously depleted Wal-Mart's stock."

"Oh it's just ugly."

"Roll down the window."

Jingle Bell Rock assaulted her ears until she managed to roll the window back up again. "Oh my. Isn't it against some law…"

"They turn off the music every night at nine o'clock sharp

255

and the lights at eleven. There's not much he can do unless he wants to make people antagonistic to all of us."

Willow gave the house one last horrified glance and begged him to take her somewhere else. She watched as he considered her request and then put his truck in gear and drove back down the street. "There's this house down the road from Alexa with lots of lights and music. You've got to see the difference."

"Oh Chad no!"

"Seriously, you'll love it. I promise."

She glanced at the truck dashboard. "Isn't it time to go to the church?"

"We've got half an hour, you nut!" He teased. His hand found hers and gave it a quick squeeze. "You've got to learn to trust me."

"Well after you took me to that—"

They drove past Alexa's house. "She did a Victorian Christmas theme this year. Every year she does something else."

"Different every year? That would be fun, but so much work." Her mind raced with the possibilities. "I wonder if I could do one of those little trees somewhere—change it every year. It wouldn't be so much work that way. What kinds of trees does she do?"

"I heard she was looking for someone to make her origami stars and doves and other Christmas ornaments, but she didn't find them in time. I guess she's trying for a rainbow Christmas next time."

"I'll have to remember that and make her some."

"Do you know how?"

Willow shrugged. "I'd probably have to pull out the book to remember, but yeah... I know the basics."

The house Chad wanted to show her sat at what appeared to be the end of a street with a sharp curve at the end. One house, covered in white lights, blinked in strange patterns. "Roll down your window again," Chad urged.

From the yard, a recording, not obnoxiously loud but loud enough to recognize, played "The Dance of the Sugar Plum

Fairy" as the lights blinked on and off with the notes. "The children from that other street were trying to copy this?"

"Probably. Poor guys."

"Next year, you should keep a lookout, and when you see them out there, walk by and see if you can get them to invite you to help. You might be able to influence a nicer look."

Chad shook his head. "That's Joe's department. He's the one with the mission to save the kids. I'm just a cop."

Willow tore her eyes from the beautiful sight and met Chad's gaze, disappointed. "I thought you were passionate about law enforcement."

"I am."

"Then you'd better consider that preventative maintenance might be a good idea."

"Time to carol," Chad muttered and whipped around the corner, retracing the roads to the church. "They need to fill the flatbed with hay anyway."

At the church, Chad and the men piled straw bales around the edge of the feed and seed's flatbed, broke open a couple to pad the bed, and mounted two battery powered lanterns on garden hooks that they plunged deep into straw bales. Willow watched, excited, as she realized that this was the modern equivalent of a hayride. For a moment, she felt a little Anne Shirleyish, but instead of enduring a "lifelong sorrow," she would soon fulfill a lifelong dream.

At the sight of Alexa Hartfield, Willow nudged Chad, stood on tiptoe and whispered, "Please tell me she isn't singing."

Chad choked back a laugh and shook his head, tears from restrained laughing streaming down his eyes. "She brings hot chocolate and cookies for us when we get back. Shh, she's coming."

"Willow! That is a lovely ruana. I've bought several but none were exactly what I wanted. Where *did* you find that?"

"Mother made it last year. I'd offer to make you one, but my loom is broken." Alexa started to reply, but Willow continued, "Chad's fixing it, though. I don't know how long it'll take him. He's kind of busy…"

257

"Well, I—"

Assuming the woman was disappointed, Willow interrupted. "But if you tell me what color you would like, I'd love to make you one when I get the loom back."

"She says she can do origami for you next year if you still want to do that," Chad mentioned as if desperate to impart that bit of information.

The woman nudged them toward the flatbed. "Go. Sing. We'll talk later. Besides, if I stand here too long, I'll start making people nervous." With a wink at Willow's blushing cheeks, Alexa hurried away from the crowd and into the church.

Willow sighed as she pulled herself onto the truck. "She's what Mother would have called a 'very classy woman.'"

Chad helped Willow to a spot at the back of the flatbed. Most people loved the front where they could jump off and on easier, but Chad preferred to sit and sing from the truck bed. The truck rolled slowly away from the building, but not a single person vocalized anything.

"When do we sing?" Willow asked curiously."

"Pick a song, Willow!" Bentley called cheerfully.

The night erupted in song as the voices of carolers sang of a night long ago. Up and down the streets they sang, telling people everywhere of the birth of our Lord. The stars above twinkled and added their own wonder as they sang of a star followed by "three kings," and hearts were tugged far away as their voices told of hay, cattle, and a babe in a manger.

As the night air grew colder, Willow inched closer to Chad, drawing her arms up against her and surprised that she felt it so keenly. "I told you," Chad murmured into her ear drawing her closer and wrapping an arm around her. "You're used to generating heat with work. You have no body fat to help you in a situation like this."

"I wouldn't say none," Willow muttered to herself unaware that he could hear. A snort from Chad made her glare at him, daring him to say it.

His attempt at ambiguity failed. "Let's just say you have none where it'll do you any good then."

She whacked his arm with the back of her hand.

258

"Chaduck."

"Chadwick."

"No, Chad plus Chuck makes Chaduck," she growled.

"Hey, I'm not anything like him."

"Talking about a subject like—"

Chad pulled her head closer and whispered into her ear, "But you're the one who brought it up. Not me. It's more like Chillow."

Their voices erupted in laughter just as Lily Allen's voice rang out clearly, "Angels we have heard on high!"

Gary Novak took up the tune. "Wildly laughing o'er the plain!"

Chad picked up the parody. "And the carolers in reply,"

Willow carried it out, "Wonder if they are insane!"

As they burst in the front door, laughing, "That was so much fun! Thank you for taking me."

"I used to go with my family every year in Westbury, but this was so much more fun. I missed it last year—had to work."

"Want another cookie? Alexa sent me home with about fifty."

"I don't know how she expects you to eat them all," Chad mused glancing around the room. "What's wrong with this picture?"

"Candles are out."

Chad held up a finger saying, "Just a minute," and rushed back out to his truck. Bursting through the door and shaking off his coat, he held up a flame igniter. "I got this so you wouldn't keep burning your fingers."

"Mother never let me light candles," Willow mused, examining the few pinkish spots on her fingers. "Not if she could help it. I'm really bad at it."

Chad demonstrated proper lighting technique until she mastered it. Once the room was aglow in candlelight, they removed their shoes, sat them near the fire, and Willow pulled on her slippers. Chad lay back in his corner of the couch,

259

covering his eyes with his hand. Slowly, he pulled it away and glanced around the room once more.

"Does anything strike you as odd?"

Willow sat up and let her eyes roam the room. She was tired and cold, but everything seemed normal enough. "Not in particular, why?"

Chad stood and slowly climbed the stairs, glancing down behind him as he went. "Where did you leave your quilt stuff?"

Willow reached down beside the couch for her basket and then looked over the edge. "That's odd. I thought I left it here. Maybe I took it upstairs with me. It's probably on my bed."

She heard him rummaging around upstairs and froze when she heard him call, "Willow, get up here!"

"What's wrong?" Willow tried taking the steps two at a time but fell. Her gimpy leg rarely bothered her, but she was obviously not ready for skipping steps.

"It's a mess up here."

"Well duh, you told me to leave it."

Willow went cold as Chad paused before asking, as she reached the top of the stairs, "Did you have your mother's papers out too?"

CHAPTER 63

Chad jerked out his phone, calling for Judith and the forensics kit. When Willow stepped into the room, he waved her back. "Don't touch anything. Go downstairs and check out the library, bookcases, and kitchen. See if you notice anything different. Try to watch where you're going."

Her voice sounded very small. "Chad, why?"

This he hadn't expected. A feisty girl like Willow should be angry, livid. She shouldn't be whimpering as though someone called her a dirty name. "You're fine. We're fine. We'll get them. Just go check the house."

He didn't notice the absent way she turned and left the room. Focused on what now felt like his job, he mentally tried to separate the things Willow had left out from the things disturbed by the intruder. Intruder. The word burned like fire in his heart. How dare someone enter her home, uninvited!

The gift bins in the spare room tugged at his heart. Her hard work now layered the floor in odd heaps. The questions followed in rapid succession. Who was it? He couldn't ignore the potential Solari connection, but it made little sense. They seemed to desire a relationship, and this was the last thing to encourage that. *Had the article prompted some kind of strange obsession? Now you're thinking like a TV drama writer,* he chided himself.

Distracted by his thoughts, he didn't hear when Judith arrived, calling out from downstairs. "Chad?"

"Up here. The mess is concentrated in Kari's room, but the spare and craft rooms were also hit." He pointed to the rooms as Judith topped the stairs. When Willow didn't appear behind him, he asked, "Where's Willow?"

"I thought she was up here with you?"

"She didn't answer the door?"

Judith shook her head. "But to be fair, I didn't really knock. Just a couple of raps and came on in. Chief is coming. He's still spooked from the Plagiarist case."

"Willow..." Chad called but heard nothing. "I bet she went to check her animals. I'll be back in a minute to help."

He thundered down the stairs, shoved his arms in his jacket pocket, and jerked open the back door. "Willow!"

Silence. Even Saige didn't run to get her ears scratched. The barn was bare, the chickens roosting, and he heard nothing that hinted at her location. He called. The wind had picked up, and it swirled around him, tossing her name through the yard and back into his own ears.

Come on, Chad! Think. Where would she go if she felt scared and violated? You aren't stupid! Where... He groaned. "Oh no! Lord, please no."

He sprinted down the driveway, his lungs complaining at the cold icy air. As he reached the post directly across from the large oak tree, he looked for Willow but saw nothing. Though his instinct was to turn back and get a flashlight—anything to help—he knew she must be at the grave. With a deep breath of a prayer, he hopped the fence and stumbled over the ground until he reached the tree. Saige bounded to his side and licked him. "Where is she girl?"

The dog whimpered and returned to the headstones. As Chad followed, he almost tripped over Willow's legs. Seeing her prostrate over the grave stirred emotions he could not afford to consider. "Hey, hey." Without hesitation, Chad pulled her into his arms and held her, rocking her and assuring her that all was well. "We'll find them. We'll protect you."

"The doors were locked," she whimpered through chattering teeth.

Chad's EMT training jumped to the forefront. He picked

her up and began carrying her across the field toward the house, but she protested. "Put me down!"

"Will you walk?"

"Yes. Why wouldn't I?"

"Why," he began patiently, "would you walk out here in the freezing cold and curl up with your mother without telling anyone where you were going?"

"Because I wanted my mother! I didn't do it because I chose to be difficult!"

"Keep up the anger," Chad encouraged. "We need it to keep you warm. You've been chilled twice tonight."

"I know the symptoms of hypothermia, and I'm not even close, Chad."

They burst into the kitchen, startling Judith and just seconds before the headlights from the Chief's car approached. "She's fine. Just out for a midnight stroll in the lack of moonlight."

Chief Varney knocked confidently and opened the door. "Miss Finley? May I come in?"

The three officers went upstairs, but Judith returned seconds later, calling for electricity. "We can't see a thing with that little oil lamp. Flashlights just don't cut it."

"Oh, sorry. I should have thought of that."

Once she flipped the circuit breaker, she grabbed a light bulb from the dining room fixture and carried it upstairs. "Is there one in Mother's—yeah, I thought it was bad. Here."

The tone turned businesslike as the three officers did their job. Willow overheard phrases like "dust for prints," "evidence bag," and "list of people with access" and wondered why nothing could be simple and beautiful as it used to be. She answered all questions thrown at her until the others were satisfied with her answers. The only people with a key to the Finley Farm were Chad, Willow, and Caleb Allen, and all three of them had spent the night away from the farm and in one another's company.

"Solari," Willow suggested. "She was here just the other day. Maybe she found a way to pick the lock or something.

Chad looked at the chief and asked, "Key mold maybe?"

"Not likely but possible, I guess. We'll send Joe out to question them in the morning."

"Can I go to bed? I'm tired." Willow's voice sounded almost petulant.

Chief Varney patted her shoulder and promised that they'd take good care of her. As she turned, Willow heard him speak low to Chad. "Son, I want you here until tomorrow at two. Your shift just changed. You'll come back at six."

"You don't have to do that Chief," Chad insisted. "I wasn't going anywhere anyway."

"But I want you here until at least two and back again by six—not leaving her alone out here after dark. At least until we check out these Solaris, Bill Franklin, and that reporter fellow... Bieler?"

"Yessir."

Chad found Willow folding her clothes and putting them away. He re-hung the jeans, replaced books, and helped clear her bed. As she grabbed her pajamas, Chad loaded the hall stove and lit a fire. "I think I'll ask Judith to bring me an air mattress. The search was concentrated in your mother's room, so I'm going to leave that until morning. Maybe in daylight we'll see it better."

Willow emerged from the bathroom wearing paisley flannel pajamas and braiding her hair. "I'm sorry our lights weren't very adequate."

"That's ok. We'll look again in the morning."

"Where will you sleep?"

Chad stared at the hallway and then at her floor. "I'd sleep out here, but you'd probably trip over me if you got up in the night, so I'll sleep at the foot of your bed."

"You'll get your cold feet on me."

Laughing, Chad shook his head. "No, on the floor you nut."

"How uncomfortable!" She didn't like the idea. It seemed rude. "You can sleep in my bed—"

"No!"

"—and I'll take the couch," she finished, shaking her head. "I'm not completely without understanding of social norms.

Unmarried people don't share beds. I get that. But you can't sleep on the floor, and I can sleep on the couch."

"I will sleep on the floor, and you will not sleep on the couch. I'd have to sleep on the floor in the living room if you moved down there, so can we just quit arguing? I'll go get my sleeping bag from the truck, and—"

"Why do you have a sleeping bag in your truck?"

"I keep one in there this time of year. It gets cold fast, and if I'm ever in an accident or my truck breaks down, I want to be warm until the tow truck arrives."

"Smart."

"Took you long enough to figure that out," he chided as he jogged downstairs.

His first snore woke her up. She listened, fascinated to the nasal orchestrations, amazed at how much louder and... resonant it was than her mother's soft snores. Sleep finally overcame her. *Now I understand why Mother called it "sawing logs,* she thought as she drifted to asleep.

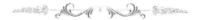

At four-twenty, Chad barreled down Willow's driveway, the tires of the cruiser, sliding at the curve. Her phone skipped to voicemail at every attempt to call, and for cathartic purposes, he shouted at her all the way. Willow rounded the corner of her house, feed can in hand, and stared at him dumfounded as he raced toward her.

"What is wrong?"

"Why didn't you answer your phone?"

"I—" she patted her pockets, looking confused. After a moment, she remembered.

"Oh, yeah. I thought I heard it ring when I was filling the water trough, so I tried to answer it, but I dropped it in the trough. I haven't fished it out yet."

Relieved, Chad grabbed her shoulders and shook them slightly, before wrapping her in a bear hug. "You scared me."

"I'm fine. Really, but your phone is ringing."

With a grin that told her they weren't done with the

conversation, Chad answered the call. She waited to hear what he wanted, but the protests of her chickens drew her across the yard to the chicken coop. "There you guys go. Get in there where it's nice and warm." Willow talked to the birds as they climbed the ramp to the coop, plugged in the oil heater, and returned the bucket to the barn.

"Come on, Willow," Chad called. "The Chief has a suspect at the station."

"I can't. I have to milk Ditto."

"Start the water and then go change. You have mud on your jeans. I'll milk her."

By ten after five, Chad led Willow into the station where Caleb Allen sat looking miserable. Another boy, slumped and handcuffed to a chair, sat next to Joe's desk. "Ryder, your parents are coming."

"Let 'em come."

"We have your fingerprint on the key Ryder. It was in your possession."

"Means nothing to me."

A professional looking couple burst into the police station, demanding to know what was happening and why Ryder was in custody—again. It took an hour to sort out the details, but eventually Ryder Hudson's parents managed to force him to admit that he'd stolen the key from Caleb.

"I read the article about her," Ryder confessed. "I thought someone like that might—"

"Stop, Ryder. Wait until Renee gets here," Mr. Hudson demanded.

As Willow turned to leave the station, Caleb Allen stopped her. "I'm sorry. It's all my fault. I knew he wasn't trustworthy. I shouldn't have mentioned that I had the key. I just wasn't thinking."

"No harm done. Not really. I hope you'll be available again soon. I might need to take a trip to the city in early January. I've been thinking I might stay over."

Pride filled Chad's heart. He knew Willow had considered going to the grand opening of *Boho Deux*. And he also knew she'd decided against it. Her request provided a way to assure

266

Caleb that she didn't blame him for the situation.

Later, in a room spit-bathed in incandescent light, Chad and Willow cleaned the mess created by Ryder Hudson in his search for stashes of cash. "He pictured you like some old miser with money hidden under your mattress, in between book pages and stuff like that."

"Fortunately he wasn't destructive. Reorganizing these papers will take hours, but they're still here. I've heard of thieves getting angry and vindictive when they don't find what they want."

"Well, Ryder is on his way. That kid needs boundaries, less ready cash, and parents who don't rely on a safe, quiet town as a babysitter to keep their bored and rejected kid out of trouble."

"I thought Joe worked with kids to prevent that." She moved her head out of the light's path in order to see well enough to wipe at the fingerprint dust on the windowsill.

Chad sighed. "He can only do what the kid will cooperate with. Ryder knows that this move was a last ditch effort to keep him out of trouble and out of their hair. He resents it."

Willow sat cross-legged on her mother's bed sorting papers. "You know, when he's done being in trouble for breaking in, see if he wants a job. He can help me assemble the greenhouse."

"Why would you hire someone who tried to steal from you?"

"You said it," she explained. "He wants something to fill his time. He wanted money for something, and maybe if someone invests some time in him, he won't feel the need to call attention to himself."

"Wow."

She rolled her eyes at him and imitated something she had heard Cheri say. "Whatever." His grin told her she'd gotten it right.

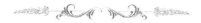

Page by page, Steven Solari made his way through the city

papers. His eyes scanned every article with the precision of a diamond cutter and the speed of a racecar driver. His eyes seemed to cling instinctively to any words that might be of interest to him, and he circled them all. Some of his associates employed people to search the Internet for them—he had a tech geek as well—but no one had his instincts. And relying on search terms alone was a solid way to miss the little things.

The Fairbury paper captured his interest immediately. The bottom quarter of the front page was devoted to a story of juvenile breaking and entry. Smoothing the paper, he read every detail, twice, and smiled to himself as he read Willow's quoted remarks. Wanda, the receptionist, stepped into the room, saw his expression, and stepped back out again. She hated that look.

CHAPTER 64

"I need to watch *The Music Man*. Do you have it?"

Chad's face drooped. "You're kidding, right?"

"No," she asserted calmly. "Aggie wants 'Shipoopie' dresses from *The Music Man*. I don't know what that means, but I need to see it."

The pieced table runners were now basted and Willow quilted them as she and Chad talked. Chad worked on the loom, his work slow and cautious. Though he had consulted with Luke regarding the best way to repair it, he lacked confidence in his skills. Occasionally he glanced up at her, watching her needle weave in and out of the fabrics. The one rolled next to her and ready to quilt, he knew must be for his mother. The colors were perfect for their dining room at home.

"Why don't I borrow that player again and rent the movie. You can keep it here for a few days until you get sketches made. You don't have to watch the whole thing. Just find the Shipoopie part."

"How am I supposed to know what a Shipoopie is? It sounds like an embarrassed mother telling her child to go use the toilet."

Chad chuckled as she wrinkled her nose and held up the quilted piece. "Looks nice."

"It's almost done."

"What is it for?" Chad thought he knew.

"Your bar in your kitchen. I thought it'd tie in nicely with

269

the rug."

Bingo! "I like it. Thanks." He paused. "Hey, I forgot to tell you. Ryder says he can start working with you on Friday, sometime after noon. He gave me his cell number." Chad pulled a paper from his wallet and laid it on the coffee table.

"I hate this phone," Willow groused as she tried to punch in the information. "Everything is different, and I forget which way I'm supposed to do things."

"Adding you to my plan was cheaper in the long run, but they didn't have your phone."

"It's still annoying." She slid the phone shut and tossed it at him. "Here, you figure it out."

"You're grumpy."

"Mother would tell me to go to bed and quit making both of us miserable. She didn't have much patience with crabby monthlies."

You set yourself up for that one Chad. Get out of it, fast! He thought to himself. Chad cleared his throat. "Well, it *is* getting late—"

"Before you go, would you see if you see anything strange around the barn? I thought I saw snowshoe prints earlier, but Saige was barking like crazy over at the chicken coop, and by the time I got back, I didn't see what I thought I saw."

The hair stood on Chad's neck. "You go to bed. Lock the doors well behind me. I'll see you Friday afternoon with Ryder."

"Not coming out tomorrow afternoon?"

He put the few remaining pieces back in the box and put the semi-complete loom in it as well. "Nope. Got a dentist's appointment in Westbury."

"Why go all the way—"

"Dr. Dunn has been doing my teeth since before I had very many." Chad explained as he rose, carrying the loom upstairs.

"Have fun!"

Chad dumped the loom in the middle of the craft room floor. "Fun? Is she serious?"

270

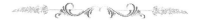

Willow froze the screen and called Chad in disgust. "This movie is silly."

"What movie?" Chad's mind was on Aiden Cox sauntering down the street carrying his skateboard.

"*The Music Man.* For one thing, they keep singing for no apparent reason half the time."

"That's why they call it a musical," Chad explained.

"And this Mayor is a pompous jerk."

"Sounds like a stereotypical politician—"

Her patience was reaching its limit. "And this 'Shipoopi' song is asinine."

"Why do you say that?" Chad's heart wasn't in the conversation but he tried.

"'A woman who kisses on the very first date is usually a hussy.'"

"Well, I guess that depends on how long you've known her," Chad commented.

"'And a woman who'll kiss on the second time out, is anything but fussy.'"

"What are you talking about?"

"This song! Get this. 'But the woman who waits 'til the third time around, head in the clouds, feet on the ground—she's a girl he's glad he's found; she's his Shipoopi'. Then they say, 'the girl is hard to get.'"

"I told you—" he boasted triumphantly.

"Well, I'm done. I got the dresses sketched. I know how to make them. I'll start after New Year's."

"Got him," Chad announced triumphantly. "I have to go. Aiden just jumped on that board again."

Willow shut her phone and stared at the screen. It seemed silly not to see how the movie ended, but she wasn't sure she could handle another song. She glanced outside to see what kind of progress Ryder had made in assembling the frame of her greenhouse. When she'd sneezed the third time, Ryder had encouraged her to go inside and let him work alone.

Friday he'd been surly but listened and followed instructions reasonably well. Saturday, he prevented her from assembling something out of order, resulting in a new camaraderie that tore down the walls he'd originally constructed. By Sunday afternoon, he worked outside, alone, and with an eye to her well-being.

Rapping on the window, Willow pulled the pan of milk from the stove, stirred in cocoa and sugar, and poured it into a cup. Ryder hurried inside. "You ok, Ms. Finley?"

"You looked cold. Have some chocolate."

Ryder sat in the chair at the table and watched Willow as she rocked and sniffled into her handkerchief. "Why are you so nice to me?"

She had expected the question. A boy like Ryder would be suspicious of anything that didn't fit his perceived ideas of justice. "Why shouldn't I be?" She asked the question, not as a stall tactic as much as a diversion onto a particular course.

"I tried to steal from you."

"Why?"

"Just wanted some money and to see if I could."

"Well, you proved you could," she began, "And if you wanted money, I provided an honest way for you to get it. I kind of thought you sounded bored, so I asked. I could do it myself with help from Chad now and then, but why not get it done faster in a way that benefits us both?" She could see that her logic made sense, but her application of it still didn't fit in his personal system of ethics.

"I like it. You have a cool place out here. When I was little, I wanted to be a farmer, but my parents stopped thinking that was cute when I turned eleven or so."

"What's wrong with being a farmer?"

Disdain dripped from Ryder's words. "If you can't get a degree in it, it isn't worth doing. My parents are university

272

snobs."

"So get a degree in horticulture, agriculture, or soil chemistry. Start a farm and develop newer and stronger seeds."

"They have degrees in farming?" Interest laced Ryder's words despite an air of studied indifference.

"Well, I don't claim to be an expert, but I've read quite a few articles by people with BSAs."

"BSA?"

Willow grinned and went to retrieve back issues of their *Mother Earth News* magazines. "Check it out. Bachelor of Science in Agriculture. Some have business management specialties, animal science, horticulture... The field is nearly limitless."

"I wonder..."

Willow's hand shot out and covered his. "Ryder, I'd never encourage someone to dishonor their parents. Once you've lost your only parent, you tend to treasure that relationship. However, if you can find a way to honor their desire for you to go to college *and* study something that interests you, I think you'd be happier."

His voice drooped and he leaned back pulling both hands behind his head. "Now if we can manage to get past the embarrassment factor for them, it might work."

"Embarrassment?"

"Sure. An MBA, law degree, medical degree, research, even stockbroker would be fine, but tell their high-class friends that their son is getting a degree in hayseed? Not exactly something they'd want to admit."

Slack jawed, Willow shook her head. "I can't comprehend that. Why would you be ashamed of a degree that helps you learn to feed the world in a more productive manner? How can you find it embarrassing to have a son who learns to utilize and maximize crop production, protect soils, and ensure that people actually eat?"

"Maybe I'll take a double major. Get a degree in accounting too. Accounting would be helpful for anyone." Ryder stood and thanked her for the cocoa. "If I'm going to get

273

that third rib done today, I'd better get out there. Thanks Ms. Finley."

At the door, Willow stopped him. "Ryder?"

"Huh?"

"If I get this farm going like I want next spring, I'll have work for you during the summer if you're interested."

January, 2001-

Willow has more energy than I'll be able to contain on this little hobby farm of ours. While I enjoy the streamlined operation and lesser burden of work as she gets older and stronger, she needs more to do to keep her occupied. She asked about growing more alfalfa crops, but I assured her that once they were in the ground she'd still be without extra things to do until harvest and then there'd be more work at our busiest time.

I don't know how to direct her. If I stifle her, she'll resent me. If I encourage her, we risk everything. I suggested she learn to master woodworking, but she's clearly not interested. I've pushed her to make more quilts, paint more pictures, sew clothes, but she has a valid point. Where would we put them? I need to encourage her fishing, and I definitely need to order some new books. I need to find something that is both intellectually stimulating and yet not a burden to read. Meanwhile, I have Dorothy Sayers mysteries on the way.

I suggested she take up speed running the other day. I explained how to mark off meters on the driveway and encouraged her to see how fast she could run the distances. She ran several races, beat her own time by several seconds, and then announced that it was good exercise, but she couldn't see spending hours every day trying to determine if she could squeeze a fraction of a second off her score. I suspect, however, that part of her lack of interest had to do with soreness of breasts. I should have told her to wrap well with an ace bandage. However, the racing and time scores brought up discussion of triathlons and decathlons. Since then, she has been turning everything into bi, tri, quad, quint, sex, sept, oct, and dec prefaced words. For some reason, she simply skips "non." We now have tri-meal-thons instead of three squares a day and anything else she can think of with

274

those prefixes. I do wonder, however, if I should have used hept instead of sex. Her attempts to use that sound so awkward – and she is clueless, of course.

Spring is busy; fall is busy. However, winter and part of summer – although much less so than winter – are fairly lazy times for us. While I don't think Willow is itching to fill them with the hyper-busyness of modern society, I do think she is a more active person than I am, and it shows at times like this.

She has unraveled all of our holey socks and is using the wool to make strange little forest animals and creatures of her own fantasy worlds. Should I be concerned that my teenaged daughter has no interest in driving a car, going out with boys, going to prom, and has never had a mid-term paper due? Is it unforgivable that she doesn't know these things are an option in her life? Is it terrible that I like her playing with her little animal creatures one moment and then debating de Tocqueville in the next? Is it too bizarre that she can survive, alone, for years in the wilderness but couldn't navigate the streets of Rockland?

Will I ever take her there? I mentioned it once a few months ago and her response was, "Why? I have everything I need here."

I suggested that someday she might like to see more of the world and she said, "Well, if you were talking about taking me to India or China, maybe, but I don't see any reason to waste a perfectly good day going into a city that you avoid whenever possible. I'd rather fish."

Will she resent me when she realizes how wrong she was? When she discovers the Rockland Arts Center or the botanical gardens, will she wonder why I didn't insist we go? Will she understand how deeply I dread that place and what a refuge our farm is to me? Can she possibly know the horror I feel as the skyline looms ahead of me as the bus rolls along that highway?

Today I speculate. Tomorrow I'll trust again. I'll pray that the Lord softens her heart if the day ever comes when I no longer feel the need to protect her from the evilness around. Some would say I've tried to create a utopia where sin never enters. How foolish the thought. Every day I see more plainly my weaknesses, failures, and sins. This little world of ours seems to magnify them and keep them from those dark secret places I had as a child. Where I hid my failures from my mother, she shares hers with me. We're open about the selfish and prideful thoughts that fill our minds, the anger that wells in our

275

hearts, and the lies. She doesn't struggle with that as much as I do. She lies to herself, but rarely has she ever lied to me. She's been much too honest at times, but I've never discouraged it. I, on the other hand, have much to conceal and therefore tend to deceive rather than speak honestly when I don't care to share. How wrong of me.

Pride is our common sin. We both think too highly of ourselves than we ought. We flip-flop across the line separating arrogance and self-righteousness from false modesty. When we stay on the path, we do well. When we flop, it's rarely on the false modesty side of pride and when it is, it's usually me. That deception thing again. It shows among our other sins as well, I guess.

Willow informed me that the wise men have reached Cyprus and will manage to reach Jerusalem by February fifth. I am so pleased. They had me worried there for a moment. Those dratted wise men never leave early enough for my taste. If they had arrived when modern storytellers pretend, fewer babies would have needed to be slaughtered. Yep. They should have listened to me. Hmmm. I think that pride thing is rearing its ugly head again. Time to quit writing and start scrubbing — something.

CHAPTER 65

"What are you doing here!" Willow's voice sounded more pleased than confused.

"I go in at ten, but at seven I woke up and couldn't go back to sleep so I decided to come out here." He glanced above her doorway, sighed, and kissed her cheek. "Mind?"

"Well, I shouldn't since I put it up there."

"No, silly," he protested laughing. Do you mind me intruding on your Christmas Eve?" The pile of journals on the floor by the couch told him he'd interrupted a memory fest.

"Oh, I thought you meant the mistletoe. Of course you're welcome!"

"Just a second, I forgot something." Chad hurried to his truck, brought several presents into the house, and stuffed them under the tree.

"You created beautiful packages!"

"Not really. Melba Torquin wrapped them. She's a bit steep, but it helps supplement her income and keeps her in heat during the winter, so quite a lot of us take our packages to her house."

Chad hunkered down on his heels and read the tags on Willow's gifts. He finally found the one with his name. "It's either a copy of your mother's journals or a book you think I should read. The shape gives it away."

"I'm not saying anything more other than that you're wrong on both accounts."

Chad shrugged off his work coat and stuffed his gloves in the pockets. His belt he hung next to them and then offered to heat some cider. At the kitchen doorway, he turned back to her. "What's with all the mistletoe? There wasn't any yesterday."

"I just put it up a bit ago. I wanted your parents to feel at home." She looked a little nervous about what that might mean to the Tesdalls.

"Willow, they're not going to make out in the middle of your living room. No worries."

"Make out?"

With a shake of his head, he refocused on heating cider for them. How do you explain making out to someone with no concept of why you'd want to do it in the first place? A thought crossed his mind. He stood in the doorway and waited for her to notice him there.

"Making out. Definition. Smashed lips leading to lip lock and then culminating in swapping spit and finally tonsil hockey. Often includes various methods of cuddling that I'd rather not get into right now."

"Kissing. Got it." A silent pause followed and Chad nearly burned his hand when her voice called out from the living room, "Did you really just say swapping spit?"

He carried mugs to the couch and handed her one. "In older vernacular, yes."

"I thought old was smooch."

"Do you really want to sit here and discuss the sixty-six terms for kissing in the English language?"

Her eyes widened in amazement. "Are there really sixty-six—"

"Oh hush, and drink your cider. What are you doing tonight?"

"You just told me to hush," she protested laughing. "I can't do that and answer your questions at the same time."

He smiled at her. "I missed you."

"I saw you last night."

"For ten minutes max."

Her brow furrowed, she leaned closer to him, sending his panic buttons into overdrive. As he floundered for a way to get out of an intimate situation, Willow sniffed his cider. "Doesn't smell fermented but…"

"Oh, knock it off. I've hardly seen you since Wednesday, and we've kind of gotten to be a nice habit of mine."

Willow set down her mug and crawled across his foot to grab his present from under the tree. "Here. It's Christmas Eve."

"I'll be here before Mom and Dad are!"

A pleading look filed her eyes. "I think I'd rather you open it now if you would."

Chad grinned. "Good answer." Reaching under the tree, he pulled his gift from the pile and handed it to her. "Open yours. I think you'll like having quiet to enjoy it anyway."

She held her gift waiting for him to open his. "Go on. I'm getting impatient now."

Chad carefully fastened the edges of paper and folded it beside him. Inside the box, in a thick bed of quilt batting, the fly case lay, reflecting the firelight of the candles all around him. "Oh, Willow…"

"I thought maybe you'd like something for your apartment, but I didn't think you'd want something stitched and my painting skills for masculine things are very primitive."

"Did you make this case?"

"Mother did. For my sixteenth birthday. I thought about buying something for the flies, but I wanted you to have a piece of Mother too."

His heart filled with emotions he wasn't ready to decipher. He leaned across the couch, hugged her tightly, and whispered, "Thank you."

Willow nodded. "There is a condition."

"What's that?"

With sly smile, she nudged his knee. "You have to actually use them — preferably with me."

"Deal. Open mine."

She teased the bow, ran her fingers over the smoothness of the metallic paper, and in short, drove him crazy as she enjoyed the textures of the package. At last, taking pity on Chad before he burst, Willow released the tape on one end and slid a box from its wrappings. She lifted the lid, folded back sheets and sheets of tissue paper, and lifted the dulcimer from within.

"Oh, Chad! Where did you find—how did you— What—"

"Actually, there's kind of an embarrassing story behind that dulcimer."

"Embarrassing to you?"

Chad nodded. "Yep."

"Let's hear it," she demanded impishly.

"Be nice," he growled. "I was thinking about the instrument thing after we talked that night, and I decided that now was a perfect time to learn one, so I went online and found—"

"You're going to have to show me the online thing. I'm really sick of Alexa's book."

Chad chuckled and continued, ignoring the interruption. "—the perfect dulcimer. The pictures were beautiful. It said, 'assembly required,' but I didn't think anything of it. I thought, pegs and strings and stuff. It arrived in precut pieces."

"You *made* this?"

"Assembled it. Yep. I went to Luke's a few times when I should have been sleeping, and he instructed me. I kind of hoped he'd take over and do it for me like he did when we were little, but I guess he figured that game out."

Her fingers plucked the strings. "Oh it's horribly out of tune. I wonder how to make them sound right."

Chad rifled through a few of the packages and pulled two out that looked nearly the same size. "Sorry. I don't know which one goes with that. I didn't think to tell her to mark it some way other than your name."

Even as he spoke, she slowly tightened strings until a better sound, however off key it still was, resonated from the instrument as she plucked it. For several minutes she plucked, tuned, plinked, and tuned some more. By the time she was finished, the strings plinked harmoniously if not in the exact notes it was designed to play.

"I love it. How did you know I've always wanted a dulcimer?"

"I didn't," he confessed. "I just tried to think of what instrument fit you and your life, and a dulcimer did."

Her hands fingered the smooth surface of the instrument. "It's so beautiful..."

Chad put his case back under the tree, retrieved the dulcimer and placed it under there with the other gifts, reached for her Bible and handed it to her. "Your turn."

"For what?"

"To read Luke."

Willow's eyes filled as she took the Bible. "But I never—"

"You can't read any worse than I do."

"I don't. I'm a much better reader actually. I've just never—"

Chad laughed at the expression on her face as she realized what she'd said. "It's ok, I know I'm not very good at it."

"Mother always read," she explained. "I don't think I've ever read the Christmas story aloud."

A fresh wave of understanding washed over Chad. He settled himself comfortably in the corner of the couch, and beckoned her. "Come here. I'll help."

She offered him the Bible as she slid across the cushions, but he didn't take it. Instead, he pulled her close, rested his hands on her shoulders, and encouraged her once more. "Go on, read it."

"I—"

Chad's voice, low and soothing, urged her. "Come on. It's not Christmas Eve without it."

She read, punctuating every other sentence with a sob, a sniffle, or the choked sound of her voice trying not to sob or sniffle. It was truly the most endearing and horrible reading of the passage Chad had ever heard. As she finished, he enveloped her in a warm hug. "I'm proud of you."

She relaxed, weeping occasionally until the clock chimed a quarter till ten. "You've got to go."

He nodded, stood, and donned his gun belt, jacket, and gloves. "Get some sleep if you can."

"I'm glad you came, Chad. It's like my first Christmas without any family, but family is still here. Not everyone has that blessing."

He crossed the floor, cupped her face in his hands, and

kissed the top of her head. "Well this family isn't going to stand for you being alone on Christmas. We're funny that way."

"Merry Christmas, Chad."

At the door, he turned, laid his finger aside of his nose, winked, and shut the door behind him. Her laughter reached him outside when she heard his voice cry out, "Happy Christmas to all, and to all a *good night!*"

Chad unlocked Willow's back door and slipped into the kitchen, using his flashlight to find the lamp on the table. Just as he'd expected, cookies and a note sat on the table.

Dear ~~Chad~~ *Santa,*

I didn't think cookies made a very filling dinner, so I left a glass of milk and a sandwich in the icebox. I hope your sleigh is warm and you can visit me again in the morning. I have company I think you'd enjoy.

Love, Willow

P.S. I was a good girl this year. Well, except for the itching powder in Mother's bed to drive Chad crazy. Shh. Don't tell.

As he inhaled the enormous roast beef sandwich, Chad reread the note, laughing to himself as he folded it and stashed it in his pocket. He rinsed his dishes and crept through the house, up the stairs, and into Willow's room. Moonlight streamed through the window illuminating her face as she slept.

His heart constricted. As much as he tried to be family to her, he was still an inadequate replacement for her mother. As much as his parents loved and invested in her, they'd never be her parents. Perhaps he'd been wrong to be wary of the Finleys and the Solaris. Chad leaned against her dresser, munched on his cookie, and watched her sleep as he prayed.

Lord, I don't know what to do. I'm torn. She needs someone here. It's not that I'm immune to her, but I'm not in love with her either — I

282

don't think. It seems so wrong to marry someone and not love them like that. Then again, it seems wrong to leave her alone so much. I practically live here, and yet I don't. I'd ask her about it, but it's not something you want to bring up carelessly. 'Marry me and then I can sleep over.' Yeah. That makes sense. I can't even think about – He swallowed hard. *I'm human, Lord!*

A strand of hair escaped from her braid, slipping down her cheek. Chad smoothed it back behind her ear before turning toward the door. "Did you find your sandwich?" she murmured sleepily.

Chad jumped. He glanced back at Willow, but she showed no sign of consciousness. "It was good, thanks."

"You're welcome," she whispered.

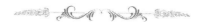

The scent of coffee woke Willow. Throwing her robe over her shoulders, she dashed downstairs. "Chad! What time is it?"

"Seven. Animals are covered. Just drinking a coffee before I crawl into your mother's bed until Mom and Dad get here."

She shooed him upstairs with a glass of milk in hand. "You don't need coffee if you're going to sleep." At the end of the hall, between the two bedrooms, she pointed to her bed. "I just changed my sheets yesterday, but I slept on them. It's warm though – if you want to climb in. I'm going to start baking pies as soon as I get dressed..."

She chattered as she grabbed her clothes and hustled from the room, dumping his duffle on the bed. He stared at it in surprise. "How'd you?"

"You taught me to be observant. Go to sleep. You've got about three hours before your parents get here. Sleep!"

Chad grabbed his sweats and lumbered to the bathroom. He was tired. This was nearly the equivalent of a triple shift, and he knew he'd be wiped by dinnertime. Once changed, he glanced at her room and then Kari's. He felt strange taking her bed. What if she got tired? She might not feel like resting on her mother's bed. Mind made up, he pulled back the covers to

Kari's bed and slipped his feet under cold sheets. His head craned around the doorframe and glimpsed the rumpled warmth of Willow's bed. Seconds later, he snuggled under her flannel sheets with the shades pulled down and room darkened. As he drifted to sleep, the relaxing cool scent of lavender wisped around him.

For the next three hours, Willow baked rolls, pecan pie, and caramel apple pie. Fresh batches of sugar cookies were ready to go in the oven immediately after lunch, and mulled apple cider simmered on the stove. She heard car wheels crunch on the driveway and hurried out to meet Chad's parents.

"Hi! I'm so glad you came," she called, waving.

"If we can't have family at Christmas one way, we'll do it another!" Marianne insisted as she gave Willow a hug. "Don't you look lovely? That sweater—tell me you didn't make it."

"I didn't. Mother did two years ago." Willow's hands ran lightly over the sleeves.

"That pattern is pretty."

"Thank you. Would you like to stretch your legs and see the barn and the animals or are you ready to get inside and have some cider?"

Christopher pointed to the greenhouse frame. "What's going there?"

"That's my new greenhouse. I have a boy from town helping me assemble it. He's been a great help."

"Ryder—the one who broke in, right? I couldn't believe you did that," Marianne said shaking her head at Christopher. "Leave the packages, we'll get them when we're done out here."

As she led them into the barn, Christopher asked questions that confused her until she realized they were related to his job—how she kept the animal smell down, what she fed them, how she processed milk and stored eggs. Outside, she showed them the pens, the coop, and even took them around the back to her "swing tree" and down to the alfalfa field. "That field..." she marked off the perimeter with her hands, "is what Chad mowed for me." She swallowed the lump that grew in her throat. "I would have died if he hadn't been such a pest about that phone. I would have died if he hadn't brought it back here that first day."

"Chad was so worried about you during that time. He called and prayed with us daily."

Marianne's words struck a special chord in Willow's heart. "He's a good friend. I am blessed to know him—all of you really. Today would be a very horrible day without you here."

Christopher cleared his throat and said, "Let's see the chickens. Chad says you let them roam around outside even as cold as it is."

Willow led them back up the hill, around the barn, past the mulched garden plot and to the chicken yard. "Looks like about half of them are out at the moment. They come in and out as they please until nighttime or if it gets too cold." She winked at the Tesdalls. "Then I treat them like children and make them do what I think is best."

Saige trotted past the chicken yard, a rabbit in her mouth. She ordered the dog to take it behind the barn and turned to the Tesdalls, shaking her head. "If I don't make her eat them back there, I get entrails strewn everywhere."

Around the house she pointed out her flowerbeds and lilac bushes, and from the porch, she pointed at the lone oak tree. "Mother is out there. If you care for a walk after lunch, I recommend going to see. Chad's headstones are beautiful."

"Headstones? Plural?"

"He made one for my dog too. Othello just didn't seem to care to live without Mother. He died soon after she did."

Willow welcomed Marianne into the house while Christopher retrieved the gifts from the trunk of their car. Marianne gushed over the house. "Oh Willow! It's beautiful in here. I just love it."

As Willow unloaded the packages from Christopher's arms and placed them under the tree, she pointed upstairs. "Chad's still asleep, I think, but I can show you around down here." She spun in a slow circle, her hands outstretched. "This is obviously the living room. We heat with that stove and mostly spend our evenings in here. Now Chad comes and tries to beat me at Chinese checkers or sex-Yahtzee.

"Sex what?"

285

"You know how there are six columns on a Yahtzee pad? We play them all at once. I thought Sex-zee—you know for six and Yahtzee—was a good name for it, but Chad's face looked something like Christopher's does now, and he suggested I find another name. I just stick with Sex-Yahtzee for now."

"I see. We'll have to see about helping you with that name. You're right, it doesn't have the kind of punch you were looking for does it?"

"Nope. I thought Sex-zee was cute but," she shrugged and then looked confused as Marianne and Christopher burst out laughing.

Mid laugh, Marianne remembered something. "Did you say Chad is asleep?"

"Yes. He's up in my bed sleeping."

At that moment, they all heard a door open, another door close, and the shower come on in the bathroom. Willow smiled. "Guess he's waking up."

She turned from her guests and led the way to the kitchen, entirely missing the look that passed between Marianne and Christopher.

Chad stretched and rolled over. The darkened room let a stream of light in around the edges of the window. He reached for the shade and pulled it letting the light flood the room. He closed his eyes in protest and waited for them to grow used to the change slowly—very slowly. A journal lay on the table next to the bed. He fluffed her pillows and curled up with it reading. "What Mom would do if she saw me reading—voluntarily," he murmured as he turned the page.

December-

It's cold now. My life is both empty and full simultaneously. I miss my mother. My heart feels lost without her when the wind rattles the shutters and sends a chill through the old windows. We really should replace those windows.

My heart is full, however. As much as I miss her, I am thankful

Chad flipped through the journal and realized it wasn't Kari's. He snapped it shut, closing his eyes. She still feels alone. I hate that, Lord. Then again, she knows she isn't. That's a beginning...

A sound downstairs jerked him from his thoughts and prayer. Laughter — his father's laughter. He jumped from the bed, grabbed his duffel, and locked himself in the bathroom.

As he lathered with the lavender soap, dried with towels hung in the upper hallway and then stored on shelves with lavender sachets, Chad smiled. She'd taken over the house with her preferences. If journals were to be believed, Kari hadn't liked lavender as much as Willow did.

Chad pulled the sweater over his shoulders and glanced at the mirror. Unable to see anything but a shadowy figure in the steamy fog covering it, he took his towel and wiped the steam from the mirror and glanced at his reflection again. He liked how it looked, though he doubted anyone would believe him. It was warm and comfortable but soft. He just hoped it wouldn't be *too* warm.

He burst into the kitchen, greeting his parents with hugs. "Mom! Dad! You found us ok. Can I get you some more cider?"

Chad refilled their cups, checked the stove's wood supply, and pulled on a jacket by the back door. "I'll be right back. The wood box is getting low."

Willow smiled. "He's very good about keeping me in wood. I almost never have to fill the box anymore. Come on upstairs. I'll give you a tour."

Chad entered an empty kitchen and listened in horror as Willow took his parents on a grand tour upstairs. *"I didn't make her bed,"* he groaned inwardly.

Marianne raved over the craft room, loved her hallway clothesline, and stepped almost reverently into Kari's room, sensing that little had changed since the woman died. "This is a lovely room."

"I see Chad realized how cold those sheets are with that room closed off," Willow commented as she straightened the

287

covers and fluffed the pillow where he'd sat on it. "I guess that means my room won't be very tidy!"

They stepped across the hall where Chad's duffel bag sat on the corner of the bed with the rest of the sheets and blankets tumbled in complete disorder. "Yep," she laughed as she zipped the bag and dropped it on the floor at the foot of her bed. She pulled the sheets up to the top of the bed as she answered questions about the wood trim, the "wallpaper," and the rugs.

"Mom? Dad?"

"Coming, laddie. Willow is just showing us the rest of the house," Marianne called back to him.

Downstairs, Chad grinned like a child. "So, presents before or after lunch," he asked glancing at the clock. It wasn't quite eleven o'clock. Too early for lunch.

"He'll never grow up," Christopher groaned.

"Better do gifts now or we'll be miserable all through lunch!"

"Who is Santa?" Marianne asked suddenly.

"I'm Santa this year," Chad insisted. "Chris gets it at home, so I've got dibs here."

He dug under the tree pulling out gifts for everyone. Seeing his name on one from his parents, Chad looked up quizzically. "But I thought we were doing our Christmas at New Year's?"

"We weren't going to bring gifts for Willow and not have anything for you. You'll just have less to open later," his mother explained. To Willow she turned and said, "You will come with him, won't you? We're all hoping you'll come."

"Of course! Thank you for inviting me. If I can get Caleb or Ryder out here, I'll do it!"

Chad passed a package to Willow from Cheri. She glanced at it and smiled before setting it aside. "Open it, Willow," he urged eagerly.

"I don't want to. I'm saving it for Christmas at your house. Everyone will feel awkward if they're opening gifts and I've already been enjoying mine."

Marianne's eyes sought her husband's once again. Willow

watched the ocular conversation, wondering how two people could communicate so well without saying anything. Chad smiled at both of his parents when they looked at him. "I know. Wow, huh?"

"Wow." Christopher agreed.

Without another word, Chad passed Willow another of his gifts. "Hopefully that's what goes with the dulcimer."

"Did I tell you? I picked out a tune that sounds like 'Greensleeves' today."

"Rock on!"

"Huh?"

"Willow," Chad began, "Your eloquence is absolutely mind-numbing sometimes."

Marianne's gift was wrapped like a Christmas cracker, and as she unrolled the paper and the cardboard tubing, she pulled Willow's table runner from the pile of wrappings. "Oh Willow! It's beautiful!"

"Did I get the colors right? I hoped — "

"They're perfect, thank you, sweetie!"

Christopher pulled a tie from his box and the Tesdalls all laughed. Willow's eyes widened. "Did I do something wrong?"

"No. We've just always joked about how no one has ever given him a tie. In fact, he swore if he ever got one, he'd wear it every day for a month," Chad explained.

"Well," Willow said, grimacing. "I hope you like brown. I would have made it a little more interesting if I had known."

"How did you get the monogram colors so perfect?" Christopher asked marveling at the almost imperceptible satin stitching at the bottom of his tie.

"I pulled strands of thread from the side of the fabric before I cut it out and used those instead of floss."

Chad couldn't resist asking — if only to show his mother how the Finley women thought of things. "What made you decide to do that?"

We always do that when we want a subtle pattern. Mother figured it out once when she couldn't match floss closely enough and just needed a little bit."

Marianne stared at her son. He saw her lower jaw fighting

289

to hit the floor, kept in place only by sheer willpower. "You weren't kidding, Chad."

"Open yours, Willow."

Willow unwrapped her box to find a CD holder filled with her old View Master cards. "This is so wonderful — how?"

"I saw them upstairs when I went to get the loom, which is finished by the way, and realized that they'd be better protected in a case."

"I am so glad Mother talked me into the old maps on that box instead of the reel I wanted. That box will still be useful — maybe for my dulcimer strings and things."

They took their time opening presents, each person opening one before the next. Willow refused to open any but Chad's final gift — the one that went with the dulcimer — and one package from Marianne and Christopher. As she pulled two tickets from the jeweler's necklace box, Willow raised an eyebrow in question.

"Chad said you liked Argosy Junction, and we heard they were coming to New Cheltenham this February, so I thought maybe you'd like to go," Marianne explained.

"You mean the singers are coming here? To Rockland?"

"They started in Rockland actually, but they're coming to New Cheltenham."

"Oh that is so exciting! Thank you! Chad can you take me?"

"I hope so! Why do you think I suggested it?"

"I should be ashamed of you, Chad," his father warned mockingly.

"But you're not." He pointed to his package. "Open it. I mean, I know you know what it is, but..."

"But I don't, do I?" Her fingers picked at the tape.

"Dare you to rip it off — shred it. I dare you."

She still picked, driving him crazy. Just as he was ready to rip it from her hands and do it himself, she jerked the whole piece from it in one motion. "Daring me is very dangerous. Thought I should warn you." She read the cover of the box. "Tuner — oh! It tells me when I have the notes right."

He passed her two triple A batteries. "It'll need these."

Chad swooped the wrappings up in the largest piece he could find and rolled it in as tight of a ball as he could manage. He shoved the wad in the woodstove and clamped the door shut fast. Then, without a word, he passed Willow her dulcimer and settled into his favorite corner of her couch, waiting.

She fumbled with the instrument, awkwardly holding it and visibly self-conscious. It wasn't fair of him and he knew it. They weren't alone. Her eyes darted to his parents at erratic intervals, yet he couldn't bring himself to retract his request. If he didn't, and he knew she wouldn't, she would do it for his sake—because he had given her a gift, and she would show her gratitude even if it meant she was uncomfortable.

However, as she played with the tuner, fighting to get each string just right, the misery that hovered around the corners of her eyes slowly disappeared. The first tentative plucks of the strings made no discernible tune. Whether she hit wrong notes or simply was not in time, he couldn't tell. However, by the chorus, the sixteenth-century song wavered softly through the room. She closed her eyes, her expression determined as she listened for where to pluck next, but it didn't help. Still, by the time she dropped her hand, the Tesdalls clapped enthusiastically.

"Excellent!" Chad called. He pointed to the dulcimer and whispered to his parents, "She's never played anything before—not just that."

"Really?" Marianne smiled. "That reminds me a little of Corinne. Remember the day she sat down at the piano and just picked out those notes from 'Joy to the World?'"

"That's right..." Christopher agreed. "If you're anything like her, you'll pick it up in no time."

"Ok, enough of me showing off what I don't know. I think it's time for sandwiches and soup."

Christopher stood and clapped a hand on Chad's shoulder as he started to follow Willow to the kitchen. "Willow, do you need Chad's help in there?"

"Oh, I'll help her; you guys go exploring. Get Chad to show you that stream. Maybe you can fish with them next summer."

Oblivious to the underlying conversation, Willow disappeared into the kitchen with Marianne right behind her. Chad followed his father out the front door, down the porch steps and into the yard. "What's wrong, Dad?"

"Well, there are a few things actually. First, you might want to find a name for your version of Yahtzee. She called it Sex-Yahtzee a bit ago."

"Well that's better than Sex-zee—barely."

"So we heard, but it's just not appropriate."

Chad nodded. "You're right. It just hasn't come up since that night, and I forgot all about it. I'll fix it."

"That's probably not going to be necessary. You're mom's in there explaining why she should call it 'Turbo-Yahtzee' or 'Brani-zee' or something like that."

"Well, that's a relief." He knew there was more to his father's expression than a poor choice of a numerical term. "What else?"

"Have you thought about our conversation at Thanksgiving?"

This he hadn't expected. His father seldom harped and never nagged. He'd watched his parents all morning, and his mother hadn't done the majority of the non-verbal dialogue. "Yes, I have thought and prayed about it, and I just can't do it."

"Because she's not attractive enough? Because you don't get along with her? Because you're immune to her? What?"

"None of that is true, and you know it. I care about Willow. She's like Cheri but better because she's here, and I don't have memories of her embarrassing me in Jr. High or have pictures of me in the bathtub with her."

"You're playing house here, Chad."

His father's words dropped between them like an anvil on both of their feet. It hurt, and neither of them could move. "What do you mean?" Chad knew exactly what his father meant, but he prayed he was wrong.

"You know what I mean, son. You're playing house. We drive up to this house where you make yourself at home, sleep in your girlfriend's bed—"

"She's not my girlfriend!"

"Chadwick, don't play semantic games with me. I am not the fool you think I am, and that I am seriously beginning to believe you are," Christopher began. "This is a young, unmarried woman's reputation. What you are doing here is nothing short of using her—enjoying almost all the privileges of marriage—but without the commitment that marriage requires. You'll ensure the best of both worlds—for you. Meanwhile, she's a wife with all of the work and emotional investment but none of the perks and yes," he added at the sight of his son's shocked face, "I mean sexual ones."

"Dad, no. She is like Kari when it—"

His father interrupted him, his voice louder and more insistent than Chad had heard in years. "She may be asleep sexually, but she's not dead. You're going to arouse in her things she might never have had to deal with if it wasn't for you, but you're denying her the appropriate ground to allow them to grow and flourish."

Chad stared at his father dumbstruck. The words hit closer to home than Chad wanted to allow himself to consider. "Dad, I don't think you understand—"

Squeezing his son's shoulders, Christopher held his son's gaze for several seconds before speaking. "Chad, I love you. I see that you love that girl. You may think you are not romantically attached to her, but if you aren't, you would be if you gave yourself half a chance. You drove away the city man; you drove away Chuck—"

"I didn't! She—"

"Neither one of you realizes it, but you did. Chuck isn't the most observant man in the world, but he's not the dumb fool you mistake him for. He's talked to me about how much Willow's friendship meant to him, and now he feels like he's lost it."

"Well that's his problem for presuming more—"

"No!" Christopher interrupted. "No. You can lie to yourself all you want. I can't stop that. However, you will not lie to me. You're using that girl, and it needs to stop now."

Chad leaned against the fence and stared across the farm. "I love it here. It's like being at Uncle Zeke's but better."

"I can see you do, son. Marry her."

"But," Chad argued, "I can't help but wonder what'll happen if someone comes along, and she falls in love with him, and I've tied her to me."

Christopher turned to walk away but paused. "And, what happens to the woman whose reputation you trashed in your selfish enjoyment of your friendship when another woman comes along and you fall in love with *her*? How will Willow feel when she's cast aside because Miss Heartthrob doesn't want you hanging around another woman all the time?"

"Oh, Dad, really! How callous do you think I am?"

Chad's father's shoulders slumped. "Obviously more than I realized. Think about it, son. I'm concerned enough that if you don't reconsider your behavior one way or the other, I'm going to consider taking this to your pastor."

The full impact of his father's words hit Chad as Christopher walked away from him and rejoined the ladies in the house.

CHAPTER 66

"Why don't you use the kid, Steve? He's right there; she'll probably be stupid and give him a key—"

"Because you don't take risks with something like this. I have a plan and we'll work that plan. She'll be begging for help by the time I'm done with her."

Nick Jaros asked no more questions. He knew when to question and when to agree. This was a time to be very agreeable. Instead, he'd have to invest in battery powered thermal underwear or something to keep himself from having frostbite of the—

"Got it?"

"Got it."

Steve eyed him cautiously. "Should I be concerned?"

"About what?" Nick ignored the trail of sweat coursing down his neck.

"Your ability to complete this job. I have others—"

"I've got it, boss." Nick turned and walked to his car. As he opened the door, a shot rang out and he slumped to the ground.

Solari glanced at the man rounding the corner of the old warehouse. "Took you too long. You can't hesitate, or you'll be the one who never drives home."

"Some kids were heading this way. I had to scare 'em off without being seen."

"How'd you manage that?" Solari rolled his eyes at the

suit jacket and slacks Ben Fischer wore. The fool had grandiose ideas of becoming a mafia hit man.

"Cop lights. I flicked them on just before they came around the corner. Ran like scared puppies."

"Good work."

"So, I go after the girl now?"

Eyes narrowed, Solari took two steps toward Ben and raised his sunglasses. "Do not harm her. If she gets a single scratch from your actions, you'll wish you were lying there next to Nick." He waited for his words to sink in for a moment and then added. "She's an attractive girl. With a good haircut and the right clothes, she'd turn every head in a room. Don't look twice. It's not happening."

"Not interested, Mr. Solari."

Steve waited until the man rounded the corner and then slipped back into his sports car. "That was the wrong thing to say, my boy. The wrong thing."

Chad reached for the deodorant but found the shelf empty. He rifled through his duffel bag and still found nothing. "Must be on Willow's sink still. Ugh," he muttered as he pulled on his shirt. He'd have to get another stick before his shift. "Might as well keep that one at Willow's—"

He stopped. His words echoed through his mind. For twenty-four hours, his father's words had taunted him. He wanted to believe his parents were wrong, but every minute that passed seemed to prove the opposite. He had made himself at home in her life, and while he didn't think Willow's reputation was truly at stake, the rest of his father's rebuke hung around his heart like a weight. He tried to protest that his parents didn't understand, and he was right. They didn't understand. Some of their concerns were valid, while others were based upon a reality that Willow hadn't entered yet.

Lord, I prayed about what to do, and ten hours later my father tells me exactly what to do. Is that You? Is it just his opinion? Am I crazy to want it and reject it at the same time? The convenience

alone –

Through the lenses of high-powered binoculars, Ben watched the farm from behind an oak tree near the road. Snow sifted down into his boots, but he forced himself to ignore it. The man—must be the cop, Chad—and the woman built a snowman in the yard. "How bucolic," he muttered to himself."

Scarf, carrot… Willow turned and almost stared directly into his lenses as a dog jumped around the base of their snowman, pawing at it until she chased him away. "Boss was right. She's not bad looking at all."

The man dug into his pocket, pulling out a cell phone. Ben's throat went dry as he turned to the girl and seemed to send her inside. Ben swore. Outdoors it was easier to observe. If they went inside, he'd have to stay out in the cold, and that dog would probably bark—again. Step one. Silence the dog.

When the couple appeared, carrying boxes to the truck in the yard, Ben jumped the fence and climbed into his car, starting the engine. His eyes narrowed as the man gave Willow a half-hug and jumped into his truck. "Didn't kiss her goodbye, eh cop? Boss'll be glad to hear that."

He pulled onto the highway and crept along the road, punching the gas as soon as the truck should have him in view. With less than a tenth of a mile between them, he turned into Fairbury just seconds ahead of Chad. Once the cop passed the convenience store, Ben tore out of the parking lot and raced back to the farm. Phase one to begin.

The temperature dropped steadily. When it fell into the teens, Willow decided to bring in the chickens before their combs got frost bitten. She pulled on her coat and boots, donned her gloves and hat, and stepped out into the yard. Her stomach lurched and her eyes widened at the sight of Saige hanging

297

from her clothesline—blood dripping onto the snow. She raced for the sink and lost the contents of her stomach.

Her hands groped through her pocket, reaching for her phone and wondering why someone would do anything—*Get a grip, Willow. You've strung up deer like that a hundred times. Well, maybe twenty anyway.*

"Chad? Come home. Now. Just—" she collapsed in uncontrollable weeping.

With a flagrant disregard for ice and safety, Chad raced down the highway and up the driveway, slipping and stumbling his way into the house. "Willow?"

"The back yard—clothesline."

Uncertain as to what he'd find, Chad stopped beside her on the chaise and brushed her hair from her face. To his disgust, he noticed that it had the same attractive windblown look that it occasionally had after she let it down from its customary braid. He had to stop noticing things like that—at least for now. "Be right back," he whispered. "It's going to be ok. Whatever it is, it'll be ok."

After one glance at the clothesline and Chad whipped open his phone and called for Joe and Judith. "I know you're busy, but this is a crime. Get the women from the church to dole out those candles. It's not a police matter. This is."

Chad returned to Willow's side, knowing nothing he could say would really help. "I'm sorry. She was a good pup."

"Why—why would?" he heard her swallow hard. "Did you take her down? I couldn't."

"I can't either. Not until the guys arrive. They were giving out candles."

"That reminds me, does anyone need wood? I have plenty of wood—"

"We can let them know," he assured her.

Willow rattled dishes, flagrantly banging them on the counter, in the sink, and into the cupboards as she washed, dried, and put them away. "Who kills a dog? That's just sick."

"Yes."

"And a sniper!" she wailed. "Someone drove out here and went to all that trouble to set up a place to kill a dog. Why?"

"To silence the dog's barking—we think." The alternative was too horrifying to suggest.

"How could a dog way out here annoy anyone? No one can hear her bark but me." She wrung what must have been every drop of water from the rag and slammed it into the sink again. "I want him caught. Whoever this creep is, I want him caught. He killed my dog."

Chad had watched her all afternoon. As though detached from himself, he observed their interaction together, their camaraderie, and, if he was honest with himself, even a bit of chemistry. He'd been blinded by proximity. He saw, in nearly everything they said or did the things that both delighted and concerned his parents. It was time to talk.

"I've been thinking about things."

"About Saige?

He groaned. Maybe it wasn't a good time. "No. Maybe I shouldn't—"

"Good. I don't feel like talking about it. She was just a dog, but you have to be a sick person to do that to an animal for no reason. I don't like the idea of someone like that anywhere near my land, and I really don't want to talk about it until we've found out who did it. I am so glad Ryder was out of town this weekend."

He needed to do it. Why was it so hard if their relationship was only the simple friendship he claimed it was? Why did he suddenly dread her answer? *Because you knew, even from the first evening you drove out here, you knew that this would happen. She fascinated you. You found her attractive. You resisted because you knew—you knew that she would hold you back if she was half the person she seemed. And you wanted Rockland. Excitement. Drama. Well, you got it now. How do you like it?*

She waited, her eyes questioning—growing afraid. Should he give her the option? Maybe he should bring it up, as something neither had much choice but to agree to.

"Let's go sit down."

"Ok." As she passed him, she started to speak, but strode to the chaise and curled up on it instead.

He took his favorite corner of the couch, the fact that he had a favorite pricking his conscience. He had to do this. With a deep breath, a prayer, and more nerves than he knew he possessed, Chad launched into his pitch. "You know, you're my best friend."

"I was thinking about that today."

"It's kind of unique, but it's good and strong, and I don't want to see anything change it."

Willow sat up straighter on the chaise."Is everything ok?"

"Come here," Chad urged, his voice low.

"What—"

"Come to me, Willow, we've got to talk."

She came, but the dread in her eyes as she started to speak cut him. "I—"

"Shh. I need to talk to you, and it's difficult for me. Just give me a second, ok?"

With his arms around her shoulders, nearly choking her at the neck at times, Chad prayed silently for strength, courage, and wisdom. This would be the hardest thing he'd ever done since the day he acknowledged the Lord's claim on his life.

"I don't want to lose you."

"But—"

He laid a finger on her lips chuckling softly. "You've never been so chatty! Let me talk.

"Well you're not exactly Mr. Orator as a general rule," she challenged turning her head to meet his eyes.

"You know, I once considered kissing you to shut you up, and if you keep it up, I might just do it."

Her eyes widened. She started to speak but clamped a hand over her own mouth, giggling as she did. Chad grinned. "That's how I can keep you in line. I'm not sure that's very flattering but—"

"Hey!"

He took a deep breath and tried to reorganize his thoughts. He'd already strayed too far off topic. "Anyway, I don't want to lose you, and yet, I... I'm just your friend—and I like that," he hastened to add. "I—"

Willow, ignoring his threats, moved away from Chad. "What's wrong? What have I done now? I can't take this suspense. I feel like I did when I was five and Mother caught me playing with matches and was too angry to deal with me."

He pulled her back to him. "Hush! I told you—"

"Obviously empty threats so just spit it out, and I'm not swapping."

He snorted. "That's a good one. Ok. Let me try this again."

"Can you just get to the point?"

"I think we should get married."

Stillness filled the room, stifling them. Chad fought to find the words he wanted to say, and he watched as Willow fought the rising panic his words had already prompted. "Chad—"

"Shh. Listen first. I may not be crazy in love with you, but... I mean, I do love you. That's kind of obvious. But I don't really feel a whole lot different for you than Aunt Libby or Cheri or any of Luke's sisters—and yet I do."

"You do what?"

"Feel differently about you than them," he tried to explain. "It's like I've told the Lord, I'm not exactly immune to you."

"What does that mean?"

His heart sank as he realized she truly didn't know what he was trying to say. "Well, you're attractive. I know that. I won't pretend that sometimes I'm not more aware of it than others."

"That's not something I am comfortable discussing."

"I know, but I needed to be honest," he insisted. "Willow, my parents made a valid point when they were here."

"What was that?"

"Dad said I was 'playing house' by spending so much time out here. He accused me of, and I confess I do see his point, of well—" The words stuck in his throat. It sounded—ugh. Maybe he should have gone with his inclination just to decide for them and pray she went along with it, but it was too late now. "Well, of enjoying all, or most anyway, of the benefits of a husband without any solid commitment behind it."

She stiffened. "I—"

301

"In my defense," he continued ignoring her interruption. "I wasn't trying to avoid a commitment to you. I'd considered all of this before and truly thought it was wrong of me to even mention it. I thought, 'what happens if she meets someone else—I've denied her.' You know what I thought."

"I told you that—"

"Yes, and I believed you and allowed things to continue as they were, but I see my parents' point. They love you. They love me. They want what is best for us, and after considering their opinions and praying about this, I think they're right. I think we should get married."

"I feel," she began, "A little like Elizabeth Bennett must have felt in *Pride and Prejudice*. You haven't told me you care about me against your better judgment or that I'm beneath you or anything, but this is a very Darcy-like proposal you've thrown at me." She frowned at him as he started to speak and continued, deepening her voice in a weak attempt to sound like him. "'I'm not in love with you, although you don't repulse me or anything, but to keep up appearances I think I should deny myself the rights of a bachelor and make an honest woman of you.' My how gallant you are, Chad. Forgive me for not being overwhelmed with gratitude."

Her sarcasm cut him deeply. She was right. He had bungled his so-called proposal. "Willow, right now, I want nothing more than to pretend we haven't had this discussion."

"Well that makes two of us. The motion is carried."

"How did you know—"

Her impatience sent her to her feet, hands on hips, and eyes flashing. "Roberts Rules of Order. On the third shelf of the center bookcase, two thirds of the way from the left. I'm not an idiot, Chad."

"You're angry with me."

"Brilliant observation."

He smiled up at her. "Come here."

"You must be joking."

"Willow," he pressed, forcing himself to speak softly and keep his voice low. "Come here. Let's talk."

"I don't really want to talk."

"Well you don't get that option. Friends don't just clam up and let things stand like this when there is a problem. They work it out." Chad couldn't believe he now echoed the very words his mother had drilled into his head—seemingly without effect. *It finally sank in now, Mom.*

"But you'll just be all nice, and I'll get comfortable again and then—"

He tried again. "C'mere, Willow."

"No."

Chad stood, scooped her off her feet, and sat once more with her on his lap. "We have to talk."

She dropped her head against his chest, tears slowly falling. "I don't want to."

"Then I'll talk. You listen."

He smoothed her hair, wiped her tears, and spoke soothingly about his idea. They were best friends, he asserted, and she couldn't deny it. They almost couldn't be more husband-wifeish if they tried. "I'd be here more. I could help more without feeling like I was overstepping." He swallowed. "I wouldn't have to go home."

"That's what I'm afraid of."

"Aww, Willow. You know I'd never—"

"That's part of marriage, Chad. It's a part I don't—can't—"

"Shh," he soothed. "Listen. I can't say that a lifetime of marriage in separate rooms will work. I'm realistic enough to know that eventually—" He took a deep breath praying for the right words. "But I am not Steven Solari Jr. I would never force—"

"I know," she whispered, the pain in her voice cutting him. "And I could never force a man into a marriage without—"

"Hey, hey," he replied, trying to calm a fresh wave of tears. "No one is forcing anyone into anything. I'm asking, and at this point I've quit begging God for you to say yes and am now pleading that He won't let you say no."

"Isn't that the same thing?"

"I wish." He pressed his cheek against her hair. "Yes is an agreement. A lack of a no just means maybe."

With her arms wrapped tight around his chest and her

head over his heart, she sighed. "Well, I can't ever tell you no, but—"

"That's enough for now, Willow. Take it to the Lord, but whatever you do, or decide, or anything, we can't let it change us—this. I didn't know how important it was to me until about thirty-two seconds ago when I thought I'd lost something amazing."

CHAPTER 67

Willow sighed in relief as Chad drove home, watching the taillights of his truck as they disappeared down her driveway. "I never thought I'd be back to being glad he's gone," she muttered to herself. "Why did he have to ruin everything?"

Her heart wasn't in it. She wanted to blame Chad for the unsettled feelings in her heart and mind, but the fact was she was just simply angry with herself for not realizing that things couldn't continue as they were. She knew that as natural as their friendship seemed, it wasn't the same she'd read in books or seen with other people she knew. He was right. Their relationship seemed more like the Tesdall's marriage than simple friends.

Headlights in the driveway frightened her. She dashed around the room, putting out the candles, turning down the lamp, and locking the doors. The lights of the vehicle were so bright that she couldn't tell who or what kind of car was out there. Unsure what to do, she crept upstairs and tried to see from her room but it was gone.

A noise came from the back of the house. Growing afraid, Willow grabbed the gun from behind her bed, hurried to her mother's room looking for a place to hide, and then dashed from there again. She started into the spare room but then chose the attic. The stairs were hidden. She could easily hide in there, no one would find her without knowing where to look for the stairs, and there was no electricity to reveal the trapdoor in the ceiling!

Once in the attic, Willow grabbed a rug, crawled to the corner of the room, wrapped it around her, and prayed. She couldn't hear the rooms beneath her. Was someone shuffling around down there? Why had mother insisted on all that extra insulation? It made things very difficult for her now.

Chad crept into her room expecting to find Willow sleeping. Her bed looked untouched. He tried calling her name, but there was no reply. He jogged downstairs again and found the front door still locked from the inside. She must be in the house but where, and why was she not answering him?

He dialed Willow's phone and then laughed at her frantic answer. "Chad, get out here. Someone's in the house."

"I'm in the house. Where are you?"

"You came back?"

As he climbed the stairs two at a time, he glanced around the upstairs rooms. "Yes. Where are you? I don't see you—" He stopped mid-sentence as the stairs dropped from the attic door. "I didn't mean to scare you."

Scrambling down the steps, Willow shook her head as she reached the bottom. "I thought, 'they've come back to get me now!' and I was sure I'd have to kill someone tonight!"

"That's why I'm back! I got to the turnoff and thought, 'You fool, you can't leave her alone!'"

Willow replaced the gun, grabbed her pajamas, and disappeared behind the bathroom door. Several minutes later, she reemerged ready for bed. "Night Chad. See you tomorrow. What time do you work?"

"Ten."

"Good, you get the goat, and I'll make the breakfast."

Chad stepped closer, his hand on her shoulder. "See, what's so bad about an exchange like that every night?"

"Don't push me, Chad. I need time to adjust—to think."

His voice cut her to the quick. "Can I still hug you?"

Ignoring the irrational warning bells in her mind, Willow leaned her head against his chest and tried to relax. "I didn't mean to make you feel bad."

"Oh hush. I just needed a hug. I hate that I've done this to you."

"You could take it back…," she urged.

"Not on your life. As awkward as the discussion was, I believe it's the best thing. For both of us." He winked at her wry smile. "What are the odds your mom has some pajama bottoms that were really big on her?"

Willow pulled out the bottom drawer of her mother's bureau and retrieved a pair of pink sweats with 'hottie' written across the backside. "They came in an order we had for some thermals. Bill called about them, but the company said to keep them. Mother never could bring herself to wear them."

"And I'm supposed to?"

"Sleep in your jeans. I don't care."

Chad snatched the pink pants from her hands and stormed into the bathroom. Willow, unwilling to miss this scene, grabbed her lamp and set it on the dresser by the door. When Chad emerged, she snorted most indelicately. "That's a lovely look on you."

He ignored her and turned to enter Kari's bedroom. Just before he closed the door, Chad flipped his shirttail displaying the word. "If the term fits, wear it," he quipped as he kicked the door shut.

"Night, Chad," she whispered as she carried the lamp back to her table, turned it off, and crawled into bed.

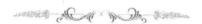

"I thought there was nothing going on with her and the cop. I mean, he gets a call and leaves and barely hugs her before he takes off. I'm more affectionate with my great aunt Phyllis — whom I hate by the way. Then late after he leaves, he turns around and comes back. I thought maybe they had a fight and broke up, but lights came on in two different rooms, so I guess he's just kind of a bodyguard or something."

Solari listened carefully. No kissing, no sharing a room. This was good. "So how did she respond to the loss of her mutt?"

"She puked."

"Good. Good. Step two. Take it to step two on Sunday. If she goes to church, while she's gone is best. Did you get a copy of the key from one of those kids?"

Ben nodded pulling a ring of keys from his pocket. "Got all three."

"I've got a guy 'apprenticing' for the local locksmith on the off-chance that she calls them, but I think you'll have to be ready to get the kids keys again."

Ben stood. "I'll take care of it."

Solaris stopped him at the door. "Whatever you do, remember. Protect the girl."

"Consider it done."

Willow burst into the kitchen shivering. For the first time, she regretted turning down a ride home. The temperature had dropped several degrees, and her nose felt the chill even through the scarf. "Glad I didn't let the chickens out while I was gone," she muttered, huddling around the stove.

As she turned to warm her backside, her eyes widened. Something was wrong. Her eyes scanned every inch of the room before she saw it. A few things were rearranged on the hutch and the teapot was gone. She found a shard of it on the cabinet, a ding in the wood, and another shard across the room.

On a hunch, she raced outdoors to the incinerator and found the remaining pieces of the teapot in there. Her mind whirled. How much money was in the pot? One thousand? Two? She'd often considered putting the money in the bank now that she had her card and checkbook but hadn't ever made it a priority.

Someone had been inside her house. They could still be in there. Where to go? The barn wasn't any safer, and it was too cold to stay outdoors for long. With a deep sigh and thankful that she wasn't sleeping there that night, Willow dug her cell phone from her pocket and dialed Chad.

"Someone's been in the house. They took all the money."

"Get out of there," Chad ordered.

308

"I can't. It's too cold and the barn is even less safe than the house."

"Not if no one is in it, get in the barn and lock it."

"And if they're out there now, I'm locked inside with them."

"You need a car, Willow!"

"Well I don't have one!"

Sounding panicked, Chad hushed her. "You don't want them to hear you if they're in there. Keep talking. I know, go down into the cellar, and take a knife."

Chad found her there minutes later as he burst into the house his gun drawn, and ready to take on whomever might be lurking. "Go out to my car, get inside, lock the doors, and get down behind the seats until I come out."

"But—"

"Go, Willow!" he yelled as he pushed her out the door.

Kitchen, pantry—irrationally the cellar—room by room, he inspected the house, looking for intruders, but found it empty. The barn showed no signs of anything off—but footprints led up to the house from the wrong direction. He waved at her, calling when she opened the door, "Get my camera from the glove compartment."

She crawled from her awkward hiding place and brought him the camera still smarting from his sharp words. "What did you find?"

"Footprints. I'll take pictures and if we find the guy, we'll find shoes or boots it looks like, and if it's a match..."

Willow hunkered on her heels and stared at the imprints. Without a word, she left him snapping pictures, trying to get the best angle and hurried to the barn, returning quickly with a shovel in hand. "Which one don't you need?"

"That one. Why?"

She scooped up the snow, carried the print to the bones of her greenhouse, and looked for an un-trampled footprint. "Chad! Over here."

Chad stumbled awkwardly through the snow as quickly as possible. "What."

"It's Ryder's. It's exactly like his."

A grim look crossed Chad's face. "I knew we shouldn't—"

"Chad," she insisted, "he didn't do this. Ryder wouldn't do this. Not now."

"But you just proved he did."

She shook her head. "No, I proved that your other footprints don't mean anything."

Deflated, Chad had to agree. Deep down, he did think Ryder had changed but the evidence had seemed so compelling. "Well, we've probably destroyed anything by the back door but—"

Chad tried retracing his steps exactly in order to avoid adding more confusing prints to the mix. As he examined the yard, the back steps, and the door locks, he returned to the front yard and stared at the steps before him. Slowly, he followed them from a distance until they disappeared beneath his tire tracks. Hugging the fence, he followed the tracks almost to the road before another half boot print showed. Satisfied, he snapped another picture of it and returned to his vehicle.

"Willow, I think you need to tell Caleb to take care of the animals tonight. We'll take your things and you can spend the afternoon with Lily or at my apartment. You're not coming back here until we get a locksmith out here."

"I'm behind them on the road between Fairbury and the Loop. I'll pass them soon and switch cars out at the rest stop. I'll need to do that again at the convenience store just outside of Westbury. Can you have a car sent there?"

"What are you driving?"

"My car."

"Ok, I'll send the SUV. You sure about destination?"

"Definitely. There was a pile of packages on the coffee table. I recognized several names."

"Westbury..." Solari's voice sounded pleased. "Perfect. What did you do in the house?"

"Broke a teapot, took almost two grand from it, and cleaned most of it up. What do I do with the two grand?"

"Keep it. A bonus."

Ben smiled and accelerated around Chad's truck. "What do you think makes her keep money like that in the house?"

"Fear. Fear is the root of all stupidity."

After he disconnected, Steven Solari glanced at his wife as she dismantled the tree in order to make way for her elaborate party decorations. Great. New Year's. "I think I may take a ride to check out a few Westbury properties tomorrow. How would you like to go along with me?"

"I've got this party —"

"Let Eva handle it. Then if that nasty Toni Bertram has anything nasty to say, you can always blame the housekeeper and rub her face in the fact that *your* husband likes to have you around."

Lynne's slow smile told him she liked his plan. "What time?"

"We'll do lunch there first. There's a great new restaurant on Churchill."

Ben arrived an hour later and passed him a slip of paper on top of a pizza box. "That'll be seventeen-ninety."

Solari snickered as he shut the door. He unfolded the paper on his way to the kitchen. The address. "Hello, Willow," he whispered.

CHAPTER 68

"They're here!" Cheri's called through the house as she raced to the car. "You took forever! Here, let me take some of those!" To her brother, she tossed an irritated look. "You need a *real* car bro! She shouldn't have to ride all the way out here smothered in packages!"

"Actually, they kept the hot air off of my face. I get so sick with that."

Chad locked the car as he remarked, "I didn't know that. Why didn't you say something?"

"Well," she began, winking at Cheri, "my mother taught me it was rude to complain."

Cheri carried the packages as she led the way into the house. Chad waited until she disappeared through the doorway, before he leaned down and whispered, "Another reason to get married. It's not complaining when you're sharing a preference with a husband."

"That's just semantics, and you know it. One day it's 'sharing' and the next it's nagging. I've read too many books with harpies for wives. No thanks."

"Hey, come on in, you two! It's freezing out here."

Chad and Willow stared at each other, snickering. Willow kissed Marianne's cheek as she passed under the mistletoe, Willow said, "Thanks for having me, Midge."

"Midge?"

Chad followed, kissing his mother's cheek and glancing

313

around the room as he did. Perhaps strategic placement of mistletoe would help melt the fearful icicles around her heart. "*While You Were Sleeping*. You've been watching it again."

Once she shut the door behind her, Marianne hugged her son. "Merry Christmas."

"Happy New Year, Mom. Oh and," he leaned closer whispering, "I talked to Willow about dad's suggestion on marriage. Maybe you or Aunt Libby—"

"Not interested?"

"More like terrified."

"I'll hand her over to Libby then. She's better with firm *and* compassionate. I seem limited to one or the other."

The sound of laughter from the living room drew Chad and his mother to see what the commotion was. Willow sat blushing on the couch, and Christopher looked smug. "Got her. She was watching doorways but missed the ceiling fan."

"Good one, Dad!"

"I think Willow looks exhausted."

"It's been a long week," she admitted blushing further.

Christopher's eyes shot to Chad's face while Cheri dragged Willow the stairs and into the guest room. "Chad?"

He shook his head holding up one finger until Willow reappeared to brush her teeth, eventually closing the bedroom door behind her. "There was the thing with the dog, the thing with the money, and she's still upset about the idea of marriage."

Marianne joined them with a tray of hot chocolate and cookies. "So you asked her, told her, got an opinion, what?"

"I told her what Dad said about playing house—"

"I was a little harsh..."

Shaking his head, Chad continued. "No, you were right. I was really mad that day. See, part of it is that you don't know how things are, and it was just too easy to rest on that fact rather than consider your concerns." He swallowed. "I had myself convinced you were wrong until I realized that I left my deodorant at her house and decided to leave it there for when I needed it."

"With all the work you do there, that makes sense though,

Chad!" Christopher didn't understand his son's logic.

"But I felt perfectly comfortable just doing it without a second thought. I didn't have a reason in mind outside the fact that I'm there. A lot. And I've been there every night this week."

"I'd hope so." Marianne hesitated before she added, "You *were* in separate rooms..."

"Yes, Mom."

Snuggled together on one corner of the couch, Chad saw a picture of him and Willow twenty years in the future with the possible exception of Willow's size. He couldn't imagine a chubby Willow. At last, Marianne's voice broke the awkward silence that had begun to grow. "You really aren't in love with her, are you?"

"No, Mom. I'm not."

"Why not! She's a beautiful, intelligent, interesting woman! She has everything going for her, you enjoy her company—"

"And he spent the first several months of his time with her resenting it," Christopher added. "I think he's in the habit of holding her aloof for whatever reason."

Chad hadn't admitted it to anyone let alone himself but his father was correct. "It's the end of my dream. It's selfish and despicable, but it's true."

"What dream, Chaddie?"

"Ever since I can remember I wanted to be a cop on the streets of Rockland. I wanted to be one of those guys busting gangs in the inner city or negotiating hostage situations." His head dropped into his hands. "As much as I want a life in Fairbury, and yes, with Willow, that life means there's no chance for the life I've worked toward for so long."

Marianne started to rise and go to her son, but Christopher jerked her back to her seat. "In other words Chad, you won't let yourself fall in love with the perfect woman for you because you are throwing a tantrum over what you can't have. You can have it all except something that strokes your pride, but that's not enough. You want the house in the country with the fishing stream, the gorgeous wife, and the respect of your community, oh, and a high profile job in the city. All at once."

"I know. I said it's despicable."

"It is. It's also understandable," Christopher conceded, "but it's selfish."

His fists clenched tightly as he struggled. His mother shoved his father's hands aside and moved to Chad's feet. Taking his hands in hers, she tilted her head until she could meet his gaze. "That's not it, Chad. It's a lie. You're lying to yourself out of some misplaced self-preservation."

"But—"

She caught her son's face in her hands and held it, gazing into his eyes. "It's a risk to open your heart. You're right. She may never reciprocate your affection. You happened to choose a girl who has reason to both be leery of men and not see any benefits to marriage. Love is a risk as well as an action. It's rolling the dice on the craps tables over and over and over until you finally get the right numbers even if it bankrupts you in the process."

"Marianne!"

"Crass analogy but it's the best I can do. Shut up." She waved her hand dismissively at her husband who chuckled behind his hand. Even Chad managed a smile. His mother's occasional feistiness always tickled his father.

"It's not that. I've always wanted a family, and Willow—"

His mother clamped a hand over his mouth and shook her head. "You can lie to yourself all you want, but you're not going to lie to me. You're afraid of love, and I'm not letting you up out of that chair until you admit it."

He fought it. Repeatedly he started to argue and then ground his teeth, forcing himself to keep quiet. His mother would surely give up if he just refused to talk. Her ideas were ludicrous and ridiculous. Why would he be afraid of love? Besides, he did love Willow and had already admitted as much.

Eyes—concerned, serious eyes—bored into him while he wrestled with the truths he fought. *I'm a man—a law enforcement officer. I'm not afraid of anything. They're crazy.* He tried to avoid their gazes but they followed him, wherever his eyes went. "I can't," he whispered.

"Can't what, son?"

316

His lip trembled, but Chad willed himself not to cry. "I—no." His head shook.

"Just face it. You're letting some fear paralyze you, and it's going to hurt both of you in the long run."

"Mom—" Determined to get it over with, the words poured from him. "I can't stand the idea of being in love with someone who doesn't love me."

"Well then, it's not a problem. Even if Willow never falls madly in love with you, and frankly, I think if you actually tried to win her affections she would, she does love you. It's evident from a million sides. She looks to you for leadership when she doesn't know what to do; she tries so hard to please you and does it all without losing her own identity."

His lips twisted as he quipped, "Maybe you should marry her."

"I would if she was the right gender and I wasn't already stuck with that old lug!"

"And don't you forget it, Mari." Christopher leaned forward, his forearms resting on his knees and his hands clenched. Chad recognized the "this is the only time you'll hear this from me" stance. "Son, you haven't given either one of you a chance to fall in love. You'll have to try. You'll have to show her marked attention, all the way from her appearance to overt flirting. You should be very good at that."

"Why?"

"Because you come from two very sappy parents who would love to give you a demonstration of how it's done if you think it'll help."

"No thanks," Chad insisted. "I think I get the gist."

Marianne and Christopher cleared the coffee table of their chocolate mugs and tray and said goodnight to Chad. "Pray, son," Christopher admonished. "Pray that you will know not only what the Lord's will is, but how to act on it."

Chad did. He prayed. For an hour, he poured out his fears, his hopes, and laid them at the Lord's feet. He sat with his hands over his head as though protecting himself from a verdict he didn't want to hear as he meditated on every scripture he could bring to mind.

Cheri came down and saw him on her way to the kitchen. She sat beside him on the couch and leaned against him. "When I was in the pit that summer, I thought I would die. I prayed I would die. I begged the Lord to release me every day and every day, the Lord said no."

"How did you know it was no? Were you hearing voices by that point?"

"I knew it was no when I woke up in the same situation the next morning."

"Why didn't you quit praying for it?" It seemed insane to him. "Why put yourself through that torture?"

"Because I knew that it might have been the Lord's will for me to live another day with the struggles I had, but I didn't want another one unless I had to."

He turned his head to meet her gaze. "And I assume there's a corollary to this?"

"When Jesus prayed for deliverance, He meant it. I trusted in that every single day that I prayed that same prayer. I believe with all my heart that His prayer to escape the coming trials was heart-felt and sincere. He wanted out. However, if out wasn't the best, He wanted the strength to endure whatever 'in' would bring."

"And that makes sense with what you did at camp that year but—"

"Chad, your 'in' is nothing compared to Golgotha. Your 'in' is the difference between winning the lottery or winning the Publisher's Clearing House. One of them will cost you something. Not much probably, but something. The other costs next to nothing—a stamp. Both are huge blessings. Don't tear up your winning ticket or your entry just because you wanted to win at slot machines instead."

"What," Chad chuckled, "Is with you and mom and the gambling analogies?"

"Well, they fit for one thing," she explained. "And we just watched *Ocean's Eleven*, which might have influenced us a little..."

"Go to bed. And thanks."

"Just a hint, laddie."

318

"Hmm?"

Cheri grinned. "Save your announcement until after Luke's wedding."

"It'll take that long to get her to agree."

"Even so," she began, "if she says yes tomorrow, wait. Luke is always in the shadow of those girls and even us. Let him have this stage moment. He's so proud of that family of his."

"Gotcha. You're right."

Cheri grinned. "I'm always right. It's about time you noticed that."

"Go to bed."

Once certain that his family was in bed, Chad turned out the downstairs lights, taking note of all of the mistletoe festooned places in the downstairs area of the house. He slowly climbed the stairs and quietly opened Willow's door. The hall light illuminated her room just enough for him to see the rise and fall of her back as she slept. He sat on the edge of her bed and prayed for her.

She stirred and rolled over on her other side facing him. Her hair was unbound and covered her face irritating her as she slept. Her hands fidgeted around her face trying to push the hairs out of the way until finally, Chad tucked them behind her ears. The restlessness settled and her breathing grew slow and even again.

With a sigh of resignation and a heart heavy with concern, Chad kissed her temple and left the room closing the door behind him. "It all sounds so easy until you have to do it..."

Doors slammed and excited voices squealed. Suddenly the house filled with a din that woke Willow from a sound sleep. She scrambled from her bed and peeked down the stairs. Aggie's children. Why hadn't she thought about them? She hadn't brought anything for them — nothing but Vannie's dress that she'd intended to send back with Luke. Of course, he'd bring his fiancée to "Christmas" morning with the family.

As quickly as possible, Willow threw on her skirt, sweater, and slippers. She pulled her hair, a hopeless tangle, into a quick ponytail and hurried to wash her face and brush her teeth. Chad emerged from his room looking sleepy and grumpy. "What's the racket?"

"Aggie and the children just arrived."

With a bear yawn, Chad hurried to brush his teeth. "Go hold the baby or something so they'll gimme a minute to wake up."

She dodged walking under a sprig of mistletoe hanging from the hall light and hurried down the stairs. Aggie handed Willow a sleepy baby Ian and hurried to corral the littlest twins down in the basement. Luke piled two plates of food from the breakfast buffet and herded a few more children after her. "Aunt Marianne, we're going to keep an eye on the little guys downstairs until Vannie and Laird are through eating."

"What about the little ones, do you need help fixing plates or something?"

"Everyone but the four of us ate at home. Blood sugar drops and car rides aren't fun."

Willow listened to the discussion as she watched the baby sleep. He'd tried to explore her entire house the last time he'd been there, but hadn't been willing to get too far from Aggie's sight. She wondered if he was bolder now, or if he still liked the security of knowing his "mother" was nearby. Somehow, that thought reminded her of herself. Learning to walk in this new world of people and friends but still holding onto the security blankets her mother kept them wrapped in for so many years.

Libby entered knocking and calling out "Merry Christmas Year!"

Wrapped in her own little world of baby cheeks and tiny hands, Willow didn't hear or notice when Libby shoved several packages under an already overloaded tree. "He's a sweetie, isn't he?" Libby's whisper and the brush of the back of her hand over Ian's hair caught Willow's attention.

"Aggie let me hold him. Wasn't that nice? I didn't know they'd be here or I would have brought—well, *something!*"

"Can you imagine their house with just a 'little something'

320

for each child? If we all did that, they'd go home with a hundred new things to find places for. I'm glad you didn't know, and I'm sure that's why Marianne didn't tell anyone."

"But to be opening gifts—how cruel to the children to be left out!"

"They'd be happy for everyone else. They got their gifts already. The littlest ones might struggle, but I think it'd be good for them frankly." At Willow's shocked face, Libby added, "But don't worry, they're just staying for breakfast and then going on over to Zeke's."

"So they won't be here—"

"No. You can stop devising gifts from thin air now."

Willow visibly relaxed and sank further into the couch. "I'll just sit and hold this little man then. He snores sometimes. Isn't that cute!"

"Looks like someone is ready for a baby or two around her house."

"If they were all like him, I'd take twenty and have them delivered tomorrow morning."

Libby's laughter brought wrinkles to the baby's brow and he snuggled even more closely to Willow. "I think you'd find twenty baby boys to be more than even you could handle."

"I don't suppose Aggie thinks she has her hands full enough and wants to let him come live with me?"

Chad watched the conversation from the dining room doorway. He couldn't hear the words but from the look on Willow's face, she was enjoying her first "baby fix." Libby's expression was indulgent and slightly teasing. He hoped his aunt would plant a seed in Willow's mind. Watching Luke with Aggie's children and the paternal air it gave him was heartwarming. Maybe...

"Mom, did you see this?"

Marianne turned from the buffet table and watched the scene before her. Her son watched Willow as she smoothed the baby's hair, brushed a cheek, or let the child's hands curl around her finger. Libby needed to talk to her.

"Libby, can you help me in the kitchen?"

321

"Are you sure you guys don't want to come with us?" Marianne paused and waited for Chad and Willow to answer.

"I don't think so, Mom."

"Thanks Marianne, but I don't think I'd make it until midnight."

Christopher, carrying two bowls and a plastic sack full of something, urged her out the door. "Let's go! I don't want to miss the sports blooper reenactment."

The house settled into a quiet hush once the door closed behind Chad's parents, Cheri, and Chuck. Willow leaned her back against the couch and covered her eyes. Chad stretched asking, "Rough day?"

"I had fun. Aggie's children were a nice diversion."

"You seemed to enjoy the baby..."

She nodded with a slight smile hovering about her lips and making her appear as though she had a secret. "I loved how he smelled and the way he just seemed to melt into me. I always dreamed about having two sons." She paused. "Don't say it."

"Say what?"

"That if I would just quit being so stubborn, I could have them."

"I wouldn't say that, Willow," Chad whispered. "I thought I made it clear that I was talking about a marriage with separate bedrooms—at least for a while anyway."

"Am I that repulsive?"

"Willow, no..."

She rubbed her temples. "Libby spent half the afternoon telling me how I'm not trusting God and His plan for His creation. How He made men to need this stuff, and I'm just not doing my part—"

"She said what!"

Willow sat brooding over the words Libby had spoken to her. "You heard me."

"Yes, but I don't believe you. Aunt Libby would not tell a girl it was her duty to marry anyone so he could fill some animalistic urge to feed his own lusts."

"Well she didn't say *that*—" Willow admitted.

"What exactly did she say?"

As Willow struggled to remember Libby's exact words, she realized that she'd deliberately taken the encouragement and twisted it in her mind to make it into something she could reject. The realization sickened her. "Oh, Chad. How despicable."

"What is?"

"I chose to hear her words and tone to mean things that are repugnant to me. It was deliberate... and ugly."

"Aww, Willow—"

"I've driven a wedge between us."

"No you haven't."

She nodded. "I did this with Mother a couple of years ago when I thought she was being too stubborn about me going to Rockland with her. I thought I wanted to see the city—"

"That probably didn't go over well."

"I was ugly. Probably the result of usually getting my way in everything. Mother was adamant. I accused her of lying about her attack, that she made trips to see my father and was just keeping me from him. I can't think about it without getting sick."

Dismay crossed his face. "Oh, Willow."

"See. You're pulling away from me just like she did."

"I haven't gone anywhere."

"No, and a week ago," she insisted, "You wouldn't be sitting across the room from me afraid to come near me."

Chad sighed. "What do you want from me?"

"I don't want anything to change."

He shifted in his seat, trying to make room for her, and gestured for her to join him. "C'mere."

"You're not going to talk me into—"

"Hush and come here."

"My you get bossy when you don't get your way," she tried to tease as she crossed the room tentatively.

He pulled her to him but they simply didn't fit in the chair. She frowned as he stood, punched the CD player, and began to two-step around the room by himself, his arms empty and awkward looking as they held an imaginary person. Willow watched for a moment and then finally gave in and asked the obvious question.

"What are you doing?"

"Dancing."

"But you can't dance alone."

"No, but right now, you're more comfortable dancing with yourself, and that leaves me dancing alone too."

Her eyes followed as he held the air and danced around the room in time with the music. At the end of the song, he made motions as though dipping his partner, which sent Willow into stitches. "Oh, Chad."

He crossed the room and stood looking down at her. "One of my favorite movies has a scene where a man describes dancing as a conversation between two people." Chad paused before quoting the line directly, "'*Talk to me.*'"

Instinctively, Willow knew Chad was communicating more than a request for a dance. "I'm afraid."

"I won't lead you anywhere you aren't ready to go."

"Even—"

He held out his hand, his eyes earnestly encouraging her to take it. "Especially there, Willow. Especially."

After a moment's hesitation—and then a couple more—Willow stood, placed her hand in his and tried to smile. "Then let's dance."

324

As Chad pulled her to him, an impish glint filled his eyes and he glanced upward. Willow's eyes followed and the sight of a sprig of ribbon festooned mistletoe. Her eyes flew to his face and widened as he leaned in to kiss her. A nervous giggle escaped when his lips brushed her forehead.

"I told you, Willow, nowhere that you're not ready to go."

Past Forward. Don't miss a single episode of this serial novel. New episodes released weekly. Check for them **FREE** on Kindle.

Volume III Coming soon!

Made in the USA
Middletown, DE
17 April 2018